Liberty's Land

*A true-life novel of the American Revolution—
where rugged frontier Pennsylvanians rose
to shape a nation's destiny.*

CHRIS YOHN

Liberty's Land
by Chis Yohn

Copyright © 2025
All rights reserved.
Published by Masthof Press.

Cover Illustration: A View of the Attack Against Fort Washington by Thomas Davies, 1776.

Library of Congress Control Number: 2025940182
International Standard Book Number: 979-8-89674-026-1

Masthof Press
219 Mill Road | Morgantown, PA 19543-9516
www.Masthof.com

Society of the Descendants of Washington's Army at Valley Forge Virginia Brigade Commander and Virginia Daughters of the American Revolution Chaplain Holly Lynne McKinley Schmidt

Liberty's Land is a true page-turner. It captures the raw frontier spirit, weaving together stories of love, grief, perseverance and patriotism in some of the harshest conditions imaginable.

The book highlights the bonds forged among families and the deep human connections formed in and around the frontier forts. What makes this book stand out is its balance between historical fact and meaningful dialogue that breathes life into the past.

Liberty's Land illuminates a side of colonial life often overlooked: the conflicts and sacrifices made far from the famous Revolutionary battlefields, but paid for with American courage all the same.

Engaging, informative and emotionally rich, *Liberty's Land* is perfect both for readers steeped in Revolutionary War history and for those eager to expand their understanding of the era. It's not just history—it's history brought to life.

★　★　★　★　★

Congress of American Revolution Round Tables (ARRT) Co-founder, ARRT of Richmond President, Author, Historian and Revolutionary War battlefields guide Bill Welsch

While most of the major engagements of the American Revolution occurred along the east coast, the interior frontier was ablaze with constant raids, massacres and smaller battles. In *Liberty's Land*, author Chris Yohn drops the reader right into that inferno. Set primarily in North Central Pennsylvania, we meet numerous characters who carry the exciting story through the end of the Revolution, with their experiences driving the narrative. Yohn's reconstruction is interesting and exciting. It will both educate and engage the reader. I highly recommend *Liberty's Land*.

TABLE *of* CONTENTS

AUTHOR'S NOTE

I'm a history fanatic and so are many of my friends and colleagues. So, I'm often asked, "Why a novel?" My response? . . . I *love* a good textbook account of a point in history and I have many favorite works of that type. But, why visit a battlefield or other historic site instead of just reading the cold, hard facts? It's to stand in the footsteps of those who came before us . . . to see what they saw. I long for those brief glimpses of time travel that are so fleeting but that I know all history buffs crave. What was it like to BE there? How did it sound, smell . . . feel? I wrote *Liberty's Land* as a novel for precisely that reason. I wanted readers to not only learn the incredible facts of this little-known history of the Revolution, but to *know* these remarkable characters. This intimate emotional connection creates time *and* place through the written word and allows the reader to truly experience the world and the circumstances in which these heroes lived. It's my greatest hope to bring that world back to life and share it with you.

Liberty's Land is a **true** story. The characters are **real** people. Extensively researched across many diverse sources, the story was teased back to life from an extremely fragmented historical record. In rare places where the record conflicts or breaks down entirely, I reasoned through the most logical scenario rather than omit a pivotal event. Similarly, where history records an important deed but omits the individual's name, I assigned a name to preserve that person's contribution and for the clarity of the narrative.

In taking this approach, I hope to illustrate the incredible hardships, sacrifices, deep convictions and bravery these amazing Americans displayed. We owe them everything.

Human history is an ongoing stream of despots and nobles who ruled through being born to privilege. Millennium by millennium . . . continent by continent . . . culture by culture, the average person lived as a slave, a serf or a peasant with no hope of advancement.

Even cultures that briefly stumbled toward democracy allowed only a small, privileged class to participate. Free will was a fantasy. Self-determination was nonexistent. In rare instances where laws did not exist to oppress the masses, strict social strata did. A person's family name had far more to do with the life they could lead than their own abilities.

Then, suddenly, the clouds parted. The times and conditions converged to create hope for all humankind. Average people rose up to embrace a cause of liberty and freedom. For the first time in human history, they created a government guaranteeing anyone could become whatever they could make of themselves. They could think, feel and worship as they wished.

While the government they established guaranteed that freedom, the reality of the breakthrough moment wasn't realized by all. The weight of the past kept many from participating. Slavery continued. It was even practiced by some who helped establish the cause. It took almost one hundred years and another gut-wrenching war to finally bring it to an end. That war was fought to realize the ideals upon which the country was founded and prompted President Lincoln to declare the conflict a "new birth of freedom." Still, despite the victory won at horrific cost, oppression continued.

Women were also largely excluded. Their struggle to vote and hold office lasted more than another hundred years. Many other groups experienced the marginalization of the past and their fortunes continued to rise and fall.

Yet, the flame was lit. The words were written. They live on because of those who continue to fight for them. In the two-and-a-half centuries of our nation's existence, vast American armies struggled and bled to ensure freedom for *others*. They did so on our own continent and around the world.

We Americans continue to embrace the words and make true progress. Decade by decade, century by century, the words become more of a reality. They remain a beacon for all who love liberty, fairness, decency and hope . . . as we continue to inch ever closer to realizing the true society they envision: all people, of all races and religions are equal. The only differentiator is self-determination and individual ability. None of that could have happened without that first watershed moment. The words were written . . . and nurtured . . . and defended.

This is the story of the average people. The men, women and children . . . the Whites, Blacks and Native Americans . . . those of all religions and professions who first came together to fight for the words that guaranteed freedom and liberty for all. They fought for free will. They fought for a new country and the new idea that all people are created equal and can advance as far as their talents can take them.

SETTING

The West Branch of the Susquehanna rises in the Allegheny Mountains and flows in a long, lazy arch across North-Central Pennsylvania. The stately river flows through rolling foothills and majestic forests until it makes a sharp turn to the south and joins the North Branch at Sunbury.

The area was opened to settlement after the 1768 Treaty of Fort Stanwix, which sought a lasting peace between the British and the Iroquois Six Nations. The treaty ratified the British purchase of a large swath of Central Pennsylvania, including parts of the West Branch valley.

This was the colonial frontier of the 1770's. Settlers pinned their hopes and life savings on the chance to buy land of their own and to establish a place in the world for themselves and their families. Dotted by small villages and farms, the valley basked in neat fields and tidy orchards.

Settlers' relations with their Native neighbors were generally good. Although, there remained a dispute over which creek served as the boundary of the purchased land. The colonial government recognized the Native's claim and barred settlement of the land in question. Some, however, refused the government's stance and pushed on to the disputed land anyway. With no recourse to government law or protection, they formed their own government they called the Fair Play system, in which three elected commissioners resolved all internal problems.

The greater conflict was with Connecticut. Royal grants ceded the same land to both Connecticut and Pennsylvania. Connecticut settlers began arriving to displace the Pennsylvanians and the Pennsylvanians refused to leave. Through late 1775, the Pennsylvanians defeated Connecticut Militia advances, expelled Connecticut settlers from the West Branch and marched on their North Branch settlements.

But, a larger conflict was brewing . . .

CHAPTER 1

July 1776

THE FAIR PLAY TERRITORY

"Odd," thought Caldwell as he reached for the bell and noticed its London manufacturer's mark. He'd handled it a thousand times before. But today it struck him. He turned the cool brass over in his hands and brushed the mark with his thumb.

"Odd, this prized possession from the old country should summon them *here*. Odd, things could ever have gotten to this point."

He shook his head and stared at the bell a moment longer. He raised his eyes to the surrounding hills. It was about noon.

"Well, it begins today," he said. And, he rang the bell.

Others picked up his signal. He heard shouts, whistles, gunshots and the shrill note of the conch shell relay through the valley.

Caldwell's forehead beaded with perspiration. He was grateful for the shade of the elm. He laid down the bell and sat by the creek with his back against the trunk.

Soon, he saw them. Men, women and children ambled onto the lanes. He watched them come, about fifty families in all. And, he waited.

As the last of the assembly arrived, he stood and motioned them to press in close. He unrolled the parchment. The whispering died away and he raised his voice above the rush of the creek.

"Citizens . . . we have drafted the following statement of our resolve."

He read:

"We, the inhabitants of the Fair Play Territory, have settled here by right of the Treaty of Fort Stanwix and the purchase of 1768.

The boundary dispute between the Penns and the Indian signers of that treaty has left us unrecognized and unsupported. We, therefore, founded our own Fair Play system. We've used that system to govern ourselves.

Though we are considered outlaws, we have defended this land against invasions of Connecticut Yankees who attempted to claim our valley as they have land on the North Branch. We will continue to defend it against all enemies of Pennsylvania.

We've furnished good men to the local militia and to the Continental Army in Massachusetts to counter the base actions of the crown. The unwarranted seizing of citizens, waging war with regulars against civilians and inciting our Indian neighbors to join in their depredations will not be abided.

As we can no longer wait for officials to respond to these outrages, we must act upon our own consciences.

Therefore, on this fourth day of July, in the year of our Lord, seventeen hundred and seventy-six, we declare ourselves to be wholly independent. Our allegiance to the crown and government of Britain is hereby dissolved and we are now and forever free."

He looked up.

For a suspended moment, his words hung in the air.

Then someone let loose with a triumphant cry, and the crowd erupted. Men laughed and shouted. Women hugged. Tears of happiness streamed down their cheeks. A fiddle squealed through a din of gunshots and barking dogs and someone grabbed the bell and clanged away in accompaniment.

Caldwell took a swig when someone bumped into him mid-reel and offered him a jug in apology.

He savored the moment.

"We did it," he thought. "We took a stand."

★ ★ ★ ★ ★

ACROSS THE RIVER

Brady was stunned when he heard the sudden commotion. He pushed a branch aside and stared across the river. He rested his hand on the shaft of his tomahawk and looked at Boone and Murphy.

"Fair Play men," said Boone.

"What the devil?" answered Murphy. "Odd time for a frolic."

"Sure is a mess of 'em," said Boone.

Murphy turned to Brady and asked, "Cap'n, you think we ought'a go see what's goin' on?"

"Na, Murph, they don't seem to be in any trouble. Must be somebody got married or somethin'. Besides, we need to get back to Fort Augusta."

Two days earlier, Brady attended the council on the worsening situation with the Indians. He suggested they contact the local tribes and reinforce the friendship they'd had with them. The committee liked the idea and asked him to look into it.

Now, he, Boone and Murphy were returning from the village on the Great Island. They'd gotten the old chief to agree to come to the fort to discuss a treaty, but the young men of the village didn't hide their disgust.

Brady glanced around.

"I been thinkin' we ought'a get off this river path and take one 'a the hollows up over the mountain," he said. "I don't like bein' out in the open like this. In fact, this looks like a good spot to leave the trail . . . plenty of cover. Be careful to cover your tracks."

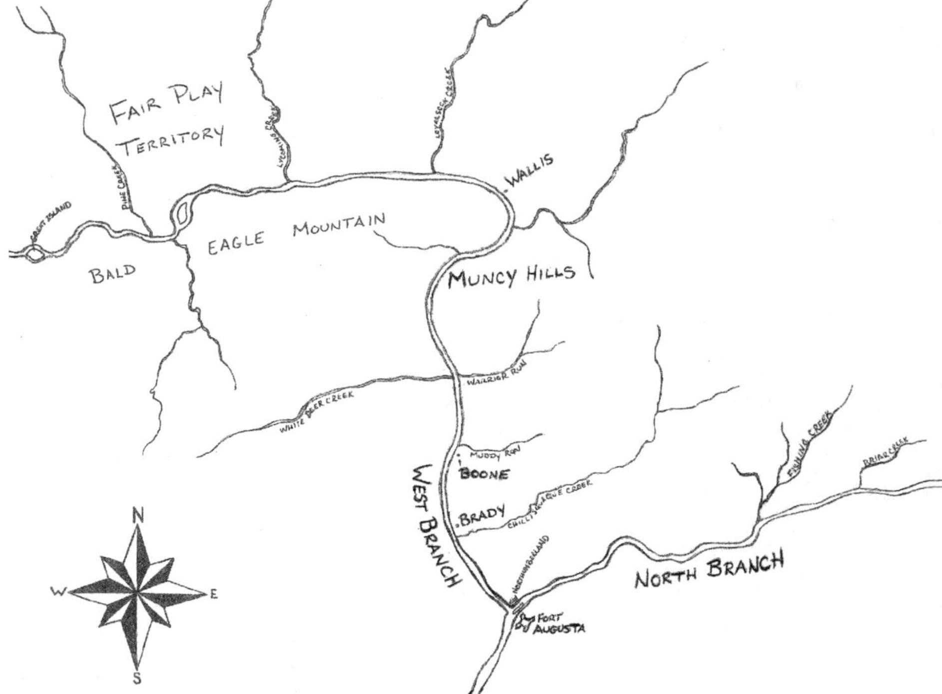

By midafternoon they were high on Bald Eagle Mountain. Suddenly, Boone said, "Hey Cap'n, look there."

"What is it?" asked Murphy.

Boone pointed down to where they'd been on the path. The others sighted along his finger and saw heavily-armed men from the village moving in a slow, measured run.

"Good thinkin' getting' off that path Cap'n," said Murphy.

"I just had a feelin' they didn't want us deliverin' that message."

"Well," said Boone, "I'm sure as hell always goin' to trust your feelin's."

"Let's get back to the fort, gentlemen," said Brady.

Toward evening they found a ravine and secured themselves for the night.

"We'll sleep in shifts," said Brady. "I'll take first watch."

The next morning, they ate a cold breakfast and got back on

the trail. By dusk, they'd weathered the day's thunderstorms and Fort Augusta lay only a few miles ahead. They pushed on to reach the riverbank directly opposite, just a little after dark.

They boarded a canoe and started across the river. As they neared the far shore, they smelled the apple pie the colonel's wife was baking in the fort.

"Amazin' what a few days on the trail can do to yer appetite in' it Murph?" asked Boone, who saw the kid craning his head in the direction of the smell.

"Well, I sure could go for a hunk o' that pie if that's what ya mean," answered Murphy.

Approaching the riverbank, Brady called up to the sentry on the outer wall, "Hello in the fort."

"Stand and be recognized," challenged an adolescent voice.

"It's Cap'n Brady, sentry, and bein' as I'm in a canoe I'm sure as hell not standin' up."

"Who's with ya?" shot back the sentry. Boone gave Brady a surprised look.

"Boone and Murphy; we're back from the Great Island and the colonel's waitin' on us."

The sentry called out, "On the gate. Three comin' in."

The men beached the canoe in front of the fort, dragged it up the riverbank and walked the last few yards of their journey. The massive gate in the outer wall creaked open and the men slid through. As they neared the drawbridge over the dry moat, Brady turned and hollered up to the young guard, "Sentry."

"Yessir?"

"Good work."

The gate closed behind them, and a heavy timber locked it in place. They crossed over the drawbridge, through the inner gate and entered the parade ground.

Candles flickered through the barracks windows as men inside wrote letters and played cards. A dog was bedded down outside the door and raised its head as they walked past. They crossed the parade, passed the officer's quarters and approached the door to the colonel's house.

Brady reached out and gave it three sharp raps.

"Who is it?" called an older female voice.

"Cap'n Brady, with Boone and Murphy; come to make a report, ma'am."

They heard soft footfalls on the floorboards and the door swung open to reveal a pleasant woman wearing a city-made dress. A fire glowed in the hearth behind her and the sweet smell of apple pie wafted over them.

"How are you, gentlemen? It's good to have you back safe."

"Thank you; fine, ma'am," said Brady.

Philadelphia furniture and real imported china shone behind the woman and caught Murphy's eye.

The lady called, "Sam . . . Captain Brady and his boys are back to see you."

"I hear 'em, Sue," he yelled. "I heard Brady bellowin' from halfway across the river."

He appeared from the next room with a grin on his face. "Good to see you, Brady. Boys. Won't you come into the office and tell me all about it?"

Before stepping into the colonel's front room, Brady and his men slid their feet along the boot-scraper embedded in the doorstone. They nodded to Mrs. Hunter as they passed and followed the colonel into his office.

Hunter took a seat at his desk and motioned for the men to sit. Murphy glanced toward the bookcases which held the colonel's library and the maps he kept rolled and tied with ribbon. Candlelight reflected from his uniform buttons as Hunter turned and asked, "Well, Brady, what have you got?"

"A chance, Sam. We met with a Seneca Chief named Waopadagh up at the Great Island. They was cuttin' down their corn and gettin' ready to head north when we got there. Waopadagh said the Brits is offerin' big money for our scalps. We told him they was bein' used and all. He seemed like he wanted to treat with us. Course his young men didn't seem too enthused."

"How so?"

"Well, let's just say they wasn't real cordial with us. But we got Waopadagh to agree to come down here on the next full moon."

"Good job," said Hunter.

"There's more," said Brady. "On the way back we saw the Fair Play men across the river actin' a fool and kickin' up a ruckus. I'm not sure what they was doin', but like Hawk said, it seemed like a strange time for a frolic."

"Didn't you go find out?"

"Na, I didn't like bein' on that river path, so we cut up over the mountain to get back here as quick as possible."

"He was right, too, Colonel," Boone chimed in. "Once we was up on the mountain, we saw a bunch a' young warriors runnin' down the path where we woulda been. They was for sure tryin' to stop the message gettin' through."

"Well, good work, boys," said Hunter. "The next full moon gives us three weeks to get this fort into shape. We've got to make it look as tough and intimidating as possible. If they think they can't tangle with us, they may be more inclined to sign. We'll get to work on it right away."

"I think that sounds like just the thing, Sam," said Brady.

"So, you didn't even get to see Mary and the kids on the way home, John?" asked Hunter.

"No, we stayed on the west side of the river and made straight for the fort."

"Well in that case you haven't had anything but trail food for a few days. Sue insisted on lighting a fire through the storms today so I said she might as well do some bakin'. You fellas want some apple pie?"

Boone jumped in, "Well, me and Cap'n Brady sure would like some, but Murph was just tellin' us he couldn't abide the stuff."

"That ain't so!" shot back Murphy. The three older men laughed as Murphy reddened and realized he'd been had by Boone again.

"Sue, how's about bringin' some a' that pie in here?" Hunter called.

Susanna Hunter appeared with the pie and then came back with some port wine. The men sat talking until Hunter realized they must be exhausted and told them to go to bed.

After saying goodnight, Boone and Murphy ambled off to the barracks while Brady paused in the parade ground. He looked up at the last-quarter moon hanging high above. "Three weeks, Waopadagh. Don't let 'em talk you out of it."

He followed Boone and Murphy into the barracks, took the first empty bed he saw, and was asleep as his head touched the straw.

★ ★ ★ ★ ★

FORT AUGUSTA

The next three weeks passed quickly. Murphy, from Northumberland, was in and out of the fort, constantly. He helped the garrison replace rotted stockade logs and reset fallen palings over the moat. He carried ammunition kegs to the bastion points and stacked cannonballs next to the newly positioned artillery.

Brady and Boone each headed back up the West Branch to tend their farms. They did their chores, attended militia musters and spent evenings at home with their families. A few days before the full moon, Boone showed up on Brady's doorstep.

Before he could knock, the door swung open and Mary Brady yelled, "Hawkins Boone, get yerself in here and have some dinner."

"Hiya Mary, I just had breakfast this mornin'."

"So did we an' that was five hours ago. Now get in here and eat."

"Yes'm."

Entering the house, Boone found the Bradys seated at their

long table. John sat at the head and pretty, blue-eyed Mary at the far end with all their sons and daughters in between.

"James, scrooch over an' let Mr. Boone have a seat," said Brady.

"Thank you, folks," said Boone. "How are ya young'uns?"

"Fine," they answered, almost in unison, while continuing to eat.

"We're havin' Dutch potpie," said Mary. "I learned it from Mrs. Derr over the river."

"Mmmmm. Mighty good, Mary," said Boone as he took the first bite.

Boone always liked James, the smart, good-natured eighteen-year-old sitting next to him. The young ladies admired his long, fiery red hair.

The older, more business-like Samuel sat across from Boone. He'd served with Murphy in Massachusetts. Concentrating on his meal, Samuel didn't look up until he finished.

Brady took pride in all of his children. From Samuel to the youngest, his boys were responsible and hard-working. He doted on his girls, who all shared their mother's character, good looks and flowing blonde hair . . . especially little Hannah.

"How's the folks, Hawk?" asked Brady, wiping potpie juice from his chin.

"Just fine. Jane sends her best."

"Tell her the same," said Mary.

"Thank you, I will."

"How's the militia company you raised?" asked Brady.

"They're doin' fine," said Boone. "Good bunch a' men. Each muster brings 'em closer to lookin' like soldiers."

"Mr. Boone?" young James spoke up.

"Yeah?"

"I heard as how you're related to Dan'l Boone, who started Boonestown out west. Is that so?"

"Yep, it is. Dan'l's my cousin and our folks was close down in Berks County, where we come from."

"Did he teach you to shoot?" asked James.

"Nope . . . I taught him."

Everyone laughed, including Boone himself. Brady enjoyed his friend's legendary bravado, but he also knew Boone was one of the few men in the valley who'd give Murphy a run for his money with a long rifle, and his claim could just as well be true as not.

"Well, dead-eye," Brady broke in, "have you had your fill?"

"Sure have," answered Boone. "Darn good dinner, Mary. I thank you."

"You're welcome, anytime." she replied.

"We'd better be goin', then," said Brady, who stood and reached for his rifle standing in the corner.

"Good to see you, young'uns," said Boone. "Mary," he added with a polite nod.

"You too, Hawkins," she said.

"Mr. Boone?" said James again.

"Yeah?"

"Do you 'spose we could go huntin' sometime?"

"I 'spose we could; only yer ma would have to get a lot bigger cookpot than that one."

There was more laughter as he waved and stepped out the door. "Goodbye," said Brady to his family.

"Bye," they answered.

"Bye, Mary," said Brady, giving his wife a kiss as he stepped to the door. "You, children take care a' your ma, now."

"We will."

"Oh, and James. . . " he said as an afterthought.

"Yessir?"

"You'd get a damn sight more game if ya'd take me along on that huntin' trip."

Everyone laughed as Brady left the house and started down the road with Boone.

A long afternoon's walk brought them to Northumberland.

They crossed the river to the fort and were impressed with its transformation.

"Looks like the colonel's been busy," said Boone.

"Yeah, when Sam puts his mind to somethin', it gets done."

"Cannon are a lot more noticeable," Boone continued. "An' it looks like they got men on permanent in each a' the bastions now."

"Yeah, an' in them blockhouses too," said Brady as he saw men silhouetted in each of the strongholds along the stockade walls that reached to the river. Walking up the riverbank, they noticed Sunbury was quiet. Most people were inside having their evening meals. Woodsmoke permeated the air as it curled up from outdoor summer kitchens.

Here and there, someone worked alone in his garden, tending to weeds and enjoying the young evening's cool breeze off the river. The muted purple and pink tones of early twilight cast a peaceful veil over the town, and one or two candles popped on as the sun slipped beneath the top of Blue Hill, across the river.

"My favorite time a' day," mused Boone.

"Yep, mighty purty in' it?" agreed Brady.

Not yet dark, the gate was open. Brady nodded to the guard, and they walked in. They crossed the parade ground and found the colonel sitting beside his house enjoying the air and an after-dinner smoke.

"Didn't expect you boys for another day or two," he said.

"Thought we'd come down an' see if ya needed a hand. . ." answered Brady, "but evidently ya don't."

"Nope, things are shapin' up pretty good," said Hunter. "Had your supper?"

"No, we ain't," said Boone.

"Why don't you go an' see the cook? Men on the wall haven't eaten yet, and I know he's got some stew cookin'."

"Thanks," they answered.

"And when you're done, come on back. We can talk over a game of All Fours."

"You mean Pitch?" replied Boone.

"Yeah, the high, the low, the jack and the game," answered Hunter.

Boone said, "You 'spose you can afford it; losin' to us *and* givin' up some a' that port wine a' yours?"

"Me afford it? I'm planning on getting a'hold a' some a' that land you've been buyin' up all over the place."

"Whoa, fellas. . ." Brady chimed in, "gentleman farmer speakin'. I think we can leave it at a friendly halfpence-per-wager game." They all laughed as Brady and Boone turned to go eat.

Returning after dark, they were ushered into the colonel's office. He was waiting in his high-backed Windsor chair, holding a deck of cards.

"Sit down, gentlemen. Let's cut for the deal." While going through the ritual, the colonel asked, "You think they'll show, John?"

"Should. Waopadagh seemed sincere enough. I think it depends on how much authority he really has with his people."

"Let's hope it's considerable," said Hunter.

"Well, in any case, we'll know in three days," replied Brady.

"Oh, by the way, gentlemen," said Hunter, changing the subject, "have you heard the news about independence?"

"You mean the Fair Play men?" asked Brady. "Yeah, we heard that was the ruckus we saw."

"No," answered Hunter. "A rider came in last week with news the Continental Congress has finally taken a stand. And, they did it on the very same day the Fair Play men did. We are, gentlemen, a free and independent country."

"'Bout damn time!" shouted Boone, smiling.

"See, Sam, things are lookin' up," said Brady. "Now, we'll make it stick."

The colonel smiled, then slapped his hand on the table and said, "Let's play cards."

The evening continued genially. After a bottle of port, and

Boone losing almost five shillings, Brady and Boone went back to the barracks to get some sleep.

For the next two days, Hunter had Boone and Brady drill the extra militia brought in for show. Hunter knew they'd have them in crack condition by the time the Indians arrived, and it freed him to attend to the final details of the fort.

About midmorning of the third day, a cry rang out from one of the blockhouses, "Indians, comin' down the river!"

Mounting the walls, Hunter, Brady and Boone saw a procession of canoes rounding the bend as far up the West Branch as they could see.

"Is he bringin' all six nations, Brady?" asked the colonel.

"It was a big village, Sam."

Finally, the end of the column appeared, and more than one hundred canoes floated toward them. As they neared, Brady could see Waopadagh and the elders leading the way. The young men followed, and the women trailed behind with the stores.

The heavily-armed Indians looked impressive. Dressed in breechcloths and leggings, the shirtless men wore colorful paint. Highly-ornamented sashes crossed over their shoulders, and they sported jewelry and long, greased hair for the occasion.

"They're in warpaint," said Boone.

"Yeah, it seems they had the same idea we did about tryin' to look intimidating," said Hunter.

"It's a good thing you made the preparations you did, Sam," said Brady.

"Drummer, beat the call to posts!" cried Hunter. "Come on, gentlemen," he said to Boone and Brady. "Let's go try to keep the peace."

Hunter, Brady and Boone worked their way through the oncoming men while the garrison formed on the parade ground and militia manned the walls. Waopadagh, the elders and the young men marched through the open gate and came to a stop, facing the officers.

Brady took a step forward and said for all to hear, "Welcome, Waopadagh. We are pleased our brothers have come to talk with us of peace."

"Thank you, John Brady," answered Waopadagh.

"This is Hawkins Boone, who you met before," continued Brady, "and this is Colonel Hunter, commander of Fort Augusta."

"Colonel, we are honored to meet you," said Waopadagh, formally.

Hunter nodded and replied, "Waopadagh, it is I who am honored. Thank you for coming."

"Let us now speak of peace between our peoples," said Brady.

Waopadagh paused awkwardly and replied, "It has been a long and hard journey for us, John Brady."

Realizing his breach of etiquette, Brady said to Hunter, "He expects a welcomin' ceremony. Do you have any kind of gift to offer them?"

"No," said Hunter. "Not much. We've no trade goods whatsoever. There's hardly any currency in the entire fort and what we've got wouldn't make much of an impression. The citizens of Sunbury are barely scraping by, so there's nothing there, either.

"Well . . ." said Brady, "let's hope he wants peace more than niceties."

Turning back to the delegation he said, "Thank you, Waopadagh, for the long and arduous journey you've endured to come and treat with us. Let us now speak of peace between our peoples."

Realizing they weren't going to be given the ritual welcoming gift, Waopadagh glanced at the elders who returned bewildered looks. Looking to his warriors, he saw them sneering in disgust. His hands were tied. He couldn't ignore this lack of protocol and maintain authority among his people.

Brady continued, "What have you spoken of with your brothers in the north, Waopadagh? And what have you decided?"

Waopadagh responded, "John Brady, we want no war with

you and your people. You say you are our friends, and the King will use us to his purpose. His men say the same of you."

Brady sighed, "Waopadagh, they are lying to you. You know we've kept faith with our Indian friends. We've been good neighbors and have honored our friendship. If they turn us against each other, both our peoples will suffer. Please, stay here as our neighbors. Support us against the King and don't believe what they say."

"When I look at this place," replied Waopadagh, "I think of the great village of Shamokin. Yet I do not see Shamokin. I see a settler's town built on Shamokin's ashes. We know not who to trust. We will not sign a treaty."

"Waopadagh, it's true settlers destroyed Shamokin. But, that was in wartime, long ago. And, Shamokin was a Delaware town. Your own people fought the Delawares for many years. It was only through conquering them that you came to control the land in these valleys. It was your people, then, who profited from the sale of that land to us."

"John Brady, we thank you for your thoughts. We must go now."

Realizing his cause was lost, Brady said, "We thank you, Waopadagh. Go in peace."

Waopadagh turned and the Indians filed out of the fort. Boarding their canoes, they solemnly headed back up the West Branch against the current.

Back in Hunter's office that afternoon, Brady said, "I shoulda thought about that damn ceremony."

"It's not your fault, John," answered Hunter. "We had nothing to give in any case. Ever since we've been supplying ourselves *and* the continentals, we've been just getting by. You gave it a damn good try."

"They may keep the peace yet Cap'n," said Boone. "He said they wish no war with us."

"Yeah, maybe," answered Brady, distractedly. "Sam, if you don't need me for a while, I wouldn't mind followin' 'em up the river a ways. I got a funny feelin'."

"Sure," said Hunter. "That sounds like a good idea."

"Another feelin', huh Cap'n? You want some company?" asked Boone.

"Na, Hawk. It might be better if I go alone. No tellin' what they're up to, an' if they double back, you'll be more valuable here than with me."

"I agree," said Hunter.

"Then it's settled. I'll get a horse and get goin' right away."

Brady excused himself. He grabbed a horse and galloped through the gate. Crossing the river to Northumberland, he set off down the road, leaving a roiling cloud of dust behind him. Riding hard along the river road, there was no sign of the Indians who'd been in the fort.

Brady couldn't help but think of his family up ahead.

"James and John could put up a stout fight," he thought. "But, there are so many Indians that if they decide to do damage, nothing could stop them."

His mind began painting the worst possible images. He tried to control it, but the mutilated bodies of victims he'd seen in the past, lying twisted and broken in front of the charred ruins of their homes, crept back to him. Only now, they wore the faces of his family.

Filled with angst and self-reproach, Brady felt in some bizarre way he might actually cause his fears to become reality, simply by seeing it all so clearly.

"Oh, God, let them be alright," he said out loud. "Help me get there in time."

Brady's horse was in trouble, but he spurred it on. He rounded a bend in the road and finally saw his farm up ahead. He quickly looked around.

"No smoke," he thought. "No scalpless bodies in the yard . . . sheep and oxen browsing quietly in the meadow behind the barn."

"Thank you," he breathed quietly for seeing the answer to all of his confused and fragmented prayers.

Slowing his horse, Brady noticed a chaotic swirl of color and motion across the river. He heard raucous voices echoing hollowly over the water. Some of the voices were angry while others just yelled and laughed nonsensically.

He realized, as he reigned-up on the riverbank, it was the warrior's red sashes and jewelry flashing in the late afternoon sun that had drawn his attention. Waopadagh's procession had pulled into Derr's trading post for the night.

Just then, James emerged from the side door of the house. He walked up to Brady and said, "They've been over there for a couple hours now."

"What's all the hollerin' about?" asked Brady.

"I don't know, but they sure have been raisin' hell," answered James. "They sound drunk to me."

"I was thinkin' the same thing, but Derr wouldn't give 'em spirits." Brady watched across the river for a few moments and said, "James take this horse over t' the barn. I'm goin' over there t' see what's goin' on. Derr might need some help."

"Ma's not goin' to like it, you goin' over there," said James.

"Then don't tell her," said Brady. "And, try to keep her away from the window."

"Yessir."

James led the exhausted horse to the barn as Brady walked toward the canoe he kept on the riverbank. He hadn't gotten forty feet when he saw the Indian women board several canoes and begin rowing across the river toward him.

He crouched in the underbrush and watched them come ashore. They unloaded ammunition and powder, rifles, tomahawks and knives from the canoes and hid them in the thickets near him.

Brady was trying to decide if these weapons were being stolen, but he didn't think Derr had nearly so many. They must have brought them with them and didn't want Derr to see them and raise the alarm. The women's task accomplished, they rowed back to the western shore.

Brady ran to his canoe and shoved it down the bank. He

pushed it into the water and jumped in, in a single fluid motion. He grabbed the paddle and dug deep into the placid water, his strong strokes leaving a wake behind him.

The low-hanging sun shone directly in his eyes and made it difficult to see. The trees and people were all silhouetted against the brilliant sky. Reaching the opposite shore, he leapt from the canoe and dragged it out of the water. He marched up the bank and was appalled to discover the jewelry wasn't all he'd seen shimmering in the sunlight.

Many of the warriors had pulled their knives and were making a sport of grabbing each other in mock scalpings. Brady watched as they made huge, exaggerated cutting motions from their *victims'* foreheads to the top of their shoulders. Then they pretended to bite at the front of the scalp with their teeth and rip it backward.

As he neared the melee, Brady's fears were confirmed. A large barrel of rum was sitting on the porch. Warriors with tin cups bunched around the barrel and dipped into the sweet, fiery liquid, downing it as quickly as they could. After two or three dips, anxious comrades shoved them out of the way and began dipping themselves.

Waopadagh was off to one side with the elders. Now it made perfect sense why the women had taken the weapons across the river. Waopadagh was trying to keep the peace. "Good thinkin' my friend," Brady thought to himself.

Spying Derr on the far edge of the porch, Brady worked his way through the crowd and said to him, "My God Ludwig, what have you done?"

The poor Dutchman had tried his best at frontier diplomacy. Now, seeing the result, he was obviously afraid for his family. He stammered, "Dey say you gif um no treat at de fort, so I dink I gif um one here. Den mebbe dey go home in bease."

Brady felt sorry for the man but was angry at his stupidity. He saw the barrel was still more than half-full and knew things could only get worse. There was only one thing he could do. He marched up to the barrel and kicked it over, dumping the liquor irretrievably into the dust.

The silence that followed cast a pall on the crowd. The warriors stared at Brady in disbelief. In their stupor, some droned incomprehensibly. One tall, muscular warrior strode up to Brady and confronted him, weaving slightly as he stood.

Brady stared back. Either through boredom or drunkenness, the young man turned and tramped sullenly away.

Brady knew, for the moment, he'd diffused the situation. He told Derr everything would be alright now, and he walked back to the river. He looked up as he boarded his canoe and saw Waopadagh. Brady threw him a respectful wave of thanks and Waopadagh nodded in reply.

The Indians resumed their journey early the next morning. They traveled out of the valley and didn't stop until they reached the home of the Six Nations.

Winter 1776-1777

FORT AUGUSTA

Mary Brady stared at the ceiling. The rest of the house lay sleeping. Her mind raced with the thoughts of John and John Jr. marching off to war in the morning.

"How could so much change in just five short months?" she thought.

The peaceful days of family life ended quickly after the incident at Derr's. First, John decided they should move to a more defendable place, further up the West Branch.

They bought land at Muncy Manor and worked through the fall building a new stockaded home. The locals already called it Fort Brady. Mary still felt the fresh layer of callouses on her hands.

Then, she'd barely seen John and the boys. They were kept busy with militia training. She took charge of settling into the new house and drilling the children in what each needed to do in case of attack.

Mary thought about the day when news of the army's defeat at Long Island reached the valley. With New York lost and Philadelphia threatened, the hope of victory seemed dim.

Congress soon called for more regiments and Mary learned West Branch men would make up the new 12th Pennsylvania. Samuel had already enlisted in the 8th regiment and she knew the rest of her family wouldn't be together much longer.

She was proud when John was given command of one of the new companies. Even now she smiled thinking about Hawkins Boone being promoted to command another.

When the regiment was ordered to rendezvous at Fort Augusta, Mary knew it would take days there before they'd actually march to join General Washington.

She could still see John's face when she announced she was coming along to the fort. He just stared back . . . and grinned.

The fort buzzed with activity as they arrived. Mary saw crews building the batteaux the regiment would use to move down the river. Others unloaded supplies. Militiamen from across the county were drilling on the parade.

Mary was elated when Jane Boone came running up to them.

"Hello, Bradys," she yelled.

"Jane," shouted Mary. "I'm so glad t' see you," she said as they hugged.

"Me too," answered Jane. "C'mon with me to the Hunters'. The colonel and his wife invited me and Hawkins to stay with them. They want you and John to have the other upstairs room."

"How nice," said Mary. "John, did you hear?"

"Yep. Mighty fine of 'em. You go on ahead, Mary," said Brady. "I'll go find Hawk."

Jane, Mary and Susanna Hunter spent most of the following days together as Brady and Boone worked with the regiment and Colonel Hunter organized supplies.

Now, as morning neared, Mary rolled on her side and snuggled next to John. She thought about how the evening began.

When darkness fell, the regiment grew quiet and reflective. Men sat around the fires. In the distance, someone played a fiddle. There were no jigs or reels in the strings that evening. It was a low, soulful sound that wove through the hundreds of men staring into the flames.

Mary experienced this before, but she'd never gotten used to it. It never became any easier. She showed a brave face for John's sake. Sure, he'd know it was an act, but she knew he'd want to remember her without tears.

They sat quietly in each other's arms and looked out the window at the fires below.

"We got plenty a' supplies laid in an' the boys are there for choppin' all the wood you'll need," said Brady, absently.

"We're fine," answered Mary.

"That's a good strong stockade we built," he continued. "I feel a lot better about you bein' there than at the old place. But, if there's any trouble, we're right there by Wallis' so don't hesitate to go there if ya need to."

"We're *fine.*"

"I know it, darlin'. I just hate leavin' you with things bein' like they are around here."

"You said it yourself," said Mary. "Somebody's got to go. If the Continental Army collapses, there's nothin' left."

"Yeah."

"I'll miss you, John Brady."

"I'll miss you, darlin'."

Staring into his eyes, she felt that familiar pain of never being able to get quite close enough to this man with whom she'd shared her life.

They sat looking at one another for what may have been moments or may have been hours. Slowly, Brady raised his hand and caressed her hair between his fingers. He leaned closer and tenderly placed his lips on hers in a timeless, longing kiss.

As the melody from the fiddle drifted plaintively through the night, they finally pulled apart. One great, round tear trickled down Mary's cheek and reflected the firelight below.

She finally fell asleep, but morning came early when the drum awoke the camp before dawn. It was December 18th, just one week before Christmas.

As the Bradys and Boones met downstairs, they smelled the comforting aroma of Susanna Hunter's biscuits baking in the oven and the coffee she had bubbling over the fire. Colonel

Hunter came from his office, and the three couples shared a brief breakfast.

No one said much.

"Feels like it might snow," said Brady.

"I was thinkin' the same thing," said Boone. "Hope the hell it doesn't. Wouldn't be so bad while we're on the river, I guess, but I don't like the thought of trudgin' through it all the way to Philly."

Then, suddenly remembering a question he'd been meaning to ask, Hunter interjected, "What ever happened to that Murphy boy who liked Sue's pie so well? Is he in the regiment, or do we get to keep him here?"

"He signed back up a'ready," said Brady. "About the same time Samuel joined the 8th.

"Murphy's with Cap'n Parr's rifle company," said Boone. Said he didn't want to wait around to get back to the fightin'."

"Sounds like we could have used both of 'em here," said Hunter.

"Yeah, an' as many like 'em as we could find," answered Brady.

There was a polite knock on the door. Susanna rose to open it, and Colonel William Cooke stood in the doorway.

"Gentlemen, I'm afraid it's time for us to depart," he said gently.

Everyone stood while Boone and Brady grabbed their rifles and accoutrements. "Good luck to you, Bill," said Hunter to the colonel.

"And to you, Sam. Watch after our folks for us, will you?"

"You know we will."

The Bradys and Boones each embraced.

"Look out for, Johnny," said Mary, "and come back to me soon."

He gave her a quick but tender kiss. "I will."

Jane Boone stood smiling up at Hawkins. She was obviously proud of her husband.

She playfully cuffed him on the side of the head and said, "Go get 'em Cap' Boone."

He held her by the chin and kissed her.

"We'll get 'em," he said with a wink.

Then he turned and stepped through the door, followed by Brady.

"Good luck, boys," Hunter called after them.

They walked with Colonel Cooke across the parade, out the gate and down to the river's edge. Colonel Hunter retired to his office, and Mary stood with Jane by the door until they were out of sight.

Every now and then, the women heard their husbands yelling orders while they organized the loading of men and equipment. Near nine o' clock the regiment's fifes and drums struck up a martial air. Clutching their heavy shawls about them, Jane and Mary went with Colonel and Mrs. Hunter to the walls of the fort overlooking the river.

Spread before them was an armada of local pride. The men stood smart with their rifles shouldered at attention while flags snapped in the breeze above them.

The squeal of the fifes and thunder of the drums infused the moment with a feeling of magnitude. Then the instruments stopped, and, as the last lingering drumbeat echoed back across the river from Blue Hill, it began to snow.

Colonel Cooke gave the order to cast off. Men loosed the lines holding the batteaux and the crews poled them into the current. Thin skiffs of ice flowed past and broke as they collided with the boats.

Jane and Mary waved. Brady and Boone, in the ranks with their companies, waved back. Mary also saw Johnny pushing hard on a pole as he looked around to see her.

Once out in the channel, the current caught the boats and carried the men on their way as the fifes and drums began to play again.

Colonel Hunter looked down the wall and nodded to a nearby gun-crew. In salute to the departing men, the cannon roared to life with an explosion of fire and a plume of smoke that billowed out over the river.

The snow grew heavier and obscured the view of the regiment as it drifted further away in the gray morning light. Only splashes of color could be made out through the swirling flakes as the flags fluttered in the wind. Then, the boats drifted around the furthest bend in the river, and they were gone.

★　★　★　★　★

NEAR WALLIS' ESTATE

It was a big day for Robert Robb. That morning he'd bathed and was now carefully dressing in his best clothes. Though he admitted it to no one, he was nervous about meeting with Mr. Wallis. The invitation had come most unexpectedly.

He wasn't sure he knew quite how to act in a private interview with someone so refined and rich as Wallis. Robb had always been proud of his hundred-acre farm, but Wallis owned six thousand acres that stretched all the way from Muncy Manor to the Great Island. And, that was just a part of his livelihood. Wallis' real money came from the shipping business he'd owned and run in Philadelphia for so many years.

Robb liked Wallis . . . as much as he knew of him. He'd voted for Wallis when he was elected to the Pennsylvania State Assembly and again when he was elected a captain in the local militia. In fact, he always admired that Wallis didn't allow his religious convictions to keep him from accepting the post. His men always joked they had the only Quaker captain in the commonwealth.

Robb worked his thick fingers through the loops at the top of his boots and shoved his massive feet into them. He pulled on his overcoat and steeled himself at the door before opening it and heading out to the barn.

Riding his stout chestnut mare, Robb picked his way along the country lanes between his farm and Wallis'. It was a cold day, and the wind pelted him with fine needles of snow, blown from the fields. He flipped up his overcoat collar and tugged the brim of his hat down over his forehead. Reaching the intersection with the river road, he turned up the valley and continued the half mile or so on to Wallis' lane.

Robb passed between Wallis' stone gateposts, which anchored fences that neatly bounded the fields on either side of the lane. Everything was manicured and stately. Robb could see the rooftop of the house over the ridgeline in front of him, and, as he crested the hill, the entire home came into view. Two stories of Pennsylvania limestone were handsomely finished with a wooden third floor. Along the roofline stood elegant dormers and a massive chimney he figured must be supported by an immense hearth inside.

Robb was astounded. He knew Wallis was well-to-do, but, here in the valley where a man was doing well to have a second room in his log home, Wallis had constructed a fine mansion. Looking around, he saw large barns and outbuildings. Beyond those were the servant and slave quarters. This estate of Wallis' was a village unto itself.

Approaching the home, Robb was greeted with a cacophony of barks and yowls as a cluster of baying hounds ran toward him. Dismounting, Robb tied his horse to an ornate hitching post and took a step toward the front door when it opened suddenly before him. He was met by a well-dressed Irish servant. Robb explained he'd been invited by Mr. Wallis and the man showed him inside and seated him in the study, by the fire.

The entry hall and study were more opulent than anything Robb had ever seen. Carpets, paintings and fine furniture were everywhere.

As Robb warmed himself, the servant appeared carrying a tray with a steaming noggin of spiced cider. For Robb, just holding the vessel between his palms felt wonderful, but then the warm, sweet steam curled up into his face and enticed him to drink.

It was delicious. The cider had been spiced with cinnamon, nutmeg and cloves . . . luxuries locals rarely experienced. Robb also tasted fine Jamaican rum, which did its part to warm him, too.

He sat, staring into the fire and savoring the drink when the servant reappeared with a pitcher.

"Drink it down and I'll pour ye another," he said. "There's a whole great cauldron bubblin' in the kitchen and I'll keep ye supplied."

"Thanks," said Robb, gulping quickly and holding out his cup.

A short time later, the servant appeared again. This time, he stood in the doorway and announced, "Mr. Robb; Mr. Wallis."

Seeing Robb beginning to rise, Wallis entered the room and said, "Don't stand up Robert. Relax and be comfortable. I appreciate you coming out here like this."

"Nice to see ya, Mr. Wallis," said Robb. "What did ya want t' see me about?"

As Wallis took the other chair by the fire, it occurred to Robb that Wallis was shorter and pudgier than he'd realized.

Wallis was dressed in a plush, burgundy waistcoat and jacket with matching breeches. Lace ruffles and silver buttons erupted from every possible niche, and silver-buckled shoes covered his finely woven stockings. He wore a supremely coifed and set powdered wig that, to Robb, lent him an air of authority.

"Well, Robert," Wallis began, "as I mentioned, I know you to be a man of character. You possess the heart of a patriot and the qualities of a leader."

"Thank you, Mr. Wallis," said Robb.

"No need to thank me. These are your justly deserved merits. I am merely observing them. Now, I have chosen to speak with you because I believe you are a man who will go to any lengths for the good of his country and that you can be trusted."

"I certainly am."

"No doubt," said Wallis, "you have heard of the King's peace commission that tried to meet with Congress a few months ago."

"Yes. I understand nothin' came of it," answered Robb.

"That is true, but the reasons are little known. Lord Howe was not granted permission to meet with Congress as a whole, so he met with a representative committee on Staten Island. That committee was made up of Dr. Franklin, Mr. John Adams, and Mr. Rutledge. I have here a notice that was printed shortly afterward in New York recounting the particulars of the meeting."

Wallis handed the document to Robb.

"You'll see it contains a disturbing account of what transpired."

"But Mr. Wallis," said Robb, "New York is in British hands. If this was printed there, how can it be trusted?"

"When you read it and know what I have come to know of these men, there is no doubt of its veracity."

"What do ya mean?" asked Robb.

"Consider for a moment, Robert: Lord Howe was offering peace. Think of the countless lives and fortunes that would have been saved had his offer been accepted. What is truly best for our country? Who stands to profit from war?"

Robb's mouth opened, but his eyes squinted as though he were trying to find his way from a dark room into the bright sunlight.

Wallis continued, "You see, through my position and from my friends in Philadelphia, I have come to learn that Dr. Franklin, Rittenhouse and many of our other leaders are rogues. They have achieved their high status through bribery and chicanery and have come to crave the power they've gained. If the war were averted, these men would be mere citizens with no authority and no position. They care nothing for the country itself, but only about what they mean *to* the country."

Robb's eyes now relaxed, but he leaned forward from the edge of his seat as Wallis continued.

"I happen to know we *can* achieve a just and lasting peace. I have it on fact that we will be recognized in parliament and share all the advantages of the empire."

Robb tilted his head, as if about to ask a question, but Wallis didn't give him the chance.

"I am a patriot, Robert. I know this is best. As a captain of the militia, I know if our men who are away at war were to return, we would be far better situated to defend ourselves against the Indians and the Connecticut settlers who have designs on our valley. I know, as you do, our safety here is in question and I will fight tirelessly for my country. I am concerned for my neighbors and friends, but I don't care a damn about a corrupt Congress that is wasting men's lives solely to advance its own members."

Robb was now completely involved in Wallis' rhetoric and waited motionlessly for his next revelation.

"Friends of mine who know of the true nature of what is happening in Philadelphia have come up with a plan to save our country. The words in the document you hold are true. Officials from every county in the state have copies. They believe if local citizens who are strong in heart and patriotic, like yourself, were to alert the population of the dismal circumstances we face, we may circumvent Congress and end this frivolous war."

"I can't believe it," said Robb, his face reddening. "The rascals! The very people we've been lookin' to for leadership are treatin' us like that?"

Robb paused and considered Wallis' words. "I'm honored you chose me for somethin' so important, Mr. Wallis, but you're way more influential than I am. Why don't you convince everybody yourself?"

"I wish I could, Robert. It is an honor I would dearly love to have. But, because of my associations in Philadelphia, I would jeopardize the whole plan and endanger my friends to the wrath of Congress. You pose no threat to them. That is why I chose to speak with you. I know you to be a man of integrity, and I know you will keep this sacred secret. If it were to get out, many good patriots' lives would be imperiled."

"No one will find out," swore Robb. "I give you my word. Now, what do you want me to do?"

"Hardly anything at all," said Wallis. "At the next Committee of Safety meeting, perhaps just inquire of the other members if they see any good in pursuing such a course of peace. If they agree with you, we may deliver our county from war. I understand the Crown will negotiate with any group of men so no effort will be inconsequential. If other counties follow suit, we may deliver the entire state."

"You can count on me, Mr. Wallis."

"I knew I could, Robert. Now if you'll excuse me, I have correspondence awaiting me in my office that must be attended to promptly."

As Wallis rose, he motioned for Robb to stay seated. "Perhaps some evening you and your wife would consent to join me for supper?" said Wallis.

"Yeah, we'd like that," answered Robb.

"We must plan it, then," said Wallis, smiling. "Please stay, have another noggin of cider and enjoy the fire. I wish I could join you, but duty calls. Farewell, Robert."

Robb did have another cider, and then another as he pondered what he'd heard. He was enraged that he and his neighbors could have been so used.

As the fire died away, he noticed the lengthening shadows out the window and decided he'd better be on his way.

Unsteadily, he rose and headed for the door. Met there by the servant, who handed him his coat and hat, Robb thanked him and went outside.

As he galloped down the lane between the fences, Robb savored the experience and the feeling that he'd been trusted for such important work by Wallis.

Discreetly, lace ruffles and a splash of burgundy appeared at the window over Robb's shoulder. From his vantage, Wallis watched him depart . . . and smiled.

★ ★ ★ ★ ★

FORT BRADY

Mary spent most of the day preparing stew. It was Muncy Township's turn to hold the Northumberland County Committee of Safety meeting, and Mary volunteered to host it at Fort Brady. Though John was away with the 12th and never was a member of the committee, she realized the fort was the most sensible location to lodge the thirty-three members. She was happy to do her part.

Mary cut vegetables she'd preserved last fall with big chunks of potato and onion from the root cellar. She used generous amounts of venison from a large buck James brought home a few days earlier and dropped it into the simmering kettle. While it cooked slowly over the fire and the broth condensed into thick, rich gravy, Mary baked bread in the hearthside oven and opened a fresh cask of ale to be served with it.

The committee members began to arrive late in the afternoon. Greeted with the aroma of the stew and warm bread, Mary welcomed them as they entered. She invited them to sit and eat while they chatted and caught up with the news from across the county.

By nightfall, Peter Smith arrived.

"Hello Mary," said Smith, as she opened the door. "Got room for one more?"

Mary smiled at Brady's friend, "Always got room for you, Peter. Were you one of the locals summoned to appear?" she asked.

"No. I just felt it was my duty to come; especially since the meeting was so close this time," he said. "For public meetings, it seems a lot a' the public don't show up."

"Well, it's nice to see ya," said Mary. "Why don't you find a seat? The benches is fillin' up an' I think they're about t' get started."

"Thank you, Mary," he answered and stepped inside.

Just as she was turning from the door, Samuel Wallis arrived.

"Mrs. Brady," said Wallis with a slight nod as he walked past her.

"Ev'nin' Mr. Wallis," she answered and watched as he picked his way through the crowded room to find a seat.

Then Mary went to the hearth, lit a taper, and worked her way around the room, lighting tallow candles to supplement the light from the fireplace.

"Gentlemen, let's bring the meeting to order," yelled Captain John Hambright as he rose from his seat at the table by the hearth.

Mary had known the man for years. He'd had a long and successful military career in the valley, going all the way back to 1756 when he commanded a company of the Augusta regiment, which came to the forks of the Susquehanna to build the fort. She knew he was a good leader and was happy when she heard he'd been unanimously elected to head the committee.

The conversation died away and Hambright continued, "Gentlemen, we have many important matters to discuss this evening, but first I'd like to extend the committee's gratitude to Mary Brady for her hospitality."

"Hear, hear." The men rejoined amidst polite applause.

"Now, then," said Hambright, "it has come to our attention that Mr. Alexander Lane and Mr. John Bullion have come into possession of a large quantity of salt which they are hoarding and refuse to sell. Are Mr. Lane and Mr. Bullion here?"

Heads turned but no one spoke.

Captain Hambright asked, "Have they been summoned?"

"Yes, they have, Captain," said Committeeman Henry Krebs, "William Sayers from our township is a good man, and he knows these men well. I asked him to contact them on the committee's authority and to summon them to this meeting. Mr.

Sayers carried out the request, but, apparently, they've decided not to oblige us."

"In that case," said Hambright, "considering the dire need of salt for preserving meat and sustaining the population, I presume these gentlemen's absence proves their purpose in not selling the salt is, at best, to hoard it until they can gain extortionist prices and, at worst, to sell it to the enemy. Therefore, I move that Mr. Sayers be given the authority to use whatever force necessary to confiscate this salt for the public good.

"When he's obtained possession of the salt, he is to sell it at the rate of fifteen shillings per bushel, but not to sell more than half a bushel to any one family. He must keep accounts of all he sells and, when the supply is exhausted, return the money to this committee. He may subtract six shillings and one pence for its transport and one shilling of every pound sold for his own trouble. Is there a second to the motion?"

"Second," replied a few stray voices.

"All in favor of passing this motion say 'aye'," said Hambright.

"Aye."

"All opposed?"

Silence.

"The 'ayes' have it. The motion is passed," said Hambright. "Mr. Krebs, will you notify Mr. Sayers of our wishes?"

"I will, Captain."

"Very well."

Captain Hambright continued down the agenda and addressed issues concerning grain supplies and pricing and how much should be permitted to be distilled after the poor received enough to survive.

When resolved, Captain Hambright said, "The next order of business concerns Mr. William Read, who is accused of refusing to associate in the militia or to bear arms on behalf of the states. Is Mr. Read present?"

"I am, sir," said a voice from the edge of the room.

Looking in that direction, Hambright saw a gaunt-faced man standing in the shadows. "Please step closer, Mr. Read," said Hambright.

Read obliged by stepping over several people to get to the center of the room.

"Mr. Read is it true that you refuse to associate?" asked Hambright.

"Yes sir, it is."

"This could be considered a treasonable act, Mr. Read. On what grounds do you refuse?"

"Well sir, I am an Irishman. Back in the ould country, I was a member a' the Hearts of Steel society. We campaigned against the mandatory unpaid work on the county roads and the consolidation of our farms for grazin' purposes by the government. When they captured six of our number and lodged them in the Belfast jail, we mustered b' the thousands an' marched on Belfast. We took the town an' liberated our mates.

"For some reason, the King didn't look upon this favorably an' he sent troops against us. They captured most of our leaders an' selected a group of us for trial. I was one a' those chosen. Some stood trial in Belfast an' were acquitted, so the government moved the rest of us to Dublin an' tried us there.

"Well, sir, the jury wouldn't convict us there, either. We were acquitted on condition a' takin' a solemn oath of allegiance to the King. We were made t' promise not t' ever take up arms against him again. So, ye see, sir, since I am a man who will not break his word, I cannot associate in a militia that is raisin' arms against that same King."

Considering for a moment, Hambright said, "Mr. Read, do you have any objections to the cause of the United States?"

"No, sir, I do not," answered Read, "and I would be as willin' as any man t' join it if I could do so without violatin' my oath."

"Mr. Read, would you consent to take an oath of allegiance to the United States?" asked Hambright.

"Of course I will," said Read, "if I can do so without obligin' myself to take arms, sir."

"Members of the committee, I make a motion that we tender Mr. Read an oath of allegiance to the United States and consider that the end of the matter," said Hambright. "Is there a second to the motion?"

"Second," replied a multitude of voices.

"All in favor of the motion," said Hambright, "signify by sayin' 'aye'."

"Aye."

"All opposed?"

Silence again.

"The 'ayes' have it and the motion is passed," said Hambright. "Mr. Read, please raise your right hand, and repeat after me."

Read raised his hand.

"I, William Read, do swear to be true to the United States of America . . ."

"I, William Read . . ." he proudly recited after the captain, repeating until he concluded, ". . . and do renounce and disclaim all allegiance to the King of Great Britain and promise that I will not, either directly or indirectly, speak or act anything in prejudice to the cause or safety of the states, or lift arms against them or be any way assistant to their declared enemies in any case whatsoever. . ."

". . . So help me, God," added Read.

"Mr. Read, you may go back to your home and family," said Hambright. "You have this committee's respect and approbation. I believe we will sorely miss having the privilege of you fighting with us."

"Thank you, sir," said Read. "Sirs," he said nodding to the rest of the committee.

Read turned and stepped back through the crowd, receiving slaps on the back and admiring comments along the way.

"Now gentlemen," continued Hambright, "I'll open the floor to any concerns the committee may have."

Pausing a moment to see if anyone was going to speak, Robert Robb stood up.

"Friends and neighbors," he began proudly, "I have two items to bring to the attention of the committee. I hold here a handbill that calls for reinforcements for General Washington's army. While we are at war, gentlemen, we owe it to our brave neighbors already in the field to encourage every able man to volunteer."

Then, Robb reached into his shirt and pulled out the paper he received from Wallis. Holding it up for everyone to see, he continued, "I also believe we owe it to ourselves t' look after our own defense. I have come across this document regardin' the peace talks Lord Howe tried to hold with Congress."

Heads snapped around. Wallis, in the back of the room, sat calm and still.

Robb, now less assured because of the reaction, continued, "Congress only allowed Howe to speak to a committee. This paper gives an account of the meeting he held with Dr. Frankling, Mr. Rutledge and Mr. Adams. It says right on it that it was printed in New York."

"It's British lies then, Robb!" cried someone from the floor.

"Hear me out!" he fired back. "The meeting was held on Staten Island. They printed this right after in New York, and it's a true account."

"What's it say then?" yelled someone else.

"It says Lord Howe wants t' offer us good conditions for peace, and the committee turned 'em down flat. It also says Howe used the committee politely, and they used him ill."

Someone yelled, "Why wasn't these peace conditions made public by Congress then, Robb?"

"Congress and their committees kept it back," he answered.

"Why would they do that?" yelled another voice.

"They only want the war t' go on because they're in power over us and don't want to lose it. I think we should look into this offer an' see if it's worthwhile."

Tension in the room escalated, and the meeting rapidly disintegrated.

"Order, gentlemen. Order," yelled Hambright over the crowd. "Mr. Robb has the floor, and we will hear him out."

"Thank you, Captain," said Robb.

"However, Mr. Robb, I'm curious," said Hambright, "do you suppose Dr. Franklin and the others didn't understand the terms being proposed to them?"

"I have it that Dr. Frankling is a rogue," spluttered Robb.

Through audible exhalations and outright curses, Robb went on. "He an' Rittenhouse an' Adams an' all of 'em are rogues. They only have their positions because a' bribery an' corruption in the conventions.

"Congress is usin' us to continue this war so they can stay in power. It's a few that runs this government, and a majority shouldn't be ruled by a few. Not t' mention we're more and more defenseless here while all our men goes off to fight with Washington."

"Mr. Robb, did you not just exhort us to persuade every able man to go and join Washington?" Hambright interjected.

"Yes, Captain. I did, but I said 'while this war goes on,' and that's true because we owe it to our neighbors. But, I also think we should take the peace offered on the good terms of Lord Howe and save our county."

"Mr. Robb," said Hambright, "I have it from Colonel Hunter, who has learned intimate details of Lord Howe's proposal, that Britain offered us nothing more than repatriation under the old system. There would be no independence so there was nothing to discuss. Now, you also said that a few should not rule a majority. How, then, do you view the monarchy that you propose we rejoin?"

"Uh . . ." Robb searched for an answer to Hambright's logic.

"I'm not for the monarchy. I simply think we should look at these good terms of peace and see if it's not in our interest to accept them. I understand the British will talk with any number of men, and that gives us the chance to save our county."

Robb realized he'd stirred a hornet's nest and now seemed to have run out of words. Hambright looked at him for what seemed a long while.

Finally, Hambright said, "Mr. Robb, we have given you every consideration to explain your feelings on this matter. It seems to me that the document you hold is highly suspect. Moreover, you … a member of the Committee of Safety, no less … have denounced Congress and openly proposed making peace with the British. You seem to hold opinions that stem from more than the information that appears on the document. I am disturbed about how you have come to attain that information … how *did* you come by that information, Mr. Robb?"

Wallis bit down hard, causing the muscles on the sides of his face to flex as he awaited Robb's reply.

"I'm not at liberty to say," answered Robb.

"He's admittin' it. He's a traitor!" yelled Peter Smith.

Robb strode through the crowd to the back of the room where Smith was seated. As Smith rose, Robb threw one of his tremendous fists into Smith's stomach. When he doubled over, Robb reached behind Smith, picked up the stool he'd been sitting on and broke it over his head. Smith collapsed, and Robb stomped and kicked him further.

Standing nearby, James Brady leapt in and pulled Robb off Smith. Seeing this, others joined Brady, and, together, they subdued him. They pinned Robb's arms behind him, leaving him flush-faced and panting while Smith bled and moaned, barely conscious on the floor. Hambright said, "Will someone please attend to Mr. Smith?"

Mary Brady was already on her way with a pitcher of water and some cloth for bandages.

"Mr. Brady," Hambright said to James, "the committee thanks you for your quick action. Will you gentlemen please escort Mr. Robb to the next building while we deliberate on what has happened here?"

"Yessir, Captain," said Brady.

James and the others restraining Robb pushed him toward the door, struggling to keep him in control. Hambright spoke to the crowd, "Would anyone like to comment on this incident?"

"He's a traitor and a bully!"

"Hang 'im!"

"Treason!" called a jumble of voices from the crowd.

Maintaining the situation, Hambright yelled over them. "We will not act as a lawless mob. From what we know, Mr. Robb has been a faithful member of this committee and of this community."

"Yeah, from what we know," came a sharp reply.

"Captain Hambright," said a calm voice from the rear of the room. Everyone turned to see Samuel Wallis standing. "I know I am not a member of this august body, but may I please address the committee?"

"Certainly, Mr. Wallis," answered Hambright. "We would be most pleased to hear from you."

"It seems to me, gentlemen, that whether Robert Robb has *seemed* to be a good member of this committee in the past is irrelevant. How can we know his beliefs but by his own words? I feel he has betrayed himself as a traitor and that he must be held accountable."

"Hear, hear!" roared the crowd.

Wallis nodded, accepting their acknowledgment, and seated himself.

Hambright said, "I agree his words were very damning. However, as we all witnessed, he took great exception to being called a traitor. Furthermore, could he have truly believed he could persuade this committee to commit a treasonous act? Would he even try if treason were the object? I, for one, am puzzled as to where he got his information and opinions."

"We can't just let him off," yelled a voice from the crowd.

"I don't intend to," answered Hambright. "What if we were to offer him the chance to prove his innocence? I propose we give him the choice of immediately joining a militia company headed for the army, or to be confined by military authority as a traitor."

The crowd murmured general agreement to the idea.

"Very well," said Hambright. "I therefore make it a motion. Do I hear a second?"

"SECOND!"

"All in favor?"

"AYE!"

"Opposed?"

"... The 'ayes' have it and the motion is carried. Now, will someone please ask the gentlemen in the next building to bring Mr. Robb back in here?"

Someone in the back ducked out the door.

"Mrs. Brady, how is Mr. Smith?" asked Hambright.

"I think he has some busted ribs and there's a nasty gash on his head, but his skull ain't shattered. We'll keep him here and look after him tonight," answered Mary.

"I'm glad to hear it," said Hambright. "It's a good thing for Mr. Robb he's not worse."

A commotion in the back of the room revealed a still obviously enraged Robb being led back into the meeting.

"Mr. Robb!" said Hambright in a voice of such authority that Robb ceased struggling and listened. "It is the opinion of this committee that you have spoken treason here this evening. Your brutal actions against a patriot and friend of this community have not helped your case.

"We have, therefore, resolved that you shall either march immediately with the militia of this county to the defense of the United States, or be committed to the care of Lt. Col. Murray, of the 2nd battalion, to be sent to some proper place of confinement. How say you?"

"I say I won't give you the satisfaction," sneered Robb. "I won't be used so by such a set of rascals, horse-thieves, robbers and murderers! I don't accept your resolution. I appeal to the state committee."

"Mr. Robb, you have sorely tried this committee's patience. You are hereby placed in the custody of Col. Murray for the length of time it takes him to deliver you up to the state committee. With him will travel a full and fair account of this night's affairs and this committee's actions. Gentlemen, please escort the prisoner back to the other building and confine him there."

Robb was once again ushered out of the room.

Hambright waited for him to leave and said, "If there is no further business to be addressed, I move we adjourn this meeting."

"Second."

"All in favor?"

"Aye."

"Opposed? . . . The 'ayes' have it; our meeting is adjourned."

CHAPTER 3

1777

EASTERN NEW JERSEY

"Cap'n Brady, 12ᵗʰ Pennsylvania," said Brady to the camp sentries.

"Payass," said a tall sergeant in a Virginian accent.

Brady reached inside his shirt and produced his credentials. The sergeant studied the paper for a moment and handed it back.

"Entah," said the sergeant with a swipe of his hand toward the camp.

"Where's Cap'n Boone?" asked Brady.

"Ovah theyah bah the fahr," answered the sergeant.

"Much obliged," said Brady.

He walked into camp and found Boone lying with his splinted leg stretched out in front of him.

"How's the foot?" called Brady.

"I'll be damned," laughed Boone. "Must be pretty bad if *you're* comin' t' visit. Am I dyin'?"

"Without a chance to get your money back from Hunter? I doubt it," quipped Brady.

The men laughed.

"The foot's alright," said Boone. "Doc got the ball out. He said it just broke some bones in there. He doesn't think I'll lose it."

"Good t' hear," said Brady. "Maybe it'll be better in time for our next march through the snow and freezin' rain."

"Wasn't that awful?" said Boone. I told ya that was goin' t' be bad. Didn't make it any easier findin' the army wasn't even in Pennsylvania anymore."

"Yeah, but what a hell of a plan," said Brady. "Pushin' the army across the Delaware on *Christmas night* and surprisin' the Hessians that way. Wish't we'd a been there in time to be a part of it."

"That woulda been somethin'," said Boone. "But I think we done our fair share. First at Princeton, but then especially after we got t' Morristown."

"Well, the Gen'ral makin' us scouts put us on the front edge, for sure," said Brady. "But, I'm just as glad he didn't coop us up with the infantry."

"I ain't complainin'," laughed Boone. "I was just sayin' we done our share a fightin' in all them skirmishes."

"Oh, I know what ya meant," said Brady. "We had some hot ones. So, how's the new outfit, anyhow?"

"You know, John, at first I wasn't so sure about havin' my company split off from the 12th to join men from all over the place. But, orders is orders, and I figured Washington knew what he was doin'. Turns out, fightin' in an all-rifle regiment has some real advantages. The redcoats don't seem t' want t' get quite so close. Them boys from Maryland an' Virginia ain't bad shots, neither. Course, they ain't quite up t' Pennsylvania snuff but they're alright," he said, smiling. "Colonel Morgan seems mighty fine, too."

"Good," said Brady. "How's Murphy makin' out as a ranger?"

"He's the same," laughed Boone. "Good kid . . . hell of a shot with that double-barreled rifle a' his . . . and still easy to needle."

Brady laughed. "Well, too bad things worked out for ya like this but I'm glad you'll be home for a while. I'll bet they can use you."

"I'm sure Hunter's got it all under control," answered Boone, "'specially since they named him County Lieutenant. Now, he's in charge a' defendin' everything from Sunbury to the New York line."

"Yeah. Think a' that," said Brady. "An' it ain't just the valley he's defendin'. If the frontier collapsed, the whole rest a' the state could fall, county by county. Washington might wake up one mornin' t' find a whole new enemy army comin' up from behind."

"I guess that's true," agreed Boone.

"Anyway," said Brady, "I hope ya have a safe trip back and heal up real soon."

"Thanks, John. Give the boys back in the 12th my best. I'll look in on Mary an' the kids for ya."

"I appreciate it."

ANTES FORT

"C'mon ladies, get yer buckets," said Abel Cady, standing by the stockade gate.

"Them cows ain't gonna milk themselves."

"Hold yer horses, Abel," answered his wife, Molly. "We're comin'."

Cady was anxious to have a few hours outside of Antes Fort. With so many settlers taking refuge there, the place was beginning to feel pretty crowded.

Cady waited with Zephaniah Miller, Isaac Bouser, and James Armstrong. They watched Molly and Mrs. Tobias gather the buckets. The ladies were headed to the island across from the fort to milk the cows pastured there. The men served as guards.

They opened the gate and ambled down the hill as the morning mist rose off the river.

After loading the buckets into two canoes, Cady and Miller climbed in one with Molly riding in the center. Bouser and Armstrong pushed off with Mrs. Tobias.

Cady could already tell it was going to be one of those oppressively hot, muggy days that were so common in the valley. But, it was still in the cool of the morning and the fresh air felt good.

Bass fed on surface insects and jumped sporadically around

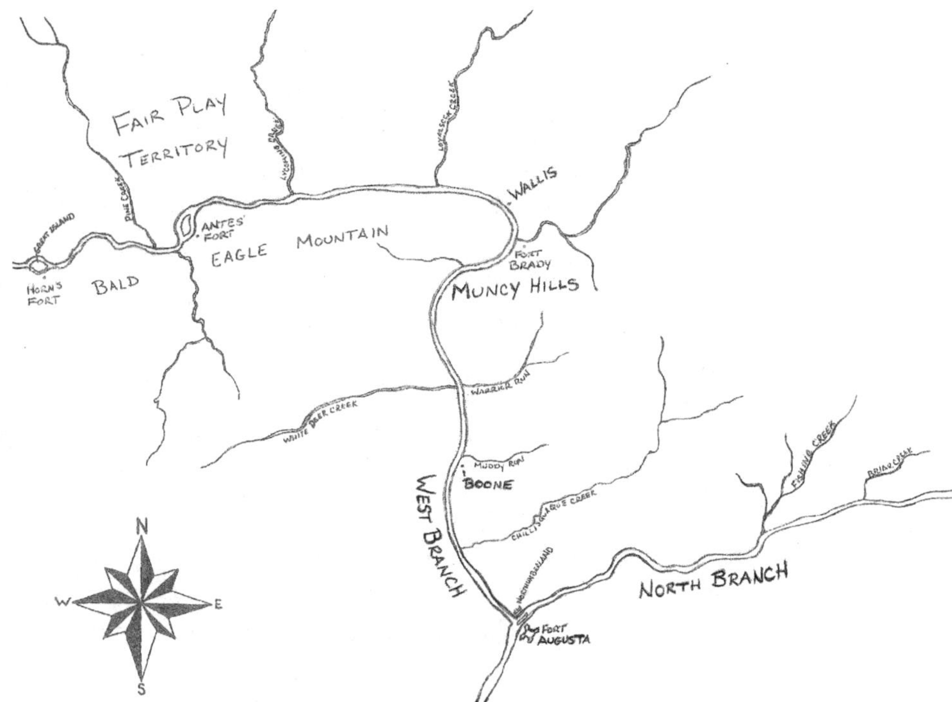

the canoes. Nearing the island, three deer startled and clattered off into the underbrush.

Mrs. Tobias closed her eyes and inclined her face to the sun. She soaked in the warmth and listened to the rhythmic sploshing of the paddles. Then, two smooth scraping sounds announced their arrival as the canoes beached on the sandy bottom.

"Alright, ladies, here we are," said Miller.

Miller and Armstrong each stepped out, grabbed his canoe and pulled it on shore so the ladies could get out without wetting their feet. Steadying the canoe with one hand, the men extended the other to the ladies and helped them out. The men in the rear passed the buckets ashore, followed with the rifles and pulled the canoes up the riverbank.

Armstrong said, "Maybe we can track some a' them deer and have venison for supper tonight."

"First things first," answered Miller. "B'sides, they're prob'ly already across the river and up into the hills b' now."

The men grabbed their rifles and formed around the ladies. Everyone carried a bucket and started across the island to find the cows. Away from the river's edge, the mist had almost completely burned away, and the heavy dew was beginning to evaporate in the warming sun, making the air thick.

The birds sang loudly around them as they followed the path through the trees to the center of the island.

". . . birds is sure makin' a ruckus," noticed Molly.

"Must be after all the bugs," answered Cady. "These damn gnats is eatin' me alive."

"I was tryin' not to notice," she answered.

They rounded a bend in the path and looked up to a grass-covered clearing to find the cows exactly where they expected them to be. They were quietly munching the long grass toward the top of the hill.

"That damn bell cow's wandered away," said Miller.

"She's sorta rambunctious," answered Armstrong. "Maybe we oughta switch the bell to one a' these others."

"Wait, I hear her," said Mrs. Tobias. "She's just in that thicket over there."

"Well, why don't you ladies get started milkin' and we'll go after the loose one," said Miller.

Molly and Mrs. Tobias each went to a cow and knelt down with a bucket. The men looked around to make sure the women were safe before heading off for the bell cow.

"What in the hell could she be eatin' in them bushes?" wondered Cady.

"I don't know but she sure must like it," answered Bouser. "Listen to that bell goin'."

"Let's just get her an' get back to the women," said Miller.

He started off toward the thicket, followed by the others.

Then, he stopped. He looked back at Cady and said, "Why don't you hang back a little an' keep an eye on the women?"

"Alright."

Miller, Bouser, and Armstrong continued down the gradual slope.

POP . . . POP, POP, POP . . . POP, POP. The women looked up, startled at the sound.

What Molly saw horrified her. Instinctively, she looked toward her husband just in time to see a musket ball explode through the back of his shirt, leaving a thick mist of blood hanging in the air. It glinted in the sun as he fell backward onto the ground.

Without thinking, she ran to him and cradled his head in her arms. Mrs. Tobias ran and hid in the field on the opposite side of the hill. Cady looked up and implored Molly to run.

"You can't help me darlin'. . . . save yourself. . . I love you," he gasped.

They were his last words. His eyes grew vacant, and his life seeped away.

Looking down the hill toward the other men, Molly saw Indians. She laid her husband's head on the ground, grabbed his rifle and ran to the field on the other side of the hill with Mrs. Tobias.

When the shots were fired, Zephaniah Miller had been just a few feet from the Indians, who'd led the cow into the thicket to bait their trap. A musket ball crushed into his temple. Isaac Bouser fared no better. He was struck in the neck and received a savage wound.

James Armstrong was shot in the stomach but somehow maintained his feet. He got off a return shot but didn't know if he hit anyone or not. He struggled the short distance back over the hill and hid in the field with the women.

The Indians charged from their cover and pounced on the fallen. A warrior loomed over Isaac Bouser, who was still alive. Bouser saw a tomahawk catch the light for just a moment before it came crashing down. He was oddly conscious of the dull thud it made, but he felt no pain. It was the last sensation he had.

Pulling his knife, the warrior cut a slit from the tomahawk wound around Bouser's ears to the base of his neck. Then leaning over his prize, he lodged his teeth under the opened skin and began to wrestle the scalp away in quick violent jerks. In Miller's case, the gunshot wound allowed another Indian to skip the killing blow and go straight to the knife.

Cady's scalping went easier. The warrior triumphantly raised the prize above his head and shouted in victory.

The men in the fort heard the Indians' volley. Looking down on the island they could see the clearing. It was a long shot but within rifle range. The defenders began a covering fire that kept the Indians on the reverse slope from Armstrong and the women while a rescue party left the fort for the island.

Free to leave the hillside, the women helped Armstrong back down the path to the river. They were just emerging from the underbrush as the men arrived from the fort.

"Is there any others?" hollered an older man in charge of the rescue party. It was Colonel Antes.

"I don't think so," Molly called back. "Abel's dead. James said Zephaniah is too. Isaac's hurt real bad."

"You folks get in the canoes. Meyers and Williams will take you back," said Antes. "The rest of us'll go see what's what."

The women helped Armstrong into a canoe, and the two men from the rescue party took the survivors back to the fort. The firing died away while they were on the water. They reached the bank, and the women ran back to the fort as the men helped Armstrong up the hill.

Later that morning, the rest of the party returned. Inside the stockade, Antes walked up to Molly. She was sitting by herself. Her husband's blood was dried on her dress.

"It all happened so fast," she said quietly.

Antes waited a moment and said, "We found Isaac, Zeph and Abel. They was all scalped. I hope it's alright with you, but we went ahead an' buried 'em on the island. We'll show you where."

She nodded.

"It was quick thinkin' to take Abel's rifle with you, Molly. The Indians took the others o' course. They shot all the cows and even took all the buckets they could find. We brought a couple back with us. I'm real sorry for you, Molly."

"Thanks. Thanks for everything you did . . . Did you get any of 'em?" she asked.

"Nah. We followed 'em back t' the other side of the island, but they'd already crossed the river. We'd a' been sittin' ducks if we followed. They was carryin' a body with 'em though. One of our men musta got a shot off."

They sat in silence. Then he said, "You're a brave woman, Molly. Abel'd be proud of you."

Her face wrinkled and reddened. She laid her head on his shoulder and sobbed quietly. He tenderly placed his arm around her shoulder and held her tightly.

The next evening, James Armstrong also expired. They took him back to the island and buried him with the others.

★ ★ ★ ★ ★

SOUTHEASTERN PENNSYLVANIA

A thick fog rose off Brandywine Creek, intensifying the chill in the mid-September air. Washington's army went into position there almost three weeks earlier.

"So why are we just sittin' here?" Johnny Brady asked his father over a sparse breakfast.

"From what I heard, the British boarded ships when they disengaged us in New Jersey," said Brady. "Howe has designs on Philadelphia."

"Then why did they send Morgan's riflemen to join the northern army?"

"Well, they said Burgoyne's leadin' an army against us out a' Canada an' Morgan can help bolster Gen'ral Gates' army up in York State."

"My God, I hope they're right about Howe headin' to Philadelphia," said Johnny. "If he turned an' sailed up the Hudson to join Burgoyne, they could split New England from the rest a' the states."

"I think that's why we stayed put in Jersey for a while. Gen'ral Washington wanted to be sure where Howe was headed," said Brady. "Word is they saw him enter the Chesapeake."

"I guess that explains why we marched south of Philly, so we could cover the city," said Johnny.

"Exactly," confirmed Brady.

"Well," said Johnny, "then we'll sure be in the thick of things when Howe shows up. Looks like we're holdin' down a main crossin'."

Suddenly, the morning stillness was broken by firing on their left, about a mile downstream. The regiment's drums came alive but no enemy appeared across the creek. The combat downstream started hot, but soon fell into a lazy firefight. Hours passed as the regiment stayed on alert for any movement across the ford in front of them.

Then . . . shouts on their right.

"We're flanked! We're flanked!" yelled outposts who came running toward them.

Just then, a messenger arrived on horseback.

"Fall back! Gen'ral Conway says, 'refuse the line and fall back!' shouted the messenger. "Gen'ral Sullivan is forming us up just back of Birmingham Meeting House!"

The men scrambled from their works and quick-timed to the new position. The brigade fell in line next to the artillery.

"There they are!" shouted Johnny. Brady snapped his head around and saw swarms of British regulars appear before them in the distance.

The cannon came to life and boomed away as the ranks of red approached.

"Steady, men," yelled General Conway riding behind the lines. "Hold your fire until they close in."

Johnny watched the enemy maneuver toward them. When in range, they stopped, leveled their muskets and fired. The Bradys heard shots whistle just over their heads. Then, Colonel Cooke shouted, "Fire!"

The 12th's line erupted and dropped scores of the enemy. But, positioned in the center of the line, they were taking heavy fire. The enemy soon began overlapping both flanks of the new position.

Colonel Cooke shouted, "Give it to 'em, boys!"

Brady reloaded and raised his rifle to fire when he was struck in the mouth by a spent ball.

"Ahhh," he yelled.

Johnny turned. "Pop, are ya' alright?"

Brady was dazed. He sat for a moment probing his tongue around his mouth. He spit out a gob of blood and several teeth. His lip and cheek were already swelling and badly bruised. He shook his head but couldn't seem to clear it.

"Col'nel," shouted Johnny. "Pop's hit. I'm gonna take him t' the rear."

"Go," yelled Cooke. "Gen'ral Conway just ordered us to pull back. Get Captain Brady to safety an' we'll follow directly."

The day ended in confusion as the continentals streamed to the rear. But, Johnny kept Brady out of harm's way.

Days later, a soldier strolled up to the fire where Brady was sitting and trying to eat.

"That's a real pretty bruise you got, there," he said.

Brady looked up to see his son Samuel grinning down at him.

"Ha," Brady reacted, happily. "Yeah, the swellin's goin' down a little. But I'm damn sure tired a' gummin' mush," he said, dropping his spoon back into the bowl that held his supper. "So, you heard, huh?

"Yeah," said Samuel. "Our division is camped just over in Paoli and I got leave to come see you for a few minutes. Hell of a fight, wasn't it?"

"It was that," agreed Brady. "If you fella's in Wayne's division didn't cover the retreat, I don't think we'd have an army left. That had to be a pretty hot engagement."

"Well," said Samuel, "I can't imagine how hot it was in the center where ya' got that souvenir. You was lucky that ball was spent. Otherwise, it'd have blown your head off."

"Yeah, I guess that's true," said Brady.

They stared silently into the fire for a few moments, just happy to be assured the other was alright.

"Well," said Samuel, placing his hand on Brady's shoulder, "you get some rest tonight. I pulled sentry duty, and I got t' head out."

"Be careful," said Brady.

"Always am," he answered, smiling.

Samuel reached his post on the edge of Wayne's camp just as it was growing dark. He pulled his blanket around him and cinched it with his belt.

He watched the lightning bugs rise from the grass accompanied by a chorus of tree toads and crickets. Then he heard a rustling sound. He turned.

A line of British troops was charging across the meadow with bayonets leveled. He barely had time to fire a warning shot before they were on him.

Samuel turned and ran, but a soldier followed close behind. He reached the edge of the field and found a rail fence blocking his escape.

In full stride, Samuel placed his hand on the top rail and swung his legs over it. The soldier thrust at him. The bayonet missed him but pinned his blanket to the fence. Samuel quickly tore the blanket and ran into the woods as the soldier struggled to free his bayonet.

When he put some distance between them, Samuel stopped and reloaded. He wasn't sure where he was. He needed to find the regiment. He moved cautiously along the edge of a swamp but didn't get far before a British cavalryman appeared.

"Halt, you damned rebel," yelled the cavalryman, pulling his pistol.

Samuel leveled his rifle and fired, dropping the man from his saddle.

Samuel heard more horses approaching. Knowing he couldn't outrun the horsemen, he waded into the swamp. He found a thicket on some marshy ground and tried to make himself as comfortable as possible for the night.

When day broke, Samuel waded out in search of his regiment. He'd only slogged a few hundred yards before he met other refugees.

"Who's there?" called a voice in a decidedly American accent.

"Sam Brady, 8th Pennsylvania," he answered.

Three men stepped out from behind the trees.

"Glad to see you," they said. "We're with the 4th. We're goin' t' find the army."

"Sounds good t' me," he answered.

The men pushed on and discovered more and more Americans who'd hidden in the swamp overnight. By the time they reached solid ground, there were more than fifty of them. They formed up and worked their way back to the American lines.

FORT BOONE

Hawkins Boone grew restless at home. His foot wasn't entirely healed, but he couldn't just wait around. He set off for New York State in search of Morgan's Rangers.

He found them late in the first week of October, dug in near

Saratoga. He reported to Colonel Morgan and was on his way to find his company when he ran into Tim Murphy.

"Cap'n Boone," shouted Tim. "How the hell are ya?"

"Fair t' middlin'," answered Boone. "Amazin' how a little walk loosens up the muscles."

"How long you been on the road?" asked Murphy.

"Couple a' weeks. Why?"

"You hear about Philadelphia?"

"No, what?" asked Boone.

"It fell. We just got the news."

"Damn," said Boone.

"I'm glad yer back, though," said Murphy. "An' just in time, too."

"What do ya mean?"

"I don't think it'll be too long before things here get int'restin'."

"How's that?" asked Boone.

"Well, Burgoyne come down from Canada. A few weeks back we tangled with him at Freeman's Farm. Gen'ral Arnold saw a weak point in their line and ordered us in. We had 'em runnin' but Gen'ral Gates wouldn't support the attack, and we ended up losin' the battle."

"Why wouldn't Gates support the attack?" asked Boone.

"Ah, hell. Some kinda craziness between 'em about Arnold's rank. Gates says he's in charge an' that's that."

"Even if it means losin' a battle?"

"Apparently so," answered Murphy. "Anyhow, I guess Gates didn't even mention Arnold in the official report, and they got into a big dust-up over it. Then Gates confined Arnold to his tent."

"Damned politics," spat Boone. "Could cost us the country."

"Not so fast," said Murphy. "After the battle, each side dug in an' we've been in a stalemate ever since. Thing is, some a' their deserters come in sayin' things is bleak in their camp. They're runnin' out a supplies and gettin' desp'rate. Meanwhile, we been getting' reinforced an' now we're almost double the size a' Burgoyne's army. It's just a matter a' time until he has to attack or surrender."

"Sounds like I did get back at a good time," said Boone. "Good talkin' with ya, Murph. I gotta go find my comp'ny."

"Good talkin' t' you, Cap. Glad yer back."

Burgoyne attacked the next morning. As the battle developed, Morgan called his captains together.

"We've been ordered around the left flank," he said. "General Poor will work around to the right. We'll attack at the same time."

Boone led his company into position, and, when Poor launched his attack, Morgan pitched in, too.

"They're not goin' easy, Cap'n," yelled one of Boone's men.

"No, but look there," yelled Boone.

He pointed to the center of the field. There was General Arnold, ignoring orders, mounted and leading a charge with three regiments he'd commandeered from nearby.

Boone watched Arnold lead the men directly into the British center. The enemy wavered. Only the demonstrations of a British general galloping along the line kept it from collapsing.

"Captains," yelled Morgan, "each of you send me your five best shots. Gen'ral Arnold says t' get Fraser . . . that mounted British general. We got t' take him out."

Boone quickly chose his five best men and ordered the rest to keep firing on the enemy flank.

As the marksmen gathered near Morgan, he explained the situation. Many of them started firing, but Tim Murphy took his time.

"I'm gonna get me a better look," he said, and he climbed a nearby tree.

Fraser was a *long* way off. Murphy calmly sighted in his target. When he was satisfied he'd gotten the mark, he slowly squeezed the trigger. The powder flashed and a split second later his rifle rang out with a loud crack.

Fraser reeled and fell from the saddle. He was hit square in the midsection and mortally wounded. As Murphy watched him fall, a British messenger rode up to the same point on the battlefield. Coolly, Tim dispatched him with his other loaded barrel.

With Fraser out of the way, Arnold renewed his attack on the British center. The Americans slammed into the enemy, broke their line and advanced.

"Arnold's hit," yelled Boone.

As Arnold was carried to the rear, the American attack lost its momentum and the British remained on the field. The Americans retired to their entrenchments and the stalemate continued. For Burgoyne and his army, however, time had just about run out.

Ten days later, Boone stood at the head of his company, drawn up in parade formation with the rest of the army. Burgoyne had surrendered.

The Americans watched as a whole British army dropped its arms at their feet and signed oaths to fight no more in the war.

That evening at the celebrations, Boone saw Murphy. He walked over to him, put his hand on his shoulder and looked him straight in the eye. "That was one *hell* of a shot, Murph," he said.

★　★　★　★　★

LOYALSOCK VALLEY

"Look, Pa," said twelve-year-old Jacob Benjamin. "Indians."

"Whereabouts?" asked his father.

"There. On the path by the crick."

William Benjamin lowered his axe and looked along the Loyalsock Creek. In the far distance he, too, saw the raiding party.

"Looks to be about twenty of 'em," he said. "C'mon. We gotta get back t' the house an' warn the others."

The Benjamins ran down the hill as fast as they could. Reaching home, they burst through the door.

"Grab what ya can," said William. "There's Indians comin'. We gotta go warn your sister's fam'ly an' get on downstream to your folks."

"Jacob, take this pouch a' salt," said Mrs. Benjamin, as she gathered their toddler son.

"Yes, ma."

"Make sure to take the powder too," said William as he loaded his rifle.

"I will," answered Jacob.

"Alright, everybody ready?" asked Benjamin. "Let's go."

Traveling along the creek, they reached the Cooks and told them of the coming attack.

"We gotta warn Ma an' Pa," said Mrs. Cook to her sister.

"That's what we plan on doin'," said Mrs. Benjamin. "Let's get goin."

The Cooks quickly gathered their essentials, and both families continued on to the Browns'.

"Indians comin'," yelled Zacharias Cook as they reached the home. "We gotta get down t' Wallis'."

The door flung open, and Mr. Brown stepped out with his rifle.

"Where are they?" he asked.

"About fifteen minutes behind us," answered Benjamin.

"Ain't no way we can make it four miles t' the river and then all the way down t' Wallis' without 'em catchin' us," said Brown. "We're better off makin' a stand here."

"I agree," said Benjamin. "Let's pool our powder an' lead an' see what we got."

The inventory was a small one. Together, they stared down at a moderate amount of powder and very few rifle balls.

"Molly, start runnin' some ammunition for us," said Brown.

Mrs. Brown looked crestfallen but knew there wasn't a choice. She motioned her daughters to help her, and they gathered the family pewter and utensils to melt and cast into bullets.

Looking out a window to the north, Benjamin saw thick, dark smoke rising from the location of his home. Another plume soon announced the Cooks' home was lost.

The women finished casting the first rounds just as the Indians appeared at the far end of the Browns' harvested cornfield. The raiders raised a war cry and fired shots into the house as they crept between the corn shocks.

The men took positions at the windows and returned fire. They held the raiders off for a time, but their rate of fire was slow as they waited for fresh ammunition from the bullet molds.

"We're surrounded," yelled Cook. "And, they're comin' with torches."

The men fired from the windows, but there were too many to stop. The Indians lofted torches onto the roof, and the building started to burn.

"Ain't no way we can fight our way outta this," said Cook. "C'mon darlin'," he yelled as he unbarred the door and ran outside with his wife.

An Indian tried to force his way into the home as they ran out, but Benjamin shot him in the chest and rebarred the door.

"Did they make it?" asked Mrs. Brown.

"Na. They took 'em captive," said Jacob, from the window. "They're takin' 'em across the field."

"I can't breathe," gasped Mrs. Benjamin through the thickening smoke.

"Get the young'un," answered William. "In the confusion, we might be able to fight our way out."

"You'll never make it," yelled Brown.

"Well I ain't staying here t' burn, neither," he said.

Mrs. Benjamin quickly kissed her mother, father, and little sister. Then she picked up their toddler and walked to the door.

"Let's go," she said.

Benjamin handed Cook's rifle to Jacob and positioned his wife and little son between them. They opened the door and rushed out.

The Indians swarmed around them and both father and son

emptied their rifles into the on-rushing crowd. The struggle ended quickly.

Mrs. Benjamin and the toddler were taken captive and led away while behind her she heard her husband's yelling cease. Hysterically, she writhed in her captor's grasp to see what was happening.

As she turned, she saw Jacob being scalped alive. She also saw her parents' home engulfed in a raging fire, but the front door remained closed. No one could survive that inferno, and she knew her mother, father and little sister were dead.

Led back across the cornfield, she held tightly to her little son. Ahead, she could see the Cooks standing with their captors. On reaching the woods, she looked back one last time to see the house fallen in on itself in a burning heap. Jacob wandered scalpless, drenched in blood, and senselessly stumbling amongst the corn shocks until he finally pitched forward on the ground.

"Please, bring him with us," she shrieked to her captors.

"Quiet," yelled one of those holding her, "or we'll kill your baby, too."

To make his point, the warrior grabbed the toddler by the ankle, but she jerked him away.

When the raiders returned from across the field, they shoved the captives in line and headed back up the Loyalsock.

Numb and unsure of what the future would hold, Mrs. Benjamin followed the procession through a grove of maples. The October wind blew gently across the valley and showered her in swirling crimson.

CHAPTER 4

January-June 1778

FORT AUGUSTA

"Fine supper, ma'am," said John Brady to Mrs. Hunter. "Thank you, kindly."

"It was nothing," she answered as she served dessert in Hunter's office. "My cooking certainly can't compare to Mary's."

"I hated being sent home from the regiment last fall." said John. "It was just a little touch a' pleurisy. And, I'll admit, nothin' coulda brought me around as quick as Mary's cookin'. Still," he said slyly, "nothin' could be as good a send off as your apple pie, an' that's a fact."

"Oh, you're just being nice."

"Not at all, ma'am, but don't tell Mary I said so," he said with a wink.

"Have a safe trip back to Valley Forge," said Mrs. Hunter, laughing as she left the room.

"It's a pity you didn't take sick before you did, John. You coulda been here with Boone," said the colonel.

"I see enough a' him at the war," Brady joked.

Hunter grinned. "You boys had it tough, huh?"

"Well, we been through some scrapes."

"Yeah, I noticed you're chewing all on one side these days," said Hunter.

"What the hell, Sam. I'm gettin' old. I woulda lost 'em soon anyhow."

The men laughed. Then Brady said, "I've been hearin' things here haven't been easy."

"Well, I'll tell you, John, we could be better off," said Hunter.

"You mean 'cause a' the supplies?"

"And the militia bein' taken all the time."

"I know it, Sam. They don't understand how bad it is here. All they see is the army meltin' away 'cause enlistment terms are expirin' and they want to replace 'em as soon as possible."

"Ain't that the truth?" said Hunter. "In the middle of last September, the council ordered me to send the first class of militia and to keep all of the other classes ready. That's just about when Colonel Kelly and his men discovered all those raiders up above the Great Island."

Brady nodded.

"Two days later, I got an order for the second class. There was no powder, ammunition or blankets to give 'em and I couldn't follow the order. I wrote and told council I needed supplies. Sure enough, in a few weeks, I received five hundred pounds of powder and twelve hundred pounds of lead, but we still didn't have enough rifles.

"By the end of October, they ordered the third and fourth classes out. I told council things were bad here. The settlers got no crops in this fall. Then those poor friendly Indian families came to us, and we were provisioning them too."

"Yeah, I heard about that," said Brady.

"Anyway," Hunter continued, "I split the third and fourth classes. I sent half of them to join the army and the other half out on the frontier. Kelly's men had served their time, and I gave my word they'd be replaced. I felt for them, John, I'll tell you. None of 'em had blankets. Most didn't have anything more to wear than their hunting shirts. It's going to be a rough winter for them."

"Yeah, blankets is a luxury item in the army this winter, too," confirmed Brady.

"Oh, and I had to ask council to send three thousand dollars. I advanced a good sum to those on the march and Kelly's men still need paid. Now, just a week ago, they called out the fifth class."

Hunter paused, not sure how to continue. He was half-embarrassed about having discussed it.

"Sam," said Brady. "It's obvious you've been up against it, keepin' the frontier defended and the militia and civilians supplied. I don't think there's a damn thing you coulda done different than you did, and I don't think anybody coulda done any better. Nobody doubts your resolve or your sense of duty. In fact, I feel a hell of a lot better knowin' you're here lookin' after things. I *know* Mary and the kids is bein' taken care of."

"Thanks, John," said Hunter. "That means a lot. And thanks for listening."

The men spoke until midnight and retired. Early the next morning, Hunter joined Brady on the parade ground. The north wind was blowing the American flag straight out, the white stars riding proudly on the deep blue field.

Hunter looked up and said, "By the way, thanks for bringing us that new ensign."

"Yeah. They just come up with that and sent some for the camps. I knew I was comin' home, so I asked for one of the extras."

Brady shook Hunter's hand, then turned and walked away.

"Nice to have a flag of our own," called Hunter.

Smiling back over his shoulder Brady nodded and yelled back, "Yeah, kinda purty ain't it?"

★ ★ ★ ★ ★

PHILADELPHIA

"More lace, damn you," snapped Wallis at his couturier. "General Howe's officers pitched in £4,000 for his farewell party, and I'll spare no expense on my appearance."

"Congratulations on your invitation, sir," said the clothier. "I understand the Mischianza is a very exclusive affair."

"Yes, I suppose it is," said Wallis smugly. "The officers not only want to honor General Howe, but they're surely trying to impress his replacement Sir Henry Clinton. As for *my* invitation," Wallis continued, "I should have been stunned *not* to be invited. After all, I procure supplies for the army. General Howe and his officers are also very grateful for the luxury items I obtain for them. In fact, Captain Andre is quite a good customer of my imported wines and trinkets for the ladies. When he was put in charge of organizing the event, he proffered my invitation as a matter of course."

"Yes, I can see how that would be the case," said the clothier.

Privately, Wallis cringed with the memory of wheedling the invitation the day Andre came to his office to order material for gowns and costumes.

"After all, Captain," Wallis remembered saying, "haven't I provided valuable information about the enemy on the frontier? By maintaining my façade as a patriot, I'm sure there will be plenty more to come."

"Yes, yes Wallis," answered Andre. "And, you've been quite happy to take payment for the information, too."

"And, shouldn't I? I run the risk."

"Of course, of course," said Andre. "Yes, you shall be invited, but I do so in honor of that fine Bordeaux you found for me last month. That and the sweet April air proved a most successful elixir with a very pretty Tory girl."

"How does that look, sir?" asked the clothier.

Wallis snapped out of his reverie. He studied himself in the mirror and said, "Yes. I believe that will do. Have it delivered to my home by 10 o'clock tomorrow morning. I won't be made late for the event."

Wallis spent the next day persecuting his servants as he obsessed over his wig and the shine on his shoes. He even daubed on a *discreet* amount of makeup, in the British style, to hide any possible imperfections. He carefully slipped on his new ensemble that afternoon and snatched his silver-handled mahogany walking stick as he walked out the door.

Wallis' anticipation mounted as he sped along the Delaware toward Walnut Grove. He alighted from his carriage and glided toward the mansion through rows of fragrant boxwood. He followed the path around the home, through the rear formal gardens, and joined the crowd at the river's edge.

Martial music and a cannonade heralded a flotilla of festooned boats. They carried the "tournament's" participants and the evening's dignitaries. Guests on the shore formed an aisle through which they disembarked and led the way to the grounds for an old-fashioned medieval joust.

British officers, adorned in silks, played the role of knights. Each championed a loyalist girl, arrayed in Turkish costume, as his lady. Wallis noticed one of the more conspicuous damsels was Andre's close companion and Philadelphia society's Peggy Shippen.

Gauntlets loosed, trumpets flourished and thunderous jousts entertained the guests. When a champion had been crowned, he and his lady led a procession through triumphal garden arches, up carpeted stairs and into the grand ballroom. Surrounded with mirrors and beribboned candelabras, light sparkled around the room. Wallis wished the poor bumpkins back in Muncy could see him now.

The herald announced the first dance, and the orchestra began to play. Wallis took advantage of the chance to fraternize with several young loyalist girls. He danced for the next hour before getting down to business.

When the time was right, he targeted the guests he thought could most benefit him. He maneuvered around the room and eased his way into any conversation he could use as a springboard to the next. He worked his way up the social ladder until the chance he awaited presented itself.

General Howe, with General Clinton by his side, was drawn into his discussion. Wallis was introduced to the new commander. As the generals moved on, Wallis followed and pulled them aside for a private interview. Wallis mentioned a matter of current business to

Howe, who then explained to Sir Henry that Wallis had been doing exemplary service for the cause.

Wallis thanked Howe for this *unexpected* compliment and, noting that Clinton seemed properly impressed, assured the new commander he would be honored to continue to perform any service that would be helpful to him. Clinton nodded politely in response. Wallis then told the generals he didn't wish to monopolize their time and bid them a pleasant evening.

Wallis was now free to relax and enjoy the rest of the evening. Music, dancing and fireworks led to a midnight banquet. Drinking and dancing continued until early in the morning, and, as dawn broke, Wallis realized he was one of the last to leave. He negotiated the path back through the boxwoods while musing *this* was how he was intended to live. He climbed into his carriage imagining future Mischianzas held in *his* honor.

★ ★ ★ ★ ★

LOYALSOCK VALLEY

John Thompson was at the far end of his field when he heard the conch shell. He spun and looked down the valley in the direction of the sound.

"Damn," he said, and ran for the house.

He grabbed his rifle and powder but left everything else behind. He ran back outside and paused to look at his two cows grazing peacefully in the meadow. He hated to leave them behind.

"Nah, they'll just slow me down," he said out loud, and took off at a measured run toward the Scott's farm at the end of the valley.

When he neared their farm, Mr. Scott, with the conch shell still in hand, was motioning him on.

"News from upriver. Raiders on the way," he shouted. "We're headin' to Wallis'."

By the end of the day, most of the upper West Branch had

shown up at the estate. Wallis' foreman directed settlers to lodgings in the manor's outbuildings and farmyard. Thompson was grateful for the shelter, but the journey was uneventful, and he already regretted his decision to leave his cows behind.

"I can't believe I just left 'em there," he said over and over to Peter Shufelt and William Wyckoff for the following week. Finally, it got the better of him and he announced, "I'm goin' back for 'em tomorrow mornin'."

"Count us in," they said.

They set out at dawn and headed up the east bank of the river.

The rest of the community at Wallis' was just beginning to stir. They were tending animals and preparing the morning meal when Michael Dean, one of Wallis' African slaves, came running and hollering that some of the horses had been stolen.

Militia Captain David Berry was sitting by the fire having a bowl of corn mush. He called Dean over.

"Alright Dean," said Berry. "Calm down an' tell me what happened."

Dean was obviously upset. He'd been put in charge of caring for the settler's horses. An older man with very dark skin and a snowy white beard, Dean was in remarkably good shape for his age. He was a proud man who carried himself with quiet dignity and, in spite of his situation, took his job seriously.

"They took the horses," said Dean.

"All of 'em?" Berry replied.

"No, but quite a few."

"Are you sure they didn't just wander off?"

"No, sir. They did *not* wander off," said Dean. "I had 'em secure in the pasture fence, and they couldn't a' got away. Besides, you can see the tracks for yourself, and there's footprints with 'em."

"Alright, Dean. Nobody's blamin' ya. Why don't we go take a look?"

Berry and Dean headed toward the pasture, accompanied by a few others who were near enough to hear the exchange. Arriving at the breach in the fence, it was obvious someone had purposely broken it.

"Odd," said Berry. "Some a' the horses stayed here. You'd think if someone was stealin' 'em, they'd take 'em all."

"Maybe Thompson took a couple horses and forgot to get the fence back up," said Thomas Covenhoven.

"I don't think so," answered Berry. "He's goin' after his cows. He can drive 'em back here just as well on foot. Besides, Thompson wouldn't be that careless."

"I think it's *meant* to look like an accident," said Captain Sharpshins. Sharpshins was an Oneida warrior, one of the two tribes of the Six Nations that stayed loyal to the American cause.

"Yeah," said Dean excitedly, "look close and you can see the footprints I was talkin' about."

"Where?" said James Covenhoven.

"Right here." He pointed to a specific spot. "And here. You see they walked ahead of the horses and then the hoofprints covered the man prints."

"He's right," said Sharpshins. "The men are lighter so don't make as deep a print, but you can see a half-covered heel mark right where he says."

"Yeah, I see it now," said Berry.

Sharpshins continued, "The man's in moccasins. Whether it's settler or Indian moccasins, who can tell?"

"I don't give a damn," said Berry. "I'm goin' to go get them horses no matter who the hell took 'em. You comin' Sharpshins?"

"I'll come."

"Anybody else?"

James and Thomas Covenhoven agreed, as did Peter Wyckoff and his son, Cornelius. As the men started back to the camp, Dean spoke up. "You ain't leavin' without me are ya?"

Berry answered, "That's mighty fine of you, Dean, but you don't have to risk goin' with us. I told you, nobody's blamin' you."

"Well, I appreciate nobody blamin' me for those horses gettin' *stole*. But let me ask you a question Cap'n Berry."

"What is it?"

"Well sir," said Dean, "what is it you're fightin' this war for?"

"I'm fightin' for my independence, same as everybody else."

"Well Mr. Cap'n Berry, I was put in charge of them horses that was bein' used in that fight, and they was taken away by an enemy, no matter how you look at it. Now, Mr. Wallis ain't here, and I don't get to make too many decisions on my own . . . but if you don't mind, I s'pose I'd like to go and fight for my independence too. . . "

"Dean . . . I'd be proud to have you along."

"Thank you, sir."

The men gathered their arms and supplies and were soon on the trail of the horses. Barely started, Robert Covenhoven caught up with them. He'd served with Colonel Kelly on the frontier the previous fall, and he'd seen this before.

"You should turn back," said Covenhoven.

Berry said, "What and leave 'em take our horses?"

"Better than takin' your scalps, ain't it Captain?"

"We're not even sure these are Indians we're dealing with," answered Berry.

"Captain Berry, it's got t' be either Indians or Tories who took them horses. How many times are we goin' to fall for the same trick?" Robert looked to his brothers to see if they were considering his words, but they just stared back.

"If that's all, we'll be on our way," said Berry.

"Well boys, I'd like to join you on this one, but it just don't feel right. I wisht you'd reconsider," said Covenhoven.

"We need those horses," answered Berry, stubbornly.

"Alright, good luck."

Robert turned toward Wallis' and the group continued on. He looked back over his shoulder and watched his brothers disappear over the crest of a hill into the muggy June mist.

★ ★ ★ ★ ★

KING'S STOCKADE

"I lost a good friend in Armstrong when he was killed at Antes Fort and I ain't gonna chance losin' you'ins," said William King when the alarm was raised earlier that month. He and his garrison of four men were determined to hold his stockade on Lycoming Creek, but he sent his wife and children to Northumberland.

"Don't come back until I send word," he'd told her.

Now, King was getting low on supplies. When some neighbors from upriver passed on their way to Fort Augusta, he said, "Tell 'em I'm runnin' out a' powder, lead an' salt. If they can get some to me, I think I can hold the fort."

King's message made it to Northumberland and Peter Smith decided to take a wagonload of supplies back up the river to him. It had been a year since Smith received the beating from Robert Robb and he still felt the effects. Still, he'd evacuated his family from the Loyalsock and was anxious to return.

"Would you an' your children like to come along?" Smith asked Mrs. King after he organized a party of five militiamen to accompany them.

"I don't know," she said. "Bill said stay here."

"There couldn't be no safer way t' get there than by travellin' with an armed guard," answered Smith.

"I guess you're right," she said. "Alright, we'll come along."

They were ready and loaded on the morning of June 10th. Smith grabbed the reigns and yelled, "Let's go."

The supply-laden wagon rolled out with Smith's wife and

six children and Mrs. King and her two daughters tucked in the back. The militiamen fanned out and the party headed up the West Branch.

★ ★ ★ ★ ★

ON THE TRAIL FROM WALLIS'

Dean and Sharpshins led the way in search of the missing horses. Their practiced eyes recognized bent grass and scuff marks on rocks that blazed their path. The horse thieves' trail joined that of three other men just before they reached the Loyalsock. The group followed the tracks to Thompson's home.

"Thompson." shouted Captain Berry as they neared the house. There was no reply.

"Shufelt?" he yelled again. "William Wyckoff!"

The men split up and rounded both sides of the home, heading toward the creek that flowed just behind.

The men met in back of the house and discovered the bodies of Thompson and Shufelt. They were laid side by side next to the back wall. Both had been shot at close range and scalped. The ground around their bodies was painted with a thick wash of blood that already teemed with swarms of flies.

"Damn," said Berry. "I guess that decides if it was Indians or not. Anybody see Wyckoff?"

"Maybe he got away," said William's brother Cornelius.

"Yeah, or was taken," mumbled his father, Peter.

"Cap'n," said Dean. "Them tracks go right into the crick. There ain't no way to tell which way they went now unless we get lucky and see where they come out."

"Well, let's split up and see what we can find," said Berry. "Dean and Sharpshins, you take the Wyckoffs and head upstream. I'll go downstream with the Covenhovens."

The groups separated. A hundred yards downstream, the air

came alive with screaming lead. James Covenhoven never knew what happened. A ball entered his right side and tore through his heart.

Berry instinctively ducked and turned toward the sound. He heard a shot whistle above him. The next hit him squarely in the forehead. He toppled forward and hit the ground, dead.

Thomas Covenhoven was wounded in the thigh and fell to the ground. The Indians stood and walked across the creek toward where he lay, reloading as they came.

Hearing the gunfire, the four other men came running from upstream to see what happened. They traded some long shots with the Indians in the creek. As they came closer, more Indians circled around and fired from behind them. It was a perfectly sprung trap. No one was hit, but, surrounded and outnumbered, the settlers realized they couldn't fight their way out.

Dean, Sharpshins and the Wyckoffs dropped their weapons and approached Covenhoven as the enemy closed around them. The Wyckoffs were relieved to see William alive with the Indians. He'd been wounded in the shoulder but was stable and able to walk.

The Indians pulled Thomas Covenhoven to his feet and forced him to walk. He knew this was the test to see if he would become a captive or a corpse. He fought the blinding pain and forced himself forward. Surprisingly, each step became a little easier and the stiff thigh began to loosen and work.

An Indian walked up to him with a rag he'd torn from Berry's shirt and some moss he scraped from the creek. The Indian chewed the moss, placed it on the wound and tied the rag around it. Thomas had passed his test.

After scalping Berry and James Covenhoven, the Indians rounded up Dean, Sharpshins, Thomas Covenhoven and the three Wyckoffs and headed upstream.

★ ★ ★ ★ ★

BETWEEN WALLIS' AND THE LOYALSOCK

"Whoa," shouted John Harris, coming out of his stockade and waving his arms.

Peter Smith brought the wagon to a stop, and the militiamen knelt down to take a breather.

"What's a matter?" asked Smith.

"You better turn back," said Harris. "I heard gunshots up the valley here this mornin' an' it wasn't no hunters. If I was you I'd turn back t' Wallis' for the night till ya can find out what's goin' on."

"Why ain't you leavin', then?" asked Smith.

"That's just what I'm thinkin' a' doin'," answered Harris. "I stayed through the alarm 'cause I figured we was safe here, but after today I'm thinkin' twice't."

"It was that bad, huh?" asked Smith.

"It was a reg'lar firefight."

"You didn't see nobody afterwards?" asked Smith.

"No," answered Harris. "An' I didn't go lookin' neither."

Smith thought it over for a moment and said, "We just come all the way from Northumberland. If we turn around now, we'd have to go five miles back to Wallis', an' we only got seven miles left to get to the Lycoming."

He looked down to the militiamen to see what they thought.

"Let's go on ahead," said Snodgrass. "We come this far."

"Campbell, Hammond, Burger and Adams . . . you boys feel the same?" asked Smith.

"I do," said Campbell, as the others nodded. "Let's go."

"That's just what we'll do," said Smith. "Thank you, Harris. We appreciate the warnin'. We'll be back from King's in a few days and settle back on our land."

"It'll be good t' have ya back in the neighborhood," said Harris, walking beside the wagon. He stopped and watched as they drove on.

Nearing the Loyalsock, the militiamen fanned out around the wagon.

"We'll water the horses here and soon get you home," said Smith to Mrs. King.

She smiled and stroked her tiny daughter's strawberry-blonde hair. "See honey," she said softly, "we'll see daddy soon."

When the horses had their fill, they pushed on.

At twilight they came to a bubbling rill flowing through a grove of plum trees.

"Just a couple more miles, now," said Snodgrass, who led the way.

He leapt the little brook, and shots rang out. He was bizarrely driven back in midair. A ball passed completely through him and lodged in one of the lead horses.

Confusion erupted as the rifles cracked. Horses reared and fell. Children screamed and buried their faces in their mother's skirts.

Campbell and Hammond were killed in the volley. The Indians charged and Burger and Adams each got off a shot from behind the wagon.

Peter Smith grabbed his little girl and jumped from the driver's seat.

"Follow me," he yelled to his wife as he ran, but she paused to help Mrs. King get the children out of the wagon.

Smith and the militiamen fell back and watched as the Indians engulfed the wagon. In the confusion, they saw one of Smith's boys drop out the back of the wagon and run off into the woods toward King's.

The screaming inside the wagon didn't last long. One after another, the women's and children's voices fell silent.

When the Indians came out, they were carrying Smith's youngest son and the tiny strawberry blonde King girl.

"Well, they spared them anyways," said Adams, who looked up to see tears streaming down Smith's face.

The survivors stole silently away as the wagon was plundered and burned.

★ ★ ★ ★ ★

ON THE TRAIL UP THE LOYALSOCK

Dean noticed the looks directed toward him that day and tried to ignore them. The Indian who took him captive argued with other warriors as they walked. The argument intensified that evening while they ate. Then, Dean's captor grew sullen and quiet.

Suddenly, a handful of warriors grabbed Dean and led him to a clearing down by the creek. The other prisoners were led in tow and made to sit in a circle around a stake surrounded by brush at its base. The raiders forced Dean up on the brush and bound him to the stake.

A raider with a burning torch walked up and set the brush on fire. Dean remained motionless and stared directly ahead. He didn't utter a sound as he endured his horrific end. His funeral pyre blazed and sent sparks sailing heavenward in the evening sky.

"That was a terrible way to die," said Peter Wyckoff to Thomas Covenhoven, sitting next to him.

"You know Peter, I was just thinkin'," he replied.

"What?"

"Dean was born a captive, lived his life as a captive, and he died a captive, but today he was a free man. I s'pose he wouldn't have had it any other way."

★ ★ ★ ★ ★

PHILADELPHIA

From the upper window of his townhouse, Samuel Wallis stared into the street. The summer heat rose from the cobblestones, causing a strange rippling effect in the pattern.

Wallis reflected on the day the British withdrew from the city. Scarlet streams of men wound their way through the neighborhoods as Union Jacks hung limply against swaying flagpoles. Booming bass drums and rattling snares echoed crazily off brick buildings in the narrow streets. It was a businesslike, unceremonious affair.

The Americans called it a retreat, but the British realized occupying the capitol was removing an entire army from operations against Washington. Since they lost an army at Saratoga, moving these troops to New York for future operations made sense.

Wallis recalled how distraught Tories ran into the streets in disbelief. For many, the choice was now to follow the army and salvage as much of their lives as possible, or to face an uncertain retribution from the rebels who would retake control.

"Thank God I've been circumspect," Wallis congratulated himself. He mused over how incredibly easy it had been to replace his British clientel with the newly-arrived American hierarchy.

General Benedict Arnold was the new commander. He'd been recognized by Congress for his heroism at Saratoga and given a new commission from Washington restoring his rank.

It was when Washington warned Arnold to shut down the black market that things became interesting. Arnold declared martial law and closed *all* of Philadelphia's shops. Then, with the clothier general, he used public funds to purchase bulk goods and sold them at a profit. The conspirators then split the profits and replaced the public funds.

Wallis saw his opportunity to not only remain in business but to make a handsome profit. He secured a meeting with Arnold and persuaded him how lucrative it would be to speculate in trade between Philadelphia and British-held New York.

" . . . and I'll have far less competition here," thought Wallis, "while my former competitors will be clambering to sell their wares *to me.*"

★ ★ ★ ★ ★

SOUTHEASTERN PENNSYLVANIA

Brady, Boone and Lieutenant Dougherty reminisced as they traveled west.

"Did ya ever see Gen'ral Warshington so mad as when Lee ordered that retreat at Monmouth?" asked Boone.

"Wooeee. He cussed better than von Steuben," agreed Dougherty.

"Yeah, but ol' Steuby cussed in two languages. Too bad neither one was English," laughed Boone.

"I'm just glad we was there to shore up the left," said Brady. "'Course, there's nothin' like goin' toe to toe with reg'lars at close quarters."

"First time I ever wished I had a bayonet," said Dougherty.

"What? Suddenly your tomahawk ain't good enough?" needled Boone.

"It was just exactly good enough," answered Dougherty. "Otherwise, I'd still be back on that field."

"That was a fight to remember, for sure," said Brady.

"How about that woman dropping her water pitcher to jump in an' help that gun crew when one of 'em went down?" asked Boone.

"Damnedest thing I ever saw," agreed Brady. "Made me proud the way the boys cheered her. Hell, in that battle I was as proud of the *regiment* as I've ever been."

"Wasn't a bad way to go out, was it?" asked Dougherty.

"I'd say the 12th did its part in the war," said Brady. "I have to admit, too, I'm glad I didn't end up assigned to the 3rd or the 6th like the rest a' the survivors. Just wouldn't a seemed right."

"Speakin' of seemin' right," said Boone, "I was glad Gen'ral Washington included me in the orders to go home with you fellas to protect the valley, even though I wasn't part a' the 12th no more."

"I'd say the raiders'll have their hands full now," said Dougherty.

"Well, if nothin' else," answered Brady, "Jane'll have her hands full tryin' to tame you back into a house critter."

CHAPTER 5

July 1-9, 1778

FORT AUGUSTA

Colonel Hunter stood on the wall and looked out over the river. The blazing sun drew sharp lines of light and shadow across the landscape. It was one of those still mornings that built heat so quickly, all of nature wilted beneath it. The buildings in the fort grew stifling.

"Even up here, there's no breeze," he thought as he came down from the wall. He stopped for a moment by the little vegetable garden he kept at the side of his house and stared absent-mindedly at his browned and withered beans.

A commotion at the gate caused Hunter to turn and see a rider galloping toward him. A disheveled man leapt from the back of the horse and lost his feet when he hit the ground. He was at least sixty-five.

He laid there for a moment with his eyes closed, then rallied himself. Hunter approached, extended a hand, and said, "You seem to be in quite a hurry."

"I'm lookin' for Colonel Hunter. I have a report."

"Well, you found him," said Hunter. "What have you got?"

"Sir, I'm Levi Sherman. I have news from Wyoming."

"Go on," said Hunter, helping the man to his feet.

"I . . . I'm a Connecticut settler, sir," he said.

"I have a firm rule, Mr. Sherman, to fight only one war at a time. We're all in this together," assured Hunter. "What's your report?"

"Well sir, it was terrible," the old man began. "We'd been

fightin' off raids and smallpox most a' the spring. A few days ago, we learned Tory Colonel Butler was leadin' an army towards us. We held a council a' war on the mornin' of the third. Hard to believe now that was just two days ago.

"Anyways, most of our fightin' men is off in the army. All we had left was old-timers and kids. Lucky for us, ol' Zeb, I mean *our* Colonel Butler, was home on leave from the army and took command.

"Well sir, some wanted to cut and run, and others wanted to fight it out, no matter how bad it looked. You know we just built them forts, and we didn't want to give 'em up so easy.

"'Well', says Zeb, 'I think we can hold 'em off till we can get help from the army. They're only just a ways off in Jersey.' That was good enough for us and we decided to fight it out. We left the women and real young'uns in Forty Fort and three hundred of us followed Zeb upriver.

"It was about four in the afternoon when we got close to the enemy. Zeb give us a rally speech and says to have at 'em. We pitched into their left and it looked like they might be givin' way. Just then, we was surprised by a bunch a' Indians firin' on us from our right. That's when Cap'n Durkee was kill't.

"We stood firm until more Indians shows up an' starts firin' on our *left*. We was damn near surrounded. We was ordered back to a better position, but when some a' the fellas down the line saw us fallin' back, they thought we was retreatin'. Then they panicked and run back to the river in as big a mess as you ever saw.

"Zeb was standin', shoutin' for us to hold the line, but it was too late. Most of us run towards Monocasy Island, with the enemy shootin' us down like sheep. Some run back towards Forty Fort but got cut off and slaughtered.

"We got t' the river and starts in t' swimmin'. Bullets was whistlin' all around us and men was gettin' hit left and right.

"They followed us t' the island. The ones who stayed there was all hunted down and kill't . . . even them that surrendered. I went on across't the river. I couldn't get enough space b'tween me an' them. I ain't yella, Colonel, but I didn't get this gray hair by bein' stupid neither.

"I hid out in the hills back of the island, thinkin' I could work my way back to Forty Fort that night. Then, when it got dark there was all kinds a' commotion and I thought I'd best stay where I was. They'd been tomahawkin' and shootin' and scalpin' men ever since we run, but at night . . . well it was awful.

"From where I was I saw all kinds of butcherin' goin' on. There was men thrown on fires and held down with pitchforks until they stopped tryin' to get up . . . . Anyways around midnight, I guess, I saw 'em round up a big group a' prisoners an' put 'em in a circle around a boulder. They had a bonfire burnin' so I saw the whole thing.

"Each prisoner was held down on his knees. Then a old woman in the middle a' the circle lifts up a tomahawk and starts singin'. I'm pret-near sure it was Queen Esther. Well, she walks real slow around the circle and tomahawks one after the other. Seein' this, a couple a' the fellas ups and runs. I think they got away, too.

"When things finally quietened down, I worked my way back to Forty Fort. Everywhere I looked houses was burnin' . . . fields was burnin'. But, I made it back. Inside the fort, they was terrible scared. People was runnin' in all directions at once.

"The night before, they was reinforced by about thirty-five militiamen. Now they was all decidin' again, 'Do we run, or do we fight?' Well, they decided to get everybody in the fort and to hold out against 'em.

"Yesterday mornin' a Indian messenger comes and says they demand the surrender a' the fort. This time there wasn't much talk. That's exactly what we done.

"We opened the gates and in marched the Tories on one end and the Indians at the other, led by Queen Esther. We stacked our arms and Tory Butler give 'em to the Indians.

"Then the Indians come around to all of us and put black paint on our faces. They told us to carry a white cloth on a stick and that would mark us as surrendered and keep us safe. I waited around most of the day tryin' to think a' somethin' useful to do when I decided to try to get word down here to you.

"I left my place in Wilkes-Barre around dark. I got to my horse just before the Indians started burnin' the village, surrender or no. From a few miles away it made a awful sight. The whole town was burnt down.

"I rode as fast as I could to get here to you. I only stopped once'd this mornin' to get some water and wash my face.

"That's it, Colonel. It's all lost at Wyoming. It was a massacre. I thought you better know."

His task complete, the old man exhaled deeply. He looked completely drained. Hunter stared at him for a long moment, letting everything sink in.

"Mr. Sherman, you're a brave man and I'm grateful to you. Would you like something to eat?"

"Well, I am kinda hungry."

"I'll see that something is brought to you in the barracks and that your horse is taken care of," said Hunter. "Why don't you go inside and get some rest?"

"Thank you, Colonel," said Sherman, and he turned and walked toward the barracks.

Hunter considered what he'd just heard. He spit on the ground and ground it into the dust. Summoning two men of the garrison, he ordered them to take Sherman something to eat and to get his horse watered and fed. Then, Hunter walked inside and called to his wife.

"Sue? . . . Susie."

"What is it?" she answered.

"Come here, will you? I need to talk to you."

"What is it, Sam?" she asked, entering the room.

"Sit down here, a minute, Sue. I just got the news Wyoming is lost."

"No."

"Yeah. Apparently, it was pretty bad."

"Oh, those poor people," said Mrs. Hunter.

"Well, it's worse than that. Without the Wyoming settlements, there's nothing between us and the Indian country on the North Branch. That leaves the West Branch completely exposed. Folks here are in no shape for a full-scale attack any more than the North Branch was, and we have no means of reinforcing them. I've decided to evacuate the whole West Branch valley."

"Oh, Sam."

"I know," said the colonel.

"Those people finally got their crops in last spring," said Mrs. Hunter.

"Susie, I *know*. But there's nothing to be done about it now. I'd sooner they lose their homes and crops than their scalps. If they were attacked now, it'd be a slaughter."

"Alright, Sam. You're the colonel. What can I do to help?"

"Well, that's the next part of it. I need you to get ready to leave here and go down river."

"But why?"

"Susie, I won't argue about this. With both branches of the river evacuated, this will *be* the frontier. It's too dangerous. Besides, I'll be able to concentrate on my duties if I'm not worryin' about your safety."

"Alright, Sam. If that's the way you feel about it."

"That's the way I feel. You can go and visit your brother for a while."

She stood and folded her arms in front of her and huddled close to her husband's chest. He hugged her for a long while. "It'll be alright, Susie. I don't know how yet. But somehow it'll be alright."

"I know it, Sam. . . I know it will."

"Now, why don't you start gatherin' the things you'll need to take with you?"

"Alright."

She pulled away from him and looked up into his eyes. "You just make sure you're safe too."

"You'll be back before you know it," he said.

She nodded, kissed him on the cheek and turned and left the room.

Hunter walked out the front door and crossed the parade ground to the gate. He called one of the men off the wall. When he reported, Hunter looked at the boy standing in front of him. He must have been thirteen. He gave him the following orders:

"Wyoming has fallen. I want you to ride up the West Branch and send word along the forts that the valley is to be evacuated. Colonel Hepburn is in command of the militia up there. I want him to make sure all above Wallis' get the word to come down river."

"Yessir."

"You're Franklin, aren't you?"

"Yessir, Charles Franklin."

"Well, Franklin, this is maybe the most important order I've given in the war, so far. Hundreds of lives depend on it being carried out. Do you understand everything you're to do?"

"Yessir. Consider it done, sir."

"Alright. Go to it, soldier."

"*Yessir.*"

As he left, Hunter noticed the boy was smiling broadly. Hunter barely suppressed a smile himself. "Thank you, Charles," he said to himself under his breath. "I needed that, just now."

WALLIS'

Early in the morning, one of the pickets shouted, "Man comin' in."

Colonel Hepburn sat by the fire. "Whereabouts?" he yelled.

"There, Colonel." The picket pointed to the road south of Wallis'.

James Brady galloped toward them. He was riding hard and leaving a trail of dust behind him. He reached camp and dismounted next to Colonel Hepburn. "Brady reportin', Colonel."

"What's the news?"

"Word just come from Colonel Hunter. He says Wyomin' has fallen and to evacuate the valley."

"What? Did he say how bad it was, or if the enemy is on the way here?"

"No sir, he didn't say. But he did ask for you to make sure all above here gets the message."

The men standing with Colonel Hepburn heard the conversation. Robert Covenhoven stepped forward. "I'll go."

Covenhoven served in the Continental Army and was with Washington at Trenton and Princeton. Then, when his term expired, he decided to return to defend the valley. He'd made quite a name for himself in Kelly's militia last fall.

"You sure, Bob?" Hepburn asked. "It's only been a couple a' weeks since you lost your brothers."

"What the hell does that have to do with anything? I can get word up to Antes Fort, and I'm volunteerin' to go."

"Alright, Bob. The job's yours." Turning to the group, Hepburn asked, "Who's goin' with him?"

"I'll go," called a young man's voice from the back of the group.

"Acker?"

"Yeah, I worked for Culbertson at his mill up there . . . I'd like to get some of my things."

"Alright with you, Bob?" Hepburn asked.

"Come on," he replied to Acker.

Turning to Brady, Hepburn said, "How's yer ma, James? She's due anytime now, ain't she?"

"Another few weeks, I think."

"Why don't you go on back to your family and help 'em get ready to move?" said Hepburn.

"That's just what I was plannin' on," said James, remounting his horse.

"Then wait 'til you see us comin', and we'll go all together."

"Alright, see you soon, Colonel."

James wheeled the horse around and was gone.

Covenhoven and Acker gathered their things and went to see Hepburn.

"Well, Colonel, we're off," said Covenhoven.

"How you figure on goin'?" asked Hepburn.

"Well, I sure as hell ain't goin' up the road. I figure on crossin' the river right here and goin' along the crest of the mountain the whole way. Then we can drop right down the hollow into Antes Fort."

"Sounds pretty smart to me," concurred Hepburn. "I plan on keepin' camp here until everyone comes from upriver. That way, we can travel in one large group and not head down the river piecemeal."

"Alright, I'll hurry 'em along," said Covenhoven.

"I'd appreciate it. Good luck," said Hepburn.

"Good luck to you, too."

Covenhoven and Acker walked to the river past settlers who were already gathering valuables and supplies. Some refused to leave. Hepburn matter-of-factly told everyone they *would* be going, so they might just as well get ready.

Covenhoven led Acker into the river. At midstream, the water reached the men's chests and they held their rifles and powder horns over their heads.

"Current's sorta strong even with the water this low, ain't it?" said Acker.

"Keep your feet, Acker. I wouldn't want to be without *my* powder on this trip."

"I'm not fallin' in. I'm just speculatin' on the current," he answered defensively.

Water ran off their clothes in streams as the men splashed out of the river. Covenhoven led the way, pressing on up the side of Bald Eagle Mountain.

"Are we racin'?" Acker asked, panting.

"Not each other, but we're racin' to save them people up ahead ain't we? This ain't no Sund'y jaunt we're on, boy."

"'Course, you're right," said Acker. "I'm sorry."

Covenhoven suddenly regretted the way he'd been talking to Acker and added, "We'll be on top soon, and the goin' will get a lot easier. Keep at it."

"Alright."

There was no path directly up the side of the mountain. Brambles and dense thickets slowed their progress. Finally, an outcrop of rocks blanketed the mountainside for the next two hundred yards.

"Well, Acker, looks like we found us a stairway," said Covenhoven.

The men walked out into the rocks, making much better time.

"Watch yer step, Acker," said Covenhoven. "You don't want to bust an ankle between these rocks."

They pushed on with heaving chests and burning thighs. Covenhoven, focusing down on his feet, caught motion out of his periphery vision. He looked up and stopped dead in his tracks. "Acker, don't move."

"What is it?"

"Snake."

Coiled on a rock at eye level in front of Covenhoven was the largest copperhead he'd ever seen. It's thick, shiny body wound at least four feet and supported its flat, triangular head. The snake was obviously aggravated. It was hissing and bearing its long sickle fangs.

Then, Covenhoven realized the rocks and crevices in every direction were alive with movement. The burnished copper backs of hundreds of snakes slithered all around them. Drawn to the natural oven of the rock-strewn mountainside, the snakes emerged from their dens to soak in every bit of warmth the July sun had to offer.

"What'll we do?" asked Acker.

"Can you see how far the snakes are behind you?"

"Oh my . . ."

"What is it?" asked Covenhoven.

"They go for at least twenty yards behind us. Maybe more."

"Alright. It looks like they're only about twenty *feet* more in front of us, so we're gonna cut straight on up the hill."

"Are you insane, Covenhoven?"

"Would you rather stay here? Besides, we walked this far through 'em without even noticin', we oughta be able to make it another twenty feet. Now just hang on a minute while I take care of somethin' here first."

While speaking with Acker, Covenhoven had been staring straight into the eyes of the big copperhead in front of him. Slowly, he reached for the handle of his tomahawk and pulled it from his belt. Then, he swung it in a vicious backhand motion. The snake reacted to the movement and struck straight out at him.

In a slow and almost dreamlike state, Covenhoven saw the snake's gaping mouth propelling toward him. Within inches of his face, the back of the viper's head rotated toward him and struck him in the cheek before falling harmlessly to the ground in front of him. The razor-sharp tomahawk had severed the snake's head in midstrike, leaving a contorting, writhing mass in front of him.

"Now we can go," said Covenhoven as he wiped the snake's blood from his cheek with the back of his hand. "Keep lookin' around and make sure not to step too close to any of 'em."

Acker sidestepped the still flexing jaw of the dead copperhead and followed Covenhoven up the mountainside. They slowly picked their way between the remaining snakes and out of the rocks. As they reached the forest, the men found a boulder and sat down to take a short breather.

"Damn stupid of me. I should have thought of snakes in there," said Covenhoven. "I was just in a hurry, I guess."

"How did we get that far into 'em without seein' 'em?" asked Acker.

"Musta been the vibrations of us walkin' that brought 'em out, or maybe they was out already and just crawled away when we got too near 'em. I don't know. Damn copperheads. I hate 'em. At least a rattler'll let you know he's there . . . anyhow, we better get movin'. We're just gettin' started."

They reached the top of the mountain, and the going was much easier. The mostly level, windswept top of the mountain didn't have such dense undergrowth. With about twenty miles to go, the men traveled as quickly as they could.

They stopped only twice more that day, both times when they came to small streams where they got a quick drink. By evening they were descending the hollow that led to the bluff at Antes Fort. As they approached the fort, Covenhoven called out to the guard. "Hello in the fort."

"Who are ya?"

"Robert Covenhoven and Acker who worked at Culbertson's."

"Come ahead."

The gate opened and the men entered the fort.

"Where's Colonel Antes?" asked Covenhoven.

"In the house up ahead," replied one of the men.

Covenhoven and Acker walked to the house and knocked on the door.

"Come on in," yelled someone from inside.

Covenhoven pressed the latch and pushed open the door. Four men were sitting at a table eating. The lamps were lit against the deepening twilight.

"Bob, how the hell are you?"

"Hiya, Colonel," said Covenhoven.

"What are *you* doin' here?" asked Antes.

"Well, we got some bad news. We just left this mornin' from Wallis' to bring you Colonel Hunter's orders to evacuate the valley."

"What?"

"Wyoming's fallen. That leaves us awful exposed up here, so Hunter says skedaddle. We got to get word on up to Horn's Fort and to anyone above there tonight yet, and everybody's gotta be ready to leave here at first light."

"Then that's what we'll do," said Antes. "You boys hungry?"

"We could use a bite."

"Why don't you go out and see Peggy Andrews, at the kettle," said the colonel. "I'll send someone up to Horn's and get everything goin'. Thanks, boys, for gettin' up here so fast. We appreciate it."

"Think nothin' of it, Colonel."

Covenhoven and Acker went back outside to the fire. They gratefully accepted heaping plates, went over to the stockade wall and sat down against it to eat.

"You know, Acker. . ." said Covenhoven.

"Yeah?"

"I mighta been a little rough on you today. I'm sorry."

"You don't have to . . ."

"Yes . . . yes I do. I been feelin' kinda ouchy lately . . . 'cause a' my brothers, I guess. I 'spose I'm just takin' it out on everybody. Anyhow, you done real good today. You should be proud."

"Thanks for sayin' so," said Acker.

"Well," said Covenhoven, "you better eat up so you can go get those things you come after."

"I . . . I don't really have any things up here. I just wanted to come with you," admitted Acker.

Covenhoven pondered this for a moment. "Well . . . I'd be proud to serve with you anytime, Acker."

"Thanks again, Bob. Me too."

They finished their meals and pitched in to help the settlers get ready for the trip back downriver.

It wasn't long before Colonel Antes walked up to Covenhoven.

"Bob, I been thinkin' on how we oughta go about this thing," said Antes.

"Yeah?"

"Well, I figure we oughta put the women an' kids in boats to keep 'em safe in the river while the men walk along shore to protect 'em. That way the men can also drive the livestock with 'em on shore. What do you think?"

"I think that makes pretty good sense," agreed Covenhoven.

"Good. Now, why don't you turn in and get some rest for tomorrow? You had a long enough day already," said Antes.

"I think that makes pretty good sense, too," said Covenhoven. "Thanks."

Covenhoven walked over to the spot along the stockade where he'd eaten. Despite the activity all around him, he curled up beside the wall and fell into a sound sleep.

ANTES FORT

"Bob. . ."

Somewhere in the distance, Covenhoven heard a voice calling him and felt something hitting the bottom of his foot.

"Bob c'mon. Are you comin' with us, or are you volunteerin' for a haircut?"

Antes had gotten little rest himself, but he'd allowed Covenhoven to sleep through the night. It was just before dawn. He stood over Covenhoven, calling to him and gently kicking his foot.

"What's goin' on?" asked Covenhoven, blearily.

"We're all packed and ready to go, Bob. C'mon, an' get up."

Opening his eyes, the situation came back to him. He looked around. Except for a woman chasing a chicken across the grounds, he saw the fort was deserted. He watched as she herded the chicken toward the gate where a young boy grabbed it and picked it up. The woman put her arm thankfully on the boy's shoulder and they walked off toward the river together.

"Everybody's ready?" asked Covenhoven.

"Everybody but you," said Antes.

Covenhoven picked up his rifle and haversack. "Why'd you leave me sleep so long, for?"

"Seemed to me like you could use it," said Antes. "... and you musta or you'd a' woke up from all the commotion that went on all night.

Covenhoven paused for a second and gave Antes half a nod. He was embarrassed to have slept so long, but he was also grateful for the chance.

"By the way," said Antes. "The folks from Horn's Fort come in last night. They lost three men in a' ambush and one more wounded. Everybody's pretty jumpy. Now since you're the one who's rested up so good, why don't you lead us on down to Wallis'?"

As they left the fort, Covenhoven was shocked. Spread out before him was a pitiful mass of people strewn along the riverbank. They clutched meager supplies and prized possessions.

One woman held a pair of candlesticks. Someone else carried a small chest. He saw the woman who'd been chasing the chicken pick up a small, rudely made cage of sticks as her boy placed the bird inside.

Most of those from Horn's Fort, who literally left at a moment's notice, had nothing with them at all.

"You think it's a good idea to let 'em carry all this stuff with 'em, Colonel?" asked Covenhoven, as they began to descend the bluff.

"How could I tell 'em they can't?" said Antes. "It's their most precious items. I told 'em they could take only what they could hold; no personal freight ... only supplies. Most of 'em spent half the night runnin' around buryin' the stuff they couldn't bring with 'em, in hopes of gettin' it back later."

Antes gestured to the shoreline. "There wasn't enough canoes to hold all the women and children, so people made do with whatever they could find."

Covenhoven noticed a woman with two small children getting ready to launch themselves off in a hog-trough. Some were still frantically trying to secure rafts they'd built out of tree limbs. Anything that floated was fair game.

Back from the water's edge, the men stood with the livestock. Horses, cattle, a few goats and a pig milled about on the shore.

Most of the men were armed, but not everyone had a rifle. Some carried smoothbore muskets. Farmer's shotguns and pitchforks were even more common. Hunting knives and tomahawks sprouted from the belts of almost everyone, but the odd sickle was also present for duty.

Antes and Covenhoven stopped a short distance up the hill from the crowd.

"Folks! " yelled Antes. "Folks, I need your attention."

The murmuring died away and expectant eyes turned toward the colonel.

"Alright," said Antes, "you all know the basic idea here."

"Yeah, get the hell away before we're all kill't. Ain't that right?" shouted a settler.

The ambush on the people from Horn's Fort and rumors about Wyoming were causing tensions to run high.

"Yeah, that's pretty much it," said Antes. "But I'll tell you what this ain't gonna be . . . this ain't gonna be no runnin' headlong panic-stricken mob, ya hear? We got us a mess a' folks here an' we can take care a' ourselves."

Antes paused for a moment and looked out across the crowd. "Sure, we're goin' to up an' skedaddle, but we're goin' to do it in as calm a way as possible. If we keep our heads, we all get where we're goin'. An' furthermore, we might be leavin' today, but we ain't leavin' for good. As soon as we get downriver and get organized, we can all start plannin' on how to get back here an' take back our homes."

Antes' words calmed the jittery crowd. He continued, "Now, Covenhoven here is gonna take the lead an' keep an eye out for anything that seems outta place. I'm gonna take the rear and keep us all movin'. You women just flow with the current and us men'll keep up on shore. You in the canoes be careful not to get ahead a' the other boats. We all stay together, right?"

Antes turned to Covenhoven. "Alright, Bob. Let's get 'er started."

"Alright," yelled Covenhoven. "You women on the rafts, spread out your cargo along the edges. It'll balance you out and give you some protection in case we're fired on.

Men . . . we go double file. Anyone without a firearm, pair up with someone who has one.

Now, let's go to Sunbury."

The men helped the women and children board their vessels and pushed them into the river. As the woman worked their way out into the current, the men fell in line. They spread the livestock out along the column and put someone in charge of each animal.

Despite the low water level, the flotilla kept a good pace, and the men had to work to keep up. After a few miles, a rustling in a laurel thicket a few yards off the path surprised the head of the men's column. Someone fired indiscriminately into the brush. On the river, a woman screamed; then others joined her.

The column stopped and men began to aim frantically into the woods in search of the enemy. Frightened from the thicket, a small doe clambered through the undergrowth and bounded up the rocky mountainside.

Covenhoven shouted, "Who fired that shot?" Looking back along the line, he saw a sheepish farmer standing with powder smoke curling up from the muzzle of his shotgun. Covenhoven gave him a brief stare and then shouted out over the river, "It's alright ladies, there ain't no danger. You're doin' fine. Just keep goin' the way you are."

Turning back to the column he said, "No one fires a shot unless me or the colonel orders you to. Got it? We'll wind up shootin' each other before you know it . . . and in some cases it'd be a waste a' powder. I'll let you know if anything needs shootin'. Now let's get goin'."

Skittish cattle and horses were brought back under control, and the column got moving again. When they got to within a few miles of Wallis', Covenhoven said to Acker, "You up to doin' some scoutin'?"

"Sure, what do you need?"

"I want you to take a horse and ride on down to Wallis'. Tell 'em we're on our way. That way they can join right in with us an' we don't have to stop."

"Alright," said Acker as he headed back along the line and borrowed a horse.

As he rode past the front of the column, Covenhoven shouted, "Acker."

"Yeah?"

"Keep your eyes open."

"I will," he said, then looked down the valley and dug his heels into the horse's flanks.

WALLIS'

Acker showed up in the early afternoon. He briefed Hepburn on everything that happened since he left the previous morning and explained how Antes and Covenhoven organized the retreat so far.

Hepburn sent Acker on down to Brady's and ordered everyone to get ready.

The settlers dragged their vessels to the water's edge. Expectant eyes looked upriver. Hepburn instructed the women to fall in behind those from Antes Fort, and the men, being on the other side of the river from Antes' column, to spread out along the whole of the group in the water. Finally, someone shouted, "There they are."

Everyone watched as the spectacle unfolded before them. Looking like survivors of a vast shipwreck, the fleet of refugees drifted toward those waiting to join them. A dust cloud slowly ascended above the trees on the other side of the river where Antes' men guarded the flank.

"Everybody get ready!" shouted Hepburn.

Some of the men started herding the animals into line while others waited with their women to help them cast off. As Antes' settlers approached, Hepburn recognized Covenhoven along the opposite shore and shook his rifle above his head in thanks. Covenhoven returned the salute.

As the flotilla drifted by, the groups stoically surveyed one another in passing. The women from Wallis' were launched in behind the others, and the men formed their column and swung into motion.

In the matter of a day, the families of the valley left everything they'd spent years building. No one stayed behind. The frontier began at the rear of the column, and its boundary diminished with every step.

The settlers from Wallis' shared rumors about Wyoming with those already on the trail. The Antes settlers told of the ambush on the way from Horn's Fort the night before. Fear spread like a shadowy mist. Then, someone noticed smoke rising behind them.

At first, white puffy wisps curled into the sky, but it soon grew black and billowing. Then another plume rose to join the first and then another after that. There was no doubt fields and farms were being consumed in wholesale destruction. The settlers now also knew the enemy was just behind them.

When the group reached Fort Brady, Mary and the girls set off in canoes while James and the other Brady boys took their place in the passing column.

Then, the boats began grounding in the shallows just below Brady's. Many of the panicked women jumped up and called to friends for help, nearly capsizing their fragile crafts.

"Sit down and be quiet, you fools," yelled Mary, who was now eight months pregnant. "Screamin' isn't goin' to help anything. Now those who are grounded simply slide over the edge into the water. The decrease in weight will raise your boat and you can push it off the rocks."

Though she was ready to deliver her next child within weeks, Mary demonstrated as she spoke, and those grounded around her followed suit. Soon, women from across the flotilla were plunging into the Susquehanna and freeing their boats. As they pushed, some fell headlong into the water, but they kept moving forward.

Mary's words of encouragement kept the women from becoming a frenzied mob. The columns on each shore organized rear guards to watch for sudden attacks, and they kept the weary men and animals moving.

At dusk, Hepburn motioned some of the women to come to shore. He sent a group of his men back out in the boats so they could get some sleep while the others continued to march. In a couple of hours when the first shift ended, they changed places with the next group of men on the shore. Antes saw what Hepburn was doing and followed suit. Eventually, all of the men were able to get some sleep while the column kept moving.

That night, the scene behind them grew horrific. The pall of smoke drifted across a pulsating red glow on the horizon. Reflecting on the water and covering the sky above, it was a hellish scene the settlers could have barely imagined. Tired and scared, they pushed on toward safety.

★ ★ ★ ★ ★

FORT AUGUSTA

"Was I too late?" thought Hunter.

It had been four days since he gave the order to evacuate the valley. Some of the nearer settlers had already shown up, but he was anxious about those in the upper valley. For the past two mornings he mounted the wall and stared up the West Branch. Both times he'd been disappointed.

This morning as he climbed the stairs, he noticed smoke in the sky to the north. He agonized over the fate of his neighbors and friends. He strained forward with his hands on the wall; then, far upriver he noticed motion on the water.

Drifting around the bend, he saw debris floating on the current. As it drew nearer, he noticed people riding on top of it. Then, he saw both shores teemed with men and livestock. The sight was almost beyond belief, but this was what he'd been waiting for. They were safe.

A single tear trickled onto his uniform coat. "Thank you, Lord," he said out loud. He wiped his cheek and went to meet the oncoming crowd.

At the forks of the river, some of the women landed at Northumberland to ferry the men across to the fort. Others headed straight for the fort itself. Hunter waited on the shore and helped the weary women from the boats. He ordered the garrison to cross over to Blue Hill to retrieve Antes' column.

The fort was soon crowded. The space between the inner and outer walls was filled with exhausted refugees who threw themselves on the ground and went to sleep amongst their animals. The nearing smoke proved the enemy followed close on their heels.

Hepburn's and Antes' arrival in the fort signaled that both columns completed the journey. They made a full report to Hunter.

" . . . and that's about it, Sam," Hepburn concluded. "I don't think many of 'em are goin' to stay. They're scared and they want to be as far away as possible."

"I understand that, Bill," said Hunter, "but if we don't hold the fort, we maybe lose the whole state. If we lose the state, we probably lose the war. I'm not leavin' here. I don't care if I'm the only one in the whole damned place."

"I didn't say *I* was leavin'," said Hepburn. "Me an' my company'll be here.

"You can count on me too, Colonel," said Antes.

"Thank you. I know I can count on you both," said Hunter. "I didn't mean to imply otherwise. And, I appreciate all you've done to bring the settlers to safety."

"Let me go start talkin' to some folks, Sam," said Hepburn. "I'll see if I can't get 'em to stay."

"I'll do the same, Colonel," said Antes.

"Thank you both. I appreciate any influence you have with your people."

Hunter spent the rest of the morning speaking to everyone he saw about staying and defending the valley. Hepburn, Antes, Covenhoven and James Brady did the same. But, by midafternoon, it was apparent most of the settlers would continue downriver.

They began leaving, singly at first and then in small groups. Eventually, throngs of people were back in the river and putting Fort Augusta behind them. There was no reasoning with desperate and panicked people.

By nightfall, it seemed as if none of the day's events ever occurred. The only difference was Northumberland and Sunbury were now also evacuated. A few hardy souls from those towns and a few settlers from the West Branch stayed with Hepburn's and Antes' militia to occupy the fort.

Ironically, Hunter had pleaded with Mary Brady and Jane Boone to leave, but both were adamant about staying.

"Mrs. Hunter has gone downriver to visit with her brother, ladies. Why don't you join her?" entreated Colonel Hunter.

"Someone'll have to do the cookin' here, won't they?" answered Mary, as Jane nodded emphatically behind her.

There was no question. The ladies were staying and that was that.

"You ladies do yourselves and your families honor," said Hunter, and he let the matter rest.

That evening, Hunter retired to his office. He settled at his desk and rested his head in his hands. He let out a deep breath, raised his head and reached for his pen and paper. His words to the Council came flooding out in a stream of perfect mental clarity and he poured his soul onto the page.

Fort Augusta, 9 July, 1778
Gentlemen,

I am sorry to inform you of the present distressed situation of this county. I suppose before this comes to hand, you will be informed of the carnage which happened at Wyoming. The inhabitants of the West Branch of the Susquehannah have suffered almost as much. Both branches are evacuated.

From all appearances, the towns of Northumberland & Sunbury are the frontiers, where a few virtuous inhabitants and fugitives seem determined to stand, though doubtful whether tomorrow's sun will rise on them freemen, captives, or in eternity. They say they will remain as long as they can without incurring the censure of suicide. Nothing but a firm reliance on divine providence and the timely assistance of the government induces the few to stand that remain.

History affords no instance of more heathenish cruelty or savage barbarity than has been exhibited in this county. The carnage at Wyoming, the devastations and murders upon the West Branch of the Susquehannah, on Bald Eagle creek, and throughout the whole county to within a few miles of these towns, I suppose must before now have reached your ears. If not, you may figure men, women, and children, butchered and scalped, many of them after being promised quarter; and some scalped alive, of which we have miserable instances amongst us.

People have been driven in crowds from their farms and habitations, many of whom have not money enough to purchase one day's provisions for their families. This has obliged many of them to plunder and lay waste to the farms as they pass along. If not speedily remedied by a reinforcement of men from below, these calamities must inevitably ruin the frontier and encumber the interior counties with such numbers of indigent fugitives, as will like locusts devour all before them.

Gentlemen, you must all know that this county cannot be strong in men after the numbers it has furnished to serve the United States. Applications to us for men were always complied with to the utmost of our abilities, and with the greatest alacrity.

Should our supplications now be rejected, I think the survivors of us, if any, may safely say that virtue is not rewarded. You may believe me, no time should be lost, or all this county is lost, and the fate of other counties hangs on as slender a thread as this did.

> *I am yr Excellency's*
> *Most humble servt,*
> *Sam'l Hunter, Lieut.*

Hunter placed his pen back in the inkwell and stared at the letter he'd just composed. This must make his point. The council couldn't ignore the needs of so many brave patriots. He read the letter and reread it.

Then, the floorboards creaked behind him, and he turned to see who was there.

"Sam, have you moved from that chair since we left?"

"Yeah, seems to me you grew fast."

"John Brady and Hawkins Boone," Hunter cried in overjoyed disbelief. "What happened, did you desert?" he joked.

"No," said Boone jovially. "Gen'ral Warshington just figured he better send somebody back here to win this war."

"Well, it's about damn time," said Hunter.

"We heard about what happened, Sam," said Brady. "We was on our way back and got the news of Wyoming. Word is, they found a wounded Tory left behind who told 'em the British is now payin' *ten* pounds per scalp. Folks there figure they lost at least two hundred an' twenty-five men, women, and children. Comin' in tonight we heard all about the runaway. Is it true the *whole* valley is lost?"

"Yes, I'm afraid it is. It's been pretty bad for us here, boys," said Hunter. "I hated giving that evacuation order but, knowing there was probably a whole army headed toward us, I didn't want to lose any more lives. With our limited resources, there was just no way to defend against a major attack."

"You done what any of us would have, Sam," said Boone.

Hunter suddenly remembered, "Oh, your families are safe. In fact, your wives are both here. John, so is James and the other kids."

"We know," said Brady. "We saw 'em comin' in. We appreciate your considerin' the folks around here so much, Sam."

"I just wish there was something that could have been done without losing the valley," said Hunter.

"Well, we'll just have to go an' get it back, then," said Brady. "Ain't that right, Hawk?"

"I sure didn't come back here to sit on *my* behind," answered Boone, with a sideways glance toward Hunter.

"You'd be surprised how trying this chair can be," said Hunter, smiling. "But I agree with you, John. Let's go take back the valley."

"Sounds good to me," said Boone.

CHAPTER 6

July-August 1778

ALONG THE JUNIATA RIVER

Samuel Brady watched the messenger thunder past his company to the head of the regiment and stop to speak with Colonel Brodhead. The regiment halted. Moments later, the messenger wheeled and galloped back to the east.

"Close up. Close up," called Brodhead.

He waited for the regiment to gather before he spoke.

"Men of the 8th," he began. "I've just received news of the collapse of the West Branch Valley. Fort Augusta held but is in danger.

"Fort Pitt can wait. We're going back down the Juniata and north up the Susquehanna to reinforce them. I know some of you are from the West Branch. We'll get there as soon as we can. Get ready for some hard marching."

"Lieutenant Brady, get the company movin'," yelled Samuel's captain.

"Yessir," answered Samuel. "Alright, you heard the captain," he shouted. "About face. Forward. March."

Samuel was stunned. His thoughts fixed on his family. "Are they alright?. . . Are they *alive?*"

The further up the Susquehanna they marched, the more grim his mood became. They passed through a strange and eerie landscape. The enemy hadn't reached below Sunbury, but the country was deserted, nonetheless.

Samuel stared at the homes plundered by fleeing and starving refugees. They stood with front doors swinging in the breeze. The debris of the chaotic flight littered the prim Dutch farms that now held none of their charm. The evidence of a catastrophe became more apparent with every mile, and Samuel grew more anxious.

★　★　★　★　★

FORT AUGUSTA

"Hell, we can hold 'em," said Boone, as he manned the wall with John and James Brady. "Them folks that floated off down the river last week just give us more fightin' room is all."

"Who're ya tryin' t' convince?" asked Brady.

"Why, you fellas," he answered. "I could hear you thinkin'."

"I do wonder why they haven't attacked yet," said James. "There really ain't many of us here."

"Yeah, but they don't necessarily know that," said Brady.

"How goes it, gentlemen?" called a voice ascending the stairs.

"Just fine, Col'nel," said Boone. "In fact, we was just sayin' we think we got 'em too scared t' attack."

"With your bluster, my friend," said Hunter, "I don't doubt it."

The men laughed.

"That reminds me," said James, "You still owe me a huntin' trip, Hawk."

"You mean the one where we was goin' to show up my cousin Dan'l?"

"That's the one."

"Well, that oughtn't a' be too hard," said Boone. "I think we could do that in a good mornin's hunt."

"Well, not too hard for *you*, Hawk," said the older Brady. "You did say you taught *him* to shoot, right?"

"That's just exac'ly right," said Boone.

"Then how come *he's* the famous one?" asked Brady.

This was an invitation he couldn't resist. Boone puffed out his chest and launched into one of his dissertations.

"Hell, that's easy," said Boone. "Unlike the *rest* a' the fam'ly, Cousin Dan'l is quite a talker. With as many bears as he says he kill't, I'm surprised there's any left down there."

"Didn't you tell me *you* kill't twenty-three when you was huntin' for the army one day?" asked Brady, smiling.

"Damn right," answered Boone.

"An' was that true?"

Boone rubbed his chin and pondered for a moment. "Well . . . alright; you got me. I *did* leave out the thirty deer."

Everyone laughed again as Boone continued. "Now Dan'l done great things, no doubt about it. After all, he *is* a Boone. But he don't mind tellin' a tale now an' then, an' he don't mind takin' some credit. Hell, he'd prob'ly tell you he taught *me* to shoot.

"An' that's another thing . . . that rifle a' his. Ever notice how folks down there slapped their name on our long rifles? That's 'cause a Dan'l. Now me, I go about my business, do what needs to be done, and don't say too much about it."

"Yes, I've observed," Hunter interjected, "you've always been the soul of humbleness."

Everyone laughed, including Boone himself, when James said, "Fellas, listen."

Instinctively, they looked upriver.

"What is it?" asked Hunter.

"I thought I heard drums," said James.

"Drums?" replied Hunter, puzzled.

"Wait, I hear it too," said Boone.

They did hear the distinct sound of drums, but it was coming from behind them. Turning and looking downriver, they also heard the unmistakable sounds of a fife, far off in the distance. Then Boone pointed and said, "There. I see 'em. It's a regiment comin'."

Looking closely, the regimental colors were visible through the haze.

"It's the 8th," said James. "It's Samuel's outfit."

Boone clasped a hand on Brady's shoulder as they watched the troops approach.

"Well done, men," said Hunter. "We held. Now, we can begin retaking the valley."

As the regiment neared, Hunter ordered a nearby gun-crew to fire a salute. In response, the regimental fifes and drums broke into a rousing version of *Yankee Doodle.*

When Brodhead's men filled the parade ground, John, Mary, James and the children ran to greet Samuel. The Bradys were as close now to being a complete family as they'd been since the beginning of the war.

They enjoyed a warm reunion at supper that evening with the Boones. After the meal, Boone, John and Samuel Brady were ordered to a conference with Hunter and Brodhead.

The evening's high humidity made Hunter's little office seem crowded. The five men worked their way into the room and tried to make themselves comfortable. Hunter opened the one small window by his desk, but there was little relief from the still air outside.

Hunter turned to his bookshelf and browsed through some of the rolled documents. Selecting one, he turned and addressed the assembled party.

"First things first, gentlemen. I'd like to thank Colonel Brodhead for so swiftly coming to our relief. I believe, Colonel, you have ensured our county will not completely disintegrate."

"Glad to be of service," said Brodhead. "As, I'm sure, is Lieutenant Brady."

John Brady suppressed a smile.

"Now," said Hunter, unrolling a map of the county, "when I saw you approaching, my first thought was that we could fully man the fort and guarantee against an overwhelming attack. But on reflection, I think perhaps your regiment should advance up the valley and project our area of influence northward. That may cause the enemy to move off entirely. What are your thoughts, Colonel?"

"I agree. We can do little good here in the fort when the enemy hasn't ventured to attack you, even in your weakened state. However, when we advance, I believe we should do so across a wide front. We could screen the fort and push the enemy back at the same time."

"That makes a lot a' sense," said Brady.

"Yeah," said Boone, pointing to the map. "If you put some men here at Jenkins' farm, by the mouth of Briar Creek on the North Branch, and the rest here at Wallis' on the West Branch, you could run a line of scouts b'tween 'em and do exac'ly what you said."

"Maybe then we could coax some a' the settlers to come back," said Brady.

"Are we all in agreement then, gentlemen?" asked Hunter.

Everyone agreed.

Brady said, "Well, if you fellas are through, I believe the lieutenant and I'll go back to our fam'ly, with your permission, a' course, Colonel Brodhead."

"Absolutely. Enjoy yourself, Lieutenant. We'll march in the morning."

"Yessir," said Samuel.

"Think I'll stay if it's alright, Sam," said Boone.

"By all means; I'd like for you to," answered Hunter.

John and Samuel returned to James, Mary and the kids. They reminisced until late into the night. Finally, Samuel said, "Well, I'm gettin' tired. I got a long day ahead a' me tomorrow so I'm gonna git to bed."

Mary looked at Samuel and James standing with their father and was both proud and scared. She felt a surge of love and a pang of loneliness. She didn't quite understand her feeling but knew she didn't want the evening to end.

Suddenly, she jumped from her seat and rushed to embrace them. Then, she looked at them through welling eyes and left the room.

The next morning, Brodhead deployed a major with eighty

men to Jenkins' farm, then led one hundred and twenty more to Wallis'.

As Samuel traveled the familiar road to Muncy, he saw the charred ruins that littered the path of the enemy's advance. Reaching the burned remains of Wallis' estate, Brodhead sent Samuel with some scouts on to Antes Fort. Not one building was left standing.

Some fields, though, had escaped the torch and remained full of ripening wheat.

"Well," said Samuel, as he returned to Wallis' and made his report to Brodhead, "at least if any settlers do come back, they'll be able t' face the winter."

Since Samuel knew the country so well, Brodhead used him as his main scout and messenger. He sent him to report back to Hunter.

"Sir," said Samuel on his return, "I've made Colonel Hunter aware the line of scouts between here and Jenkins' is established."

"Good," said Brodhead. "Any message in return?"

"Yessir," answered Samuel. "Col'nel Hunter reports the Supreme Executive Council ordered four hundred militia from Lancaster County and a hundred an' fifty from Berks to march for Fort Augusta. Congress also ordered Colonel Hartley's regiment of regulars from Philadelphia to Sunbury. Colonel Hunter expects their arrival any day and is plannin' to send messengers to the surroundin' counties that the valley is secure and the settlers can come back."

"Thank you, Lieutenant," said Brodhead. "It looks like when the reinforcements arrive, we can resume our march to Fort Pitt."

★ ★ ★ ★ ★

PHILADELPHIA

Hartley answered the knock at the door. He opened it to reveal a well-dressed businessman.

"Colonel Hartley?" said Wallis.

"Yes?"

"It's a pleasure to meet you, sir. I'm Samuel Wallis. I own land on the West Branch, and I understand your regiment has just been deployed there. I wanted to introduce myself before you left Philadelphia."

"It's a pleasure to meet you as well," said Hartley. "I'm aware of your contributions to the cause here with the army, and I've heard you were one of the leading citizens from the West Branch."

"Why, thank you. Yes, I was a captain in our local militia and a member of the state assembly. I try to do my part."

"It certainly seems so," complimented Hartley.

"Knowing your regiment is on its way to reclaim our valley, I feel it's safe to return. I wanted to offer my hospitality to you whenever it may be of service."

"Thank you, Mr. Wallis. That's very kind."

"I will, of course, be rebuilding my home and out-buildings since I understand they've all been destroyed. And, that brings me to another offer I'd like to make."

"And what is that?" asked Hartley.

"While we've got a formidable stronghold in Fort Augusta, the remaining defensive positions that dot the countryside are but simple stockaded homes. I feel our greatest need to securing a true and lasting defense is to have a proper fort built on the upper West Branch. To make that a reality, I would be willing to allow the use of my land for the purpose."

Even as he spoke, Wallis could barely suppress a smirk. "Should he accept," he congratulated himself, "there would be a fort within rifle shot of my home to protect my property. My devotion to the rebel cause will be even further solidified because of my *selfless* offer, and, in politics as in business, there is no better position than to have one's enemy as close as possible. Then, you may know his intentions . . . and use them against him."

"That's most generous, Mr. Wallis," said Hartley. "Do you feel such a fort would have made a difference in the recent attack?" "I think there's little doubt that it would have," said Wallis. "Had the settlers had such a strong place of refuge, the enemy wouldn't have dared to attack it. It would have saved the entire valley below the Loyalsock."

"Very interesting thought," said Hartley. "I will certainly consider its merits. Let's discuss this further when we both arrive on the West Branch. We march tomorrow."

"We absolutely should," agreed Wallis. "And remember, Colonel, you're always welcome at my home."

"I'm most appreciative," said Hartley. "Thank you for stopping by."

★　★　★　★　★

FORT AUGUSTA

"Colonel Hartley, am I glad to see *you*," said Hunter as he welcomed Hartley into his office.

"I'm pleased to meet you, Colonel Hunter."

"Call me Sam," answered Hunter as they shook hands.

"Then, please, call me Tom."

"Well, Tom, you're the ranking officer here now. Being that the other reinforcements are milita under General De Haas, he and all of the troops in the vicinity will report to you."

"Very well," said Hartley. "I've been studying the situation as best I could from a distance, and I've got some ideas I'd like to discuss with you."

"You mean building a fort at Wallis'? I'm all for it," said Hunter.

"Why how in the world . . . ?"

"Mr. Wallis just left here this morning, on his way up the West Branch. He told me you were planning to build the fort."

"Oh, is that right?" Hartley chuckled. "I guess he really was anxious to have that fort built. Yes, I do believe it would be a great step in shoring up the valley. What other defenses have we got?"

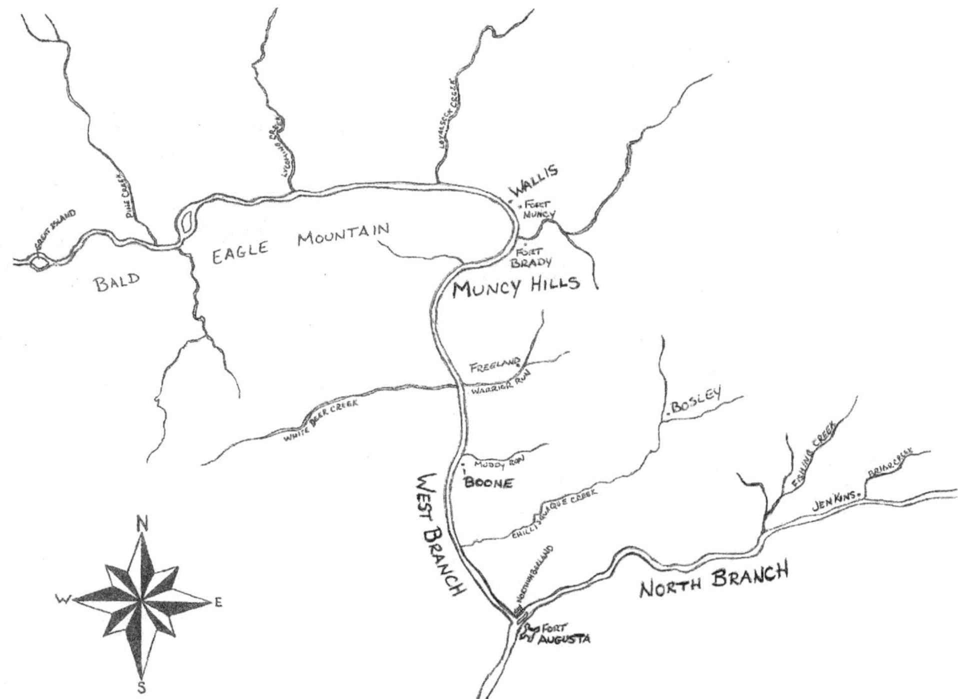

"Well, Colonel Brodhead was the first to arrive after the runaway. He deployed half of his regiment at Jenkins', on the North Branch," said Hunter pointing at the map, "and the other half at Wallis'. He's keeping scouts on the trail between them to patrol the countryside."

"Impressive strategy," said Hartley. "I think we'd do well to continue it. But, that's a lot of country to patrol. Why don't we build another fort midway between the two . . . say, here at the forks of this creek, and garrison all three?"

"That's the Chillisquaque," said Hunter. "There's a fella named Bosley who built a mill there. I haven't heard if it survived the recent attack or not."

"Little matter," said Hartley. "Doubtless he'll be happy to have a strong defensive presence on his property."

"I'm sure he would."

"Excellent," said Hartley. "As for the fort on the West Branch, I'll order Captain Walker's company, of my regiment, to march for Wallis' in the morning. They can relieve Colonel Brodhead and begin construction of the fort."

★ ★ ★ ★ ★

WALLIS'

When Samuel Wallis arrived at his estate, he was pleasantly surprised to find his indentured servants and slaves busily repairing his home.

"The frame and walls were still alright," said the foreman. "It was relatively easy to bring back under roof. Now, we'll just need to finish and refurnish the interior."

Captain Walker reached Wallis' the next day and began building the fort exactly where Wallis suggested: a low knoll overlooking the main road, about two hundred yards from Wallis' home.

A few days after that, Hartley arrived.

"Excellent work, Captain," said Hartley. "You've already got the rough outline of the fort taking shape."

"Yessir," said Walker. "When the earthworks are completed, we'll raise the stockade and then build the barracks and other buildings inside that."

"Very well," approved Hartly. "This will do a lot for the morale of the valley. I understand the locals are already referring to it as Fort Muncy."

"I'm happy to hear it, sir."

"Yes, well, carry on," said Hartly. "I'll return to Fort Augusta and leave the rest here to you."

"Thank you, sir."

★ ★ ★ ★ ★

FORT MUNCY

"I sure am grateful for the loan, John," said Peter Smith, who just came back upriver. "I know it's a lot a' money, but ev'rything I owned was in that wagon an' I need that much t' get back on my feet."

"Think nothin' of it, Pete," said Brady, not even able to imagine how horrible it would be to lose his wife and children and become financially ruined at the same time. "We'll get by until ya can pay it back."

"I'm hopin' t' get a start on it right away. I got grain just waitin' t' be harvested up at my place. I'm plannin' on roundin' up a harvestin' crew and askin' Walker for a guard t' go with us. Then once I get my place rebuilt and bring my son an' daughter up from Northumberland, I think I can start repayin' you."

Brady thought of the little Smith children who survived the ambush, and his heart ached for them. "I told you, pay when you can."

"Thank you. You're a good friend, John."

"Did I hear someone mention a harvestin' crew?" asked James Brady, walking up behind them. "Captain Walker's been runnin' 'em like scoutin' parties. We bring in the grain *and* patrol the trails. It's pretty smart."

"Are you volunteerin'?" asked Smith.

"I been on enough of 'em. No reason not to go help a friend," he said. "C'mon, I'll help ya round up the crew and we'll go talk to Captain Walker about the guard."

The next morning, James and Smith left Wallis' with thirteen armed harvesters. Walker's Sergeant McNett led the guard of four regulars and three militiamen. A solid march had them on the Loyalsock by midmorning.

"Hiram, take the militiamen and guard the next field," ordered McNett. "I'll watch this one with our men."

"Yessir," acknowledged Corporal Johns.

Soon, the men were hard at work, spread across both of Smith's fields. As James leaned with his scythe to slice the wheat off at the ground, he periodically wiped the sweat from his forehead. The work was back-breaking in the hot August sun.

In the late afternoon, Smith called, "That's enough. Let's finish the rest off in the mornin'."

Their work completed for the day, the men settled in by the ruins of Smith's home to have supper and turn in.

The next morning as James awoke, Smith asked, "How'd ya sleep?"

"Never better," said James, stretching. "Nothin' like a hard day's work and a cool night's air for a sound sleep."

"Ain't that the truth?" agreed Smith. "Well, we made good progress yesterday. A good mornin's work an' we oughta be done."

After a quick breakfast, the men shouldered their rifles and scythes and headed back into the fields. James followed Corporal Johns back toward the spot where he'd left off the day before.

"Don't wander into a tree," said Johns, as the men walked along the edge of the field. "I never seen a fog like this."

"Yeah, it's a heavy one," agreed James. "I think I just saw a catfish swim over my shoulder."

When the others stopped and leaned their rifles against a tree, Smith noticed James kept walking.

"James, you gonna carry your rifle with you while you work?" asked Smith.

"It won't do me much good half way across the field," he answered.

When the men had been at work for about an hour, Johns thought he heard a twig snap. He looked off into the mist but couldn't see anything. He ventured a few steps forward and peered through the thinning fog.

"Indians," he yelled, running back through the field.

Unable to reach their guns, the others ran for cover behind the militiamen near Smith's home.

"Come on, James, let's go," hollered Smith, as he ran.

But, James ran for his rifle. As he sprinted to within a few yards of where he'd placed it in the field, three Indians jumped from the underbrush in front of him. One leveled a gun.

James lived the next moments in amazing detail. He saw the warrior's finger tighten on the trigger. He saw the pan flash in a jagged yellow flame and the explosion of smoke roll from the muzzle pointed directly at him. Oddly, while he took in so much visual information, he didn't hear any sound.

Then, he felt a searing pain in his side. His legs, already in motion, carried him away from the Indians. But, within twenty yards, his body wouldn't allow him to continue. He collapsed in the field with the Indians nearly on him.

Johns stopped and raised his musket, but a shot from across the field struck him in the chest. Another shot from the Indians hit one of the distant militiamen. Both he and Johns died where they fell.

The three warriors fell upon James. One stabbed him with a spear. Another pulled his tomahawk and swung it at James' forehead. It chipped a small section of bone toward the top of his head, but it was a glancing blow.

The attacker didn't take time for another. He pulled his scalping knife.

The men in the next field followed McNett and their guards toward the attack and got there in time to see James being scalped.

McNett's men fired on the Indians, who retreated, leaving Johns' and the militiaman's scalps intact. As they disappeared into the woods, James' bright red hair bobbed mockingly from the warrior's belt.

The settlers were stunned when James stirred, stood and walked back toward Smith's home. Blood-drenched and swaying, he stumbled into the group. Peter Smith was distraught. Others were simply amazed he'd lived.

Jerome Van Ness caught him by the arm. "Come with me, James," he said. "I'll tend you."

James incoherently went with Van Ness, who led him to the creek. Seeing the water, James threw himself down and drank deeply. Van Ness searched among the trees until he found a patch of lush moss. He stooped and gathered as many large pieces as he could.

"Come, James. Let me fix you up," he said, gently pulling at his shirttail.

James raised himself to his knees and looked out at the current as Van Ness tenderly placed the moss on the gaping wound where James' scalp had been. He cut James' shirt and used it to bind the moss in place. The spear wound was to his upper chest, near the shoulder. Once the bleeding was stopped, it didn't seem to be of immediate concern.

The gunshot had entered his lower right side and traveled through the fleshy area at his waist, exiting a few inches away. This wound also didn't seem to be life-threatening. Van Ness wrapped the remaining bandage around James' waist, then helped him to his feet and supported him as they walked back to the group.

"Get ready ev'rybody. We're goin' after 'em," said McNett.

"Don't be too hasty, sergeant," said one of the militiamen. "That's just what they want you to do."

"They killed two of our men," countered McNett. "I can't let that stand."

"There ain't enough of us t' fight a whole raidin' party," said the other militiaman. "This was prob'ly just scouts that caught us by surprise. They'll want t' lead us back to the main group."

"So you just want t' let 'em go?" said one of the regulars.

"No. I wanna kill the bastards. But, I know we have a lot better chance a' gettin' 'em if we go back t' the fort an' organize a full response from there."

"Might be you have a point," said McNett.

"I'll stay here with James until ya come back," said Van Ness.

"Thank you," said McNett. "Alright, let's get goin'."

Van Ness and James watched the men march off to Wallis'.

"Well, I might as well tend t' the dead," said Van Ness. "Can't just leave 'em there. You sit here, James, an' I'll be back after bit."

Van Ness ventured into the field and retrieved the rifles the Indians left behind in the confusion.

He carried them back and said, "Here's your rifle, James. They didn't get it."

James took it and held it close.

Then, Van Ness went back to the bodies of Johns and the militiaman and dragged them to the edge of the field, where he started to dig.

As the hours drifted by, James' thoughts grew more fragmented and confused, and his head ached even worse. Slowly, he began to drift to sleep.

That afternoon, Walker led the party back from the fort. As they approached, they startled James who jumped up and cocked his rifle.

"No, James," cried Van Ness. "It's our men come to get us."

James stood, dazed, with his rifle pointed at them. Then, he relaxed and slumped back to the ground where he'd been sitting.

"Mr. Van Ness, I thank you for your bravery in staying here with Mr. Brady," said Walker.

"It was nothin'," said Van Ness. "I was able t' gather up the rifles they left behind and I went ahead and started buryin' the dead."

Walker turned to his men. "First squad; finish the burials Mr. Van Ness has begun. Second squad; build a stretcher so we can carry Mr. Brady back to the fort. It's too late in the day to mount a successful pursuit."

"Yessir," they answered.

"I'll build the stretcher," said one of the militiamen with Walker. It was Robert Covenhoven. "I can make him a halfway tolerable one."

"Very well, Mr. Covenhoven; please do so," replied Walker.

"I've been thinkin'," said Van Ness, "we should get word to the folks up Muncy Crick. Could be the raidin' party is headed that way."

"It's been taken care of," said Walker. "When Sergeant McNett and his men arrived with news of the attack, I determined to come back here. I asked Captain Brady to organize the defense. As we were leaving, he called for a volunteer to warn those on Muncy Creek. The men standing nearby just glanced at one another. Then, a voice finally broke the long silence. It was Rachel Silverthorn. She was determined to warn her neighbors and no one objected. Captain Brady insisted she take his horse, and, in a moment, she was off. It was an incredibly brave display. I'll never forget it."

When Covenhoven finished crafting the stretcher, he, Walker and Van Ness tried to make James as comfortable as possible. Two soldiers grabbed one end of the stretcher and Covenhoven and Van Ness lifted the other. They carried it the whole way back to the fort.

James was in agony but bore up bravely. He was constantly thirsty and drained the canteens of many of the soldiers who marched beside him.

Within sight of the fort, a man came running out to meet them. It was John Brady, who had been watching for their return.

Brady took Van Ness's place and carried James the last short distance to the fort. They found a cool, shady spot and set him down.

Brady was shaken to see just how badly hurt his son was. Earlier that day, Smith had described James' wounds, but Brady wasn't prepared to see this. A deep crimson stain oozed from his side and another from his shoulder. Trails of dried blood streaked his face from beneath the moss on his head. Brady bit his lip to fight back the angst and rage he felt building inside him. He closed his eyes.

James looked up, puzzled, and said, "Father?"

Opening his eyes, Brady quickly swallowed his emotion.

"Yes, son. It's me."

"Father . . . my head hurts."

"I know, son. I know. You try an' rest now."

"Alright," he said and shut his eyes.

"John," said a voice from behind him.

Brady turned. He stood and walked over to Covenhoven, who was a few yards away.

In hushed tones, Covenhoven said, "I know I don't need to tell you, this don't look good."

"I know."

"Van Ness did good work in savin' his life, but he's lost a *lot* a' blood, an' now he's gettin' feverish."

"Yeah."

"It might not be for me to suggest, but isn't Mary down in Sunbury?"

Brady realized what Covenhoven was driving at. Of course, he should try to reunite the boy with his mother while he lived.

"Yeah . . . maybe she could even bring 'em back around," said Brady.

"I wouldn't be surprised," Covenhoven answered.

"I'll go get a canoe," said Brady.

"John," said Covenhoven, "why don't you stay here with James? I'll tend to everything we'll need."

"You're comin' with me?"

"'Course I am," he said, turning.

"Bob," Brady called after him. Covenhoven looked back.

"Thanks."

It had already been a long, fatiguing day when Brady and Covenhoven gently lifted James' stretcher and placed it in the canoe. They pushed off into the gathering dusk with almost thirty miles of river between them and Sunbury. The humidity had dissipated, and they paddled into the darkness beneath a blanket of stars. Now and again a meteor blazed the path in front of them.

Neither man said much on the journey. For a long while the only sound was the hypnotic splosh . . . splosh . . . of the paddles in the water and the chorus of tree frogs and crickets that accompanied it.

"Indians," hollered James, suddenly.

Both men started and looked around before realizing James was staring straight up into the sky.

"Sshh, James. It's alright," said Brady.

"They're comin'."

"Nobody's comin', James. You're alright now."

It was no use reasoning with him. James was delirious. Covenhoven, in the front of the canoe, didn't say anything. He kept paddling as Brady occasionally dipped his hand into the cool Susquehanna and trickled it over his son's face and neck.

This continued for hours. James went through periods of quiet, when the men thought he'd fallen asleep. Then he suddenly screamed incoherently and fought the enemies confronting him in his fevered mind. Brady spoke to James, and it seemed to calm him, but the episodes continued.

After what seemed like an eternity on the river, the men came within sight of Fort Augusta. It was very late at night. They planned to take James into the fort and place him in the barracks, where he could rest quietly.

As they neared the shore, Covenhoven could just make out someone standing in the darkness. It was a very pregnant woman. As they beached the canoe, he spoke to her. "Mam, are you alright?"

"I'm alright. Is everything alright in Muncy?"

"Mary?" Brady asked, incredulously. "What are you doin' out here all alone?"

"I couldn't sleep. I knew somethin' was wrong. What is it, John?" Her voice was wavering.

"It's James, Mary. We brought him to you."

"Is he dead?"

"No. But he's hurt pretty bad."

"Oh, no," she gasped, and started to cry as she rushed down the bank toward them.

The men lifted James out of the canoe and carried him into the abandoned home where Mary had been staying with the kids. She clutched his hand the whole way. Inside, they lit a lamp and Mary saw the full extent of his injuries. She moaned and sobbed piteously as she pressed James' hand to her cheek. Covenhoven excused himself as Brady held Mary from behind and began to cry himself.

After the initial shock had passed, Brady told Mary what happened. They tried to comfort James, who was still delirious. His fever worsened and his wounds were becoming infected. They stayed with him through the night.

James finally fell into a belabored sleep just before dawn. Physically and emotionally exhausted, John and Mary slept, too. When they awoke, Covenhoven was there, tending to James.

"Mornin'," he said, when he noticed they'd awoken.

"Mornin', Bob," said Brady. "How's he doin'?"

"'Bout the same, I'd say. The Hunters and Mrs. Boone have been in to help, too. Why don't you folks go an' get somethin' t' eat? I'll watch over James."

"No, thanks," answered Mary. "We're fine here."

"Well then," said Covenhoven, "I'll have 'em bring you somethin'. You gotta eat, Mary."

James hallucinated and slept for the next four days while the Bradys kept vigil at his bedside. The Brady children, the Hunters and Jane Boone each came and went. They cared for James and the Bradys throughout the ordeal. On the fourth night, James slept soundly. He awoke the next morning entirely lucid. He saw his mother and smiled as he reached out for her hand.

"Hello, Mother," he said.

"Hello, darlin'."

"How long have I been sleepin'?"

"A few days. Your father brought you down here to me."

James looked over to his father and smiled.

"They surprised us. I thought I could get to my rifle, but they caught me."

James recounted the whole fateful event to his parents. When he was through, he said, "I don't remember much after bein' carried down the road by the soldiers. I've been havin' the strangest dreams, though. I was runnin' and runnin', and Indians was chasin' me through the night. There were all these stars and I heard the sounds of water and the night animals real loud."

"Sshh honey, now. You're alright," said Mary. "You'll be fine, now."

She gazed at his gentle face looking back at her from beneath the blood-encrusted scalp, which had grown attached to the dried and crumbling moss. She smiled as she looked lovingly into his deep blue eyes. The stench of infection permeated the air.

"Mother, is it gettin' foggy in here?" asked James. "You're gettin' farther away."

"I'm right here, darlin'," said Mary, clutching his hand.

Brady placed his hand on Mary's shoulder, and both parents had tears in their eyes.

"Mother . . . I can see . . ."

His voice trailed away as his eyes darted back and forth and then . . . stopped. The Bradys stood motionless, looking at their son. Dumbfounded at the fragility of life and the sudden finality of death, it was almost incomprehensible to them that James was gone.

Being a soldier, Brady had seen death many times before. He thought he understood. But, this was a new and unreal feeling, a feeling of emptiness and disbelief.

Almost involuntarily, the Bradys stood and left the house. Emotionally drained, they walked into the fort and told their friends and children that James had died.

That evening, there was a simple, dignified ceremony for him. Hunter spoke of the sacrifice James made for the cause of freedom and for the friends and neighbors whose lives he valued above his own. Hartley arranged an honor guard to fire a salute. The report echoed up the river and carried with it the news of the valley's loss.

The gilded clouds of sunset drifted over the river as James' body was lowered into eternity, just outside the walls of the fort.

CHAPTER 7

August-October 1778

SUNBURY

"Ahhhhh!" yelled Mary Brady, who went into labor just days after James' death.

She grasped the rope tied to the bedpost as she pushed.

"C'mon, darlin'," she coaxed through the pain. "Come an' greet the world."

"You're doin' fine, Mary," said Jane Boone. "You're doin' real good. You're gonna have a fine, healthy child."

"This one's a fighter," said Mary, grimacing. "Ahhhhh."

"I can see its head," said Jane. "Push . . . just a little more."

"AHHHHH!" yelled Mary again as she delivered the child.

"It's a girl, Mary. It's a girl."

"Call John," said Mary, as she received the baby in her arms.

"John!" yelled Jane. "Come inside."

Brady rushed into the room.

"Meet yer new daughter, John," said Mary. "She's feisty an' strong."

"Praise be," said Brady. "An' you're doin' alright?"

"I'm fine. I give birth to twelve children b'fore. One more ain't gonna do me no harm."

"Well, that's for sure," said Brady.

The couple fell silent and stared at the newborn.

"What'll we name her?" asked Mary.

"Well, I been thinkin'," he said. ". . . the world is so full of strife and oppression. The past two years have brought so much agony . . . but there's *such promise* ahead if we prevail."

He turned and looked at Mary.

"I couldn't wish her anything more precious than a long life of happiness an' freedom," said Brady. "That's what we're fightin' for. . . . That's what James died for.. . . Let's call her Liberty."

"I think that's perfect," said Mary. "Liberty Brady."

FORT AUGUSTA

Hartley scrutinized the map on Hunter's desk. He could almost see the forts rising out of the landscape at Muncy, Bosley and Jenkins.

He gathered his thoughts and sat down to make a report to the Supreme Executive Council:

Sunbury, 10 August, 1778
Gentlemen,

In my last to you, I mentioned the steps I had taken & the situation of these frontiers. Since then, I have ordered the militia to different posts. Every man of my own regt., who could possibly go, I have also sent upon command.

We have lent every aid to reap & get in the harvest. Much more will be saved than I could possibly have imagined.

Berks County has furnished its quota of militia. Lancaster County has fallen far short. Northumberland County, distracted & distressed with many of the inhabitants fled & not returned, could afford but few men to act in the general scale of militia. From all these causes, our exertions must fall short of the services wanted by an unhappy & intimidated frontier.

All the people of the West Branch above Wallis' have fled & evacuated their settlements. Those about Muncy and below are wavering and doubtful. So on the North Branch, all above Nescopeck Falls are gone.

I was resolved to hold posts at both these extremes and have an intermediate one on the head waters of the Chillisquaque. There had been a small work begun at Jenkins', about five miles from Nescopeck Falls, near Briar Creek. This I have garrisoned. I have troops at the forks of the Chillisquaque, but the left flank on the West Branch, which was most exposed & where the greatest present danger appeared, I visited.

Indians are appearing there daily. No women or children have ventured to return. The inhabitants strongly pressed that they should have troops amongst them, & that some fortress should be built to cover that part of the country & afford asylum to their families in case of necessity. None of the houses are properly situated for a stockade fort of any real use.

Genl. Dehas was with me & we found those settlements in danger. They were useful from their fertility of soil & the industry of the inhabitants, besides being the frontier. If these people give way, there would not long be an inhabitant above Sunbury or Northumberland. A valuable country would be depopulated & some thousand persons ruined. Added to this, if the settlements toward the Bald Eagle & Great Island were to return, there was a necessity for a secure post about mid-way.

Upon the whole, we agreed that a fort ought to be built near Saml. Wallis', about two miles from Muncy Creek. I therefore, directed one to be laid out, a rough plan of which I enclose you. My men there are at work with the militia & inhabitants. The public will have to pay but a small expense though thousands of pounds and many lives will be saved.

The savages have again appeared in some force. They have gained so much plunder & have met with so little opposition, I imagine they are induced to pay another visit to these frontiers.

I am happy to agree well with the militia. I hope they will do as much good as can be expected from them.

It will be necessary to have at least two iron six-pounder cannon for the work I have mentioned, and also ten or twelve swivels. I hope you will be pleased to send them as soon as possible. We will endeavor to get them up by water or some other means. The attacks upon the frontiers have really become serious.

We are subject to some inconveniences here, but shall do all the good we can. The harvest prevented me from sending a scouting party on the Indian paths last week. We hope to attempt it at the close of the present week. The bearer, Col. Antis, will be able to give you further information.

I am, with great respect,

Yr. Honors most obed. &

Mo. Hble servt,

THOs HARTLEY, Coll.,

Commandant.

P.S. Aug. 10th. By several fresh advices, we shall probably soon have some of the barbarians to attack the settlements.

Hartley also received a letter that day from Colonel Zebulon Butler. He read Butler's account of how he'd escaped the massacre at Wyoming and that he'd now returned with twenty regulars and forty militiamen. Butler said most of Wyoming's inhabitants fled to Connecticut, but he planned to re-establish the North Branch settlements.

"Thank God," thought Hartley. "That strengthens the flank."

Hartley replied to Butler and said troops were on the march

from Easton that he could add to his force. He told Butler he should hold his position. In case of trouble, though, he ordered Butler to retire down the North Branch to Fort Jenkins.

★ ★ ★ ★ ★

FORT AUGUSTA

"How can they be so short-sighted?" spluttered Hartley throwing Council's reply to his letter on the desk.

"This is the frontier, Tom," said Hunter. "They always think there are greater needs elsewhere."

"I can't believe they won't fund the building of Fort Muncy and I *don't* believe the fitting out of privateers has taken *every* available piece of artillery."

Hunter sympathized, but he wasn't surprised. He'd heard it all before. He sat quietly while Hartley weighed the situation.

"Well, there it is," he said. "We have a half-completed fort with no cannon to arm it, we have two small garrisons, manned by militia and fragments of my own regiment, and we have Colonel Butler at Wyoming with fewer than a hundred troops . . ."

Hartley trailed off as he stared down at the map that had become so familiar to him.

"Sam, you've got a map of the state here somewhere, haven't you?" he asked suddenly.

"Yeah, right here," said Hunter, retrieving it from the bookshelf and unrolling it.

"You remember Colonel Morgan is about to attack up the Cherry Valley in New York State, right?" asked Hartley, jabbing a finger at the map.

"Yes."

"And, Brodhead is about to strike north through Western Pennsylvania?"

"Yes. I can see that might put the Indians back on their heels but there's a lot of ground in between to think they wouldn't still attack us here."

"That's exactly right," said Hartley. "That's why we need to attack *them*."

"What?" said Hunter. "We barely have enough men to secure the valley. How can we mount a campaign?"

"Reason with me for a moment," said Hartley. "If we strike into Indian country at the same time the other forces make their attack, we'll become the center of a broad advancement. That will push the enemy back on all fronts and protect the valley far better than if we stay here and tried to defend it."

"Tom, that's brilliant," conceded Hunter.

"It's our only choice," said Hartley. "Besides, I think we can make it happen rather easily. Fort Muncy exists, with or without official funding. We can man it with a relatively small garrison and use the residual troops to mount the campaign."

"Why don't we send one of the four-pounders we have here up to Fort Muncy?" said Hunter. "At least they'd have one piece of artillery."

"I think we should," agreed Hartley. "Now, if you'll please arrange a party to transport the gun, I've got to plan the appropriate troop movements and send orders to Colonel Butler."

"Consider it done," said Hunter, as he rose and left the room.

Hartley fired off a series of orders as the plan formed in his mind. Then he wrote to Butler.

Sunbury, August 22, 1778
Sir,

> *My firm intention is to act offensively against the enemy adjoining these frontiers. I go to Muncy tomorrow and am collecting a clever body of men there.*
>
> *The attachment of my regiment in Northampton County is now ordered to Wyoming. I order Captain Bush*

of my regiment to join them. This will strengthen us with upwards of 100 good men.

My plan is this: that on the 31ˢᵗ of August, I march with all the force I can collect to Wyalusing, where we will arrive on the 2ⁿᵈ or 3ʳᵈ of September. To provide against any misfortune, you are to remain in garrison at Wyoming with between 80 and 100 of those men who are worst prepared for an expedition to the woods.

Captain Bush should take command of all the remainder of the forces at Wyoming – regulars and others – and march on the same 31ˢᵗ of August towards Wyalusing. He is to effect a junction with me on the 2ⁿᵈ or 3ʳᵈ of September – taking care to send on scouts to inform me of their approach and situation.

The troops that move from Wyoming must draw forty rounds of cartridges per man; carry four days' provisions on their backs, and twelve days' more of flour with them on packhorses. If a few beefs could be driven with them with convenience, it might be done; otherwise they must trust to Providence who, I make no doubt, favors us.

I should be happy of your company on this expedition but it is of the last consequence to support the post of Wyoming, where you are so well acquainted, and I must deprive myself of your assistance.

The expeditions from the north and the west into the Indian country will appear about the beginning of September and our movement may have a happy effect. I trust these frontiers will soon be cleared of the savages.

My orders are that you have everything in readiness for the proposed expedition by the 31ˢᵗ of August. The troops are not to march till they receive my further instructions. If anything should happen in your quarter which would make the proposed expedition improper, you are to send an express to Wallis', at Muncy, giving me information by the 30ᵗʰ of August.

These matters require the utmost secrecy. From your character, I dare say you will consider them accordingly.

I am your mos.

Obed. Servt.

THOs Hartley, Coll.,

Commandant.

★ ★ ★ ★ ★

FORT AUGUSTA

Delays in troops and supplies pushed back Hartley's timeline. As September arrived, he made his next report to the Council.

Sunbury, Sepr 1ˢᵗ, 1778

Gentlemen,

Since my last, I have been out with several detachments up the West Branch. Though we are not certain we killed a single Indian, it would have been in our power several times had we some horse. The barbarians have frequently appeared in open ground & do fairly outrun most white men.

I am clearly convinced of the utility of horse. For however sagacious the Indians are, they cannot always choose their own ground. The horsemen should be armed with a sword, two pistols & a short rifle.

The latter would intimidate the enemy, & the soldier might occasionally act on foot. I have written to the Board of War to send an officer & 12 horsemen here. I hope they will comply.

Captain Walker has been so industrious at Muncy as to have completed all the earthworks, & nearly all the stockade. I never saw as much work done by so few men in so short a time.

We have a four-pounder mounted there. If we had four swivels to place in the bastions the place would be very secure with a small garrison. I most earnestly wish that you would send up twelve swivels for the county. In case the militia withdraws, they will be essential. Since this work has been begun, no person has been killed within our line of posts.

I am inducing the people to put in some fall crops. Several are returning to their habitations, but with great diffidence.

Yesterday morning three German militia, without arms and without permission, went out of Fort Muncy to dig some potatoes. Though within sight of the garrison, they were immediately attacked by one white man and some Indians. The enemy discharged all their pieces at once. One militia man fell and was scalped, one ran off, and the other was seized. He had a tussle with a stout Indian but was rescued by the troops.

Several Indians and Tories have appeared about Wyoming. One family has been killed 15 miles on this side of it, & two near the garrison.

No medicine has yet arrived. The militia are very sickly.

The bearer Captain Brady can inform you of any other matters from this county.

I have the Honor to subscribe myself

With the utmost Respect,

Your most obedt

Humble servt,

THOS. Hartley,

Coll. Commandant.

P.S. As we are just now on the recovery here, I dare say the state will endeavor to replace some of the militia whose times are out. Otherwise hundreds of families will need to be maintained as paupers. The western and northern expeditions will grant no present relief.

Yours as above,

T. Hartley.

★ ★ ★ ★ ★

WALLIS'

The refurnishing of Wallis' home was progressing nicely. Hartley gratefully accepted Wallis' offer to be his guest whenever he traveled up the West Branch.

One evening, after a pleasant meal, the two men retired to Wallis' study. They fell into a congenial conversation.

"Splendid port, Mr. Wallis."

"Thank you, Colonel. I brought it with me when I returned from Philadelphia. I import it myself. It's playing the odds as to whether a shipment will make it through the British patrols, but I consider it worth it if even half of it does."

"Well," said Hartley, "here's to hoping we'll soon be victorious, and that situation will be a thing of the past."

"I will drink to that, sir."

They sat by the window in reflective quiet, their crystal glasses sparkling pleasantly in the twilight. Hartley broke the silence.

"Mr. Wallis?"

"Yes?"

"When we met in Philadelphia, you said you'd been a member of the Pennsylvania Assembly. Is that not so?"

"Why yes, it is," answered Wallis.

"And, you were a militia captain as well, correct?"

"Yes, why do you ask?"

"Nothing really," said Hartley. "It just strikes me as odd that you were able to remain in Philadelphia during the occupation."

Wallis was stunned. This was completely unexpected. He fixed Hartley with a steely gaze and remained very calm as he answered.

"Do you question my loyalty, sir? I was there looking after my business, at great risk to myself, I might add. In doing so, I was able to procure vital supplies *and* arranged to have them smuggled through enemy lines to our soldiers. It *would* be rather difficult to run a shipping business from anywhere but the coast, after all."

Wallis was a good actor, and Hartley perceived he'd offended his host.

"Do forgive me, Mr. Wallis. I insinuate nothing. I was merely asking. You've provided safety for area inhabitants and have gone so far as to lobby me to build the adjacent fort. I must, however, be circumspect. I'm sure you can understand."

"Circumspect?" asked Wallis. "In what regard?"

"Mr. Wallis, you are very familiar with the surrounding countryside, are you not?"

"Yes, of course, I am."

"What I am about to tell you must remain in the utmost of confidence. Do I have your word as a gentleman?"

"Yes . . . absolutely." This was another unexpected turn. Wallis waited, in complete stillness, for whatever choice piece of information he was about to receive. The intervening moment hung frozen before him, and he felt the blood pound in his ears.

"I've been planning a strike into Indian country," said Hartley.

"Excellent," answered Wallis, trying not to seem too excited or too indifferent.

"I feel," continued Hartley, "that for us to stay here to await the constant harassment of the enemy is foolhardy. We must take the fight to him. We must force him to fall back to his own country."

"I heartily agree, Colonel. How may I help?"

"My plan is to march up the Loyalsock and to take the Wyalusing Path to the North Branch. I'll join with troops arriving there from Wyoming. Together, we'll proceed up the North Branch to Chemung, where our intelligence tells us the enemy lies in strength. We'll destroy the countryside between Wyalusing and Chemung, including the village of Tioga. I've been some distance out the Wyalusing Path and have found it to be very agreeable, though I am told it becomes rather mountainous. In respect to your knowledge of the area, what is your opinion of this idea?"

Wallis paused. He needed to sound enthusiastic but at the same time protect his interests and his Tory friends. While he maintained a calm and thoughtful expression, his mind raced to contrive an answer. He drew in a long, pensive breath and spoke.

"As for the effect it will have on our residents, and on the enemy for that matter, I find it to be very promising. But with all humility and respect, Colonel, I feel the logistics of the route are somewhat questionable."

"In what respect?" asked Hartley.

"Well, sir," Wallis continued, "first of all, you've heard correctly. The Wyalusing Path does become very mountainous. In fact, it crosses the section of the state called the *Endless* Mountains, and it becomes quite rugged."

Wallis was gaining confidence. He pressed on as the sound of his own voice reassured him.

"While you'll encounter mountains no matter which path you take, I feel the Sheshequin Path, up the Lycoming, would be a far more inviting route for an army. Also, once on the Sheshequin, taking the left fork will take you almost directly to Chemung. I would think you could affect a far greater surprise by suddenly emerging from the woods and sacking the village than you could by destroying the whole valley for fifty or sixty miles before reaching it."

Wallis was laying a perfect trap for Hartley. The Wyalusing Path did go through the Endless Mountains, but it wasn't overly taxing. The Sheshequin Path, however, was strenuous and demanding.

Wallis reasoned if he could convince Hartley to head up the Lycoming, his army would get bogged down and become a ripe target for ambush. Wallis also planned to get word of the approaching rebels to Chemung long before Hartley arrived there.

With the idea now fully formed in his mind, he concluded confidently, "Having destroyed Chemung, you could then return *down* the North Branch and destroy the enemy country in detail, while heading back to Wyoming."

Wallis fell silent and allowed his words to take effect. Hartley looked absently out the window at the dying light.

After some minutes, he turned to Wallis and said, "Thank you for your input, Mr. Wallis. I will take what you've said under serious consideration."

"I hope I have been of some assistance," said Wallis.

"You have, sir. And I regret if I, in any way, impugned your character earlier. Please understand how very careful I must be in these situations."

"Nonsense, Colonel," said Wallis. "Of course, I understand."

"You do your country proud, sir. Now if you would excuse me," said Hartley, "I believe I will retire to my room. I have to be up very early tomorrow, and I must attend to some unanswered letters from home."

"Of course. Sleep well, Colonel."

Hartley considered what Wallis said. It made good sense to keep the element of surprise. Destroying the Indian territory on the way back was also smart because he'd be headed toward friendly territory as he progressed. Finally, if the Sheshequin Path was in better condition than the Wyalusing, he could avoid unnecessary delays and keep his troops in better condition.

Hartley awoke early the next morning and returned to Fort Augusta.

He didn't discuss his plans with anyone. He spent time alone with Hunter's maps and soon made up his mind. He'd take Wallis' advice and use the Sheshequin Path but not follow it clear to Chemung. If he did, he'd be forced to cross the river in the face of the enemy.

Hartley decided to follow the right fork of the path and gain the North Branch just below Tioga. This would give him the option to cross the river and attack Tioga before advancing northward, or to sidestep Tioga all together and cross the river at some obscure point. In any case, the river crossing would be made below Chemung. Following this plan may sacrifice the element of surprise, but it was more militarily sound.

His plan set, Hartley composed his final orders to Colonel Butler at Wyoming.

> *Sunbury, September 10, 1778*
> *Sir,*
>
> *Upon full consideration, I have come to these determinations: It is absolutely necessary that the troops at Wyoming, and those on the West Branch should unite before they proceed against Chemung. I understand a great part of the plunder taken from Wyoming, and a body of Indians and Tories are collected there.*
>
> *I mean for Chemung to be approached by the Lycoming Path to the mouth of Towanda Creek, that it should be attacked and, if possible, destroyed. The troops should then sweep the country, down the river to Wyoming. This will give relief to our frontiers, and intimidate our enemies.*
>
> *You will detain thirty regulars of those who are least able to march and fifty militia or inhabitants to compose your garrison. Captain Bush, with the residue of my regiment and the other troops at Wyoming, will march off from thence on September 14th to Muncy Fort, near Wallis'. They are to bring all the packhorses, saddles, etc. with them.*
>
> *Previous to their march they are to draw and cook four days' provisions. Provisions will be provided for them afterwards. It is expected they will arrive at Fort Muncy the third night of their march, or the fourth day.*
>
> *It will be impossible to tell the troops or people where they are to march. You must induce the militia to go. Say they are marching to some Indian town. I am informed*

many of our people have the highest inclination to go against some of the Indian towns, that besides serving their country they may avenge the murder of fathers, brothers and friends.

After they have marched, the garrison are to be informed the men have gone to the West Branch to support the people there who have been attacked by the Indians. The route to Muncy will justify that and the Tories will be deceived.

You will act in the best manner you can during the absence of the troops. A garrison will still be continued near Nescopeck. You may communicate this letter to Captain Bush under the strictest injunction of secrecy.

The inhabitants who go on this expedition will be back in time enough to put in some fall grain.

I am your mos.
Obed. Servt.
Thos. Hartley
Coll. Commandant.

★　★　★　★　★

FORT MUNCY

Hartley awoke at 3:15 on the morning of September 21st. He'd ordered the army to be ready to march at 4:00. As he dressed in the cool darkness, he heard rain pattering on the window. It wasn't a downpour, just a steady drizzle that crept into the valley overnight.

Leaving Wallis', Hartley crossed through the abatis that encircled Fort Muncy. The sharpened entanglements were disconcerting to pass between, let alone attack.

"Walker did alright," thought Hartley, as he came to the earthworks and surveyed the stockade fence in front of him. He entered the fort and saw his men stirring amongst the smoking, sputtering fires.

"Captain Bush, how are you this morning?" asked Hartley, seeing Bush with the newly-arrived Wyoming men.

"Ready to go, sir," said Bush.

"Good man."

Hartley noticed his cavalry in the far corner and walked over to them.

"Good morning, men," he said.

"Good morning, sir," answered those nearest to him while the others gathered.

"Are you looking forward to your new role?"

"Yessir," they answered.

"Well, I'll miss having you in the ranks of infantry, but since Council didn't see fit to send us any regular horse troops, I thought it best to create our own. I felt the seventeen of you were best suited to the job and I know you'll provide valuable service."

"Thank you, sir," they answered.

Fort Muncy's gates opened at 4:00 a.m. precisely.

"March!" shouted Hartley.

A drum beat the cadence, and the force strode with an easy gait out onto the road.

As Hartley galloped along the line, he nodded to Brady and Boone. They were still in the regular army but now marched with friends and neighbors. Some rows behind them marched Robert Robb, who amazingly won his appeal in Philadelphia and was allowed to remain out of the service. He then, inexplicably, volunteered as a militiaman and joined Covenhoven, Antes, Hepburn and the rest of the West Branch men on the march.

At the Loyalsock, Covenhoven looked wistfully up the creek, where his brothers had been killed. Brady also couldn't help but glance toward the field where James was mortally wounded. Looking quickly away he said, "Rain's pickin' up a little."

"Yeah," said Boone.

Boone knew Brady's imagined version of his son's attack

had burned itself into his mind and played over and over... and over ...

Many of the men that morning were passing the scenes of the deaths of their friends and family members and the burned-out shells of their homes.

There was no sunrise. The sky merely lightened by degrees to a thick and murky gray. Conditions deteriorated. The soaked and mud-splattered men sank above the tops of their shoes into the morass churned up before them.

Reaching the Lycoming, the army turned north and pushed a few miles up the creek before going into camp. Hartley was pleased with the first day's results. After a cold meal, the men did their best to get comfortable and tried to get some sleep.

It was still raining the next morning, and the army awoke wet and cold. The creek was running fast and swelled to the edge of its banks. The force resumed its march and pushed up into the mountains. It was soon apparent the path wasn't in very good shape.

They marched through a tangle of undergrowth, and the terrain was quickly becoming challenging. The horsemen were especially having a difficult time. Colonel Hartley waited along the path until the West Branch men came along.

"Captain Brady," Hartley called when they approached.

"Yessir, Colonel?"

"Do you have any knowledge of the conditions ahead?"

"No sir, Colonel, I don't. I know it goes to the North Branch, but I never took it myself. You haven't either, have you Hawk?"

"No, not me," answered Boone. "I done my surveyin' mostly along the river."

"Antes . . . Hepburn? How about you gentlemen? Have either of you taken this route?" asked Hartley.

"Not this far up," answered Antes.

"Me neither," said Hepburn.

"I have," Covenhoven spoke up. "Me an' Van Campen scouted up here when we was with Colonel Kelly last fall."

"What will we find ahead?" asked Hartley.

"It gets a *lot* worse 'n this, Colonel. The thickets get heavier an' this is still pretty level compared to how it's gonna get. We'll have a fancy piece a' work to get them horses through the mountains up ahead."

"Do you think it's a possibility?" asked Hartley.

"Yessir. We can do it," said Covenhoven.

"Well then, Sergeant Covenhoven, since you've been up this path before, I'd like you to join the captains, here, in leading us," said Hartley. "Keep in mind the horse must be able to follow."

"Yessir," answered Covenhoven. "If I may, sir?"

"Yes?"

"I think we oughta get a detail of axe-men up front so they can open the way when they're needed."

"Yes, I agree," said Hartley.

"We can take the point just ahead of 'em," Covenhoven continued.

"Very well."

"An' one other thing."

"Yes?"

"You musta seen the Delaware Indian with us by the name a' Job Chilloway. He was with Kelly last fall, too. He's a good man an' he'd be useful up front with us."

"By all means, pick your squad, gentlemen," answered Hartley.

Covenhoven, Boone, Brady, Antes and Hepburn called Chilloway and fifteen Northumberland militia from the ranks. They hurried along the column to the front. Meanwhile, Hartley gathered a squad of ten men with axes and sent them forward, too. When the column was reorganized, they moved out.

Within the hour, they were forced to stop. The axe-men, now designated *pioneers,* swung into action while the new advance guard fanned out around them with rifles at the ready. The pioneers cut saplings and vines to clear the path for the next half mile.

The column advanced through the cleared swath, over the crest of a hill, into a more open section on the north-facing slope. This set a rhythm for the march that became familiar.

The hills became more daunting as they continued northward. Then the path disappeared into a sheer rock face ascending directly from the creek. It was impassable. Covenhoven halted the column and sent for Hartley.

Hartley called, "What is it, Sergeant, why have we stopped?"

"Well sir, we can't go on this way. We could go back and up over this hill, but the pioneers would be at it for some time gettin' us through. Or, we could ford the crick. It looks like we could cross right back there a hundred yards or so."

"I don't want to waste time in backtracking and ascending that mountain. We'll ford. And from now on, you needn't consult me. Just choose the most expedient path."

"Yessir."

The column advanced into the thundering water. Men and horses struggled to keep their feet as the current swept through the boulder-strewn rapids, but they crossed safely to the other side. Soon, though, the call of "Pioneers!" rang out again.

Time and again, the trail wound itself out and forced another crossing. When fording the stream became commonplace, Covenhoven sometimes chose it as a desirable alternative to hacking through more underbrush. The hardest part of the march came when the valley narrowed, and both sides of the creek were impassable. Then, the column was forced to cut its way up over the mountain.

The pioneers cut a zigzag path for the horses up the steep slopes. When they finally reached the crest, the troops from the southern part of the state were relieved, but they quickly learned going back down was just as hard.

Carrying heavy packs down a steep trail of mossy stones and roots wasn't only difficult, it was dangerous. Men fell, dragged themselves to their feet and continued on. It was a miracle none of the horses broke a leg. Rejoining the creek, the men forged on through the wild country.

The next days brought more cold food, wet clothing and little sleep as they climbed, forded and hacked their way north. The rain finally stopped, but the days remained cool, cloudy and damp.

Then, on the morning of the 26th, the advance guard ran into a party of about twenty Indians coming toward them. Both sides were caught by surprise, but the Northumberland men got off the first shots. Seven Indians fell, and the rest ran back up the trail.

The fallen were summarily scalped by the militiamen. Brady, Boone and Covenhoven grimaced. But, they did nothing to stop them.

Hurrying along the path, they came to a camp that hosted at least seventy warriors the night before. The raiders had been on their way to the valley. The Indians who escaped up the trail had warned the larger body, and they were nowhere in sight.

"We've got to get to Sheshequin as soon as possible," said Hartley.

"We just need to cross one more mountain and follow a tame little stream down to the village, Colonel," said Covenhoven. "Hopefully, the raiders stayed on this path and didn't head that way."

When they reached the trailhead at Sheshequin, Hartley fanned his troops out along the woodline on both sides of the trail and advanced directly toward the village on the river's edge. They surprised and surrounded fifteen Indians.

While the village was ransacked, Hartley sent for Chilloway. "Mr. Chilloway, do you speak the Iroquois language?"

"Enough to talk with 'em," he said.

"Ask them what they've heard about our expedition."

Chilloway walked up to the smallest of the captives and fixed him with a menacing glare.

"These soldiers lost their families in raids on the West Branch," he said in the Seneca's language. "They want revenge. If you tell the truth, I'll try to keep them from killing you and the others."

The warrior tried to look brave but winced under the pressure. Chilloway grabbed him by the jaw and pulled his face very close to his own. Slowly, in a low and steady voice, he asked, "What do you know about this army?"

The Seneca stared back blankly for a moment and then spoke, very quietly. Chilloway listened, then turned to Hartley and said, "He says a man deserted from Wyoming and told 'em we were coming."

"Damn!" said Hartley. "And, after all the precautions we took to maintain secrecy."

Hartley looked off into the hills. He took a breath and looked back at Chilloway. "Ask him how long ago the man arrived."

Chilloway asked the question.

"He says a few days ago."

"Ask him if he knows where we're going?" said Hartley.

Chilloway asked. "He says, 'Here … Indian country, to destroy their homes.' That's why they're still here. They were trying to save their crops before we came."

"And where are the rest of them?" asked Hartley.

Chilloway questioned the Seneca.

"He says, 'Run off, up the river.'"

"Very well," said Hartley. "Secure the prisoners and keep them under close guard."

Hartley decided to push on to Tioga, five miles to the north. He quickly organized the column with half of his horsemen in front and the other half as a rear guard.

The trail along the river was wide, flat, and easy to travel. Soon, men in the vanguard saw Indians running from them in the distance. A small squad from the advance horse galloped ahead but found no ambush awaiting the column.

The Indians kept running and were closing in on Queen Esther's town. The horsemen swung down on them, but the Indians plunged into the river and began swimming across. Two of the horsemen rode in after them and captured one of the refugees before he got in water deep enough to force their horses to swim.

They held him until Chilloway arrived to interrogate him. The conversation between them was long and animated. Just before the army reached Queen Esther's town, Chilloway finished with the prisoner and turned to Hartley. "He says they knew about us coming."

"Yes, from the Wyoming deserter," said Hartley.

"I don't think so," said Chilloway. "He says they found out quite a while ago from a Tory white man, come up from the south."

"From what place?" asked Hartley.

"He doesn't know. Just said he came up from the south."

"He could have come from anywhere," said Hartley. "That's at least two security breaches."

"I also asked him what news he had of Morgan's northern raid," said Chilloway. "He said there was no northern raid."

"They didn't attack? That means we're exposed," said Hartley. "Any enemy within a hundred miles could concentrate on us."

"That's the next part," said Chilloway. "He says Tory Butler was at Tioga just a few hours ago with three hundred green-coat rangers. He left for Chemung to join at least two hundred Indians and they're waiting for us there."

"Thank you, Chilloway. You've been very helpful."

Hartley was deep in thought as the troops entered Queen Esther's town. It was near dark. He called a halt to the column and sent out scouts to inspect the village and its surroundings. When everything was found to be safe, he ordered the men to make camp.

Then, Hartley sent for the officers. They met in a large Indian longhouse they referred to as Queen Esther's Palace. It was obviously the most important building in the village.

The men sat on the floor as Hartley laid out the situation.

"Men," he said. "We've come a long way to sit at the hearthside of our enemy. While our purpose was to take Chemung and destroy the enemy's ability to cause us further pain, we must be satisfied with what we've already accomplished. The enemy knows of our approach and is waiting for us with at least five hundred men in defensive works.

"We're fortunate the rumor of our approach was larger than our actual number, and the enemy has fled from us. We've disrupted his plans and prevented further attacks on our frontiers. But now, I see no alternative but to destroy all the crops and dwellings here and in Tioga and then retire down the river to Wyoming. Are there any questions?"

"Yeah, Colonel. I got one," said Boone.

"Yes?"

"Just who *was* the Tory son-of-a-bitch that give us away?"

"Unfortunately, there was more than one," said Hartley. "One deserted from Wyoming after our troops left there for Muncy. He should be relatively easy to pinpoint. The other is more difficult. He is described as a 'Tory white man' and he arrived here from the south."

"We all arrived here from the south," said Brady. "He coulda come from Wyoming, Muncy or Philadelphia for all we know."

"Yes, that is exactly the case," answered Hartley. "But now is not the time to consider such things. A full investigation will be made when we return. Right now, we have a job to do. Let's all get some sleep, shall we?"

Hartley left the building and retired to a cabin he took for himself. The rest of the officers stayed and bedded down in the longhouse.

To Brady, it was a strange feeling to lay by the fire and stare up at this ceiling, as the raiders of the valley had done on so many previous nights. He looked around the room and visualized his enemy living here. Through the shadows, he could see them cooking, and eating . . . and sleeping. His son's killer might have called this place home. Perhaps he slept in this very spot.

His mind wandered. He could see himself back in the canoe on the way to Sunbury that terrible night. He saw himself relentlessly paddling, though his back and shoulders ached. But, James was lying mutilated and dying before him and there was nothing else he could do.

He saw the stream of stars above him, reflecting in the elongating river that began to twist and rise and swirl around him, as though it were a living entity trying to catch him in its coils. He paddled harder and tried to focus on Mary on the distant shore. Finally, he rested the paddle across his knees, for just a moment, and looked down at his quivering hands. When he looked up again, the paddle was gone.

Suddenly, he was all alone in the tiny canoe being carried swiftly along the current that rose and twisted in ever-tightening circles. The stars swirled around him. As he reached its zenith, he plunged down the gushing torrent that swallowed him in a funnel of blackness . . .

Brady awoke the next morning to the sounds of men stirring around him. He had terrible dreams all night, and, though he slept for hours, he didn't feel rested at all. The officers were up quickly and went to rouse the troops.

Tioga lay on the point at the confluence of the Chemung River and the North Branch, directly across the river from Queen Esther's town. A large detachment was sent across to Tioga while the rest of the army stayed on the western shore.

From early morning, smoke began to curl up from the river valley. Vast apple orchards were cut and set ablaze, along with fields of corn and squash. The villages were ransacked for anything of value. Whatever wasn't useful or practical to carry was placed in the buildings and burned.

Soon, nothing but scorched fields and smoldering ruins remained, and the army turned back down the river, marching and destroying as it went.

Hartley resumed the march with the army organized into three small divisions and the horsemen split between the front and rear guards. Many of the troops, including Brady and Boone, descended the river in captured canoes.

When the Tory Butler realized Hartley had withdrawn, he left his defenses in Chemung and began a pursuit. Days later, Butler closed in and attacked.

Indian troops pitched into Hartley's rear guard. The soldiers gave ground slowly but were being pressed toward the main body.

"First and third divisions," shouted Hartley, "take that high ground on the enemy flank. Second division, advance to support the rear guard."

As Hartley was about to attack from the heights, Brady saw what was happening from the river.

"Northumberland men," he yelled, "land next to the enemy. Send up a big cheer and fire into their flank and rear."

The Indians, seeing troops arrive from the river and hearing yelling and firing from all directions, thought they were surrounded. They broke and ran, leaving their dead on the field.

★ ★ ★ ★ ★

FORT AUGUSTA

"Incredible," said Hunter, on the evening Hartley returned. "In just two weeks, your men marched three hundred miles through wild and rugged terrain. They destroyed a swath of enemy country, returned with captured supplies, and prevented at least one raiding party from reaching the valley."

"We were fortunate," said Hartley. "We'd been betrayed at least twice, and the enemy was aware of our approach before we ever got there. Furthermore, the northern attack was never made, and we didn't have the cover we anticipated."

"Nevertheless," said Hunter, "the strategy worked. Now, what do you propose to do?"

"I'll send Walker and his men back into garrison at Fort Muncy so they can build the barracks, magazine and storehouse. I suggest we allow the militiamen and our local officers to complete their harvests and fall planting."

"I agree," said Hunter.

★　★　★　★　★

FORT BRADY

The October air was like a tonic to Brady. He paused from his harvesting and stared up the valley. The autumn color shone beneath a bright blue sky. He walked to the edge of the field, near the river, and sat down with his back against an ancient walnut tree he'd left standing for precisely this purpose.

For the first time since July, he almost felt normal. Rage drained from his body and was carried away on the breeze.

"This country *is* worth fightin' for, James," he said out loud. "I haven't been so sure of that since you left us, but I know *you* always was. And, I know you're right, too. We'll win our freedom, and we'll build a new land of rights and justice. You won't have died for no reason. I promise. I'm proud of you, boy."

Two tears trickled down Brady's cheek. They fell to the earth in front of him and seeped slowly away.

CHAPTER 8

October-December 1778

WALLIS'

"**B**it of a chill this morning," thought Samuel Wallis as he looked out at the year's first frost.

Normally, he would have already retired to Philadelphia for the winter, but October was dwindling and Wallis was still on the Susquehanna. He told the locals he was staying to direct the completion of his home. It was an easy excuse, but Wallis' motives were more complex.

He was more determined than ever not to allow the rebels to take this land from a power that recognized privilege and status.

"Obviously," thought Wallis, "they have no way of defending themselves or local interests. And, trying to conceive of a government based on the theory that *these* oafs are *my* equal is beyond ridiculous."

He thought back to the night when Hartley spoke with him about the campaign. That was the night his plan coalesced. After Hartley left for Fort Augusta the next morning, Wallis followed him downriver.

Wallis knew of a Northumberland County Militia Captain named Burton who was secretly a Tory. It was one of the choice pieces of intelligence he'd discovered through his associates in Philadelphia. Burton lived on the eastern shore of the North Branch, just a little more than 20 miles upstream from Fort Augusta. Wallis dropped in unannounced.

Burton's home was impressive for the area, but it didn't compare to Wallis'. Wallis drew great satisfaction from this as he rode up to the front door and dismounted.

He knocked sharply. Moments passed. He was about to knock again when the door flung open before him.

"Yah?" said a pudgy Pennsylvania Dutch woman wiping her floury hands on her apron.

"Mr. Samuel Wallis to see Mr. Burton."

"Yah, I just been at the hearth," she said holding her palms up to Wallis, "Mr. Burton can't go a week without some a' my schnitz pie."

"Yes, I'm sure. Could you announce me to him please?" asked Wallis impatiently.

"Yah, alright," she said, feeling the snub. "Mr. Burton," she called back through the house, "Mr. Wallis is here t' see ya." And, she walked off to the kitchen without a look back.

Wallis shook his head at the lack of protocol. At the same time, he took pleasure in the contrast to his own estate. "Any servant of mine that treated a guest in such a manner would be thrashed severely," he thought.

As he stood musing, Burton poked his head around the corner from a back room and then walked out to the door.

"Sam? What are *you* doin' here?"

"Hello, Captain Burton. I'd like to discuss something with you."

"Alright, have a seat," said Burton.

"Wallis opened the conversation with small talk and played his hand shrewdly. He kept the conversation friendly for some time before he struck. Then, when it would have the greatest possible effect, Wallis said, "Captain Burton, I am aware of your treachery."

Burton was stunned.

"My . . . treachery?" said Burton. "What are ya talkin' about?"

"You know very well what I'm talking about," said Wallis matter-of-factly. "I know all of your contacts in Philadelphia and I'm happy to name them for you, if you wish."

Burton sat dumbfounded. Wallis let him sweat.

"You see," continued Wallis, "I was talking with one of my business associates last summer who mentioned your name because we come from the same county. I know that person is suspected of being a Tory so I drew him into further conversation."

Burton was really becoming alarmed and Wallis decided it was time to ease the pressure. Now, he'd make Burton feel he was the one in control.

"I was disgusted by the destruction of my home," said Wallis. "I feel there is no way to win this war, and I've come to the realization that life under the British was at least secure and certainly preferable to what we have now.

"I've happened upon some information that may be of service to his Majesty," continued Wallis. "I've never done anything like this before, and I'd like to ask your guidance."

"Oh . . . I *see*," said Burton, who was both relieved and flattered. "Of course, I'd be happy to advise you."

Wallis shared that he'd just learned about Hartley's upcoming raid.

"I wonder if we should send a messenger to Tioga with word of the army's approach?" asked Wallis.

"I know just the person," answered Burton. "He's a local man. . . . one of my runners to Philadelphia. I'll send him to Tioga with the information."

"Very well," said Wallis. "Thank you for your help."

"Not at all. Thank you for your service to the Crown. You've made a wise choice," said Burton.

Wallis left feeling very proud of himself. He'd gotten Burton to warn the Tories of Hartley's campaign and kept himself out of it. Part one of his plan was underway. Part two could wait for the time being.

Now, more than a month later and with Hartley's raid concluded, Wallis invited Burton to his home.

On the appointed day, Burton arrived smug and confident.

He relished the idea of having such an impressive follower. Burton rode down the lane to Wallis' estate and dismounted. The door was answered by the Irish servant.

"Yessir?"

"Captain Burton to see Mr. Wallis."

"Yessir. Mr. Wallis is expectin' ye. Won't ye come in?"

"Thanks," said Burton.

"Right this way, sir."

The servant led Burton into the newly completed study, now even more opulent than before. Burton looked around as casually as he could manage, but he hadn't expected to see anything like this.

"Won't ye sit by the fire, sir an' I'll bring ye some refreshment," said the servant. "Mr. Wallis'll be down shortly."

"Thanks," said Burton again.

Wallis, who was waiting at the top of the stairs, smirked to himself. He'd instructed the servant to treat Burton as formally as possible. While pretending to be subservient, Wallis wanted to keep the psychological advantage as his superior.

He waited until Burton received his drink and then descended the stairs.

"Thank you for coming, Captain," said Wallis as he entered the room.

"Thanks for the invitation, Sam."

"How was your journey?"

"Very nice. The West Branch is a beautiful valley, 'specially at this time a' year."

"I'm glad you enjoyed your ride," said Wallis. "I suppose you can assume the subject I wish to discuss with you."

"I guess it must be about the raid. I heard it went pretty good for Hartley," said Burton.

"You assume correctly," said Wallis, who got right to the point. "Upon his return, Colonel Hartley conducted an investigation into how word of his army's approach *somehow* reached the enemy.

Hartley discovered some traitorous soldier from Wyoming deserted and gave warning shortly before they arrived.

"However, what disturbed Hartley more was that the enemy concentrated in numbers that couldn't have been gathered in that short amount of time. He learned a 'white man came from the south' and arrived some time before the deserter. He warned the enemy of the impending attack."

Wallis sadistically paused here for effect.

"And what'd they find in the investigation?" asked Burton.

. . . Another short pause.

"Nothing whatsoever," said Wallis, jovially. "The information was far too vague for it to be of any use. Your man covered his tracks well."

"Well, that's good t' hear," sighed Burton.

"In fact, he did an excellent job," continued Wallis. "If it weren't for Colonel Hartley's good grasp of the situation, the results of the raid would have been very different indeed."

"Better luck next time, I guess. So go the fortunes of war," mused Burton in his sagest tone.

"Interesting you should mention the next time, Captain."

"How so?" asked Burton.

"I told you of some of my Philadelphia business contacts' political leanings?" began Wallis.

"Yeah?"

"It so happens I've learned of a plan within another county's militia to contact British officials and openly switch sides. I only mention it because I thought you may want to go in with them; depending on your depth of influence with your men, of course. Your joined forces would constitute at least a full battalion."

Wallis paused for a moment and said, "Can you imagine a whole battalion suddenly switching sides in the middle of the decisive battle? It goes without saying that when the war is over, the leaders of this militia would be most highly thought of by the new royal governor. Do you suppose you have that kind of influence?" asked Wallis.

"I'll tell ya, Sam," said Burton, "where I lead, my men follow."

"Very good," confirmed Wallis. "Who knows? This could foster a full-on counterrevolution. I presume being one of its leaders would be a very fortuitous position in which to find oneself. Would you like to be placed in contact with those involved?"

Burton thought for a moment. So flagrant an action wasn't to be entered into lightly. Yet, as Wallis described it, there was so much to gain.

Burton began to envision being awarded property and perhaps a title. Who knew how far this could take him?

"Alright," said Burton. "I'm interested."

"I thought you might be," said Wallis. "The head of the plot is Colonel Rankin of York County. He's nearly ready to contact the British. I suggest you make a trip to York and pay the colonel a visit."

"Should I tell him you sent me?" asked Burton.

"By no means should you tell him that," stammered Wallis.

Recovering, he added nonchalantly, "My name will mean nothing to the colonel. Rather, I'm sure he's *heard* of me, but I would seem a complete outsider to him, and he'd surely feel his plan was compromised. No. You should use the name of your contact in Philadelphia. He's in on the plan, and his would be a *safe* name to use."

"Fine," said Burton. "How much time do I have?"

"The sooner the better. Surely you've enough time to discuss matters with your men, but don't be too long about it. I understand Rankin intends to make his move in a matter of weeks. In fact, if you began to organize your plans immediately, it wouldn't be too soon."

"Thanks, Sam," said Burton. "I appreciate you bringin' this t' me. I'll see to it you won't be left out of the rewards when matters are finished."

"No. No reward is necessary for me," said Wallis. "I'm happy to play my part for the good of the country and wish you to take full credit in the matter."

"That's very kind," said Burton, incredulous at his good fortune.

"Now, if you'll excuse me, Captain, I must get back to my packing. You see I'm preparing to move back to Philadelphia for the winter and have a great deal of arrangements to make. I hope you won't consider me rude for not offering to have you spend the night, but you'll need to be rushing off anyway, won't you?"

"Yeah," said Burton awkwardly. "I've got to be going. Have a good trip, yourself."

"Thank you," said Wallis, rising. "And, the best of luck to you, sir. My man will see you out."

As Burton rode back down the lane, Wallis contemplated what it could mean for him if the militia around Muncy could be persuaded to join the plot.

"Maybe," he thought, "Robb could encourage them in the idea."

But then, he reasoned, with Brady so near, there probably was very little chance indeed.

★ ★ ★ ★ ★

FORT FREELAND

"I'll be damned," said Garrett Freeland when he returned to his property after the runaway and found his gristmill, his sawmill *and* his home still standing. "They must not a' come this far up Warrior Run."

"Well, Pop," said one of his sons, "since we don't need to rebuild the house an' mills, we might as well go ahead an' build a stockade around the house. Wouldn't hurt t' have another fort around here."

"Not a bad idea," agreed Freeland.

By the end of October, the completed enclosure covered half an acre and housed not only the Freelands but the Vincents, McKnights and Durhams, too.

"It's such a nice mornin'," said Margaret Durham, "let's take the baby down t' see Aunt Sue in Northumberland."

"That's a fine idea," said Emily McKnight.

"Been a lot a' rumors of raidin' parties, ladies," said Freeland, having overheard the conversation.

"Yeah, an' there ain't been one actual raid," answered Margaret. "We'll be fine."

The ladies rode out of the fort on horseback. Margaret held her infant in her arms.

"Oooh, it's nice t' be out a' the fort. Ain't it, Marg?" said Emily.

"Yeah, an' havin' a day off from milkin' an' cookin' and preservin' ain't bad either," she said.

They laughed and talked as they passed along the creek. When they reached the river, they turned south along the wagon road.

A mile further, their conversation was interrupted by rifle shots in the nearby field. They turned, expecting to see hunters, and heard a ball whiz over their heads. Margaret felt a jolt in her arms. Looking down, she saw blood splattered on her dress. Her baby had been shot in her arms.

"Aaahhhhhhh!" screamed Margaret.

The horse reared and she fell to the ground. Emily started for the nearby Williams farm but realized Margaret hadn't moved. In the distance, she saw three Indians rushing toward them. She yelled, "Margaret, come on! They're coming!"

Margaret didn't seem to hear her. Bound in horror and grief, she was patting the dead infant's cheek and trying to revive it. Emily knew if she were going to escape that *now* was the time. She left Margaret and rode to the farm.

Margaret sat kissing her baby and smoothing its matted hair, oblivious to the danger. When the three warriors reached her, she never looked away from her baby until one of them grabbed her by the hair. With her face to the sky, she didn't see the knife and really didn't feel any pain. She was mostly aware of the violent jerking at her scalp.

Then she felt a burning sensation that intensified as she lay there. Her baby lay at her side. She wrapped her arms around it and buried her face in its neck as the Indians ran off.

Emily made it to the Williams' farm.

"Help! Help!" she screamed.

Peter Williams and his son Elias ran outside.

"What's the matter?" asked Peter.

"Indians," yelled Emily. "They attacked us on the road."

"C'mon," said Peter to his son.

They grabbed their rifles and ran down the road. As they reached Margaret, they saw a baby on the blood-soaked ground with a thimble-sized entrance wound on top of its head. Holding it in her arms was the body of a still, scalpless woman.

Suddenly, the woman raised up and stared at them with wild and pleading eyes. Blood covered her face and dress.

"Please . . . bring me some water. I'm *so* thirsty," she said.

Startled, Peter said, "Elias, go down t' the river and get some water." Then he knelt down and reassured her, "You just hang on ma'am. We'll take care of you."

Elias waded a few steps out into the river, plunged his hat into the water and brought it back as quickly as possible. Tenderly raising the woman in his arms, Peter said, "Here's some water ma'am. Take a drink."

Margaret turned her face toward the upturned hat. Elias held it as she placed her face inside the brim and drank insatiably. When she drank all she could, she seemed to come to her senses. She began to cry and rock her baby.

Peter steadied her and said, "Ma'am, we got to get you t' the doctor's. We'll take you down t' Doc Plunket's in Northumberland. He'll fix you up."

"We got t' take my baby," she pleaded with the men.

"Don't worry, ma'am," said Elias, calmly. "We'll look after your baby."

Peter stood and gently lifted Margaret in his arms while Elias took the baby.

Margaret passed out again as they hurried back up the road to a canoe they kept on the riverbank. Emily called to the men, "How is she?"

"Fainted, but alive," answered Peter.

"How 'bout the baby?" she asked.

Elias shook his head. He didn't want to take the chance that Margaret might still hear him. Emily began crying softly. Turning to Elias, Peter said quietly, "Put the baby in the shed. We'll bury it when we get back."

Elias did as he was told.

Peter looked at Emily and said, "Would you go in an' get a couple a' blankets from my wife?"

Emily ran inside. She returned with Mrs. Williams and the blankets about the same time Elias came back from the shed.

As they placed Margaret in the canoe, Peter folded a blanket and laid it under her head. Easing her back, he spread the other blanket over her to keep her warm. Peter said, "Mrs. McKnight, you stay here with my wife while we take this lady down t' Doc Plunket's. Who is she, anyhow?"

"Why, this is Mrs. Durham," she answered.

"Poor woman. I didn't even recognize her," said Peter. "Stay in the house and bar the windows, alright?"

Mrs. Williams nodded in response.

The men pushed off and headed down the river. Margaret passed in and out of consciousness. When she awoke, she begged for more water. Each time, Elias rested his paddle, refilled his hat and poured slowly from the folded brim so she could drink.

He did his best to refresh her by pouring water on her face and neck. He washed the dried, crusted blood from her cheeks. Then, he picked up his paddle and resumed pulling toward Northumberland.

They arrived in a few hours. Landing on shore, the men picked up the unconscious Mrs. Durham and carried her to Plunket's home, a few hundred yards away.

They pounded on his front door and called to him.

"Doc!"

"Doc Plunket!" they shouted.

The door opened and the old doctor brought them inside.

"It's Mrs. Durham from up Warrior Run," said Peter.

The men followed him into a first-floor room and laid her on a bed. Plunket began dressing her wound. "How long since this happened?" he asked.

"Couple a' hours," said Peter.

"Has she had any water?"

"Yeah, she drank an awful lot durin' the trip," answered Elias.

The doctor proceeded with his work as he spoke. "Remarkable," he said. "The wound's already begun to scab over nicely. She seems to have lost a lot a' blood, but I don't think she's lost *too* much."

"You mean she'll live, Doc?" asked Peter.

"Too soon t' tell for sure," he said, "but I believe she's got a chance. Did you elevate her head on the journey?"

"Yeah, we folded a blanket as a pillow t' try an' keep her comf'table," said Peter.

"That helped stop the bleeding," said Plunket. "She also needed a lot a' water, and it looks as if you treated her as good as she coulda been."

"Well . . . I just hope she'll be alright," said Peter awkwardly.

"I think she's got a chance," said Plunket.

"Well, if there's nothin' else we can do, Doc, we oughta be getting' back. My wife and Mrs. McKnight are there alone an' I'm feelin' kinda uneasy about it," said Peter.

"By all means," answered Plunket.

"Thanks, Doc," said Peter in departing.

"Thank *you*, men."

The Williams' walked back to their canoe and climbed in for the return journey. They arrived, exhausted, by early evening and found the women safe inside.

"How is she?" asked Emily.

"Doc said she could make it," responded Peter.

"How are you?" asked Mrs. Williams of Peter and Elias.

"Tired, but alright," said Elias.

"Well, I got some supper ready. Why don't you sit down an' eat, an' then get some sleep?"

The men nodded thankfully and sat while Mrs. Williams set out the meal.

"Where are we gonna bury the baby?" asked Elias.

"We'll put it in the fam'ly plot. If the Durhams want, they can leave it there. I'll set to makin' a coffin in the mornin'. Shouldn't take too long . . ."

★ ★ ★ ★ ★

FORT AUGUSTA

"Well, the line is intact," said Hartley to Hunter as he returned from a reconnaissance, "clear from Jenkins to Fort Muncy."

"Thank God," said Hunter. "I'm surprised they'd mount a raid so late into the season. How much damage did they do?"

"They destroyed some settlements on the North Branch as far as Fort Jenkins," said Hartley. "Then, seventy broke off from the main body and laid siege to Fort Bosley. I took the relief force up the Chillisquaque and drove 'em off."

"Well done," said Hunter. "That's a fitting end to your action here in the valley. I sure wish you hadn't been ordered back."

"And, I regret having to leave," said Hartley. "But they've consolidated some of the decimated regiments, including mine, into the new Pennsylvania 11th. I must go look to its organization.

I'll leave Captain Walker here through the winter and send for him when the new regiment musters in the spring."

"Thank you," said Hunter. "And, good luck. We'll miss having you around."

"Thank you, Sam."

A few days later, Hunter, Brady, Boone and Covenhoven accompanied Hartley out of Fort Augusta and walked with him down to the water's edge. Hartley tossed his belongings into the waiting batteau and turned back to Hunter. "Colonel, it's all yours again."

"Tom, you've been tremendous. We can't thank you enough."

"Nonsense. They merely gave me some resources to work with. *Not nearly* as many as we could have used, but a damned sight more than they ever gave you."

"Well . . ." said Hunter, awkwardly.

"You're the ones who have been tremendous;" continued Hartley, "you and your men here, defending this valley with next to nothing and being successful for so long. Hopefully, now they'll take your requests more seriously."

"Well, Council's been stretched pretty thin everywhere," said Hunter, "but you're very kind to say so."

"All true, sir. All true," said Hartley. "I wish you well." Hartley extended his hand and Hunter took it.

"The same to you," said Hunter. "Have a good journey . . . and thanks."

"Thank *you*," replied Hartley. He turned and boarded the batteau, taking a seat in the center. Hunter and the others helped the crew shove off and then stood on the shore as they paddled down the river.

When Hartley was away, the men turned and walked back toward the fort. They got to the gate and paused amongst their horses before going their separate ways for the winter.

"Been a hell of a year," said Boone.

"Hadn't it just?" answered Brady.

For a moment, no one spoke as their thoughts turned to those who didn't live to see the winter. But, Covenhoven broke the silence and tried to cheer things up a bit.

"Well, I say things'll look a damn sight better this time next year."

"Hope you're right," responded Boone.

"We may not all *be* here this time next year," grinned Brady.

"I will," said Covenhoven, "I'm too damn stubborn to die."

"Ain't that the God's honest truth," said Boone, slapping him on the back.

"You'd better *all* be here, gentlemen," said Hunter.

Brady laughed and mounted his horse. The others followed suit.

"Gentlemen," said Hunter before they rode off, "Colonel Hartley was correct, you know."

"How's that?" asked Boone.

"You have all done tremendous work for our country . . . and our valley. I'm very appreciative of all you've done."

The men smiled. Brady spoke up and said, "We all feel the same about you, Sam. You have a nice winter, now."

"You men as well," he replied. "And happy Christmas to you and your families."

★ ★ ★ ★ ★

NEW YORK CITY

"Yes, Mr. Sower, Colonel Rankin is my brother-in-law," said Andrew Furstner when he arrived carrying Rankin's offer to the British.

"And you say these York County men will switch sides whenever we feel it to be most beneficial?" queried Christopher Sower. Sower was an open loyalist and prosperous Philadelphia printer who followed the British to New York when they left the city.

"That's right. And, it's not just the York County men," Furstner continued. "We got Captain Burton and his Northumberland County men throwin' in with us, too."

"Interesting," said Sower, as he diligently took notes. "Thank you, Mr. Furstner. I'll take your proposal to General Clinton and will have his reply for you tomorrow."

The next day, Sower handed Clinton's written response to Furstner. On Furstner's arrival back in York County, Rankin opened it and read,

> *"The commander-in-chief directs you inform the gentlemen that his Excellency will save them harmless from all penalties denounced against rebels. He requests them to continue in their respective posts under the present usurped authority.*
>
> *It is his pleasure they increase the circle of their acquaintances and furnish him with all important intelligence that may come to their knowledge."*

★ ★ ★ ★ ★

PINE CREEK VALLEY

Andrew Fleming awoke and went out early Christmas morning. He decided to gather some trailing pine and surprise his wife and child by decorating the house. It was the kind of lighthearted activity he'd been needing. He'd had enough seriousness lately.

Living in the Fair Play Territory, he'd been there when they signed the declaration. He served in the militia here and in New Jersey. He and his family had been part of the big runaway, and he'd taken the war to the enemy on Hartley's raid to Tioga. Now he was ready to enjoy some happy time with his family and to forget about the war for a while.

He bent to add to his armload of trailing pine when he noticed a flake drift to the ground in front of him. When he stood, he noticed a few more. It began almost imperceptibly as bits of lace floating on the early morning air.

Fleming chuckled to himself. It made him happy. In childlike wonder, he stood perfectly still and thought maybe he could just hear the icy crystals reach the ground. Heading back, the quickening flakes made everything seem almost magical.

He followed the path to his door and reached out with his foot to give it a few taps.

"Deborah, open up. My hands are full."

"Comin'."

The door opened.

"Where you been?" she asked playfully.

"It's Christmas, ain't it?" he said, holding out the trailing pine.

"Come inside before you freeze," she laughed.

"Hi, Pa!" cried a little voice from the corner. It was his four-year-old son.

"Hiya, Matthew! Happy Christmas!"

"Happy Christmas to you, too, Pa! Whatcha got?"

"This is trailin' pine. We use it to decorate the house up real nice, and then, boy, does it smell good, too."

"You better get to decoratin' 'cause I got cookin' to do," said his wife.

"Whatcha cookin'?" asked Andrew.

"Well, the best I could manage was rabbit stew for dinner, but I plan on bakin' some apple pies."

"Rabbit stew doesn't seem like a very nice Christmas meal."

"That's all we got," said Deborah.

"Well, let's just see if we can do a little better," he said smiling. "How's roasted venison sound to you?"

"Oh, Andrew. You're going huntin' now?"

"Why not? I bet I can get a deer real quick. It just started snowin' and already dusted the ground. I'll be able to track 'em real easy. Then you can make a nice big roast, and we'll have plenty left over to salt an' store."

"Well, if you're sure you want to go . . ." she said.

"Yeppur, I am. We're gonna have us a real nice Christmas meal. How's that sound to you, boy? You like venison for Christmas?"

"I sure do!"

"Well, then I'll go an' get you some." Fleming walked to the corner for his rifle and slung his powder horn over his shoulder.

"Pa?"

"Yeah?"

"Can I go with you to shoot the venison?"

Fleming tried not to laugh. "Well, do you know what a venison looks like?"

"Sure, I do."

"Why don't you tell me then?"

"Well, it's sort of like . . . uh . . ."

"Does a venison look like a cow?" he prompted.

"No. Not like a cow."

"Does it look like a deer?"

"No. Not like a deer."

"How 'bout like a bear?"

"No. It don't. It looks like a venison."

Andrew and Deborah laughed. He leaned over and scooped up his young son.

"Let me tell you what."

"What, Pa?"

"I'm afraid if you'd come along, we'd wind up gettin' all the venisons an' then there wouldn't be none left for later. Why don't you stay here an' help your ma? She's got cookin' *and* decoratin' to do and she'll need some help from a big fella like you."

"Alright, Pa."

"Good. Now you be a good boy till I get home."

"Alright, Pa."

He lowered him to the floor. Grabbing his wife by the waist, he pulled her close and kissed her. "I won't be too long."

"You better not be," she said, smiling.

He opened the door and said, "Happy Christmas!"

"Happy Christmas!" called the boy.

"Happy Christmas," said Deborah laughing. "Now get goin' so you can get back."

He closed the door behind him and headed back into the woods.

Deborah busied herself at the hearth for a while and, when she reached a stopping point, turned to the boy. "Matthew, should we decorate?"

"Yeah!"

"Alright. Here, take some a' this pine, an' put it on the windowsill."

She hung trailing pine from the mantel and over the door and windows. Then, while she was draping it from the loft in long swaths they heard a rifle shot. It sounded like it was from the next hill, and it echoed down the valley in a weakening rumble.

"I think Pa's just got us our venison, Matthew."

"Yeah!"

She finished hanging the garland and went back to the hearth. An hour later, she was standing by the window looking for him.

"Is Pa comin' home soon?"

"He'll be here soon, honey."

There was no sign of him when the pies were finished, and now she was beginning to worry. At first she thought maybe he stopped to dress the deer in the woods.

"That makes sense," she thought. "It would be lighter to drag then." But by the time it grew to be midday, she decided she had to go and look for him. She bundled her child and took the path to her nearest neighbor's house.

"Where are we goin', Ma?"

"It's Christmas. We're goin' t' go visitin' a little while."

"But what about Pa and the venison?"

"He'll be there when we get back.

Fleming's neighbors, the Neals and the McRays, lived close to one another. They were celebrating at the McRays' home. Deborah knocked on the door, which was answered by Susan McRay. Deborah quickly asked her and Constance Neal to take Matthew up into the loft to play with their children. The women were confused but did as they were asked. When left alone with Leonard McRay and Michael Neal, Deborah explained the situation.

"I'm really gettin' worried," she said.

"Don't worry, we'll find 'im," said Michael. "You stay here and get warm by the fire."

"Are you sure?"

"Sure, we'll find 'im," said Leonard. "We heard that shot this mornin', too. It didn't sound like he was that far off."

"Yeah," added Michael, "we oughta be able t' track 'im pretty easy."

"Thank you," she said. "I'm sorry to interrupt your holiday."

"Don't give it a second thought," said McRay.

Deborah went up into the loft as the men ventured out into the snowy afternoon. Walking to the next hill, they began searching.

"There," said Neal.

He pointed up ahead in the snow where there were fading footprints. They followed them a short distance and saw the tracks wound far along the ridge and then dropped into the hollow directly beneath them.

"We can save some time here," said Neal as he started toward the sheer embankment.

"I ain't goin' down there, Michael."

"No? Why? It's just down there a ways," said Neal.

"Yeah. Over snow an' ice," said McRay. "Andrew had enough sense t' go around an' you should too."

"Well, we shouldn't split up."

"No, we shouldn't," McRay agreed, "an' I ain't goin' that way. He's in no trouble that another ten minutes is goin' t' make any difference. Now let's get movin'."

The men went the long way around the hill and were just getting back to the spot beneath where they had been.

"Ah, my God," said McRay suddenly.

"What?"

"Up ahead."

Looking up, Neal saw the snow at the base of the hill was covered in a garish red stain. Beneath a fresh dusting they could see their friend. As they approached, it was obvious he'd been scalped. When they rolled him over, they saw a huge exit wound on his chest. He'd been shot in the back. There was no life in him.

"Well, at least it looks like it was quick for him," said Neal.

"Yeah," agreed McRay. "Probably never felt it."

The men picked up their friend and began the grim task of carrying him back to his home for burial. They used Fleming's own tools to complete the job, then started back to McRay's.

After walking for some time in silence, Michael looked up at McRay and asked, "How're we gonna tell Deborah?"

CHAPTER 9

April 1779

FORT BRADY

The sun hung low to the river and silhouetted Brady. He leaned against the trunk of the old walnut tree with one foot propped behind him and his rifle rested across his knee. He was lost in thought.

The night before, little Hannah looked up at him quizzically.

"Pa?" she asked.

"Yeah, darlin'?"

"How come ev'rybody's fightin'?"

"What do ya mean? Is yer sisters at it again?" he said, smiling.

"No."

"Well, what then?" he asked.

Liberty sat in his lap, playfully batting at his cheek.

"Well," continued Hannah, "I keep hearin' ev'rybody talkin' about raids an' people gettin' killed, like James did. How come they's fightin'?"

Brady looked at Mary. He hadn't expected this. "How do you explain a war to a four-year-old?" he thought.

He considered for a moment and took her by the hand.

"Well, darlin', it's like this. We're buildin' a new land."

"How, Pa? The land is here already, ain't it?"

"To be sure, darlin'," he answered. "I don't mean the actual land. I mean we're buildin' a new country. Ya see, there's them that wants t' tell us how we can live, an' what we can do and what we can't. We're fightin' t' build a new country where we can live an' do as *we* see best. We're buildin' a land a' liberty an' freedom."

"For Liberty, Pa? It'll be Liberty's land?"

Brady smiled broadly and gently stroked her cheek. "Yes, darlin'. It will be Liberty's land . . . and *yours*, and mine. It'll be for all of us. We'll *all* be free."

Mary smiled.

. . . Now, as he felt the sun's warmth on his face, he kept hearing Hannah say, ". . . people gettin' killed . . . like James did."

Brady drew in a deep breath. James' death no longer dominated his thoughts, but, when he was alone like this, he couldn't help but dwell on the loss of his son. He kept his thoughts to himself so as not to burden Mary, who was still grieving in her own way.

In his mind, Brady traveled back to before his boy was gone. He could see himself laughing and talking with James as they crunched through the woods. He relived the hunting trips and days at the swimming hole and even saw him take his first steps all over again.

"That was back in the old house at . . .". . . He was jarred from his reverie by a rustling on the riverbank.

Looking up, he saw a whitetail buck picking its way through the brambles. Brady raised his rifle and leveled it at the front quarter of the animal. He pulled the hammer back to full-cock and fired. Through the smoke, he saw the deer wheel and bolt back into the woods.

Brady trotted over to the spot where the deer had stood and inspected the ground for signs of blood. Finding none, his gaze worked its way up the side of an oak tree that had been directly behind the deer.

He soon discovered a neat, round hole on the freshly marred bark. He poked his finger in and felt the hard metal of his rifle ball. He'd missed. Missed at thirty feet!

"Serves me right for not keeping my mind on my work, I guess," said Brady out loud.

The venison would have been a welcome addition to the family table. It had been a long, sparse winter.

He reached into his shot pouch for another ball and found he only had three left. He knew his powder horn was also very light. As he reloaded, he had just enough for the charge and primer. He coaxed the last few grains from the horn and carefully pulled the frizzen back over the pan.

He looked at the glowing western sky and turned from the river to head back in the dusk. He crossed the field and was home in a few minutes. Mary was waiting for him at the gate.

"Heard the shot. What's for supper?" she asked, smiling, seeing he was carrying no game.

"Whatcha cook?" he answered.

She could see he was a bit depressed and tried to cheer him up. "How's sauerkraut soup sound to you?"

"It'll have to do, I guess."

"It's already made."

"Thanks for the confidence, darlin'," he said with a sarcastic smile.

"I made it to go with whatever you brought home. We'll just have it with bread now, that's all."

Brady laughed, shook his head and put his arm around her as they walked into the house.

"I'm scrapin' bottom on powder and shot," he said.

"Salt's almost gone, too," she answered.

"I'll go up to Fort Muncy and get some supplies for us tomorrow."

As they spoke, the children were busy setting the long table for dinner. Mary ladled the soup into pewter bowls and placed them neatly before each seat. Hannah carried the spoons. The fire crackled as everyone took their place, joined hands and gave thanks for their meal.

When dinner was over, Brady went out into the stockade to organize the morning supply trip. From the families staying with them at the fort, he recruited a driver and two guards to ride with the supplies. Peter Smith agreed to go with Brady behind the wagon.

"Why don't you stay and talk a while?" asked Smith.

"No, thanks. We'll be talkin' all day tomorrow," said Brady. "Why don't you get some rest?"

"Nah, I'm not tired. I was just thinkin' a takin' a walk, anyway," said Smith, grabbing his coat.

"Alright. Well, be careful. I'll see ya tomorrow," answered Brady who, with a slap on his friend's shoulder, turned and headed back to his house.

Brady entered and yelled, "I got an idea. Let's make some popcorn."

The kids giggled when Hannah let out a gleeful squeal. Mary smiled and brought down the special jar of popping corn, Brady went to the other side of the room and came sauntering back with his fiddle.

"What's gotten into you tonight?" asked Mary.

"I dunno. Just feel like actin' a-fool, I guess."

"I would have thought your marksmanship would have taken care a' that for the day."

"Oh, Mary, my dear, you know how to hurt a man," he said with a huge grin and a touch of the brogue.

The kids enjoyed the playful sparring. They laughed and nudged each other as they eased the skillet over the coals.

Brady sat down in a chair by the fire and propped his feet up on a stool. He cradled the fiddle in the crook of his arm and began to saw away. The aroma of the popcorn wafted around them, and the friendly crackling was the perfect accompaniment to the chain of jigs that poured from his fiddle.

The kids happily munched the hot popcorn, and Hannah took special pleasure in feeding handfuls to Brady as he played.

Mary mused, "This almost feels like Christmas, don't it?"

Hannah looked up and shouted, "Are we gonna get presents, Pa?"

Brady laughed and said, "Well, I don't think a 'hold in your hand' kind a' present, but if you ask real nice, you might get an even better kind a' present than that."

"What, Pa? What?" she asked, barely able to contain herself.

"Come here an' I'll tell you."

Hannah cocked her head as Brady leaned over and whispered something in her ear. Her face transformed from solid concentration to pure delight as he shared the secret.

"Go on an' ask 'er," Brady prodded.

"Momma? Will you sing us a song an' give us a better than a 'hold in your hand' kind a' present?"

Mary looked at Brady and smiled. "Well, I suppose I *could* sing just one."

"You know the one I wanna hear," said Brady.

"It's been a long time, but I s'pose I could remember it," she said.

Uneaten popcorn rested in the kids' palms as they waited in anticipation. Brady began bowing the strings slowly and mournfully. The melody was the most beautiful thing the children ever heard. That is, until their mother started singing.

The old Irish lullaby was indescribably lovely and haunting at the same time. Mary's lilting voice and the fiddle music seemed to entwine in the air before them. There were many verses.

Mary looked straight at Brady as she sang, and he at her. If not for the flickering firelight, he may not have even seen the small tear that trickled down her cheek as she finished the last verse. He played through the melody once more and the song wound down to its beautiful and melancholy end.

Brady held the bow in place for a moment in the pronounced silence. No one breathed. Then he rested his arm in his lap, and the children jumped up and clapped.

"Do it again, Momma," shouted Hannah.

"No, dear. It's a one-time present. That's what makes it special. B'sides, I think it's time for some Brady children to be gettin' t' bed."

After the usual protests to stay up longer, the kids trundled up the ladder to the loft. Brady laid down his fiddle, and Mary sat in his lap. They didn't speak. They just sat contentedly still in each other's arms and stared into the cheering flames.

Morning arrived just a few short hours after Brady finally fell asleep, but he was up with the dawn and the smell of freshly baked biscuits. Opening his eyes, he saw Mary at the hearth, quietly placing the warm morsels into a hamper.

Brady walked over to Mary and gave her a hug. She smiled and walked outside with him, where the supply party was hitching the wagon and checking their arms. "You boys have any breakfast?" she asked.

"Hot biscuits, boys," said one of the men, who was standing closest to the hamper.

Each man, in turn, came over and took a few.

"Thank ya, ma'am," they said as each received his portion.

"You're welcome fellas. Be safe, now, an' have a good trip."

Brady put his arm tightly around Mary's waist. She looked up at him with a broad, happy smile and he gave her a quick kiss.

"Let's get goin', boys," he said, swinging up onto the cream-colored mare Smith had waiting for him.

The party pushed off into the early morning light. The rising sun at their backs cast long shadows before them that secretly made them feel like giants. Brady asked Smith if he wanted to ride double on his horse, but Smith declined.

"No, I been cooped up all winter," he said. "I need a good limberin' up."

They stayed fifty feet behind the wagon and kept watch. It was only about three miles to Fort Muncy, but the cumbersome wagon was slow on the rutted road that wound over the hills.

Brady and Smith whiled away the time in conversation, and by midmorning they crested the hill near the fort. It was an imposing sight. Walker and his men had done well.

Even now, a detail was adding another row of abatis while riflemen peered over the walls and kept watch over them. Friendly cook smoke curled up from inside. These were men who meant to stay.

Brady and Smith closed the distance to the wagon, and they all arrived together.

Challenged by the pickets as they neared the fort, the men were admitted and drew the wagon to the center of the parade. Brady dismounted and handed his reins to Smith. He saw Captain Walker coming toward him.

"Captain Brady, how have you been?" asked Walker, with his hand extended.

"Pretty fair, Cap'n Walker, an' you?" he answered, shaking hands.

"It's been quite a winter since our journey to Tioga," said Walker. "I've never seen so much snow or felt quite so bitter a wind."

"Yeah, it's been a tough one," agreed Brady. "I see you're still workin' on the defenses."

"Yes, some of the works didn't fare so well through the weather. The outer earthworks compacted. We've just finished raising them an additional foot and a half. Now we're bolstering the abatis."

"Nice work, Captain," said Brady. "I don't think a squirrel could sneak in here without you knowin' it."

"Thank you, Captain," said Walker. "What brings you here today?"

"Well, we're gettin' short on powder an' ammunition. *And*, if you can spare it, we could sure use some flour an' salt too."

"I think we can spare enough to get you through until we're resupplied from Fort Augusta."

"Thank you, kindly, Cap'n," said Brady. "We appreciate it."

"Not at all." Walker turned and called to a man a short distance away. "Sergeant."

"Yessir," he answered.

"See to it these men are well supplied with powder and ammunition, and give them any flour, salt, and other foodstuffs we can spare."

"Yessir."

"We sure appreciate this, Captain," said Brady.

"Nonsense," said Walker. "We're all in this together. We must keep each stronghold viable."

"Well, I'm glad you feel that way, an' I agree," said Brady, "but thanks just the same."

"My pleasure."

Walker paused and said, "Captain Brady, why don't you have your men go with the sergeant while you accompany me to my office? I'd like to discuss some things with you."

"I'd be happy to," answered Brady.

Brady instructed his men to load the supplies. He turned to follow Walker and motioned for Smith to come along. Smith quickly said something to one of the men and handed him the reins to Brady's horse. Then he followed Walker and Brady into a small room on the end of the officer's quarters.

It was sparsely furnished with a roughly hewn bedstead and straw mattress and a campstool against the wall. A campaign chest completed the suite and functioned as a desk, footrest or dining table as the case warranted. Walker pulled two more campstools from beneath his bed, unfolded them and invited the men to sit.

Walker wanted to make sure he and Brady had the chance to share whatever intelligence they had. They compared notes and discussed strategies for their common defense. When the business was complete, they fell into an amiable chat.

Eventually, Brady said he should be getting back. They walked out to the parade and found the supply wagon had gone. Brady was a little surprised his men would leave without him and Smith, but everything seemed quiet on the road that morning, and he wasn't too worried.

Brady mounted his horse and asked Smith again if he wanted to ride but got the same answer. They said goodbye to Walker and started off after the wagon. Once they were on the road, Smith said, "Seems like a nice enough fella."

"Who, Walker?"

"Yeah."

"Yeah, I think he is," said Brady.

They wound up over the hill and passed a burying ground the locals had been using for a few years. The stones overlooked the broad valley in front of Bald Eagle Mountain.

"We should go rabbit huntin' sometime, Pete," blurted Brady, forcing his thoughts from his friends and neighbors who lay beneath the sod.

"That'd be nice," said Smith. "Though I don't know how good I'd keep up with this bum leg."

"You seem to be doin' alright today."

"Yeah, but that's on the road, not through the underbrush."

"Is that still from Robb?" asked Brady.

"Yeah, that dumb bastard really messed me up. That's why I wanna walk on it, to loosen it up as much as I can."

"Oh."

Smith suddenly chuckled and said, "You shoulda seen James pull him off a' me. That was somethin'. Didn't hesitate a bit."

"Yeah, he was a brave boy," replied Brady, the thought of the incident bringing a grin to his face.

Smith continued, "Same as the day they got 'em on my farm. Didn't hesitate. Just ran for his rifle instead of runnin' away like most of 'em done. You'd a' been proud."

"I am proud."

Smith paused. "I'm sorry, John. I don't mean to talk on it. I was just thinkin' a' how much I admired him."

"Don't be sorry. I like hearin' about him, too."

They crested the hill and Smith said, "You know, the wagon

would lose a lot of time following the road down to Wolf run and comin' up the other side. If we take the footpath here, we could probably catch 'em by the time it joins the road again at Muncy Crick. It's quite a bit shorter."

"Let's give 'er a try," agreed Brady.

The men veered to the right and followed the path down a gentle slope. They entered a heavy growth of trees and thickets as they reached the run. Smith suddenly ran the last ten feet to the water's edge, took two quick hops over the rocks, and darted to the left.

"Where are ya goin', Pete?" asked Brady, who was just reaching the run.

Poppop!

Smith spun toward the sound and saw Brady careen off the back of the mare. He ran back to the path and caught Brady's horse as it came galloping toward him.

"Well done, Mr. Smith," said Wallis, emerging from the thickets with a rifle in his hands.

"Well done?... Well done?... I just killed my best friend," yelled Smith.

"Actually, *we* killed your best friend, didn't we?" said Wallis, who turned to Robb and added, "Go get his rifle, and make sure he's dead."

"Yessir, Mr. Wallis," answered Robb.

"You don't know how close I came to not goin' through with this," said Smith.

"Yes, and then you'd still owe him all of that money, and your estate and bounty wouldn't be awaiting you in Canada, would it?" sneered Wallis. "You've gone from destitute to quite well-off in a matter of moments, Mr. Smith. Now, I suggest you complete the plan so you can take advantage of the situation."

Smith looked down at Brady, lying bloodied and twisted in the water. He swung up onto Brady's horse and took off at a gallop toward Fort Brady.

Wallis stepped back off the path and retrieved his own horse, which he'd concealed in the underbrush.

"He ain't movin'," said Robb.

"Give me the rifles, you fool," Wallis barked impatiently as he mounted.

Robb reached up to Wallis who, already holding his own rifle, accepted Brady's and Robb's.

"Well, Mr. Brady," said Wallis, looking down at him, "let's see if your neighbors are as steadfast in the cause without you."

Robb stood gaping up at Wallis, not sure what to do next.

"Get out of here!" snapped Wallis. "Go home, and be quick about it." Wallis wheeled the horse and galloped back up the path.

Rather than run for home as instructed, Robb delayed. He knew Brady wasn't moving, but he wasn't sure he was dead. If there was any chance Brady was conscious, he could have seen Robb when he retrieved his rifle. Not sure what to do next, Robb wandered back up the path a short distance and waited in the brush.

By this time, Smith had continued across Muncy Creek and covered the remaining two hundred yards to Fort Brady.

"Open the gate! Open the gate!" he screamed.

The gates parted, and he saw Mary standing with the supply party. They'd heard the shots. She saw Smith on Brady's bloodstained horse.

"John!" she screamed. "Peter, where's John?"

"In heaven or hell, or on his way to Tioga," said Smith. "Indians ambushed us at Wolf Run. They shot him."

"John!" yelled Mary, who ran through the gate, followed by the men.

Smith collapsed from the horse in a heap on the ground. He rolled on his back and stared up into the April sky. He was overcome with guilt and disbelief that he'd actually listened to Wallis. He looked away when he saw the blood on the side of the horse standing over him.

Forcing himself to his knees and then to his feet, Smith followed the others. He stumbled forlornly over the ground he'd just crossed. As he neared the run, there was a knot in his stomach. It was an odd, sick feeling that made him wonder if he was going to throw up or faint. He approached the party huddled around Mary, who was cradling Brady in her arms.

Seeing Smith arrive was too much for Robb. His mind already worked itself into a frenzy about the possibility of being discovered. He thought his best chance was to establish an alibi.

Robb burst through the underbrush and rushed down the path. Hearing the noise, several of the men leveled their rifles in his direction.

"How is he?" called Robb. "Will he live? I was on the road and heard the shots."

The men lowered their rifles when they saw it was Robb. No one answered, but one man shook his head.

Mary silently held her husband in a last farewell.

Smith approached one of the men in the party and asked, "Eb, is he dead?"

"Yeah," he replied. "We found 'em in the water there b' the rocks. The Indians musta left in a hurry 'cause they didn't scalp 'im or even take his shot pouch or gold watch . . . just his rifle. I'll tell you, this don't look like no random attack. They was waitin' on *him*."

Smith stared down at Brady.

"We know you said go on ahead," the man continued, "but we feel terrible we left Fort Muncy ahead a' you. We shoulda waited."

Smith was crushed. As he listened to the man talk, the voice seemed to drift far away, and his vision became blurry.

"I . . . I didn't want ya t' have t' wait for us," said Smith, woozily.

His knees suddenly went weak, and he collapsed into the man's arms.

"Whoa, now," he said as he caught Smith and held him up.

"He didn't feel nothin', Pete. He took two rounds right between the shoulder blades. Woulda been dead b'fore he ever hit the water."

Smith clung to the man for a moment and then regained control of himself. He patted him on the shoulder and weakly said, "Thanks, Eb."

Mary looked down at her husband. She said tenderly, "You've won darlin'. You've done all you could, an' your dream'll never die. It lives in all of us, an' it always will. This *will* be Liberty's land. . . . Tell James I miss him an' that we'll all be together by an' by."

Mary laid her husband gently back down to the earth. She rose and walked back toward Fort Brady. The group parted and allowed her to pass.

"Will you please bring him home?" she asked no one in particular.

The next morning was overcast. A cold wind blew out of the west, driving slate-gray clouds before it. Word of Brady's assassination had passed quickly through the valley, and, early in the morning, the inhabitants of Fort Brady heard muffled drums in the distance. It was Captain Walker leading a detail of regulars, complete with color guard, from Fort Muncy.

They marched to the gates of Fort Brady and halted, though the drums continued a quiet and mournful dirge. As the guards opened the gates, Mary approached and accepted Captain Walker's condolences.

Cordially he said, "Mrs. Brady, we are all deeply saddened at the loss of your husband. He has been instrumental in preserving this valley for the patriot cause and he will be sorely missed. If we may, we would like to show our gratitude and respect by participating in his services."

"I thank you, Captain, for your attendance an' your words. My husband an' I would be proud to have you participate in his memorial service. In fact, if I may impose upon you, I'd be most grateful if you'd *conduct* the service."

"It would be an honor, ma'am," said Walker.

The detail broke ranks, passed through the gates and entered Brady's home, where his body was laid. They sat in reverent silence as Brady's neighbors and friends eulogized him. When everyone who wanted to speak was through, Walker stood and led the group in prayer.

He concluded the service with an old and familiar hymn. The singing brought tears to the eyes of almost everyone. When it ended there was silence.

Then Walker ordered his men to attention. They lifted Brady's coffin and carried it out of his home, placing it in the back of the very same wagon that carried the supplies the day before. As the crowd emerged, the wagon began a slow and steady procession from the fort.

Fort Brady's residents followed the wagon. Mary and the smaller kids rode in a carriage drawn by Brady's cream-colored mare and driven by Peter Smith. Mary held Liberty in her arms.

Walker split his soldiers evenly before and after the funeral party. The muffled drums accompanied their progress to the little burying ground on the hill overlooking Fort Muncy.

On the way, a grieving friend stopped by the roadside and picked a simple bouquet of wildflowers for Mary. She graciously accepted them and placed them in her lap.

When the procession arrived, they gathered around a freshly dug grave at the top of the hill. The troop waited respectfully in formation while the color guard stood just behind Walker at the head of the grave. Soldiers placed Brady's coffin on two beams laid across the open grave, and the service began.

Walker read passages from the Bible and led the group in reciting the Twenty-third Psalm. It seemed as if he were about to end the proceedings, but then he paused.

"I'm no preacher," he said as the flags snapped in staccato counterpoint to the dark clouds racing above him, "but something keeps coming to mind and I'd be remiss if I didn't mention it. This book teaches there is no greater love a man can have than to lay down his life for others. We've all lost family and friends in this conflict, but I can think of no man who was fighting for more selfless reasons than John Brady.

"I didn't know him well, but I know he wanted to make this earth a better place, and he was doing that by fighting evil and oppression and despotism with his whole heart and being. John Brady has my greatest respect and thankfulness for all he accomplished and all that he was."

Walker looked directly at Mary as he finished speaking, and she returned his look with gratitude and satisfaction for his insight and kindness. Walker ordered his troops to fire a volley. The pans flashed a brilliant yellow-orange against the gray landscape and powder smoke blew through the crowd. The drums began again, and the gathering slowly headed back down the hill.

Still holding Liberty, Mary remained still for a moment and then approached the coffin. She tenderly laid the bouquet of wildflowers on top, kissed her fingers and placed them gently down beside the flowers before she turned to leave.

The children followed in her wake, but, suddenly, little Hannah broke ranks and ran back to her father's coffin. Going after her, Mary found she was fumbling in her dress pocket.

"Hannah, dear, what are you doin'?" asked Mary incredulously.

"I have somethin' for Pa, too," she answered earnestly.

"You do?"

"Yeah, here it is."

She wrestled her hand free from the material, and it was closed in a tight fist. She reached up as far as she could to the edge of the coffin and opened her hand, when out fell a little handful of popcorn.

It was the closest Mary came to crying all day. She knelt down, hugged her close and whispered, "I'm sure Pa will like that very much, darlin'. . . . Now let's go home."

CHAPTER 10

April-June 1779

FORT FREELAND

"C'mon, James," called William McKnight to his teenaged son. "It's milkin' time."

James was hard at work at the wood pile, but he and his father drew milking duty that afternoon. He was happy to take a break.

"Comin', Pa," yelled James.

He sank his ax blade into a log and ran to help his father with the buckets.

Fourteen armed guards accompanied them into the pasture.

"Least they didn't wander too far away," said William, as they reached the herd.

The guards fanned out around them while James and William crouched down and started milking.

The afternoon sun felt good on James' back. It was warm and comforting after his hard day's work. He could easily lie down and fall asleep. James filled a few buckets and stood to stretch.

He looked across the field and noticed some of the guards passing the time talking. Others gazed peacefully off into the distance. James stretched his neck from side to side, then knelt down and got back to work.

Suddenly, a crash of musketry ripped across the pasture. Shrill yells came from all directions.

"Raiders!" shouted James.

"Stay down," yelled William, who stood to see what was happening.

James heard the guards fire a few shots in reply.

"They got about half the guard, an' they're closin' in," said William, ducking back down. "Get back t' the fort. "Run!"

James did. He stayed low and darted between the cows. A raider saw him, pulled his tomahawk, and closed in from behind. William lunged out and tackled the pursuer.

Straddling the raider's chest, William got one hand on the tomahawk and the other on his throat. The raider used his free hand to push McKnight off. They jumped to their feet and faced one another.

The raider swung his tomahawk in huge, wicked arcs. The air parted with a whoosh as McKnight ducked out of the way and counter-punched, landing direct hits on the raider's jaw. Staggered, the raider drew his knife with his other hand and renewed the attack.

McKnight saw his only chance was to get in close. He rushed the Indian and knocked him into one of the cows. The frightened animal kicked. The hoof landed squarely on McKnight's thigh and sent him sprawling to the ground.

Before he could recover, the raider sprang, sinking the tomahawk inches into McKnight's temple.

James worked his way to the edge of the herd. He couldn't see any guards. Men in the fort were firing on the raiders, who were scalping their victims and scavenging their weapons.

James thought he saw a chance to escape. An open path lay before him to the nearby woods. He looked back for his father who was nowhere in sight.

Taking a deep breath, James bolted from the herd. A raider saw him and sprinted after. Nearing the woods, James felt him just on his heels.

He bounded into the treeline and realized the Indian was no longer behind him. Turning, James saw him lying, dead, about fifteen yards away. He'd been killed by a shot from the fort.

James ran on to the creekbed, out of sight of the enemy, and was back inside the fort in moments.

"Who else made it back?" James asked the guard.

"You're it," he said.

PHILADELPHIA

One early May evening, Joseph Stansbury heard a curious knock at his front door: four slow, measured raps followed by two quick ones. The knock wasn't unfamiliar. It was a code used amongst a select circle of loyalists to identify themselves to one another using the first line of *God Save the King*.

Stansbury owned a glass and china shop. When the war began, he wasn't in favor of independence. By the time the British took Philadelphia in 1777, he was a solid loyalist. He accepted a civil role in General Howe's occupying government.

Known for his wit and humor, Stansbury was a regular at the officers' social gatherings. However, he'd been circumspect enough to be able to stay behind when the British left Philadelphia. He took the patriot oath of allegiance but continued to help the British in every way he could.

Stansbury rose and crossed to the door. Peering through a sidelight, he recognized Samuel Wallis standing on his stoop.

"Mr. Wallis, it's a pleasure, sir," he said, opening the door. "Come in, won't you please?"

"Yes, thank you," Wallis answered.

Wallis knew Stansbury through business, having imported china for him over the years. Wallis always felt superior to the little shopkeeper and it rankled him that Stansbury experienced so meteoric a rise in the loyalist universe. Their standing, in official British eyes, was vastly far apart.

The men were aware of one another's political leanings, but Wallis decided to remain on the periphery of Stansbury's work in the cause. He was determined to make a bigger impact on his own. Recently, however, Wallis reconsidered. . . .

His attempts to raise his profile with the British hadn't gotten him very far. Despite his role in saving the Tory-Indian army from Hartley's invasion last summer and his work to ignite a grassroots counter-revolution, he remained on the outside of official British circles.

Now, he thought, why *not* use Stansbury's position and influence to better his own? He wouldn't think twice about it in the business world, and this certainly should be no different.

Stansbury was genuinely pleased to see Wallis. He helped him off with his cloak and invited him to have a seat.

"There's still a bit of a chill in the evenings isn't there?" queried Stansbury.

"Yes. Yes, there is."

"Would you care for a drink, Mr. Wallis? I have a most delightful sherry to offer you."

"That sounds very agreeable, thank you."

Wallis observed his host scurry about the little room. Stansbury produced two small matching glasses and an impressive crystal decanter filled with a rich crimson liquid. Obviously, they were an example of the best his shop had to offer. The vessels caught the flickering candlelight.

Holding the empty glasses in one hand, Stansbury poured two generous drafts and offered one to Wallis. Wallis accepted it with a nod and a forced smile. Retiring to a nearby chair, Stansbury continued to exchange pleasantries.

"Well, Mr. Wallis, how *have* you been?"

"Just fine, thank you," he answered before sampling the sherry.

"You look well," said Stansbury. "Well, indeed."

"Thank you," said Wallis.

"How has your business been faring?"

"Business is fine, thank you."

"And your home on the frontier?" asked Stansbury. "How very enchanting that must be?"

"It's very nice, yes," said Wallis. "But perhaps I could come to the point of why I'm here."

"Oh, why certainly. Please proceed," said Stansbury.

"Well, Joseph, through our mutual friends I believe we are both well aware of one another's *political activities?*"

"Yes, quite so," said Stansbury. "I've been hoping for some time to coordinate some *activities* with you, but you always seem to be so busy with your business while in town. And, then, of course you spend so much time at your home on the frontier that it has been quite difficult . . . "

"Yes. Yes, I understand," Wallis interrupted. "I *understand* you have access to the very top of the British command in New York."

"Why, yes," said Stansbury, matter-of-factly. "What have you got in mind?"

"Solely through my own effort," said Wallis, "I have had many important successes in our cause."

"Yes, I'm aware of that," said Stansbury, genuinely. "Most impressive work."

"I believe the time has come for me to work more closely with official channels," continued Wallis, "and, in so doing, could make even greater contributions."

"Splendid," rejoiced Stansbury.

"Therefore," said Wallis, "I have come to officially offer my services to General Clinton. Can you get that message to him?"

"I most certainly can, Mr. Wallis. And, allow me to say I find this most heartening indeed. This is a great day for our cause."

"Indeed," agreed Wallis. "Of course, I would expect that my service, in the face of great personal risk, would be met with *liberal* acknowledgments."

"I suspect that could be the case," said Stansbury. "I will certainly inquire about it."

Wallis sat for a moment in quiet satisfaction and then suddenly drained his glass.

"Thank you, Joseph, for your hospitality," he said, rising. "I'll look forward to your reply. You know how to contact me."

"Oh . . . yes. Thank you for stopping by," said Stansbury as he retrieved Wallis' cloak and helped him on with it. "This is a great day, a great day indeed."

"Good evening, Joseph."

"Yes. Yes, good evening, Mr. Wallis."

FORT BRADY

Mary spent the first days after the funeral in quiet disbelief. She went about her daily chores and took care of the children just as she'd always done. In many ways it was as if he was away hunting or on another campaign, and her mind could wander into that safe place of normalcy and routine.

The difference this time was that friends and neighbors kept stopping by to share condolences. It was these well-intentioned reminders of reality that made her eventually come to grips with the fact she would never hold her husband again. She soon realized there was no real need for her to remain on the frontier.

With John and James gone, Mary Brady decided to take her children and move to her parents' home in the Cumberland Valley, in the southern part of the state. After packing her belongings and bidding goodbye to the others at Fort Brady, they were off.

The first night along the way, they stayed at Fort Boone and visited with their old friends. The Boones were heartbroken. They sat with Mary and talked late into the night, comforting one another as best they could. The next morning, Hawkins kissed Mary on the cheek, and with tears in his eyes said, "He was the best man I ever knew, an' I'll miss 'im terrible."

Hawkins, Jane and Mary stood hugging one another for a long time. Finally, Mary pulled away, squeezed each of the Boones by the arm, then turned and left.

Soon, Mary and the children were passing their old farm across the river from Derr's. It was excruciating to see this place of happier times. Yet, in some way it was also comforting. Images of the family seated at the long dinner table crowded in on her, and she smiled through her tears.

By late afternoon they'd reached Northumberland and crossed the river to Sunbury. They spent that night with friends, too.

Welcomed by the Hunters, they ate a solemn meal, and the children went off to bed. Mary stayed up visiting with Colonel and Mrs. Hunter. The next morning, after breakfast, Colonel Hunter took her gently by the arm and said, "Mary, I'd like to send a man to accompany you."

"No, thank you Col'nel," she replied. "You need ev'ry man here. I know that as good as anyone. Don't worry after us."

"You're a remarkable woman, Mary," said Hunter. "This is a dangerous country, but I know you'll be fine. You're every bit as brave as John, and I'm proud to have known you both."

Mary and the kids boarded a batteau and crossed the river. As they reached the far shore they disembarked and, without a backward glance, turned south.

★　★　★　★　★

WHITE DEER VALLEY

"Raiders, Colonel," said Sergeant Christian Van Gundy, looking up from the tracks they discovered on the White Deer path.

"Recent?" asked Kelly.

"Within a day, I'd say."

"How many?"

"Pret-near forty or fifty, anyhow."

"We got t' warn Mr. and Mrs. Sample," said Kelly. "They're up here all alone."

"You'd think they'd a' left when ev'ryone else did," said Van Gundy.

"Well, they're old," responded Kelly. "Prob'ly pretty rough on 'em t' be on the move."

"Why don't I take a squad an' go get 'em?" suggested Van Gundy.

"That's just what I was thinkin'. Pick your men. We'll meet you back down by Derr's."

"Yessir, Colonel."

The rescue party arrived that evening and Van Gundy knocked on the door. It was opened by a white-haired man carrying a shotgun, with his wife tucked in behind him.

"Mr. and Mrs. Sample . . . good evenin' folks. I'm Sergeant Van Gundy. We're part a' Col'nel Kelly's outfit an' we come to take you off from here."

"Well, I don't know . . ." said the old man.

"Where ya plan on takin' us?" asked Mrs. Sample.

"Anywhere's you want. We can get you to any friends or family you might have south a' here, or we can take you to Fort Augusta if you want."

The old man studied for a while and Van Gundy added, "It really ain't safe up here all alone, you know. All your neighbors is left and there's been raids all around."

"I s'pose that'd be all for the best, Sergeant," said Sample. "We'll go with ya, an' thanks for comin'."

"Fine," said Van Gundy. "We'll leave at first light. Too late to start now. Now let's see to securin' the premises."

Van Gundy ordered his detail to fill every container in the house with water and carry it up into the loft. The men began running back and forth to the creek. When that was done, Van Gundy turned his attention to the door.

"Set that heavy chest up against there and pile the rest o' the furniture on it," he ordered. "Get them winda shutters closed, too."

Just after nightfall, when everything was secured to his satisfaction, the men sat down and waited.

"Do ya expect a raid tonight, Sergeant?" asked Mr. Sample.

"Can't tell. There've been some around here lately an' I sure ain't takin' no chances there won't be."

"Rrrr . . . ruh ruh ruh . . . ruh ruh."

"You got a dog, Mr. Sample?" asked Van Gundy.

"No, we ain't."

The barking continued and something was rubbing against the door.

"You think that's Indians?" asked Mrs. Sample.

"We ain't gonna test an' see," replied Van Gundy. "If it is, they been watchin' us since before dark and they know we're in here. Just ignore it."

The barking soon ceased.

"We oughta try an' get some sleep," said Van Gundy. "We'll keep two awake at all times and switch ev'ry three hours. I'll stand the middle watch by myself."

With two men picked for the first watch, the Samples, Van Gundy and the others fell asleep. Just after midnight, Van Gundy was awoken for his shift.

He stared across the room . . . his mind working.

"They could just be waitin' until we're asleep t' surprise us," thought Van Gundy. "If I lit a fire, they'd see the smoke an' know they won't catch us unawares."

He stood and walked to the wood box. When he got the fire going, Van Gundy stepped to the window, carefully opened the shutter, and looked across the fields. The smoke curled up into the moonlit sky.

In the pale blue light, Van Gundy saw a line of warriors step from the treeline. He saw the same thing in the other direction and again at the window on the other side of the house.

"Ev'rybody up!" he shouted. "We got comp'ny."

The men scrambled to their feet, gathered their weapons and deployed around the house. Mr. Sample manned one of the windows with his shotgun while his wife huddled on the floor next to the hearth for safety.

"Look here, Sarge," called Tietze.

Van Gundy ran to the man's position and looked out the window. He saw four raiders shouldering a log and running headlong toward the door. The defenders opened fire and wounded two of them.

The others staggered under the weight of the log, and it dropped into the door with a thud that made the house shudder. The Indians jumped to their feet and retreated while the settlers fired out the windows after them.

At the same time, a lone raider stole behind the house and set it on fire. Through heavy smoke, Van Gundy climbed into the loft and broke through the roof. Using the water stowed there earlier, he climbed out and fought the fire.

Backlit against the pale sky, Van Gundy was a perfect target. Shots whistled past him from every direction, but he quenched the fire and headed back for the hole in the roof. As he knelt, a shot hit the stone chimney and ricocheted along the roofline, striking him in the leg just below the knee. He dove through the hole and into the loft.

Van Gundy peeled down his stocking and examined his leg. The ball hadn't broken the skin, but he was left with a huge, swollen welt. Satisfied it wasn't serious, Van Gundy stood and took his place with the others.

Accurate rifle fire kept the Indians at a distance through the rest of the night. By daylight, there were varying opinions on whether to stay in the house and continue to fight or to make a run for it. Van Gundy decided to put it to a vote. As they stood at the windows, Van Gundy asked, "All for makin' a run for it?"

"Aye."

"Aye."

"Aye."

"Nay."

"Aye."

"Nay."

"Aye."

"Alright. The 'Ayes' have it," said Van Gundy. "We run for it. Vandyke, help me get to the door," he ordered.

They pulled the furniture away and opened the door to find a dead raider lying directly in front of it. Van Gundy grabbed his rifle, and Vandyke took his powder horn. Yells filled the air, and they looked up to see the Indians attacking from across the misty field. Everyone in the house scattered.

Van Gundy made for the creekbank and called for the old couple to come with him, but they followed some of the other men. Van Gundy reached the bank and slid over the edge without being followed. He looked across the creek, trying to decide what to do next.

Peering back over the edge of the bank, he saw the old couple had been killed and scalped. His men spread in all directions. Van Gundy decided to try to make it back to Kelly's militia on his own. With his two rifles primed and ready, he crossed the creek and set off through the forest.

Van Gundy avoided the main path and went miles out of his way to keep clear of the Indians. He came out at Derr's that afternoon and made his report to Kelly.

★ ★ ★ ★ ★

FORT AUGUSTA

"Thank you, Captain," said Hunter as Boone entered with the post. "Welcome back,"

"Yer welcome, Col'nel," said Boone.

Hunter opened the sealed papers.

"It must be important," he said. "This is from General Washington himself."

Boone stood quietly while Hunter read the orders. Then, Hunter looked up and said, "Since Hartley's raid provided some relief last fall," said Hunter, "the general's decided to mount an all-out campaign against the Iroquois and finally push them back from the frontier. General Sullivan will organize and lead the campaign.

"Sullivan will remain in Easton where the troops assigned to the expedition will join him. Then he'll march to Wyoming. Once he's supplied and organized, he'll head upriver and meet up with even more troops from Cherry Valley in New York State."

"This sounds big," said Boone.

"And, listen to this," said Hunter. "Before that can happen, we need to get the supplies to Wyoming. They're using Fort Augusta as the main supply depot for the expedition. We're ordered to organize men here for the *boat service*. They'll build batteaux and shuttle the supplies to Wyoming so they're waiting there for Sullivan's arrival."

"What men are we gonna organize?" asked Boone. "There ain't hardly nobody here."

"There's going to be fewer," said Hunter. "The remnants of Hartley's regiment have been ordered to join Sullivan."

"What? That means Forts Muncy an' Jenkins will be abandoned," said Boone. "There ain't no one t' take their place."

"I'll base Kelly's Rangers at Bosley's Mills," said Hunter. "At least we'll have that."

"Yeah, an' Fort Freeland an' my place," said Boone. "But that ain't much t' hold the valley."

"That's true," said Hunter. "But, I think it'll be enough. I'll still have thirty men here to hold the fort after Hartley's men leave, and if the campaign draws the enemy's attention from the valley, this might be just the remedy we need."

★ ★ ★ ★ ★

PHILADELPHIA

Wallis couldn't believe his good fortune.

"Clinton should pay me well for this," he thought after another visit to Stansbury's. "Council President Reed shares Washington's strategy with me *and* asks me to provide a map Sullivan can use to plan his attack. Not only have I warned Clinton of the plot, I've already sabotaged his enemy's campaign."

He chuckled out loud and walked down the street toward his office.

Stansbury closed the door behind Wallis and sat down to write to Clinton.

> "*. . . Mr. Wallis is a gentleman of large estate in this province and better acquainted with the Indian country than almost any other person. As such, he was applied to by the council to furnish a drawing of the country and to assist them in their plan of the Indian expedition. To have refused would have exposed him to sufferings.*
>
> *His drawing was laid by Reed before Washington and the expedition formed on it. He leads them by it to 100 miles southwest of Tioga. His corrected copy of this drawing will be ready by return of your next communication. As it will be large it will require some address to get it through . . .*"

CHAPTER 11

Early July 1779

OUTSIDE FORT MUNCY

Covenhoven slipped out of the tree line and entered the thigh-high corn. He was just three hundred yards from the fort but was sure enemy scouts were close. He lowered himself to the ground to make the last part of the trip on his belly.

The first glow of light washed over the Muncy Hills and the ground between the furrows was wet with dew. Covenhoven slogged along as quietly as he could. He neared the far end of the field and paused just inside the edge of the corn.

He was a hundred yards from the gate. Through the remaining stalks, he could see the outline of the guard on the wall against the lightening sky.

Covenhoven raised his cupped hands to his mouth and blew into the small opening at his thumbs. "Oooh . . . oooh . . . oooh, oooh," he whistled, creating the perfect imitation of a mourning dove.

Crack!

A shot pierced the morning stillness, and the rifle ball bit into the ground within feet of where he lay.

"Hold yer fire, ya damned fool!" he shouted.

"Who goes there?" demanded a voice from the fort.

"It's Covenhoven. Who the hell do ya think it is?"

"You used the wrong signal. We changed it yesterday."

"Well how in the hell d'ya expect *me* to know that?. . . Woods, is that you?"

"Yeah."

"Well, open the damned gate b'fore I get scalped out here."

"On the gate," shouted Woods, "one comin' in."

Covenhoven heard the log being removed. He jumped up, sprinted the final distance and slipped through the gates just as they opened. Behind him, the cornfield was still.

"Little jumpy ain't ya, Bob?" asked one of the guards.

"Ast Woods up there who's jumpy. Hepburn up yet?"

"Should be."

"Thanks," said Covenhoven as he strode off toward the officer's quarters, wiping mud from his clothes.

Hepburn was just reaching for the doorlatch when someone knocked from the other side. He pulled it open, and Covenhoven filled the doorframe.

"Mornin' Bill," said Covenhoven.

"Mornin' Bob," Hepburn answered. "I just heard a shot outside and then some yellin', but I couldn't make out what was goin' on. What happened?"

"Oh. Woods got excited and thought he was gonna get scalped from clear over on the edge of the cornfield."

"Damned fool," said Hepburn.

"Funny. That's what I said."

"So, Bob, what'd ya find out?" asked Hepburn. "Was it true?"

"Yeah, it's true," said Covenhoven. "I went up the Lycoming clean to the far side of Laurel Hill. From there I could see into the valley, just where the crick makes that big bend to the south."

"Yeah?"

"Well, there was a mess of 'em just layin' in there. Had to be a hundred an' twenty warriors, at least, along with about half as many rangers in those Tory green uniforms Butler's men wears."

"Shit. I knew it."

"Yeah, an' that ain't all," Covenhoven continued. "There was ten or twelve regulars with 'em. I could see their damned red coats standin' out against the rest of 'em, just as plain as day. They had a couple a' Hessian aides with 'em, too. . . Oh, and the Indians also had some a' their women with 'em."

"That ain't just a raidin' party. That's a campaign," said Hepburn.

"All told, there's gotta be two hundred of 'em coming right for us. I don't see how we can hold the fort with just these few settlers," said Covenhoven.

"I know," agreed Hepburn. "I hoped the locals would be enough to hold the fort after Hartley's men left, but there ain't no way we can stand up to a major attack. How far behind ya are they?"

"I dunno. . . A day or two, maybe."

"Let's get organized," said Hepburn. "We'll clear the valley an' head down to Fort Augusta."

"Another big runaway, huh?" asked Covenhoven.

"Nah. Ain't as many of us as last year. This'll be a little runaway," said Hepburn. "I don't see what else we can do. We'll gather the folks as we move downriver and send runners to warn those back up the cricks. That way we can keep movin' an' get down to Fort Augusta as quick as possible."

"Sounds right," said Covenhoven as he turned to go.

"By the way, Bob," said Hepburn, stopping him before he could get out the door.

"Yeah?"

"Thanks for goin' to check for me. With that many out there you musta had some close calls."

"Real close . . . I'll go get things movin'," he said as he turned and stepped outside.

By early afternoon the population was already slipping into the river, leaving Fort Muncy abandoned. Like the previous summer, the men kept guard on the shore while the women and children floated on the current.

The refugees kept a nervous watch as they passed the Muncy Hills and the heavily-wooded Black Hole Valley. Further south, they warned the settlements they passed on the way and sent a runner up Warrior Run to warn Fort Freeland. They continued through the night and finally reached Fort Augusta the next morning.

This time, not everyone left. Fort Freeland's settlers decided to stay put. So did Hawkins Boone, holed up in his fort at the mouth of Muddy Run.

It had been a tough month of raids, but when Hepburn told Hunter the enemy was approaching in force, Hunter knew it was time to get some help.

Fort Augusta, 23 July, 1779
Colonel Matthew Smith

> *Dear Sir, we have really distressing times at present, occasioned by the late depredations committed by the savages on our defenseless frontiers.*
>
> *On the 3rd, they killed three men, & took two prisoners at Lycoming. On the 8th, they burned the Widow Smith's mills & killed one man. On the 17th, they killed two men and took three prisoners from Fort Brady. The same day they burned Starrets Mills & all the principle houses in Muncy Township. On the 20th, they killed three men at Freeland's Fort and took two prisoners.*
>
> *The enemy sticking so close after the continental troops marched to Wyoming has intimidated the people so much they are really on the eve of deserting the county entirely. There is no prospect of any assistance, or for the people on the frontiers to get their harvests put up. I thought the army marching to Wyoming would draw the attention of the savages from us, but I think it never was worse than at present.*
>
> *Without reinforcements being sent from some of our neighboring counties soon, it's not probable the little forts we have at Freeland's and Boone's can stand. I suppose I've*

never seen the people of this county behave so spirited than they do at present, being reduced to so few.

I have just arrived after being on a scout along Muncy Hill & we made a great discovery where the savages had been along the frontiers & taken off a number of horses. We are scarce of ammunition, especially lead, of which there is none.

I am yr Most humble servt,
Col. Sam'l Hunter

★　★　★　★　★

LYCOMING VALLEY

The Hessian wasn't used to this kind of terrain. The path along the creek forced him to scramble over boulders and climb steep hillsides, his sword rattling in its scabbard and his boots slipping with every step. It was bad enough marching with the army through this wilderness, but heading out on a covert mission by himself didn't even allow the comfort of an evening fire. His feet ached and sweat streamed down his face as his thoughts returned to the Rhine.

Life there, when he'd been plain Hans Zeiler, had been austere, but at least he was with his family. He hadn't even gotten to say goodbye to them after the press-gang grabbed him in town that day.

He was told he was being given the honor of fighting for the Landgrave of Hesse-Cassel and that he was now a member of the Hessian army. He found himself in training the next day.

He'd done well in the army, despite the circumstances of his *enlistment*, and he was made a junior officer. Then, he was on a ship bound for America to fight for a cause in which he had no part. He proved himself in battle and was eventually assigned to a British officer at Fort Niagara.

Things there were actually rather comfortable, but now they were back on campaign. The hodge-podge collection of Indians,

Tories and British attacked the trail with relish. For Hans, the contrast of his enthusiasm for this raid was as striking as his powder-blue uniform was to those of his allies.

Then things took another turn. His commanding officer chose him to get a message through to some Yankee traitor on the Susquehanna.

"This is highly classified information," said the officer. "We can't risk writing it down. You must memorize it exactly."

Hans nodded.

"Find the gentleman from Philadelphia," the officer continued. "He's our man. He'll be at the estate on the West Branch."

"Eshtate?" questioned Hans.

"Estate. He lives in a mansion . . . a big fine house. It's the only one, so you'll have no trouble finding it. Go to the door and knock like this: tap, tap, tap, tap . . . . tap, tap. Then deliver the message precisely as it was given you."

That was two days ago. Now Hans was within a few miles of the mouth of the creek, and he grew more concerned. He'd be travelling through enemy country dressed in full uniform.

"Don't remove it and you can't be hanged as a spy," they said.

He began to catch glimpses of the valley ahead. He was told to get to the river, turn left and follow it until he found the estate.

Hans noticed movement on the path ahead. He darted into the underbrush and waited until he saw it was a small Indian scouting party. Here was his chance to get some better directions.

Hans stepped out onto the path as the Indians neared. He didn't speak their language, and his English wasn't all that sturdy either.

"Hello," he called raising his hand.

The Indians didn't look surprised to see him.

"Why you hide, blue coat?" asked one of the raiders. "We see you stumbling down the path a long time ago."

Hans grinned uneasily and said, "Oh. I didn't zee you. I zaw only people moving and I dink I hide."

"Where you go?" asked the raider.

"I have message for yahnkee in big house. I go left on river, yah?"

The raider paused, then turned to his party and discussed this for a moment in his native language. He turned back and said, "Which big house you go?"

This floored Hans. He'd been told there was only one.

"To eshtate. Big, fine house."

The Indian turned back and discussed the situation with the other raiders. One pointed downstream but two others shook their heads and gestured in the other direction.

"Dhey say turn left on river to find house," offered Hans helpfully.

The Indian turned back to Hans and considered for a moment.

"Two big houses. One this way," he said pointing downriver toward Wallis', "and one this," he said pointing upstream. "They say you turn left on river. First must be *on* river."

Hans now seemed hopelessly confused. He was asking directions in his second language from a man who was answering in *his* second language. Hans hadn't followed the logic.

The Indian saw the predicament.

"Blue coat, look," he said as he knelt. "We here." He jabbed at the dirt with his forefinger.

"You go down crick," he said while tracing with his finger, "and get *on* river." He swept his finger to indicate a right turn up the West Branch. "Then, turn left *on* river at island," he concluded. "We just come from there. You'll find canoe hidden in the brush on the riverbank. Cross the river and follow *that* crick. Big house there."

Hans stood staring at the map for a moment and then slowly nodded. After all, he'd never been to this valley in his life. His allies knew every inch of it.

"Yah," he said. "Yah, danke," he smiled as the Indian stood.

Eyebrows raised, the Indian nodded his head as if to ask if Hans was now sure of himself. Hans nodded back confidently and smiled.

"Good luck blue coat," said the Indian as he walked past Hans, followed by the others.

"Yah. Goot luck, too," he answered pleasantly.

Hans' heart was lighter. The path was smoother ahead and now he had an idea of where he was going. Following his directions, he got to the river and turned upstream. A few miles brought him to a split in the river as the channels wound around both sides of an island. Working his way along the riverbank, he found the canoe, just as his guide had said.

Hans pulled the canoe to the water's edge and placed one foot in the bottom. As he pushed off, his other foot stuck solidly in the muddy bank and nearly pulled off his boot. He jerked at his foot and the release of the suction pitched him forward. He landed face down in the canoe as it drifted into the current.

Hans righted himself and chuckled at his nautical prowess. He picked up the paddle and crossed the river on the downstream side of the island. He got out of the vessel, a bit more gracefully than he'd entered it, and pulled it up the bank.

A quick glance downstream assured Hans he hadn't passed the creek he was told to follow. He headed upstream and found it just ahead. "Turn left," he said to himself as he reached the creek.

The path wasn't too taxing, but Hans was tired. Every root and stone grabbed at his feet and every foot of elevation weighed on him. In about three miles, he came to a clearing. The tree branches gave way and revealed a home that was larger than any he'd seen on the frontier.

Exhausted, Hans decided to refresh himself before delivering the message. He knelt by the stream and took great handfuls of water and drank. Then, he scooped them over his head and washed the sweat from his face and hair. While he did so, Hans didn't realize he was being watched from inside the house.

The Foresters hadn't gotten the message about Fort Muncy's evacuation, but a ranger scouting party had just passed through and advised them to head downriver. As his wife packed some valuables, Mr. Forester kept watch out the windows. The last thing he expected to see was a lone Hessian soldier come clattering through the woods to stop and wash in the stream at his doorstep.

"Clara, someone's out here. See 'im there b' the crick?"

Forester's wife came to the window.

Time and circumstances had rendered the older couple overcautious and, perhaps, a bit eccentric.

"He's a soldier," gasped Clara.

"He's a *Hessian!*" answered Forester. "I heard about them fancy blue uniforms. But, what in the hell is he doin' here alone?"

"What are ya goin' t' do?" asked Clara.

"I ain't lettin' 'im come in here t' kill us. That's fer damn sure. Go on in the other room, now."

Clara did as she was asked while Forester quietly opened the window and pointed his rifle toward Hans.

Hans thought he heard a sound behind him and turned to greet whoever was coming from the house. But, when he turned, he didn't see anyone coming out. Then he noticed the rifle barrel pointing out an upstairs window.

He called, good naturedly, to the man in the window.

"Hey, Yahnkee. I come . . ." Hans saw a streak of flame leap from the rifle barrel. He careened backward and slid down the creekbank to the water's edge. Then he felt the horrible stabbing pain just below his breastbone.

The cold springwater lapped at his head. Moments later, he felt no more pain, just the warmth that oozed out of him. He looked up through the canopy of trees into the clear blue sky, and . . .

"What happened?" called Clara.

"I got 'im."

"He's dead?" she asked.

"He ain't movin'."

"What do we do now?" she asked, re-entering the room.

"Well, we sure as hell can't leave 'im there," he answered. "We'd be marked. We couldn't ever come back. . . . We need t' bury 'im."

"But if we bury 'im anywhere nearby, they'll notice the fresh dug grave," she said.

The couple stood in silence and tried to decide what to do.

"I got an idea," said Forester, suddenly. "Here, hold my rifle."

He went downstairs and left the house. Clara watched out the window as her husband walked to the creek, grabbed Hans by the arms and dragged him toward the house. Once inside, he closed the door and caught his breath.

Mrs. Forester had come downstairs, and the couple carefully checked Hans' pockets for any clue as to what he was doing there. Finding none, Forester looked up at his wife.

"Clara, open the cellar door."

Forester again grabbed Hans by the arms and started pulling him downstairs. Hans' boots beat out a dirge as they fell from one tread to the next. Forester reached the bottom of the stairs and dragged him into a small cold-storage room on the edge of the main cellar.

"Why are you bringin' him down here?" asked Clara.

"Can you think of a better place? We can knock out the masonry around the doorframe and seal up the wall so no one'll ever know the diff'rence."

"But he'll always be here in the house."

"And he'll never be *found*," he answered.

After a moment of anguished silence she said, "I guess you're right."

Forester spent the rest of the day removing stone from a fence near the house and carefully working it into the doorway of the room in his basement. When there was just enough of an opening left to slide through, he brought his wife down for a brief but proper burial service.

In the dim candlelight, she saw he'd respectfully laid Hans in the center of the little room with all of his belongings around him. Forester read from the Bible, commended Hans' soul to the Lord, and bade him rest in peace. They exited the burial chamber, and he covered the opening.

When the last of the stones was mortared in place, Forester leaned his forehead against the hard, cool, seamless wall and said a silent prayer. Then he turned and slowly ascended back into the world of the living.

CHAPTER 12

Late July 1779

FORT FREELAND

James Watts heard a low, distant rumble. . . Then, he heard another.

He couldn't stop thinking about how the war caught up with Fort Freeland this year. He thought about the milking party being attacked in the spring. He thought about everyone's decision to stay, earlier this month, when the runner came saying Fort Muncy was evacuated and an enemy army was on the way. And, he thought about how, just a week ago, they'd lost three more neighbors in another ambush.

James relived that attack many times in the past week. This time, it was as if he somehow saw it all unfold from above. He saw himself and the others working in the fields just outside the fort. He saw the raiders lurking behind every tree and pressed into each small undulation of the earth.

. . . He heard another rumble. This time it was louder.

From his vantage point, he looked beyond the Indians and saw an army of British regulars drawn up in line of battle surrounding the fort.

On a nearby hill, powder smoke rose above an artillery battery. He saw flashes of red and shining brass as soldiers manned the guns with brutal precision. He watched in horrified admiration as the entire line swabbed the barrels, placed the charges, loaded the shot and rammed them home in unison.

There was no doubt they'd ranged in on their target and he and his friends had but moments to live. The deadly dance concluded as the line of men stepped up to the guns with one arm stretched high above their heads. They held raging fireballs in their hands and lowered them to the guns. The flames reached the fuses and there was a flash of light and a violent explosion . . .

James opened his eyes and heard rain dappling on the roof. It was before dawn and another midsummer thunderstorm was pummeling the valley.

He took in a sharp breath, held it for a moment and realized he'd been dreaming. The patter of the rain was soothing as he regained awareness of his surroundings. Even the sharp cracks of thunder were comforting now as they echoed down the valley.

He exhaled and laid his head back to breathe in the cool, fresh smell of the rain. The storm passed rather quickly. He listened a while longer to the soft dripping from the eaves until the sun rose and he decided to start his day.

Quietly pulling on his shoes, he went outside and walked to the stockade. Looking through a gunloop in the south wall, he tried to find his sheep in the meadow. No luck.

He stepped to the west wall and tried again. Still, no luck. He walked to the gate, said good morning to a guard and explained his sheep had wandered off again.

The guard helped him unsecure the gate and Watts passed through. Glancing to the north, he saw nothing of his sheep along the tree line. He ambled toward the meadow on the south side of the fort, guessing they'd moved down to the creek.

Hearing movement behind him, he looked back over his shoulder and saw Jacob Freeland and John Dough leaving the fort and carrying buckets toward the spring. As he turned back, the sun broke through the clouds, and he caught a glint of metal just ahead in the underbrush. He stared quizzically for a moment to see what was causing it.

Suddenly, he turned to run back to the fort, but it was too late. Crashing through the brush, an Indian sprinted the short distance between them.

"Ambush!!!" cried Watts. "In the fort! Ambush!!"

Warning the garrison while trying to fend off his attacker, Watts resisted but was no match for the younger, stronger raider. Overpowered, Watts was thrown to the ground and watched the sharp blade of a tomahawk gash the air before it burrowed deep into his skull.

The Indian placed his foot on Watts' chest and tugged on the handle, wresting it from its grisly sheath. With his back to the fort, he straddled Watts, reached behind him and pulled the long scalping knife from his belt. Suddenly, he felt a searing pain in the small of his back.

A split second later, he heard the report of the rifle that fired the shot from inside the fort. Leering over his shoulder, he deliberately turned back and finished the work he'd begun. He lifted Watts' scalp over his head and defiantly shook it at the fort before staggering back to cover.

On their way to the spring, Freeland and Dough were just a few feet from the fort when they heard Watts' cries. They turned and ran back through the gate. Freeland stood for a moment in the opening to get a glimpse of the enemy and saw a distant flash.

Dough and the guard were dumbfounded when Freeland fell. They dragged him back from between the gates and got them secured. Dough looked down at the lifeless body of his friend.

"To your posts!" shouted the guard. "We're surrounded!"

Men grabbed rifles and ran to take their places on the wall. There were twenty-six of them. They peered through the gunloops and saw at least one hundred Indians, scores of green-clad Tories and even some regulars facing them.

The shot that hit James Watts' attacker started an eruption of fire on the fort. The garrison replied, but it was never more than a trickle compared to the overwhelming flood of incoming. The settlers had precious little lead. They had to make every shot count.

The women knew the situation. Mary Kirk and Phoebe Vincent calmly gathered every pewter plate and spoon in the fort.

Sitting by the hearth, they pushed aside the breakfast they'd been preparing and placed a pot directly in the hot coals.

One by one, they consigned their prized utensils to the flames, as others in the valley had throughout the war. Wedding presents and family heirlooms disappeared in the silvery, coagulated mass at the bottom of the pot. When their molten stew was ready, Mary reached into her apron pocket, pulled out a bullet mold and laid it on the stone hearth.

Phoebe ladled the precious liquid into the holes on top of the mold, carefully preserving every drop. As the mold cooled, they broke it open and quickly filed any irregularities from the seams back over the pot. The product was perfectly round, shiny rifle balls ready for use by the men outside. Mary shuttled the new ammunition to them while Phoebe continued making more.

Though sporadic, the defensive fire was effective. Any raiders brazen enough to approach the fort were swiftly neutralized by the riflemen.

★ ★ ★ ★ ★

FORT BOONE

Five miles from Fort Freeland, Hawkins Boone was doing his morning chores. It was a peaceful morning along the river after the booming thunderstorm that rolled through the valley at daybreak.

As he knelt milking, he thought he heard still more distant thunder. It was muffled and came from the northeast. He glanced in that direction, but the sky was clear.

Then he heard it again. Keeping very still and listening intently, he heard it more clearly. The morning atmosphere had been playing tricks with the sound. Now, he distinctly heard the sound of battle.

Boone realized it was coming from Fort Freeland. He called, "Sam ... Tom ... com'ere."

Samuel Dougherty had been serving with Boone since the days of the 12th Pennsylvania. They'd always been good friends but had become even closer since Brady died. They both held the rank of captain, but Boone commanded the twenty-one militiamen stationed at his fort.

Captain Thomas Kemplin commanded a small ranger force, which only recently mustered in. He and his command happened to be at Boone's. In fact, a small handful of his men had already reinforced Fort Freeland after the raid there a week earlier. One of them was John Brady's brother, old Sam Brady.

"What's a' matter, Hawk?" called Dougherty, as he came from the mill. Kemplin trailed behind him.

"They're raidin' Freeland. I was out milkin' and heard it."

"Let's go get 'em," replied Dougherty, matter-of-factly.

"Hold up a minute," cautioned Kemplin, "how do we know there's not a party headin' here too? We can't jist up an' leave."

"What d' ya think, Sam?" asked Boone.

"I think there's upwards of fifty women an' children at Freeland we might be able to save."

"You got women and children here too, Sam," said Kemplin. "Not to mention this is the last fort before Northumberland. We can't chance losin' it and lettin' Fort Augusta with no perimeter at all. Why don't you let me take the rangers up to Freeland an' see what we can do while you fellas stay here?"

"Makes sense, what yer sayin'," said Boone, "but this sounds like a pretty big party. With yer small company, you could jist be sacrificin' yerself for no reason. Besides, if we all go in at once'd we can drive 'em, like we done when they attacked our rearguard on Hartley's raid. If we surprise 'em, an' hit 'em hard, they'll run."

Boone paused as Kemplen looked down.

"We can send out some scouts to cover our flanks on the way an' make sure nobody's comin' back this way," said Boone. "Any thoughts?"

"Like I said, let's go get 'em," said Dougherty.

Boone gave him a quick nod of acknowledgment. Glancing back to Kemplin he queried, "Tom?"

Kemplin studied for a moment and said, "Sounds like you're pretty set, Hawk. I don't dispute yer thinkin'. I agree. Let's go get 'em."

"Good," answered Boone. "How 'bout we split yer rangers an' send 'em out as the flankers, while me an' Sam take the militia straight up the middle?"

"Suits me," said Kemplin.

"Good, let's form 'em up." answered Boone.

Within moments, Kemplin was shouting, "Rangers, fall in."

Dougherty mustered the militia. "Riflemen," he shouted, "fall in."

Boone went inside to gather his arms. He reached for his rifle, standing in the corner. From a nail on the wall above it, he pulled down the powder horn he'd etched with a map of the West Branch Valley and looped it over his head.

He grabbed his possibles bag, holding his rifle balls, extra flints, powder measure and patches and strung it over his other shoulder. He stuffed a few biscuits from that morning's breakfast in his shirt, and, from the top of the mantle, he pulled his tomahawk and placed it in his belt across from his hunting knife.

Somehow, placing his tomahawk in his belt always made him feel complete. He was now balanced, like a tightly wound watch spring ready to uncoil in precise and unstoppable action. Somehow, it triggered for him a sense of inevitability. This was his duty, . . . his destiny, and he was once again being called to it.

Boone paused. He placed his hands on the mantle, bowed his head, closed his eyes and said a quick prayer. He thought of the men, women and children at Freeland he could possibly save. He thought about the men under his command, men with families and responsibilities of their own who were following him to an uncertain fate.

He thought about his country and the cause for which it was struggling. Then he gave thanks for having been blessed with his wife. He prayed for her protection and that she'd be well-cared for if he didn't return. Out loud, he concluded, ". . . but as in all things, Lord, let thy will be done."

"Goin' somewhere?" came a voice from behind him.

He turned and saw Jane standing in the doorway.

"It's Freeland," he said.

"I know. I heard on my way back from the summer kitchen. Be safe, Hawk."

"Always am," he replied with a wink and a grin.

She crossed the room and fell into his arms. He held her silently for a lingering moment. As she pulled away, he gave her a tender kiss.

Then, he gently held her by both arms and said, "Now listen. We're takin' the whole kit an' caboodle with us on this one. We need as many men as possible to push 'em off. We're goin' to send scouts out on both flanks to cover any attack that could be comin' this way, but I think you'd better round up the women an' children an' take 'em to Fort Augusta jist in case. That way you'll all be safe, an' the men can fight without havin' to think about their women and kids back here alone."

"You included?" she asked.

"Me mostly," he said with a sheepish smile. "I love ya, darlin'."

"I love you too, ya big lummox," she answered while pressing herself back into his chest. Then, taking a step back she looked him square in the face and said, "Now get goin'."

Boone quickly patted his accoutrements as he made a mental inventory of everything he needed. Satisfied, he placed his hand on the back of Jane's head and gave her another quick kiss, then turned and stepped out into the sunlight.

In the stockade, a group of about thirty men was assembled. They were standing in formation awaiting the order to move out as their families looked on.

"Men," announced Boone, "you know I ain't much of a one for makin' speeches, an' we ain't got a lotta time to waste in hearin' one. But, the folks up at Freeland is in it again an' it's up to us to go help 'em out. There's a lot a' women an' children up there that can't be left to be carried off as pris'ners.

"As we move out, we're goin' to split you Rangers up an' send a company out on each of our flanks. One's goin' up the river road to Warrior Run an' the other is goin' up Muddy Run an' then cuttin' across to meet the first company on the plains overlookin' Freeland. The rest of us will cut straight across an' meet you there.

"In the meantime, Jane is goin' to roust up all yer fam'lies an' take 'em down to Fort Augusta, jist in case a raidin' party somehow sneaks in b'tween us. So ya can rest assured they'll be safe. God be willin' an' the crick don't rise, we'll be back here this evenin'."

He paused for a moment.

"I don't have to tell ya," he said, "if we can't drive off the enemy, we'll lose the whole valley down to Fort Augusta. With so few men, Fort Augusta could fall too an' wind up losin' us half the state. I don't think Gen'ral Washington an' the continentals could last out the attacks that'd come from their rear if that happens. It could cost us the war.

"I know we all come here lookin' for a better way a' life . . . lookin' for a place to raise up our fam'lies where they can live free an' not have t' answer to anyone fer what church they go to, nor what fam'ly they come from, what language they speak or what color their skin is. In fact, if ya think on it for a minute, I always thought that's what made us strong.

"Here we got folks comin' from all diff'rent countries an' situations . . . all of 'em lookin' for the same dream. We got all kinds a' folks bringin' what they do best to one common cause. We got neighbors helpin' neighbors.

"This is our chance to keep that dream alive a little longer, an' them's *our* neighbors up at Freeland . . ."

Boone stood staring at the men, suddenly embarrassed he'd

gone on like a politician. He stood silently, feeling awkward and not sure how to proceed. He'd somehow tapped into his personal feelings on the entire war, but what he didn't realize was that he'd touched a chord in all of them.

The families of the men gathered around the formation had tears of pride in their eyes. The men themselves stood ready to march off to save their friends, their homes, and their country.

"Let's go get 'em, Hawk," came a sudden cry from the ranks.

It was Dougherty. He'd broken the stillness. The men erupted in a roaring cheer, and Boone shouted, "Let's go."

They left the stockade and split off on their pre-assigned routes as Jane stood in silent admiration of her husband. Just as he reached the gate, he stole a glance back at her and she blew him a kiss, which he accepted with his usual wink. When they were gone, Jane turned back to the women and children.

"Gather 'round," she called and began to organize them for the trip down to Fort Augusta.

★　★　★　★　★

FORT FREELAND

The situation in the fort was quickly growing dire. The raiders were closing in. The defenders held back the superior force, but ammunition, and the women's ability to supply it, was running out. Return fire was noticeably slowing.

Suddenly, shouts came from the gate.

"White flag!" they called.

The defender's fire slowed.

"Cease fire!" yelled Captain Little, and the order was passed up and down the lines.

The musketry ceased and there was a sudden silence on the field.

Peering through the low-hanging smoke, Little saw two unarmed men striding down the road toward the fort. One of them was wearing a red lieutenant's uniform and carrying the white flag. Next to him walked one of Butler's men, wearing the Rangers' green coat with red trim and white cross belts.

Little looked at John Vincent, a man of about eighty, who was one of the original settlers on this land, and said, "Come on. Let's go see what they have to say."

Little and Vincent laid down their rifles and went to the gate. As it opened, Little nudged his sergeant and said, "McKean, take stock of the casualties an' ammunition. An', have the men keep their positions. This could jist be a diversion."

"Yes, sir," said McKean.

Little and Vincent left the fort and walked up the road. Vincent looked around to see if they were about to be ambushed, but Little kept his eyes fixed on the Tory captain. They met in the road about fifty yards from the gate.

Before Little could say anything, the Tory spoke, "Sirs, I am Captain John McDonell of Butler's Rangers, in the service of His Royal Majesty King George the Third," he said imperiously. "This is Leftenant McIver. To whom do I owe the honor?"

"John Little, captain of the county militia.

"John Vincent . . . American."

Vincent's title drew a contemptuous look from McDonell, and he continued to address Little. "Sir, you are hopelessly outmatched. You must see your situation is untenable. I have prepared terms for the capitulation of your fort, which I believe are most generous. If you accept them now, I will guarantee the safety of your noncombatants. Otherwise, I cannot do so."

"Ya seem pretty confident in takin' us, Captain." said Little, trying to sound out the mindset of his opponent.

"Come now, Captain, let's not play games," came the sharp reply. "You have put up a valiant resistance thus far. But, we both know you are vastly outnumbered, outgunned and facing a superior force of well-trained, undefeated soldiers and unpredictable Natives.

"From our little reconnaissance exercise," McDonell continued, "we know you've little more than a handful of men standing in defense and I presume their loved ones are also present. It is solely out of decency for them that we are even holding this conversation. Now do you wish to consider my terms, or shall we simply overrun you?"

Little paused and looked off in thought. There was going to be no bluffing his way out of this. He looked back at McDonell, drew in a deep breath and said, "Let's see your terms, Captain."

"Leftenant McIver."

"Aye, surr," came the quick reply from the regular in a thick Scottish brogue. He produced a document from somewhere in his tunic.

The lieutenant stood holding the terms in his outstretched hand, but Little looked straight back at McDonell. After a pause, Vincent reached out and retrieved the terms.

"Go ahead, John," prompted Little.

Vincent unfolded the paper and began to read out loud.

"First: The men in garrison are to march out an' ground their arms in the green in front of the fort, which is to be taken possession of immediately by His Majesty's troops.

Second: All men bearing arms are to surrender themselves as prisoners of war to be sent to Niagara.

Third: The women and children are not to be stripped of their clothing nor harassed by the Indians and are at liberty to move down the country where they please."

Little considered what he heard while continuing to look directly at McDonell.

"That's it," said Vincent.

"Thanks, John," Little replied.

McDonell broke the silence. "That's plain enough, isn't it, Captain? Do you accept the terms or not?"

Little saw no way out of the situation. He sensed McDonell actually seemed to be trying to do the decent thing by offering terms instead of forcing the issue and precipitating a massacre. However, he felt if he could just buy some time, anything could happen.

"Well, Cap'n McDonell," said Little, "they sound like reasonable terms, for a fact. I appreciate you offerin' 'em. But ya know we can't do things here quite like you folks do. I command the militia, but I don't command the citizens who live here.

"John, here, helped clear this land and built this farm from a wilderness. There's other fam'lies inside those walls that done the same. I can't jist surrender to you without talkin' to them first. Can you give me a couple a' hours to talk it over with 'em an' then I'll have an answer for you?"

McDonell was quickly becoming frustrated. He had a good relationship with his Indian allies but could only control them to a certain degree. He didn't want to see a massacre at this place. He didn't want that kind of warfare attached to his conscience or to his name.

At the same time, he needed to keep tight control on his command. He couldn't afford to lose the respect and authority he held with the Indians.

"You have exactly one half-hour to discuss the matter with the parties concerned, Captain," answered McDonell. "When that time has elapsed, I will recommence the attack if I have not received an answer from you. Is that plainly understood?"

"Yes it is, Cap'n," said Little. "But one more thing . . . we got a couple a' old timers in there who couldn't make it all the way to Niagara. Will ya let them loose with the others?"

McDonell looked at Vincent for a long moment.

"Anyone as old as him may remain with those being freed," said McDonell. "Have you any further questions?"

"Can I take the terms along inside to talk 'em over with everyone?"

"You may."

Little gave a quick nod, turned to Vincent and said, "Com'on, John, let's go hash it over with 'em."

The men parted and returned to their own lines.

Back inside, Little asked, "Sergeant McKean, what's the situation?"

"Five men killed sir, Jim Watts and Jacob Freeland just as the battle started and John McClintock, Bill McClung and Jim Miles durin' the fightin'. There's a few with minor wounds who can keep goin'."

"Alright," answered Little, "that takes us down to twenty-one men. What about ammunition?"

"'Bout two thirds of the men is out. The rest is down to maybe a shot or two, an' the women are outta stuff to melt for more."

"Thanks, McKean. Keep a guard posted and call the rest a' the men together inside."

"Yessir."

The air was thick from the morning showers, and the atmosphere was stifling in the cramped room as more than thirty people crammed inside to hear what Little had to say. They remained silent as he described the situation and laid the options before them.

" . . . McDonell says if we surrender, the armed men marches to Niagara as pris'ners, but the women, children and those incapable of fightin' goes free. He says he'll hold the Indians from a killin' spree an' guarantees the safety of our fam'lies. Then again, if we hold out it's possible we could get help from Fort Bosley or Boone. Someone had to hear somethin' from the fight. So, what do we want to do?"

Old Samuel Brady was the first to speak. "I don't put much stock in the word a' this McDonald, an' I damn sure don't admire marchin' t' Niagara as pris'ner. That's even if we get that far. They could jist let us surrender our weapons, take us over the next hill an' shoot us, then turn around an' kill ev'ryone in the fort too. If we keep fightin', we at least have a chance."

"I'm with Sam," called Isaac Wilson. "B'sides, we can't jist give 'em the whole valley."

"That's jist it, Isaac" said Cornelius Vincent, a militia sergeant who also happened to be defending his own home, "you're with Sam."

"What the hell is that supposed to mean?" challenged Brady.

"It means if I was in the Rangers with you fellas, I'd probably feel the same way," said Vincent. "You're here fightin' without yer fam'lies standin' beside you, but the rest of us has our women an' children here with us and if there's even a slight chance a' gettin' 'em out safe, then that's what I want to do.

"You saw the numbers out there," continued Vincent. "There's no way we hold out for even another half-hour a' fightin' before they take the fort. We're almost outta ammunition now. You know damned well if those Indians overrun us in a fight, we'll all be killed. At least this way our folks has a chance a' makin' it out."

"I think that makes good sense," said Elias Williams. "I don't want my fam'ly t' die for a few more minutes a' pointless fightin'."

"Well," said Little, "we heard both sides. Let's put 'er to a vote. All in favor a' fightin'?"

"Aye" came a smattering response.

"All in favor a' trustin' McDonell to his word an' surrenderin' the fort?"

"Aye" was the overwhelming result.

"That's it, then," said Little, "we surrender. Now, we still have a little time left to destroy what supplies we can. Make sure t' dump any powder that's left, mix it in t' the dirt an' pour water on it. When that's done, we can say our goodbyes."

Everyone dispersed to find their families.

Little went to Vincent and asked, "John, did you get the terms copied down?"

"I did."

"Good. Since McDonell's lettin' the older men go with the rest, I want you t' take 'em down t' Colonel Hunter at Fort Augusta. Tell 'im I'm sorry."

"It ain't yer fault, John. There ain't nothin' you coulda done. If we fought on, we'd all be dead in an hour."

"Tell 'im anyway," said Little.

"I will."

As they prepared to leave, the women put on as many clothes as possible. With each new layer, they stuffed their pockets with valuables. The men went about destroying everything of military value and whatever couldn't be smuggled out with the women and children.

As Mary Kirk was going through her clothes, she got an idea. She grabbed her sixteen-year-old son, William, and pulled him to one side of the room. "Here, Bill. Put this on."

William, who was still in the gangly teenaged stage, was frail in comparison to most of the other boys. He had long curly hair and a thin face.

"No, Ma. I ain't wearin' no dress."

"Don't sass me, now. Put it on."

"Aw, ma," he protested as he pulled the garment over his head.

His mother rigged him up with an especially fine bonnet pulled down close to his eyes, allowing his long curls to spill over his shoulders. It was a huge risk. If he was discovered, it would be a breach of the agreement, and everyone could be massacred.

Little realized his allotted time was drawing short and he called to his men, "We got to git movin'. Let's everybody say our goodbyes an' we'll go."

The men grabbed their wives and children to give them a last kiss and some words of encouragement.

Recently married, Anglechy Vincent was distraught with grief and fear. "I'm afraid I'll never see you again," she whimpered.

"You'll see me again," her husband Daniel comforted. "Nothin's gonna keep me from you." He hugged her close and whispered, "I'll be back for you. I promise." The tears welled up inside her and she could only nod. He leaned over and gave her a tender kiss, held her for a moment longer then turned and left.

"Sergeant McKean, muster the men and get the noncombatants lined up to leave the fort," said Little.

"Yessir," answered McKean. "Fall in. Everyone in formation," he shouted.

Families made hurried plans as men instructed their families to go to Fort Augusta or to relatives in other counties.

"Don't worry about me. I'll see you after the war," they said. They clutched their wives close and knelt down to embrace a daughter and tousle a son's hair one last time. The chaotic moment came to an end when Sergeant McKean called, "Formation, damn it. Formation!"

McKean began physically pulling men into place and to direct the noncombatant family members to the rear. John Vincent folded his copy of the articles of surrender and put them in his shirt. He went to his wife, Elizabeth, who was sitting on a chair in front of the house. She was crippled and couldn't walk more than a few feet on her own.

Vincent knelt beside her and motioned for her to climb on his back. She looked at him incredulously and said, "John, are you gonna carry me clear to Sunbury?"

"They'll never let us keep the horse an' I ain't lettin' you sit here. I'll do what needs done," he said.

When everyone was ready, Little addressed the crowd.

"All right, ev'rybody," he said. "This McDonell give me his word an' so far he's kept it. We don't have no reason to doubt him keepin' it the rest of the way. Everybody stay calm an' go where they say. God bless us all, an' we'll see you after the war." Turning, he shouted, "Open the gate!"

The stockade doors opened.

"Forward," intoned Little, and the disheveled band began to move. Reluctantly, Elizabeth Vincent rode through the gate on her husband's back, not knowing what would become of either of them. A roar of derisive shouting erupted as they emerged from the timbered walls, and the Indians rejoiced in victory.

The prisoners cast anxious glances in anticipation of attack, but none came. McDonell was true to his word. Lieutenant McIver, with a small contingent of thirty or so men, moved down the road and met Little not far from the fort.

McIver directed the militiamen and rangers to continue up the road to a spot on the hill. He then escorted the families to a remote spot, not far from the fort.

As the last of the refugees cleared the gates, the Indian women rushed the fort, followed closely by some of the warriors. They scavenged for anything they could use. The women cut and removed the mattress ticking from the beds to use as sacks to carry anything of value. The men searched for weapons.

Some of the warriors didn't enter the fort but approached the women and children instead. One or two raiders physically accosted them in search of trophies. William Kirk stood dumbstruck in his dress as a stocky raider approached him and stood inspecting him for what seemed like an eternity. Looking him square in the face, the raider suddenly reached up and snatched the bonnet from his head.

Several women gasped in dread, but the raider merely held his prize aloft, shouted in triumph and ran off to give it to his wife. Mary Kirk calmly reached into her pocket, produced another bonnet and redid the youth's hair.

Given the duty of protecting the refugees, McIver shouted, "Forrm tight arrr-oond them, men. Noo-one molests the civilians."

On the hill overlooking the fort, McDonell awaited the surrendering force. He formed his men on each side of the road and directed the prisoners to march between them. At the end of the formation, the prisoners were directed to lay down their weapons and move to a holding area.

Little approached McDonell and held out the original surrender document, which both men signed.

One by one, rifles and tomahawks hit the ground with a dull thud. As the men at the end of the line came along, their weapons clattered upon those already there. When all were disarmed, the prisoners stood unbound but guarded by a squad of McDonell's men where they watched as the fort was plundered.

★ ★ ★ ★ ★

OUTSIDE FORT FREELAND

Boone and his militia crested a knoll and found Kemplin's men just arriving on the hill across the stream from the fort. The squad that covered their right flank was taking its place in line next to those who had gone up the river road on the left.

"Looks like your plan worked, Hawk," said Dougherty.

"Yeah, luck's on our side today," remarked Kemplin.

Boone and Dougherty shot each other a glance.

Up ahead, one of the rangers was waving them forward. The men quickened their pace and fell in to the right of Kemplin's men. They found themselves in a thicket overlooking Fort Freeland. Warrior Run trickled in between.

"Cover, elevation *and* tucked in behind a crick. We're in the perfect position," whispered Kemplin.

"Yeah, but we can't stay here too long," said Boone. "Once'd we surprise 'em, we got to drive 'em. If we wait here an' fight defensive, they'll jist flank us."

The men realized the fort had already been surrendered. They saw the women and children held a short distance away and the men under guard on the far hill. The raiders' women had plundered everything they could use and newly liberated kettles already simmered with the victory feast they were preparing down by the stream.

Kemplin saw Boone was right. Masses of warriors milled amongst a whole regiment of Tories. "Hell," said Kemplin, "they even got some reg'lars over there."

"See," said Boone. "There's no other way we stand a chance."

"Well," said Dougherty, "are we jist gonna sit here an' hope we git invited to dinner?"

"Let's go," replied Boone.

Dougherty stood, calmly leveled his rifle and fired. His target fell and lay motionless. Then, Boone's entire line erupted.

Across the stream there was panic. Indian women screamed and ran up the hill toward the fort, while their men fell all around them. Boone's men quickly reloaded and fired again. The enemy was scrambling.

"We got 'em runnin'," shouted Boone. "Charge!"

He ran down the hill and crossed the bridge to the fort with his men close on his heels. They covered the low ground and rushed to the base of the hill beneath the fort just as a formation of Tories moved out from behind the fort, leveled their guns and fired a volley at close range.

With his men falling around him, Boone shouted, "We gotta drive 'em, boys . . . Fire!"

Using rifles at that range, Boone's men did terrible execution to the enemy. But those who weren't hit were disciplined. They stood their ground and reloaded.

Then, from behind the Tory line, another formation of green-clad troops appeared, this time joined by regulars. It was becoming a battle of attrition Boone's men couldn't win. Just as Boone saw the new formation, a wave of warriors swarmed around the other side of the fort and bore down on his dwindling force.

The original formation of Tories unloosed another volley and advanced. More of Boone's men fell, and, somewhere in the ranks, someone shouted, "Fall back!"

There was nothing else to do. Men who in other battles stood firmly against British regulars now turned and fled. Those closest to the Tory ranks were taken prisoner before they even had the chance to run.

The remainder quickly ran back to the bridge. Raiders fell upon the dead and wounded in a melee of scalping.

Across the bridge, the only cover for the retreating men was the marshy thicket that reached for hundreds of yards up and down the creek. Boone's men waded into the underbrush and hid. The raiders waded in right behind them.

★　★　★　★　★

OUTSIDE FORT FREELAND

On the hill where the fort's surrendered men were being held, many of the guards impulsively joined the ranks to meet Boone's attack. Just four remained. With only one guard between himself and a clear path to freedom, Sam Brady saw his chance to escape.

Brady made his own diversion by looking directly past the guard and uttering "Oh, my God." The guard naturally turned to see what caused Brady's reaction. Seeing nothing, he turned back, and Brady landed a haymaker to his chin.

As the guard lay senseless on the ground, Brady picked up his musket and fled across the open fields. The other guards remained focused on the battle in the opposite direction.

Peter Vincent and Francis Watts saw Brady escape, and they also ran off and hid in the nearby woods. One of the guards saw them.

"Hey, the prisoners are escapin'," he yelled, leveling his gun at those who remained.

The other two guards turned and forced the remaining captives to sit on the ground between them. Regaining consciousness, the guard on the ground called to three warriors milling nearby and pointed off in the fields where Brady was getting away.

The three instantly gave chase. Brady was very swift, and already had a significant head start, but the warriors were determined not to allow a scalp bounty elude them. The first and second warriors were even faster than Brady and began to make up ground on him. The third, who was slower than all of them, quickly saw the futility of the chase and dropped out.

Brady glanced over his shoulder and saw he was being pursued. Looking back after another hundred yards, he could see his lead was eroding. Not wanting to leave himself completely exhausted, he maintained his steady pace instead of accelerating.

The first warrior broke into a full sprint. He outstripped the other and gained more ground on Brady.

In another hundred yards, as Brady turned again, he stumbled and fell. He sprawled headlong on the ground and the musket went flying beyond him. As he collected himself, he saw his closest pursuer was only forty yards behind him and closing fast.

Brady calmly picked himself up, walked over to the musket and raised it to his shoulder. The warrior, in full stride, reached for his tomahawk and wielded it menacingly as he closed the distance between them. Brady cocked the weapon and steadily squeezed the trigger as the warrior rushed toward him.

Brady might as well have fired a cannon.

He dropped the musket, walked over to the dead warrior and picked up the tomahawk that, moments before, was destined to take his life. He looked up at his remaining pursuer, who was now within fifty yards, and shouted wildly at him while brandishing the tomahawk.

"Come on ya murderin' bastard. Ya want another Brady? Well ya ain't gettin' one today. Yer friend here looks pretty compared t' how you'll look! Come on!"

As the warrior closed to thirty yards, he paused. Brady was out of control, screaming and crazily swinging the tomahawk about him. This would be no easy bounty for the warrior to collect. Then Brady rushed *him*.

Shocked and confused, the warrior simply turned and fled. Brady quickly gave up his own chase when he was sure the warrior would continue running. He picked up the musket, tucked the tomahawk in his belt and completed his escape.

★ ★ ★ ★ ★

FORT FREELAND

As the battle waned, McDonell surveyed the landscape. He'd been careful to watch for resistance, but Boone's attack surprised him. He was fortunate there were so few of them.

He scanned the battlefield and saw the dead of both sides strewn below the fort. Across the creek, warriors were sifting through the underbrush trying to find Boone's men.

The Indian women were also moving back toward the creek. Some were kneeling and weeping over the corpses of their husbands. Others tried to salvage the feast.

McDonell saw Lieutenant McIver still at his post guarding the surrendered women and children. Now that there had been bloodshed, he knew they were in greater danger than before. He didn't want to see them senselessly slaughtered.

He approached McIver and said, "Leftenant, escort your charge to the far side of the stream and release them. See to it that no harm befalls them as they depart."

"Aye, surr."

John Vincent once again lifted his wife on his back and started off with the rest of them. With longing waves and stolen glances back to their loved ones on the far hill, they followed McIver toward the bridge and freedom.

They endured withering looks from the raiders as they passed. Were it not for McIver's guard and McDonell's word, none would have survived.

They crossed the bridge and walked up the hill where McIver halted his troop and freed the prisoners. John Vincent was already winded. McIver looked at him and said, "Ye can't be carryin' yerr Missus all the wae t' safety kin ye?"

Vincent replied, "We have a horse at the fort but knew we couldn't take it with us. That's the only way she can get around."

McIver studied for a moment and said, "Git yerrself oot of siet in those wooods and let me see what I kin doo."

The settlers followed the creek downstream. Vincent stayed with them until they were out of sight of the fort, but he could carry Elizabeth no farther. The others bid the old couple farewell and told them they'd send help back from Fort Augusta.

"Sorry, darlin'," said Vincent, when they'd gone. "Guess you got yourself a broke down ol' horse."

"John, I don't want you to carry me no farther. Leave me here an' go with the rest of 'em."

"Maybe I can't carry you no farther, but I damn sure ain't leavin' you neither," he said. "Now we'll jist wait here an' rest a while. Then we'll see what we can't do from there."

★   ★   ★   ★   ★

FORT FREELAND

McDonell sent scouts in all directions. They plundered and burned everything in their path, including Fort Boone.

That evening, they returned with supplies that would feed their families for some time. Then, McDonell ordered Fort Freeland burned, too.

The blaze lit the wild celebration that took place that night and created a diversion for Boone's remaining hidden men, who crept from the underbrush and escaped to Sunbury.

About midnight it began to rain. On the far side of the creek, John and Elizabeth Vincent lay huddled in the tall grass and did their best to keep warm.

The next morning, the Vincents heard the unmistakable sounds of McDonell's troops departing. Cold and shivering in the wet grass, they waited for John to gather the strength to carry Elizabeth a little further. Then, they heard a strange sound. "Haloo, Misterr an' Missus? Arre ye heerre?"

John warily sat up and peered through the grass. Some distance away, he saw McIver holding a horse by its mane. Vincent said, "Well, I'll be damned. That redcoat feller brought us our horse."

"What?" said Elizabeth, incredulously.

"Yeah, an' it's actually *our* horse."

Vincent stood up and waved to McIver, who smiled and brought the horse to them.

"Heerre you arre," he said. "I'm sorrry, but I cooldn't git a bridle foor ye."

"We'll be jist fine," answered Vincent. "Thank you kindly."

"Think nothing oof it," replied McIver. As he turned and walked away he added, "Goood luck t' ye."

"To you too, young man," called Elizabeth.

Vincent led the horse to his wife and helped her mount. He walked to the nearest hickory tree and stripped lengths of bark he used to make a rough halter, which he placed on the horse. By late afternoon, the couple was in Sunbury.

★ ★ ★ ★ ★

FORT AUGUSTA

Colonel Hunter was meeting with young Moses Van Campen, one of Kelly's Rangers. Already known as the best wrestler in the county, Van Campen was also making a name for himself as a leader.

Last summer, Hartley put Van Campen in command of the Lancaster County Militia that patrolled between Fort Muncy and Fort Jenkins, despite them having higher-ranking officers among them. This year he'd been given an even more important role.

"Sullivan did well to choose you to be his quartermaster," said Hunter. "You've done a fine job."

"Thank you, Col'nel," said Van Campen.

They were interrupted by a knock on the door.

"Colonel Hunter, sir," called a voice.

"Come in," said Hunter.

"Colonel, I'm sorry to interrupt you, sir," said a militiaman, "but there's a whole group a' women an' children just come in from Fort Boone. They say Fort Freeland's been attacked."

Hunter looked at Van Campen, and they rushed from the room. In the parade ground they met Jane Boone and got the details of Boone's rescue attempt.

Soon, John Montgomery and his family, whose farm was a few miles from Freeland, came in and told how they'd heard the fighting, approached the battle, and witnessed Boone's attack.

"They was wiped out, Colonel," said Montgomery. "There wasn't nothin' we could do. We wasn't seen, so we rounded up the fam'ly an' come here."

Later, Sam Brady and some survivors from Boone's force made it to Sunbury. They added more details before the women and children from Fort Freeland arrived to tell their story.

The next day, John and Elizabeth Vincent arrived.

"I have a message for you from Captain Little, sir," said Vincent.

"Yes?"

"He said he was sorry, and he wanted me to give you this copy of the articles of surrender," said Vincent.

"Thank you," Hunter answered, taking the document. "Little's a good man. I'm sure he did all he could."

"He did sir. If we'd fought on, we'd all be dead. There was too many of 'em."

"Thank you, Mr. Vincent."

"There's something else, sir."

"What is it?"

"I don't know if you know it yet or not, but I'm sorry to report that Captains Boone and Dougherty are both dead, sir."

"Are you sure?"

"Yessir. I saw 'em as we crossed the battle ground outside the fort. The rest a' the folks was intent on gettin' across the bridge, but

I was walkin' slow on account a' carryin' my wife. I saw both their bodies layin' scalped on the ground. I counted our dead an' could see there was at least ten of 'em."

"That squares with what we've been able to put together here," said Hunter. "Of the total relief force of about thirty-five men, sixteen have reported back here in the last two days. Stories vary a little, but we estimate five or six were taken prisoner. That leaves your estimate of dead to account for most of the rest. . . . We hadn't heard about Boone and Dougherty, though."

Hunter paused for a moment. "What can you tell us about those in the fort?" he asked.

"Well, there was about thirty of us on the muster rolls," said Vincent. "They killed five during the battle. Then, they let me, Art Taggert, George Pack an' Garrett Freeland loose on account of us bein' too old to make it to Niagara. So, that leaves what . . . twenty-one taken prisoner?"

"Yeah," said Hunter, "but Brady, Francis Watts an' your boy Peter all escaped durin' the battle and came in here last night."

"Thank God," said Vincent.

"Anything else?" asked Hunter.

"No sir, I think that's about it."

"Thank you, John. I appreciate your help. Now why don't you go an' tend to your wife?"

"Thank *you*, sir."

The old man turned and left Hunter's office, and Hunter sat down heavily in his chair.

"You alright?" asked Van Campen, who was sitting with him when Vincent arrived.

"Yeah."

"I know you was close."

"Yeah, we were," said Hunter. "Me an' Boone an' Brady used to spend quite a bit a' time here. Hard to lose Dougherty, too. . . So many good men gone . . . so few left to take their places."

Pulling himself back to business, Hunter tried to figure out how he would strategically handle the situation.

"Well, I know Sullivan will say he needs all the troops he has, but I guess it can't hurt to ask," said Hunter, reaching for his pen.

Van Campen said in a low voice, "Sam, we're leavin' within a day 'r two ourselves."

Hunter turned quickly and looked at Van Campen. "Are you sure?"

"I'm sure. I'm leavin' tonight for Wyoming with the last of the supplies. Our movin' north will take the pressure off you here."

"I agree it should. I'm writin' my letter anyhow," said Hunter, "jist on principle."

"Go ahead," said Van Campen, "I'll take it with me."

Sunlight poured through his office window as Hunter composed an overview of the events of the past two days. Then, he asked Sullivan for assistance. When he was finished, he sealed the letter and handed it to Van Campen.

Van Campen took the letter and rose to leave. When he was almost out the door, Hunter said, "Moses."

Van Campen looked back.

Hunter approached him, placed his hand on his shoulder, looked him in the eye and said, "Good luck."

"Thanks," he replied, looking back at him. He turned and left as Hunter sat back at his desk and stared out at the sunlit hilltops across the river.

Van Campen traveled through the night and arrived at Wyoming the following afternoon.

The next day, Hunter received Sullivan's reply. In part, it read:

> *. . . with the Disagreeable intelligence of the loss of Fort Freeland, your situation must be unhappy. I feel for you, and wish to assist you, but the good of the service will not admit of it . . .*

Nothing can so effectually draw the Indians out of your country as carrying the war into theirs. Tomorrow morning I shall march with the whole Army for Tioga.

CHAPTER 13

July 31, 1779–February 1780

WYOMING, PENNSYLVANIA

The men were up before dawn. They ate, filled canteens, checked their rifles and secured personal belongings.

"Fall in!" yelled an officer.

Sullivan gestured toward the fort as the first light crested the hills. A signal gun fired and Van Campen's heavily-laden batteaux shoved off into deeper water.

Sullivan motioned again and a second gun boomed. The army stepped off with a hearty "Huzzah," to the burr of the drums. Adrenaline rushed through the men's veins as the shout echoed up the valley.

The spectacle was breathtaking to the settlers who remained in the fort. The sun rose at their backs and bathed the ranks in golden light. Flags floated above the soldiers' heads and the fifes struck up an accompaniment to the drums as they passed the fort.

The army spent the next days in a determined march.

When Sullivan's men reached Tioga, they crossed the ford and fell out of line to sprawl on the grassy point between the rivers. Indians and Tories were gathered at Chemung, just eleven miles further upstream.

Now, Sullivan halted his march to await the rendezvous with the army from Cherry Valley.

★ ★ ★ ★ ★

FORT AUGUSTA

Colonel Matthew Smith answered Hunter's plea for help. He marched into Sunbury with his troops from downriver just days after Fort Freeland fell. Smith determined to follow the raiders the next day. That evening, he sent a report to Council President Reed:

> *I have arrived at Sunbury with sixty Paxtang boys. The neighboring townships are turning out a number of volunteers, and Cumberland County will give considerable assistance.*
>
> *Tomorrow at 12 o'clock is fixed for the time of march. Provisions is scarce, but we intend to follow the savages. The number of cattle they have taken from the country is great and they must make slow progress on their return home.*
>
> *I enclose a copy of the capitulation at Fort Freeland. Captain McDonald of the Rangers was formerly a Sergeant in Col. Montgomery's Regt. of Highlanders. His humanity has appeared in this one instance – perhaps the first in the war. Fifty-two women and children came safe to this place, and four old men was also admitted to come back. The enemy supposed them not fit to march to Niagara.*
>
> *Enclosed is a list of the number of Capt. Boone's party killed. This account I believe is the fact as the party out yesterday, that buried the dead, gave me the list.*
>
> *The distress of the people here is great and scarcely can be told. Sunbury now composes Northumberland County. The enemy have burnt houses, barns, rice and wheat in the fields, stocks of hay, etc. All is consumed.*
>
> *Such devastation I have not yet seen. For my part, I think the distresses of Northumberland County people equal, if not superior to anything that has happened to any part of the continent since the commencement of the war.*

Smith and his men left the next morning, but they were back in Fort Augusta just a few days later.

"Well, they outdistanced us," said Smith.

"What did you find?" asked Hunter.

"We followed 'em as far as Muncy an' saw where they camped at Wallis', but they'd already left the valley by the time we got there. Funny thing, too," mused Smith. "That was the one place they didn't burn."

★ ★ ★ ★ ★

TIOGA POINT—*Confluence of the Chemung and Susquehanna North Branch*

"State your business," said Sullivan's aide, Major Adam Hoops, as he stooped out from beneath the tent flap.

"I'm Van Campen. I understand the general sent for me."

"Ah, yes, the quartermaster. You're aware our scouting parties are being ambushed as they journey upriver?"

"I am," answered Van Campen.

"The general's heard you're an experienced scout and he desires to know if you'd be willing to volunteer for a special mission."

Van Campen smiled. "Willin' an' able," he said.

"Good. In that case, you are to select a party of your choosing and to advance six miles upriver to a wide flat. This is where our scouts have been repeatedly ambushed. General Sullivan desires you to *ambush the ambushers*."

Van Campen smiled even wider.

"The general's plan is for you to station a member of your party in the top of one of the oaks that dot the flats, while the rest of you remain hidden," explained Hoops. "When the lookout sees the enemy approach, he will lower a line with a piece of white paper attached to it. The number of feet the paper descends beneath a fixed point will represent the number of enemy he sees. Your men can respond accordingly. Have you any questions?"

"None at all, sir," said Van Campen.

"Go to it, then."

By the time Van Campen rejoined his men, he'd already mentally chosen his squad. He called for fifteen of his best men from the boat service and explained the mission to them. With one exception, these were valley men he'd led in the past. They were men he could trust.

They struck out just before nightfall, planning to arrive at the flats in the early hours of the morning. They'd choose their ground and be ready to spring their trap at dawn, when Van Campen believed the enemy would arrive to set their own ambush.

Once on the trail, formalities were dropped.

"Say, Mose . . . ," called one of the men.

"Yeah?"

"Whyn't you tell us again 'bout how you met ol' Marshall?"

James Marshall was the one in the party who wasn't from the valley. The rest of the men began to chuckle. The man himself winced good-naturedly, as he'd become accustomed to this routine.

"Ol' Marshall . . . ," Van Campen intoned. "Well, it was a sultry day last June when we'd been gatherin' and loadin' supplies. It was late in the afternoon of a hard day's work an' I was about as tired as I'd ever been."

"Oh, go on," groaned Marshall amidst the laughter of the group.

"Tired an' weary," continued Van Campen, ignoring the interruption. "Jist as I dismissed the men an' was about to call it a day myself, I turned an' looked right in t' the middle a' some fella's barrel chest."

This brought more laughter, as witnesses to the event knew Marshall had stood on a log for the *introduction*.

Van Campen went on. "I kept lookin' up till I finally come to a face. The fella had bent forward, and I was so far under his big forehead that if it'd been rainin' I coulda kept nice an' dry."

The men could barely contain themselves, and Marshall knew any response on his part would only make it worse.

"So, as I'm standin' there wonderin' what this fella wants," Van Campen continued,"he says down t' me 'how'd ya like t' be knocked flat on your ass?' Well, I never seen this fella b'fore in my life. I figured he musta heard I was a wrastler an' was lookin' t' make a name for hisself. I figured he musta come a long way t' find me an' I didn't want t' disappoint him after such a long trip, so I says 'if you can do it fair, have at it.'

"Well, we was right on the edge a' the riverbank an' it was pretty steep where we'd been loadin'. We starts t' circlin' an' this fella waves his big, long arms at me a couple a' times, an' that was nice 'cause the breeze was nice an' cool after all that work I'd done. I figured the least I could do was return the favor 'cause he was prob'ly hot from his long trip t' find me.

"So, I let him back me up almost t' the edge a' the bank, an', sure enough, he charges at me. Well, I jist sits back an' lifts the fella over my head with my feet an' tosses him right down in the drink."

The men erupted in laughter and slapped Marshall good-naturedly on the back.

"I'm lucky I didn't land on one a' the boats," said Marshall, red-faced.

"As I recall," said Van Campen, "you did land pret-near under one."

"Yeah," said one of the men, "an he didn't have t' eat no supper that night either, 'cause when I picked him out from under that boat he'd already eaten about a bushel a' muck from the river bottom."

This brought more laughter and everyone, including Marshall, enjoyed it immensely. Soon Van Campen said "All right boys, we'd better pipe down. We're gettin' far enough outta camp t' keep 'er quiet now."

They reached the edge of the plain before dawn and Van Campen determined no enemy was present. He looked back at the men and said, "Anybody want t' volunteer t' be lookout?"

"I'll do it," said Marshall.

"You sure?" asked Van Campen, believing this could be a reaction to the ribbing he took from the group. "Could be kinda touchy out there alone."

"I been watchin' you stump-jumpers long enough to know how to keep myself safe," he answered.

Not wanting to embarrass the man, Van Campen agreed. "Alright then," he said, handing him the weighted line with the paper attached. "We're in a good spot here overlookin' the plain. Why don't you make for that big oak about a third a' the way across't?"

"Alright," he said, turning to go.

"Marshall," said Van Campen.

"Yeah?"

"That bare limb about twenty feet up. That's our marker branch. We'll count ev'ry foot below that as one a' the enemy."

"Alright."

"Now, when you lower the line, keep 'er close t' the trunk so only we can see it."

"I will," he said, turning again.

". . . and Marshall."

"Yeah?"

"Go quiet. It don't look like anybody's out there, but that don't mean they ain't."

"I'll be alright."

"Good luck, then," said Van Campen.

The men chose a comfortable spot to wait while keeping an eye on Marshall as he crossed the plain.

"I guess he did learn a few things from us, Mose," said Colley, one of the men in the party.

"Yeah, not bad," agreed Van Campen, as they watched him work his way to the oak and begin to climb it. When Marshall disappeared into the boughs, the men settled in and kept watch.

Van Campen had everyone recheck their rifles as the wakening birds broke the silence. It had been just about an hour since they'd taken their position, and the plain was becoming visible beneath the lightening sky.

Colley whispered, "There's the signal."

Everyone looked at the oak and watched the bit of paper on the end of the line slowly descend. It stopped about five feet below the marker branch.

Van Campen turned toward the men and was about to speak.

"Not so fast, Mose," said Colley. "There she goes again."

The line descended further, and the men mentally counted off the number of feet the paper dropped until it stopped.

Van Campen again turned back toward the men to give orders.

"Hold on. There she goes again," noticed Colley.

The signal paper continued to drop and when it finally stopped it was about fifteen feet below the marker branch.

"I don't see anybody out there," said Van Campen.

"Look, Mose," said Colley again.

The signal dropped again, but this time as they watched, they saw a rustling up in the boughs and heard the sound of limbs breaking. Marshall came crashing down through the branches, almost headfirst, and hit the ground with a thud.

"Was he shot?" asked Van Campen. "I didn't hear no gun."

"Noo he ain't shot," replied Colley, incredulously. "He fell asleep."

The men heard groaning. Aside from a startled flock of birds in the field, everything was quiet.

"Tub," said Van Campen to Colley, who, despite his nickname, was tall and thin, "come with me an' we'll see if he's alright."

Van Campen and Colley quickly covered the ground to the oak and arrived to find Marshall stunned but alive.

"You all right?" asked Van Campen.

"I think I busted my shoulder," said Marshall, in obvious pain.

"You're lucky you didn't bust yer neck the way you come down outta that perch," said Van Campen.

"You sure come down quicker 'n you went up," said Colley, trying to suppress a chuckle.

"Musta been up past his bedtime last night," said Van Campen. "Come on, Tub. Let's pick 'im up an' see if anything else is busted on 'im."

Marshall didn't dispute that he'd fallen asleep. He winced in pain as Van Campen and Colley gently pulled him to his feet.

"Can you walk?" asked Van Campen.

"I think so."

"Good, let's git you back to camp. If there'd been any scoutin' parties out, we'd a' seen 'em by now."

"Yeah, or they'd a' seen us," said Colley, scanning the plain.

They helped Marshall back to the rest of the men, who greeted him with smirks. Though no one said anything at the time, Marshall knew it'd be a long time before he lived this down.

Van Campen led the men back to Tioga. He sent them to get some rest and had a doctor take a look at Marshall before going to headquarters to make his report. He waited at Sullivan's tent as Major Hoops retrieved the general from inside. When Sullivan appeared, he asked, "Well sir, how was the hunting?"

"Not so good this mornin'," answered Van Campen.

"Oh?"

"No sir. We arrived b'fore dawn an' had a good position. As daylight came on we didn't see any enemy whatsoever."

"What do you think of the plan, in general?"

"I think it's a real good plan. In fact it was workin' real good."

"How so, if you didn't see any enemy?"

Van Campen chuckled and recounted the whole episode to the general, who didn't find it amusing.

"Why the devil didn't you shoot him?" Sullivan asked hotly.

"Sir . . . you didn't give me orders to shoot my *own* men," said Van Campen.

Sullivan and his staff broke into laughter.

"Alright, you're dismissed, Van Campen," said Sullivan. "Thank you for your efforts. Go get some rest and stay ready for further assignments."

"Yessir, General."

That evening, Van Campen was called back to headquarters. This time he was asked inside.

"I am told," remarked Sullivan, "that you are not only rather talented at these nocturnal ventures, but that you also rather enjoy them."

"They do rouse a bit of excitement, sir," said Van Campen.

"That being the case, I don't feel too badly in asking you to take another such journey this evening."

Van Campen grinned.

Sullivan continued, "I'm interested in learning the disposition of the enemy. We believe they're concentrated at Chemung, some five or six miles further upriver than you were last night at the flats. It was there the enemy concentrated against Hartley and forced him to turn back last year. If the enemy is there, they are practically on our doorstep.

"Being in a somewhat vulnerable position, I'd like to eradicate the threat. But, we need accurate information on this village. How many of the enemy are present, how are they positioned, things of that nature. Are you up to the task?"

"I am, sir," answered Van Campen.

"Good," said Sullivan. "I'll leave the details up to you, with the added request that you take at least one other man with you. I don't have to tell you this is a dangerous assignment. Having another man along increases our odds of retrieving some information in the event of your capture."

"Yessir. I know just the man to volunteer."

"Good," said Sullivan.

". . . and sir?"

"Yes?"

"There won't be the event of my capture," said Van Campen, grinning again.

"I certainly hope not," said Sullivan. "You've proven yourself an efficient quartermaster and are rapidly proving yourself more valuable still. Take care, and report back here in the morning."

"Thank you, sir."

Van Campen left Sullivan's headquarters and strode back to his side of camp. When he spotted Colley, he motioned him away from the rest of the men. Strolling down by the river, Van Campen began the conversation.

"You get some rest after our adventure last night?"

"Yeah, I'm feelin' just fine," said Colley with as straight a face as he could muster, knowing there was more to the question than a general inquiry into his health.

"Good," said Van Campen. "You feel like goin' for another little jaunt tonight?"

"Sure. Where we goin'?"

"Chemung. Countin' heads."

"Just us?" asked Colley.

"Yeah, I don't want too many with us, makin' noise."

"Sure . . . I think I'm free this evenin'."

"I thought you might be," replied Van Campen as they started back toward camp. "Here's how we'll play it," he continued. "I figure we'll rig ourselves up to look as much like Indians as we can. That way if we're spotted, we might not arouse too much suspicion, at least from a distance."

"Sounds good," agreed Colley.

"All right. Let's get our outfits together an' be ready to light out about sunset."

"I'll be ready."

That evening, Van Campen and Colley ate a solid meal, donned their disguises and left camp. This time, rather than follow the trail, they forded the river and hiked up into the mountains. They headed upriver but stayed to the tops of the ridges.

They moved silently, making good time. Shortly after midnight, they found themselves on the heights across from Chemung.

Spread beneath them, on the far side of the river, was a sea of campfires. Van Campen turned to Colley and said, "Here's where I go on alone. I need you t' stay here an' count up how many fires they got goin' while I slip down and get a headcount on how many's at a single fire. When I get back, we'll add 'er up and git an overall number."

"You sure?" asked Colley.

"Dead sure," he replied. "If you hear shots, or I ain't back in two hours, you head back t' camp an' let Sullivan know how many fires they got. That'll at least give him a good idea a' their strength."

Colley knew Van Campen was right and let the matter drop.

"All right," he said, slapping Van Campen on the shoulder. Van Campen nodded once and departed.

Colley watched his friend disappear into the night. He saw him again as he emerged from the woods at the bottom of the ridge and watched him recross the river.

Colley saw Van Campen reach the eastern shore and melt into the trees near the village. Then, he got down to business and began counting fires.

Van Campen worked his way around the village to enter through the fewest number of outlying camps as possible. He made mental notes and tried to get a sense of the ratio of Indians to Tories. When he slipped into the village itself, he counted the houses and noticed the fires there were surrounded by women and children.

Taking in all the details, he began to work his way back toward the river.

This time, however, Van Campen moved straight through the camps. In the first, he walked through the sleeping enemy toward the fire. Just as he was about to take stock of the numbers, he unbelievably snapped a twig.

A warrior sat up. Van Campen coolly continued to the fire, picked up a log and placed it on the banked coals. As he made a pretense of poking the fire, the warrior stretched and lay back down to sleep. Van Campen quickly counted nine warriors and took his leave.

At the next camp, he was happy to find the ground covered with pine needles. He glided over the soft carpet and quickly counted twelve snoring men. Though tempted to continue through several more camps, there was just one more between him and the river. He felt with an average of the three, he'd have a solid survey, and he didn't want to risk not getting the information back to Sullivan.

He entered the last camp, which was more exposed to the river breeze. Through the night, the men had moved close to the fire. Van Campen carefully wove through the tangle of slumbering warriors and counted ten of them.

Satisfied with his results, it was time to leave. He chose his steps and placed his foot in a space between the heads of two warriors who were sleeping back-to-back. As he did, one of them stirred.

The warrior sluggishly raised his head. Van Campen matter-of-factly continued a few paces more and sidled up to a tree. Keeping his back about three-quarters to the camp, Van Campen slid his breechcloth to one side and relieved himself. The warrior, thinking nothing of it, rested his head on the ground and fell back to sleep.

Van Campen recrossed the river and soon joined Colley on top of the mountain.

"I was startin' t' wonder about you," said Colley, as Van Campen approached.

"So was I," said Van Campen.

Colley gave a look but said nothing.

"How many fires do you make out?" asked Van Campen.

"Right around eighty, near as I can figure."

"That includin' the ones in the village?"

"Yeah."

"All right, there was jist about ten men per campfire. There was about ten campfires in the village itself, an' they had women an' children around 'em. So, take away ten, that gives us seventy with ten men a piece, an' we're lookin' at right around seven hundred enemy."

"What about the houses?" asked Colley.

"I figure the warriors and soldiers was camped around the women an' children an' that the houses was filled with women an' children too."

"Sounds right."

"Now," said Van Campen, "near as I could tell, there was about a seventy-thirty split b'tween Indian fires an' Tory fires. That gives us about . . . what . . . five hundred Indians an' two hundred Tories?"

"Sounds jist about right," agreed Colley. "Makes sense too. Was it Butler's Tories?"

"Yeah, damn green-coated bastards," said Van Campen. "Let's git back an' fill in Sullivan."

The men sped along the ridge, retracing their steps to Tioga. They arrived opposite camp just as the sky was lightening.

They waded into the river and Van Campen curled his lips. He imitated a cardinal to get the sentry's attention. He wanted to make sure he knew they were friends before they came too close.

They reached the eastern shore, and the sentry walked down to the water's edge. He extended a hand to Van Campen. "Bein' pretty careful, ain't ya? I knew you was comin'," said the grinning sentry.

"I jist didn't want you t' think we was attackin'," replied Van Campen with a straight face.

The sentry smiled and said, "You was safe. I don't see how I coulda mistook those get-ups for the real thing."

Van Campen smiled back.

The sentry continued, "The general left word, he's waitin' on your report."

"I'll head right over," said Van Campen. "Come on, Tub."

The men were happy they didn't have to wait for the general to wake to make their report. They reached headquarters and were escorted inside.

"Well," said Sullivan. "I'm relieved to see my quartermaster is still with us."

"Thank you, sir," replied Van Campen. He continued, "General, this is Tub Colley."

"Sir," said Colley with a nod.

"Colley, I appreciate your efforts in this."

"Thank *you*, sir," he replied.

Sullivan got to the point, "Now, gentlemen. What news have you for me this morning?"

"Well," said Van Campen, "they're concentrated at Chemung all right. We figure 'em at about seven hundred ready for combat."

"Any idea of a breakdown of forces?" asked Sullivan.

"Yessir. Near as we kin tell, it looks like about five hundred Indians and two hundred a' Butler's Tories. They must have at least seven hundred women an' children with 'em, too. They're all in the village with the men camped on all sides around 'em."

"Did you see any regulars or artillery to speak of?"

"None to speak of, sir."

"Very well," said Sullivan. "Gentlemen, I'm very pleased with your results. And, I'm happy to see you back here, safe. You're dismissed. Please see my mess officer for a good breakfast, and go get some sleep."

"Thank you, sir," they answered.

Van Campen and Colley left the general's tent. The air was filled with the smell of frying ham, eggs and potatoes. They gave each other a look and, in a moment, found the mess officer. He'd been expecting them. He looked up and, taking note of their appearance, said, "I take it this is a raid."

"I think we gotcha surrounded," said Colley.

They dispatched three helpings each before Van Campen laid

down his plate. Colley looked at him, stood and returned to the mess officer for a fourth. As he sat back down, Colley said, "I woulda thought you'd a' been hungry, Mose."

"Why don't you put sides on that dish?" said Van Campen. "You might be able to get more on it."

Colley's only response was the sound of his fork working against the metal plate as he forged his way through the last helping.

Completing the meal, the men stood, thanked the mess officer and walked to their side of camp. They changed clothes and turned in for some much-needed sleep. Both slept soundly until midafternoon, when Van Campen was awakened by someone nudging his arm.

"Van Campen," said a voice. "Sorry to waken you, but you must get up."

Van Campen turned and opened his eyes enough to see a figure standing over him.

He squeezed them shut again to push back the sleep and then reopened them in a better-focused effort. This time he saw it was Major Hoops.

Van Campen sat up and involuntarily stretched. He asked, "How can I help you, Major?"

"The general would like to see you."

Van Campen got to his feet and said, "Thank you, Major. I'll be there shortly."

"Very well," said Hoops, and he departed.

Van Campen straightened his clothing and strolled over to the water barrel where he took generous handfuls and washed his face. Feeling more himself, he began the familiar walk to Sullivan's headquarters. As he arrived, the general said, "Well, there's the scout. Are you well rested?"

"Yes sir," replied Van Campen cheerfully.

"Good. Good," said Sullivan. "Are you ready for another adventure this evening?"

"Ready as ever."

"Very well. It appears you now know the way to Chemung," he said with a smile. "More importantly, you have the knowledge of the main enemy defenses, and you know where there may be possible ambushes on the way."

"I do, sir."

"I plan on raiding Chemung this evening. How would you feel about leading the way?"

"That suits me, sir," said Van Campen.

"I thought it might," replied Sullivan. "General Hand, of the Pennsylvania Line, will be commanding the strike force. In all there will be about eleven hundred men. I'd like for you to organize a detachment of twenty-five to guide them. Go put them together and be ready to move out. We'll leave at sunset."

"Yes, sir."

"Any questions?" asked Sullivan.

"No, sir."

"Very well, then. Go to it."

"Yessir," said Van Campen. He headed back to his men, where he found Colley still asleep. Van Campen nudged him with his foot.

"Tubby, let's go. We got work to do."

Colley turned and said, "We got breakfast ready?"

"You'll have time for somethin' b'fore we leave. Git up and git the men together."

"While you make breakfast, you mean?"

"Jist git up an' git the men," said Van Campen. "Have 'em meet up over there by the river."

"Alright, alright."

Colley roused himself and soon had the men gathering around Van Campen. As the last few strolled up to the group, Colley brought up the rear, munching on a dried ship's biscuit and some salted beef.

"Git yerself all squared away, Tub?" called Van Campen with a grin.

"All that sleepin' made me hungry," he replied.

The men laughed and Van Campen got down to business. "Boys, we got some work to do. The general wants us to lead the army up to Chemung tonight. It'll be up t' us to get 'em there and t' look out for ambushes on the way. Ev'rybody feel like takin' a little walk?"

"Yeah," they responded.

"Marshall, if you want, you can stay here an' rest your shoulder," said Van Campen.

"My shoulder's rested," said Marshall. "I'm goin'."

"You oughta be rested," called Colley. "You got more sleep than any of us while you was up that tree."

The men laughed as Marshall reddened and nodded in response.

"All right," continued Van Campen, "check your rifles, powder an' ammunition. You'll need 'em tonight. We'll light out at sunset. So, get somethin' to eat an' be ready to go."

The men dispersed to prepare for the night's work. As the sun dipped low to the horizon, Major Hoops appeared again. "Are your men ready?" he asked.

"Ready an' waitin'."

"It's time to assemble," said Hoops. "General Hand's men are forming on the edge of camp and, as soon as you take your position, we'll strike out for Chemung."

"Thank you, Major," said Van Campen.

Turning, Van Campen shot a look at Colley, who was just finishing his supper.

Looking up, Colley gathered the situation, quickly shoved in the last two spoonfuls and jumped to his feet. Chewing rapidly, he grabbed his rifle, possibles bag and haversack and assembled the company.

"We'll be there in a minute," Van Campen said to Hoops.

"I'll let them know. Good luck," he said as he turned and left.

"Thank you, major," Van Campen replied.

Colley soon had the men in formation and took his place in the front line, next to Van Campen. The men were ready and determined.

Van Campen said, "Boys, we're gonna be leadin' General Hand's men tonight. There'll be about eleven hundred of 'em, and we're the lookouts. Ev'rybody knows what to watch for. We'll have to be quick an' quiet an' keep a sharp eye out for ambushes. Once we get 'em to Chemung, we can finally take this war to the enemy's doorstep instead a' defendin' our own."

This statement brought low, but audible, approval from the men.

"Are we ready?" asked Van Campen.

"Yeah," they said.

"Then let's go."

Van Campen fell back in line next to Colley and led the men through camp to the assembly point. General Hand's men were already in line when they got there. The riflemen marched past the formation and took their position at the front.

General Hand approached Van Campen and said, "You're the eyes of the column, Lieutenant."

"Yes, sir," Van Campen replied.

"I'm told you are a very adept scout," said the general.

"I'm still here, sir."

"Yes, I suppose so," said Hand. "We want to keep surprise on our side. Can you get us to Chemung without bringing on a general engagement?"

"I can guide you up the trail an' make sure you don't wander into an ambush," said Van Campen, "but the enemy may already have seen you standin' here all lined up an' ready to march. Keeping surprise on our side, I can't guarantee."

"Fair enough," said Hand. "Take your men ahead, and we'll follow your lead."

"Yes, sir."

Van Campen turned to his men, who kept a strict formation in the presence of the regulars, and said, "Let's go."

They stepped off and headed up the trail. For the third straight evening, Van Campen was on his way toward the enemy. When the riflemen were out of sight, General Hand gave the order to march.

About midnight they passed the plains where Marshall had taken his fall. Van Campen split his company and sent half, under Colley, up one side and took half with him up the other.

Meeting again at the far side, no one had seen any sign of the enemy. This was the most dangerous point on the trail, and it appeared to be clear. They halted and waited for Hand's men to come up. Van Campen sent Colley with two men back to the lower end of the plain to await the general.

The regulars arrived about twenty minutes later. Colley informed the general all was clear, and they could proceed across the plain. Reaching the far end, Colley and the others rejoined their own company, and the march resumed.

They reached the village at daybreak. Van Campen halted his men and waited for the general to come up. "Chemung just ahead, sir," said Van Campen, when he did.

"Thank you, Lieutenant. Well done."

The general tried to grasp the lay of the village in the landscape. He looked to Van Campen and asked, "You've been in the village?"

"Yes, sir. Last night."

"What do you believe would be the best approach?" asked Hand.

"Well, if these was my men," answered Van Campen, "I'd form 'em up right here in a few lines spreadin' along the edge a' the village and hit 'em all from one side."

"I concur."

As the men came up, the general directed them off to the right and formed them three lines deep. On the left of the formation,

Hand stayed on the path and asked Van Campen and his men to accompany him into the village.

Hand gave the order, and the formation moved forward. Within moments they were in the village. Standing among the still flickering campfires, the troops were chagrined to find the village empty. It seemed the enemy had done some scouting of its own.

"So much for surprise," said the General.

"They didn't leave very long ago," said Van Campen. "In fact, you can see fresh tracks over there on the path where they moved on up the river."

"Damn," uttered Hand under his breath.

The general chose a detachment to ransack and burn the village, then said, "Lead on, Lieutenant the enemy lies ahead."

"Yes, sir," said Van Campen.

The scouts continued up the path, a short distance in front of Hand's column. They smelled the burning village behind them as thick black smoke wafted through the woods. Two miles further, the path squeezed close to the river and climbed a ridge to the right.

Van Campen's men started up the ridge when an enemy volley rang from the thickets on top of the hill. More than half of them fell. Van Campen ordered his men to take cover behind the riverbank.

As they slid over the edge, he said, "Be patient, boys. Don't shoot till we got somethin' t' shoot at."

A group of Indians soon left their cover and descended on the killed and wounded. Just as one of them pulled his knife and straddled Marshall's dead body, Van Campen shouted, "Fire!"

When the smoke cleared, the Indians lay dead beside the men they were about to scalp. Hearing the gunfire, General Hand came on at the double-quick with bayonets fixed. He brought his men in close to the enemy and ordered them to halt.

"Poise weapons!" he shouted, and his men swung their muskets off their shoulders and held them vertically in front of them. Extraneous shots whistled through the underbrush as the enemy took advantage of the plentiful targets.

"Cock firelocks!" Hand shouted, and the formation pulled the hammers in unison. An officer was shot in the face. Enemy fire slowed, however, as some broke and ran off through the woods.

"Take aim," Hand ordered, and the men brought their muskets to firing position and honed in on the puffs of smoke that came from the shots they'd been receiving.

"Fire!" The line erupted in a flash of light and a rattle of gunfire.

"Charge!" yelled Hand.

The men erupted with a simultaneous "Huzzah." They rushed into the wall of gunsmoke and broke through it with the glittering points of their bayonets. The remaining enemy ran. Hand pursued them for a short distance but soon ordered his men to stop and regroup.

Hand's casualties were one officer killed and one wounded. Ten of Van Campen's men were wounded and six more were dead. Hand saw Van Campen kneeling over one of the dead.

The general crossed to him and placed his hand on Van Campen's shoulder. "Your men took a heavy loss today, Lieutenant. You should be proud of the job you've done."

"We are, sir," he answered, looking down at Colley, who lay motionless. "We all are."

The general formed the men and marched them back to Chemung. They found all of the dwellings fully engulfed in flames and the surrounding fields and orchards cut and burned. Hand's army began its countermarch to Tioga, bearing the dead with them.

★　★　★　★　★

TIOGA POINT

In mid-August, Sullivan's troops were stunned to find the Susquehanna suddenly running full.

"Musta been a hell of a lot a' rain upstream," said the men.

Sullivan himself realized the rest of his army was about to join him.

"Lieutenant," said Sullivan to Van Campen, "I'm sending General Poor with nine hundred men up the Susquehanna to meet the army from Cherry Valley and safeguard its approach. I'd like for you to lead your scouts at the head of his column."

"Yessir, General."

On the trail, a few mornings later, Van Campen heard activity in the woods ahead. He turned and motioned for his men to fan out and be ready for an ambush. Van Campen advanced a short distance from his company as they deployed.

Suddenly, he saw a body flash between the trees in front of him and he knew he was being flanked. On his left, he saw what he thought was a good position, some fifteen yards away. He noiselessly sprinted to the spot and took cover behind a tree. He waited, not knowing if he'd been seen or not.

He scanned the terrain. Motion caught his eye some thirty yards ahead of him. It was the barrel of a rifle being pointed at him from behind a boulder. Van Campen ducked back behind the tree and rolled to the other side, where he drew a bead on his would-be assailant.

The rifle barrel he'd seen was still there, but he couldn't get a good shot at the person behind it. Van Campen studied the situation for any slight advantage he could find. Then, a wry smile crept across his face. He even allowed himself a chuckle as he realized the rifle pointed at him had *two* barrels.

He tucked himself firmly behind the tree and loosed a shout that rang through the forest. "Haloo Norry!" he yelled in a call that flushed birds and animals for at least a mile around.

"You dumb son of a bitch, I almost shot you!" shouted a voice in reply.

Van Campen laughed and came out from behind the tree.

"Almost shot *me*? This was nearly the end a' the great Tim Murphy."

The men came out from cover and met with a hearty handshake. "Mose, you ain't no Northumberland man, how'd you know our call?"

"I hunted with enough a' you fellas, how could I not know it?"

The two old friends had a good laugh over the episode, and, slowly, Van Campen's and Murphy's men came out from their hiding places and greeted each other as well.

"How'd you know we was comin'?" asked Murphy.

"When the river swelled, Gen'ral Sullivan figured you boys musta dammed it t' ride the current," said Van Campen.

"That's just what we done," said Tim. "So, how's ol' Cap'ns Brady and Boone doin'?"

Van Campen drew in a breath. He knew Murphy was close to them.

"They're both killed," said Van Campen. "Brady was waylaid at the crick just outside his fort last April, and Boone was killed trying to relieve Fort Freeland just before we come."

Murphy reflected for a moment. "They were some a' the good ones," he said.

Van Campen nodded.

Word passed back along the lines that the armies had met, and the combined forces faced downriver and headed for Tioga.

When the first of the Cherry Valley men's batteaux came into view, the armies erupted in volleys of cannon fire and cheers. Fifes and drums played, and Sullivan declared a holiday. It took the next three days to reorganize the now completed force. The campaign was ready to begin in earnest.

★ ★ ★ ★ ★

NEW YORK STATE SOUTHERN TIER

The army marched through the ashes of Chemung and on up the path into the heart of enemy territory. In the next few weeks, Sullivan's men burned villages, storehouses, fields and orchards as the outnumbered Iroquois fled before them.

Van Campen and Murphy and their men kept the point and scouted ahead of the main army.

"Hey, Mose," said Murphy.

"Yeah?"

"Does that pass up ahead look funny to you?"

"Where?"

"There, where the path runs between that hill an' the river."

"Yeah," said Van Campen. "The brush on the hill is half-dead while everything around it is green."

"Look closer," said Murphy. "That's an entrenchment. They cut that brush and used it to disguise the works."

"You're right," agreed Van Campen. "Let's tell the major."

Parr halted the column and called for General Sullivan. When he'd been briefed, he turned to Murphy.

"Good work, soldier," said the general. "If undetected, the enemy could have poured a devastating flanking fire on us."

"Thank you, sir," said Murphy.

"Now, Major," continued Sullivan, "I'd like your riflemen to open fire on the position. Pin 'em down. I'll bring up the artillery to shell the works, and we'll flank it with the main army."

"Yessir," said Parr.

The riflemen kept up the diversionary fire through the shelling until the main army was in position. Then Sullivan launched a bayonet charge that sent the enemy scrambling.

Murphy and Van Campen walked ahead to inspect the abandoned works after the battle. They came across members of the

1st New Jersey who were milling around the corpses of two very large Indians. Two soldiers were kneeling next to the bodies and skinning them from the hips down.

"What in the hell are ya doin'?" Van Campen asked one of those standing and watching.

"We're gonna tan 'em an' make 'em into boots for our officers," he answered.

Van Campen looked at Murphy, who seemed just as stunned.

"I guess the enemy don't have all the savages in this war," said Murphy as they walked away.

★ ★ ★ ★ ★

GENESEE, NEW YORK

The army finally penetrated all the way to the village of Genesee, just 75 miles or so from the Tory base of operations at Fort Niagara. Sullivan added the village to the list of destruction, then turned his army and headed back for Tioga.

"Wish't we coulda taken Fort Niagara, too," said Van Campen as the column headed east.

"Well, we done pretty good," answered Murphy. "We burned more 'n forty Indian towns with all their winter stores clean across York State. I think Sullivan was pretty smart t' turn back. Winter comes mighty early up here, and I wouldn't want t' be stuck waitin' out a siege when it does."

"Well, that's true," Van Campen agreed. "Besides, it'll take 'em a while t' recover from this. They shouldn't bother us in the valley any more this year."

When they reached Tioga, the army rested for a few days and celebrated its success. There was music, feasting and plentiful rum rations.

On the evening before the armies left, Van Campen took a stroll away from the frivolity to a solitary spot over the riverbank where they'd interred the dead. He stood for some time in the twilight, staring out at the golden-violet light swirling on the current.

"Well, Tub," he said out loud, "we struck a blow for the folks at home, anyhow."

"That we did," said a voice from behind him.

Van Campen turned and saw Tim Murphy.

"Visitin' a friend?" asked Murphy.

"Yeah, Tub Colley . . . the night we took Chemung, b'fore you fellas showed up."

"I knew Tubby," said Tim. "Went huntin' with him once'd. I think he ate a whole quarter a' venison in one sittin'."

"That's Tub," laughed Van Campen.

"Shame to lose 'im," said Tim. "He was one a' the good ones, too."

"He was that."

They fell silent and watched the sky deepen to a soft reddish-purple. The last of the birds raced across the sky on the way back to their nests, and the sound of crickets and tree toads filled the air.

"So what's yer plan now?" Van Campen asked Murphy.

"I gotta head back to Cherry Valley," replied Tim. "There's work there to do yet."

"Plenty a' work back in the valley, too," countered Van Campen. "We could use you back there."

"It's temptin', Mose. I miss home, but there's something about bein' up here that's startin' to feel like home, too."

"What's her name?" asked Van Campen.

Tim grinned and said, "I gotta stay here. Besides, with me here and you takin' care a' things back home, the enemy don't stand a chance."

Van Campen chuckled.

They watched the lightning bugs rise out of the grass.

Finally, Van Campen extended his hand and said, "You take care a yerself, Tim."

"You too, Mose," Murphy answered as they clasped hands.

Van Campen looked Murphy in the eye, slapped him on the shoulder and walked back to camp.

The next morning, Sullivan's troops headed down the Susquehanna while the Cherry Valley men marched for home. At Wyoming, the main army headed back to Easton and Van Campen and his men stayed on the river until they reached Sunbury.

★　★　★　★　★

FORT AUGUSTA

"Get your wood laid in for winter?" asked Hunter.

"Yep. Wood's cut an' the butcherin's done," answered Van Campen, who'd spent the past weeks with his family at Fort Jenkins.

"How are you, Moses?"

"Just fine, thanks."

"I heard it went well," said Hunter.

"We pushed 'em back from Tioga to Genessee," said Van Campen. "Gave 'em a taste a' their own medicine."

"Yes, I heard," said Hunter.

"And, *I* heard the enemy hasn't been back to the valley."

"So far, that's true," said Hunter. "I hope it lasts. Our defenses still aren't back to full strength."

"What's the plan?" asked Van Campen.

"Well, after Forts Freeland and Boone were destroyed, I felt we needed another stronghold between the North and West Branches. Montgomery's farm seemed best because of the spring there."

"Makes good sense," agreed Van Campen.

"I assigned some of the returning militia to fortify the position. They started work on a stockade fence around the spring, but then we learned a regiment of regulars was assigned here from Wyoming."

"Oh, is Hartley back?"

"I wish," said Hunter. "No. It's the German Regiment."

"The Pennsylvania Dutch boys? They're good soldiers," said Van Campen.

"Oh, I'm not doubting them," said Hunter. "But, Colonel Weltner has some unique ideas about how they should be used."

"How do you mean?"

"Well . . . here," said Hunter, handing him a letter. "This is a copy of my report to Council President Reed. It explains everything."

Van Campen took the letter and read:

Sunbury, November 27ᵗʰ, 1779
Sir,

Yours of the 20ᵗʰ, I received informing me of what you had done in regard of procuring some troops for the safety of this county. The Board of War has ordered the German Regiment from Wyoming to this place, and desired the commanding officer to advise with me in stationing his troops in such manner and places as would be deemed most proper.

When the Colonel and I met upon this, I made mention to rebuild Fort Muncy and garrison it with one-hundred men, with twenty at Fort Jenkins, a sergeant's guard at Bosley's Mills on Chillisquaque, another sergeant's guard at Titzol's Mills in Buffalo Valley, and the remainder where the commanding officer resided.

I was informed the regiment consisted of two-hundred men but, instead of that number, there was but one-hundred & twenty effective men, exclusive of officers. Therefore, we have but sixty men to order out to the frontiers as the commanding officer is resolved to keep one-half with himself in Sunbury to relieve the others monthly.

So, we'll have but forty men at Montgomery's Fort and twenty men at Fort Jenkins. Captain Kemplen and his

*company of fourteen Rangers are stationed at Mineger's place
on the West Branch, about seventeen miles from Sunbury.*

*I remain yr Excellency's
Most humble servt,
Sam'l Hunter, Lieut.*

"He's keepin' half with *him*?" said Van Campen.

"He is," answered Hunter.

"So the forty at Montgomery's is finishin' the stockade?"

"Actually, that's some positive news," answered Hunter. "They're under Captain Rice. He felt they could do better than just the stockade, so they finished that and then proceeded to gather surface limestone to put a building directly over the spring. He plans to raise it to two-and-a-half stories."

"Now, that'll be a good fort," said Van Campen.

"I agree. In fact, we're calling it Fort Rice."

★ ★ ★ ★ ★

PHILADELPHIA

Wallis sat alone in front of the hearth and stared into the flames. A half-empty decanter sat on the table next to him. Outside, snow choked the streets.

It had been a frustrating year. He thought about the riches and accolades he'd expected in return for his service to the British, but none of it materialized. His counter-revolution never got started. Even with Brady out of the way, the locals remained stubborn in their cause and McDonell's raid didn't do the damage he'd hoped.

Wallis poured himself another glass and brooded that his false map didn't bring Sullivan to ruin, either. He'd learned the general received so many varying maps of the Iroquois country that he didn't trust any of them. On the trail, he simply relied on his guides.

"Well, at least there's Andre," said Wallis to himself. "Plan a Mischianza and you get to be head of British Secret Intelligence," he laughed.

CHAPTER 14

March-April 1780

FORT JENKINS

"I think we better git workin' on the new house," said Van Campen's father when the deep snows finally melted. "We can get 'er built this spring, put in a crop, and start gittin' things back to normal."

"I ain't so sure, pop," answered Moses. "Them Indians ain't gonna be too happy about us burnin' 'em out last fall. Luggin' supplies up the crick and bangin' around in the woods don't seem like the safest thing to me. . . . At least until we know if any raidin' parties are startin' back this way."

"Well, I ain't too happy about 'em burnin' *us* out two years ago, neither," said the elder Van Campen. "Now's when we got to get it built to still have time to get the plowin' and plantin' done. Besides, youins' whupped 'em all the way back to Fort Niagara, didn't ya?"

"Yeah, but that don't mean they can't come right back," said Moses.

"Leave 'em come. Our land is just layin' out there empty while we sit here in this fort. We need a house and I'm ready to build it whether you want to come help or not."

"Pop, you *know* I'll help," answered Moses.

"All right, then. Let's get 'er built. Your Uncle Jacob and Peter Pence each wants t' rebuild their places, too. We'll all go together."

The group left Fort Jenkins and started up Fishing Creek a few days later.

Arriving at a graceful bend in the creek, Moses, his father and his little brother reached their home site. They bid farewell to the others and soon were hard at work felling and dressing trees.

That night, it snowed another four inches of light powder, but it didn't slow them down. The Van Campens raised the walls to the height of three logs by noon the next day.

"How's that one comin', boy?" shouted Moses' father. "Did you git them branches cut off yet? I'm outta logs."

"Almost, Pop," answered Moses' little brother. "I'm comin'."

"Comin'? You still got half a trunk left to do. Here, lemme help you," he laughed.

Moses chuckled to himself as he felled another tree. He loved the camaraderie and good-natured ribbing. He was happy to spend this time with his family.

Moses laid down his axe and wiped the sweat from his brow. When he looked up, he was stunned to see an Indian raider rushing toward his father with a spear. His father and brother were bent over the log and didn't see the Indian running toward them.

"Pop! Behind you!" shouted Moses.

Moses stood helpless and watched his father turn at the very moment the Indian thrust the spear. His father stood motionless for a moment and careened backward.

Other raiders grabbed Moses from behind before he could even react. More rushed in and held his brother. His father writhed painfully on the ground.

The attacker grabbed the end of the spear and rocked it slowly back and forth and laughed. Then, he dropped to his knees over Moses' father, withdrew his knife and scalped him.

When the trophy was secured, the Indian placed the point of his knife under the man's ear and cut a deep gash across his throat. Slowly, the struggle and suffering ceased.

Moses kept silent during his father's torture, but his little brother wept. When the old man's movements ceased, the boy turned to Moses and sobbed, "Father's dead."

Moses' heart sank. He knew his brother's demonstration sealed his fate. A moment later, one of the Indians raised his tomahawk and struck the boy's head.

Twisting in pain, he'd barely fallen to the ground before undergoing the same brutal scalping that so terrified him moments before. Then, they threw the boy on the fire he'd built to burn the branches cut from the logs. Moses watched him feebly try to pull himself from the flames.

The Indian who killed Moses' father wrenched the spear from the corpse and leveled it at Moses. He ran at Moses, who was still held by two other Indians. Moses twisted as the warrior thrust the spear, and it grazed his side.

The two Indians holding Moses pulled him from his attacker, bound him and led him up the path. Scarlet streaks gashed the snow where his father lay and the horrid smell of his brother's burning remains clung in Moses' nose.

The raiders collected the Van Campens' belongings, packed everything on Moses' horse and followed.

When they reached the home sites of his uncle and Peter Pence, Moses saw they'd also been attacked. His uncle and cousin lay mutilated, and the raiders busily gathered the settlers' supplies.

Moses saw Peter Pence tied to a tree. Peter also noticed Moses, but both knew better than to react. When the scavenging was over, the group moved out.

They traveled far up Fishing Creek and finally stopped at dusk. The Indians gave the captives a few morsels of food and told them to go to sleep.

When he closed his eyes, Moses still saw his butchered father. . . and his brother struggling to free himself from the flames. The scenes played themselves over and over.

Moses was already awake when he was nudged the next morning. He'd gotten very little sleep. He stood and felt more exhausted than he ever remembered being. He looked up through the trees and took a deep breath. Then, a cuff in the ear got him headed up the trail.

The morning was brisk and raw. The bracing air was like a tonic. It penetrated deep into Moses' lungs and restored his strength and clarity.

At the headwaters of Fishing Creek, they saw smoke curling into the sky from across a meadow. It came from a settler's camp. The Indians stopped and planned for what seemed like another easy raid.

From the edge of the woods, they watched a man and his wife busily tapping sugar maples and boiling the sap in a large kettle over the fire. The couple had a small child, wrapped in blankets, sitting beneath a tree.

An Indian pointed his knife at Moses.

"Yankee, call him," he said.

Moses dreaded the idea of luring more innocent people to the raiders, but he had no choice. He glanced at Pence, drew a deep breath, and stepped out into the edge of the meadow.

"Hey, come here," he yelled.

The man turned.

"What d' ya want?"

"Com'ere," called Van Campen.

The man looked hesitantly at his wife and then came trotting down the path.

"You alright?' asked the man as he reached Van Campen.

"You not alright, Yankee," yelled a raider as the Indians rose from the underbrush. Terrified, the man fell to his knees and begged for his life.

"Oh, my God. Don't kill me. Please," he moaned.

Clasping his hands together he reached toward the Indians imploring them.

"I've got a wife and child who need me," he pleaded. "Oh God, oh God, oh God. Pleeeease."

Rarely seeing a demonstration like this, the Indians broke out in laughter. They hauled the man to his feet and shoved him back up the path toward his wife. The woman knew running was futile.

"Sarah," the woman called to her child. The toddler steadied herself against the tree and teetered toward her mother. The woman gathered her into her arms just as the raiders arrived. One of the warriors struck the man from behind and sent him sprawling on the ground at the woman's feet.

The child squealed.

A raider immediately snatched the toddler from her mother and held her by the feet. He swung her in a great circle, intending to smash her head against a tree.

"Nooooo!" screamed the horrified mother as she lunged into the path of her child. She caught her mid-arc and pulled her free from the stunned Indian's grasp.

He turned on the woman and pulled his tomahawk when another raider grabbed his arm and ended the attack. The brave woman stood her ground and glared back at them both.

The Indian who intervened walked to the boiling kettle and dipped some sap out into the dust. After giving it a moment to cool, he knelt and worked it into a thick paste which he used to paint a mark on her forehead.

"You very brave," he said, admiringly. He looked at her husband, who was now weeping, and shook his head.

"You go," he said turning back to her. "Take little one and go. Follow path to river and go find Yankees. No Indian hurt you now."

The woman looked at her husband in a silent farewell. Then, she turned and walked down the path. The man was on his knees.

"Thank you, thank you, thank you," he repeated fervently with his face to the sky.

As his wife and child disappeared into the woods, the man pulled himself to his feet.

"What the hell'd you call me for?" he yelled at Van Campen.

"I didn't have a lot of choice," answered Moses calmly. "I'm sorry. What's your name?"

"Pike."

"I'm Van Campen; that's Pence."

"No talk," shouted the captor next to Van Campen, hitting him across the face with the back of his hand.

As before, the raiders plundered the settler's valuables and continued along the path. By early evening, they arrived back on the North Branch.

The raiders waded into the underbrush and retrieved several canoes they'd hidden there. They glided out under the deepening crimson sky and paddled to the far side of the river.

Moses was puzzled why the raiders pushed on when it would soon be dark. Then, in the fading light, they arrived at a campground. Instead of the friendly fire and welcoming comrades the Indians expected to find, there was a pit of cold ashes surrounded by four slain Indians.

Moses realized the dead were part of the same raiding party. They must have taken prisoners who'd been able to kill their captors and escape.

The Indians' mood made it clear things just got worse. Even if they weren't killed right away, they'd be the first captives in Niagara since Sullivan's raid. Their fate was easy to imagine.

While the Indians tended to their dead, Van Campen spoke with Pence and Pike.

"We gotta git outta this mess as soon as we can," he whispered.

"That's for damn sure," agreed Pence. Pike looked at them with his mouth agape.

Pence continued, "We can wait till they're sleepin' an' grab the guns."

"No good," answered Moses. "There's ten a' them. The first shot would wake 'em and there ain't no way we'd have time to kill 'em all."

Pike's head was on a swivel as he gazed from one man to the other.

"Well, how do you figure it, Mose?" asked Pence.

"I see it this way. When they fall asleep, we take their tomahawks and knives. Then, we can each kill three of 'em while they sleep. Even if they start to wake up, they'll be too groggy to be able to fight before it's over."

"I still like the idea a' gettin' the guns," said Pence.

"Alright," answered Van Campen. "Then why don't me and Pike take our places amongst 'em while you go to the stack a' guns? We'll kill as many as we can before they start to wake up. When they do, you start shootin'."

"Sounds good," agreed Pence.

Moses turned and said, "Pike, sound good to you?"

"I . . . I don't know," he stammered.

Pence spit in disgust, but Moses remained calm.

He explained, "If we don't do nothin' we don't stand a chance a' survivin', Pike. This is our only hope a gettin' outta this. If you ever want to see that wife and little girl a' yours again, this is how it'll happen."

"Well . . ." Pike drew a deep breath and nodded.

Just then, an Indian with an ax strode toward the prisoners. Moses turned, ready for a fight, but Pence laid a hand on his shoulder.

The Indian raised the ax, handle first. He shoved it toward Van Campen and said, "Cut wood, Yankee."

Pike exhaled.

"Get more axes there," said the Indian, pointing. "Go Yankees. Cut wood."

Moses, Pence and Pike chopped wood and stoked the fire for the next hour. When they were told to stop, each was given a bit of food and some water. Then, they were told to lie down. Each had an Indian between him and the next captive.

Another raider came along and bound each of the captives, hand and foot. He used a long rope confiscated from the settlers and, each time, cut the length he needed with his knife.

After tying up Pike and Pence, he came to Van Campen and cut two more pieces of rope. The Indian dropped the knife and began securing him. After tying his feet, the Indian motioned to Van Campen to sit up and put his hands in front of him. Van Campen did as he was told but, at the same time, turned his feet so they covered the knife.

The Indian made sure the ropes were as tight as possible. When he finished, he said, "That hold you. Now sleep."

"Did you have to make it so tight?" complained Moses, diverting attention from the hidden knife.

"Maybe not tight enough, Yankee," the Indian responded. "Sleep."

The Indian walked to the other side of the fire and laid down.

Loud snores soon permeated the woods around the fire, but Van Campen lay still. Knowing this was their best chance to escape, he wanted to make sure all the Indians were sound asleep. Hours slipped by as he watched the clouds race past the moon.

Finally, Moses raised himself to one elbow. No one stirred. He sat up and, for the first time since he was bound, moved his feet from above the knife. He reached down and grabbed it with both hands.

Silently, he sawed away at the rope binding his feet. It fell to the ground. Then, he held the knife handle firmly between his feet and worked on the rope around his wrists. He was free.

Pence sat up. Moses rose and quickly freed him. Pence stayed in place while Moses went to loosen Pike, who stared wide-eyed through the darkness back at him.

As the last of the ropes fell away, Van Campen and Pence took their places. Both looked at Pike and motioned him to get ready.

Pike stood and took a step. The Indian next to him stirred, and Pike lay back down. Knowing the Indians could awaken and unravel the entire plan, Van Campen moved back to Pike's position, grabbed a tomahawk from the Indian's belt and raised it.

Pike saw the polished metal reflect the firelight just as Moses plunged it into the Indian's temple. He finished his victim with a quick slice of the knife across his throat. Moses repeated the procedure on the now awakening Indian on his other side.

Blood-spattered, Pike cowered and drew himself back as far as he could while Moses leapt to his original place and quickly disposed of his own three targets.

Now, with the odds evening, Pence could wait no longer. Standing by the stacked guns, he opened on the five remaining Indians still sleeping on the other side of the fire. Grabbing one gun after another, he got off three headshots in rapid succession before the Indians could even get to their feet.

The last two rose and lurched toward him as he scored another perfect headshot on the first. To his surprise, the lone remaining raider ran right past Pence into the woods. Van Campen knew if he got away, it wouldn't be long before more raiders would be on their heels. He hurled the tomahawk at the retreating Indian and struck him in the neck.

Van Campen sprinted after the raider, who sprawled on the ground, and threw himself on top on him. The Indian turned and wrapped his hands in a vice-grip around Van Campen's throat. Rolling, the Indian was now sitting on Van Campen's stomach.

Van Campen reached up with his foot and shoved him off. While Moses regained his feet, the Indian ran off through the woods.

Turning back toward the fire, Moses saw Pike kneeling amidst the carnage with his hands outstretched to the heavens. Pence stood over him and berated him with the most *unholy* language Van Campen had heard in a long time.

"It's good to see you're doin' somethin' useful, Pence," said Moses wryly. "It didn't occur to ya to give me a hand did it?"

Pence's tirade on Pike quickly lost steam.

"Aw," said Pence, "I knew you wasn't gonna let the last one git ya."

"We'd better git movin'," said Moses. "Won't be long till he rounds up his friends and comes back after us."

Moses casually reached down into the belt of one of the dead raiders and pulled a knife. He tossed it so it landed at Pence's feet and said, "Let's git to work."

The two men quickly scalped the dead as Pike fervently prayed. Trophies taken, Moses strung the scalps on his belt and retrieved those of his family. They gathered what food and weapons they could carry.

Ready to move, Moses walked up to Pike, reached down and took him under the arm. Gently, he raised him to his feet and said, "It's over now, but we got to go. We need ya to carry some a' this stuff with us."

Pike murmured, "Amen," and accepted tomahawks and knives tucked into his belt and bags of shot and powder placed over his shoulder. Moses led the way out of camp and headed downriver until he was sure they couldn't easily be found. Then he said, "Let's git some sleep."

By dawn, the men were already on their way to Wyoming. There, Pike found his wife and child. Moses and Pence secured a canoe and headed home.

In Fort Jenkins, Van Campen and Pence were met with celebration.

Moses went to see his mother, who he found sitting by the fire.

"Ma?" he said delicately as he entered the room.

Turning, the woman's face twisted with emotion. She lurched from her chair and flung herself on her boy.

"We thought you was dead for sure," she choked out pitifully between her sobs. "Yer Pa and brother . . ."

"I know," he said, as her voice trailed off.

"It was horrible," she continued.

"I know," he said again. Then added, "I got them that did it."

She hugged him long and hard.

A few days later, Moses traveled to Sunbury to report to Colonel Hunter. Word of his arrival preceded him. Whoops and cheers greeted him as he reached the fort. Moses spent the next few days shaking hands and sharing more than one jug with those who were eager to hear the details of his escape.

The day before Van Campen's return to Fort Jenkins, Colonel Hunter called him back into his office.

"Moses," said Hunter, "I've just received these orders for you. You've been assigned to Captain Robinson's company. It's a good thing you made your escape," added Hunter in a fatherly tone.

"Why's that?" asked Moses.

"If you'd been off gallivanting in Indian country when this arrived, you'd have been arrested for dereliction of duty."

Moses looked deadpan at Hunter for a moment, then broke into a wide grin.

"Yeah, I guess that's so."

"Moses," said Hunter. "I'm very happy to see you safe. We need you."

Moses stood awkwardly, not knowing how to answer.

"Now, take care of yourself," said Hunter, "and best of luck in your new company."

"Thank you, sir," he answered.

CHAPTER 15

May-December 1780

OUTSIDE PHILADELPHIA

Wallis jostled inside the carriage as the road stretched along the Schuykill River. When he finally reached Fairmont Park, he was impressed. General Arnold had purchased the estate for his bride, Peggy Shippen.

"Not a bad wedding present at that," he said to himself.

Wallis was summoned by the general, but he didn't know why. He pondered it all morning.

He'd cultivated the relationship with Arnold just after the general was given command of Philadelphia.

"In fact," thought Wallis, "if it wasn't for me, his trade through British lines with New York would never have been successful."

Wallis considered the irony of how that trade made him a small fortune and ended up getting Arnold investigated by the Pennsylvania Council. And, that investigation caused Arnold to begin sharing intelligence with the British.

Stansbury confided to Wallis that he was Arnold's messenger to Andre and General Clinton. Arnold passed information on American troops and strategies and even suggested British responses.

Wallis admired the general. He laughed when he thought about Arnold representing himself at his court martial a few months ago. He'd given such a performance, the court acquitted him of all but two minor charges and sentenced him only to receive an official reprimand from General Washington.

Wallis stepped down from the carriage and climbed the elegant stairs to the door. He knocked. The door was answered by a pretty, young servant girl.

"Samuel Wallis to see General Arnold," he said.

"Yes, Mr. Wallis. The general is expecting you. This way."

Wallis followed the girl into a drawing room and found Arnold at his desk.

"Mr. Wallis. How good of you to come," said Arnold.

"It's my pleasure, General."

"I'll come right to the point," said Arnold. "I know you are acquainted with Mr. Stansbury. I expect you share his political sympathies."

"I've never given any indication . . ." parried Wallis.

"I know you haven't," said Arnold. "That's why I want to work with *you*."

"I'm sorry?"

"Mr. Wallis. I need a straight answer. I'm about to include you in an opportunity that could make you most valuable to General Clinton. Now, are you a loyalist?"

Wallis stared back at Arnold.

"I'm a damned good one, General," he said. "In fact, I'm good enough to know of your activities. I admire how you've kept your cover at the same time. It's what I've done myself."

"I'm aware of that," said Arnold. "Like I said. . . that's why I want to work with *you*."

"In that case," said Wallis, "I'm listening."

"Good," said Arnold. "When I was acquitted of the charges against me, I lobbied General Washington for a new command. He offered to put me at the head of the American troops joining French General Rochambeau at Newport. I told him my wound wouldn't permit it, and I asked, instead, for command of West Point."

"Outstanding," said Wallis, who already deciphered Arnold's plan. "That's the key to the continent."

"Quite," said Arnold. "I'm optimistic about receiving the post.

In the meantime, I've been communicating with Andre and Clinton about Rochambeau's arrival."

"Hasn't Clinton been in South Carolina?" asked Wallis.

"Yes. It's been complicated," answered Arnold. "I gave my messages to Stansbury. He passed them through Captain Beckwith to General Knyphausen, in New York, and *he* forwarded them to Andre and Clinton. But, replies were very erratic. Military communication is routine. It's Stansbury's reliability I question."

Wallis smiled. Now, he knew why he was here. ". . . and, to take Stansbury's place makes it even more delectable . . ." he thought.

"Now that Clinton is back in New York," Arnold continued, "I must rely on good communications and, of course, discretion. I'd like to entrust this project to you."

"I'd be honored to work with you, General."

"Good," said Arnold. "This letter contains my first mention of West Point to General Clinton. It will begin the bargaining process. I'd like for you to get it to Andre."

"That won't be a problem, sir," said Wallis.

"I thought not. Now, I'd like you to hear part of this," said Arnold. "Obviously, it's in veiled language, but it's easily deciphered when you know its meaning." He read:

The bearer, in whom confidence may be placed, is instructed to fix on a plan of safe conveyance and operations.

I have advanced several sums already, without any profit. It is now necessary for me to know the risk I run in case of a loss. I expect you will pay into the hands of the bearer 1,000 guineas.

As life and fortune are risked by serving his majesty, it is necessary a compensation for services be agreed on; and the mentioned sum advanced, which Sir Henry will not, I believe, think unreasonable.

I have great confidence in the bearer. He will bring

me 200 guineas and pay the remainder to Andre, who is requested to receive the deposit for Mr. Moore.

"There now, Mr. Wallis," said Arnold. "You know what is expected of you. Take all pains to deliver this directly to Major Andre. Never, under any circumstances, refer to me by name. If necessary, you may refer to me as Mr. Moore. Be sure to secure the deposit you will be given. It is but the beginning. When we've completed our task, there will be plenty to go around for all of us."

"Yes, sir, General," answered Wallis.

Wallis hadn't understood Arnold wished him to *personally* deliver the letter. He was adept at arranging shipments through the lines, but he was less sure about making the trip himself. He knew what it would mean to be caught with such sensitive information. Still, he wasn't about to let this opportunity pass.

"Be off now, and be quick with a response," said Arnold.

"Of course, sir."

Wallis accepted the message and returned to his office. He settled in to meticulously plan every detail . . . and he lost precious time in his deliberations.

Days passed. Stansbury arrived at Arnold's home with a message from Clinton. Arnold tore it open, devoured its contents and stood dumbfounded. "He mentions nothing of my proposal," Arnold seethed.

Arnold replied immediately, and more plainly, through Stansbury.

I received a letter without date or signature, informing me that Sir Henry ----was obliged to me for the intelligence communicated and that he placed a full confidence in the sincerity of my intentions, etc., etc. On the 13th instant I addressed a letter to you expressing my sentiments and expectations.

The following preliminaries must be settled previous

*to co-operation: Sir Henry will secure to me my property,
valued at £10,000 sterling, to be paid to me or my heirs
in case of loss. For my services, five hundred pounds per
annum will be secured to me for life, in lieu of the pay and
emoluments I give up.*

*If I point out a plan by which Sir Henry shall possess
himself of West Point, £20,000 sterling I think will be a
cheap purchase for an object of so much importance. At the
same time, I request £1,000 to be paid to my agent. I expect
a full and explicit answer. The 20th I set off for West Point.*

Stansbury passed Arnold's letter to Andrew Furstner, one of
his own agents, to take to Andre. Furstner quickly made the trip to
New York and delivered the letter on July 23rd.

Wallis had still yet to make his own delivery. Furstner received
a reply the next day and headed back to Philadelphia.

In his reply, Clinton informed Arnold:

*Your letter of the 15th is arrived; that of the 13th is not
yet come to hand. Should we, through your means, possess
ourselves of West Point's 3,000 men and its artillery and
stores, the sum even of £20,000 should be paid you.*

*You must not suppose that in case of detection or
failure that, your efforts being known, you would be left a
victim; but services done are the terms on which we promise
rewards. In these you see we are profuse; we conceive them
proportioned to the risk.*

*As to an absolute promise of indemnification to the
amount of £10,000 and annuity of £500 whether services
are performed or not, it can never be made. Your intelligence
we prize and will freely recompense it. £200 shall be lodged
in your agent's hands as you desire, and £300 more are at
your disposal.*

On July 28th, Wallis finally completed his journey through the lines with Arnold's letter. He reached John Odell's Wall Street home and used the familiar knock at the door.

"Mr. Odell," said Wallis. "My name is Samuel Wallis. I've come on behalf of Mr. Moore. I understand you work closely with Major Andre."

"Welcome, Mr. Wallis," said Odell. "I do, indeed. Won't you come in?"

"Thank you."

"Unfortunately, Major Andre is busy with General Clinton planning a response to counter a French landing at Newport, Rhode Island."

"Oh, I see," said Wallis.

"No matter," assured Odell. "I'm sure I can help. What is the situation?"

"I was told to deliver this message to Major Andre only. Is it possible to get a message to him?"

"Why, certainly," said Odell, "but it will take some time."

"Very well," said Wallis. "Please let him know I have a message for him from Mr. Moore and am expected to return with the first payment."

"I will certainly get that message to the captain. In the meantime, why don't I send for Captain Beckwith? He should be made aware of this as well."

"If it will speed things along, that is acceptable," said Wallis.

When Beckwith arrived, he sat down with Wallis.

". . . and so you see, Captain, I'm expected to return with the first payment," said Wallis.

"Yes, I do see," said Beckwith. "Well," he said, reaching inside his coat to produce the requested £200, "if you'll sign a receipt, I'm happy to expedite the matter."

"Sound business, sir," said Wallis, as he signed. "Sound business."

"Travel safely, Mr. Wallis," said Odell.

"Thank you, sir," he answered. "I believe Mr. Moore will be pleased."

Wallis walked along Wall Street and began thinking about going back through the lines with £200 in his pocket. He certainly couldn't risk losing it.

"I'll find Coxe," thought Wallis.

Daniel Coxe was another of Wallis' cohorts.

"Here," said Wallis, when they met. "I'd like for you to keep this £200 on account for me. It is destined for one whose actions will likely decide the outcome of the conflict," he boasted. "As I am trusted implicitly, I cannot risk travelling back through the lines with such a weighty amount. I was harassed by patrols on my way here and extorted out of £10. I can't risk losing this payment."

"Certainly, Samuel," replied Coxe. "It's as safe with me as if it were in the bank."

"I don't doubt it."

"Safe journey, Samuel."

Wallis arrived back in Philadelphia and learned Arnold had left for West Point.

Weeks later, Wallis heard a knock at his door. He answered it to find Stansbury shivering on his stoop.

"What is it?" asked Wallis.

"May I come in, Samuel?"

"Yes, yes. Come in," said Wallis standing aside.

Stansbury slipped through the door and took a seat before it was offered.

"What is it?" Wallis asked again.

"It's Major Andre," said Stansbury. "He traveled up the Hudson to meet Arnold near West Point. By the time they'd completed their meeting, Andre's ship had been shelled, and it sailed off without him. Andre was forced to travel back to New York by land with the plans to the stronghold in his boot. He was captured."

"What of Arnold?" asked Wallis.

"He barely escaped."

"Thank God," said Wallis.

"Yes, but Andre's been hung."

"What?"

"He couldn't very well travel in uniform, so he donned civilian clothes. The Americans held him as a spy. They offered to trade him for Arnold, but Clinton wouldn't go back on his word. Andre was hung in his stead."

"Oh, I see," said Wallis. "Well . . . thank you for sharing this with me. Now, if you'll excuse me, I've got some affairs to attend to."

Stansbury looked up at Wallis. He was astonished. Without another word, he stood and left, leaving the door open behind him.

Wallis closed the door and took a seat at his desk.

"So," he said out loud, "it seems I'm out my two best connections. I'll have to make the most of those that remain."

He picked up his pen and wrote . . .

Dear Captain Beckwith . . .

Wallis' relationship with Beckwith flourished. In fact, Wallis grew in prominence and his rewards grew in size. Finally, he answered the letter that confirmed he'd reached the status he'd craved for so long.

Wallis savored the moment as he read his last paragraph over and over:

> *I thank his Excellency for his offer of the 200 guineas annually and accept it as a mark of his approbation for my conduct. I also thank him for his further offer of paying me for any essential service which I may render to government.*
> *Your most humble sv't,*
> *The Gentleman from Philadelphia*

★ ★ ★ ★ ★

FORT RICE

"Them Dutchmen sure can lay stone, can't they?" said Gagnon, a ranger garrisoned at the fort.

"Yeah, but it left us mighty thin when they was ordered back east," answered Carr. "I'd feel better if there was more than twenty of us."

"Still," said Gagnon, "I'm glad we ended up here. This place is solid."

Tallow candles flickered in the dusk as the men ate their evening meal.

To the east, under cover of the darkening sky, a force of three hundred Indians and Tories crept out of the woods and moved toward the fort.

"Indians," yelled Corporal Stine, from his post at one of the gun-loops. "Lots of 'em."

The calm was shattered by the clatter of dinner plates and cutlery as men scrambled for their rifles and took position for battle.

Muzzle flashes darted from the darkness amidst the shouts of the attackers.

"Blow them candles out," shouted Sergeant Donohue. "We're lightin' up the gun-loops."

"Well, just how in the hell are we gonna see what we're doin', then?" yelled Gagnon.

"Then blow out most of 'em, damn it."

The rangers' fire kept the enemy under cover.

"Pace yourselves," cautioned Donohue. "They can't get in here unless we run outta ammunition. Don't fire unless you see a good, clear target."

Donohue knew they could hold. They were secure behind the thick, stone walls. They had a good supply of food, powder and ammunition and an endless source of water from the spring below.

With the attack stalled, enemy detachments ventured off to destroy whatever they could find.

The sound of the attack didn't go unnoticed. Colonel Kelly marched with his men from Fort Jenkins. Shortly after they left, they saw flames rising behind them.

"Looks like we lost Fort Jenkins," said one of his men.

"Yeah," answered Kelly. "Look, there on the horizon. I think we lost Fort Bosley, too."

When they reached Fort Rice the next morning, the enemy was gone. The garrison came out as Kelly and his men arrived.

"We're sure glad to see you," shouted a ranger.

"Looks like you scared 'em off," replied Kelly.

"We done some damage," said Donohue, "but I think it was these walls that changed their minds."

"Yeah," said Kelly. "They're pretty pock-marked but don't look any worse for the wear. How many of 'em was there?"

"Oh, pret near three hundred or so," said Donohue. "Wouldn't ya say Folkrod?"

"Ya, that's right," the ranger agreed. "There sure was a mess of 'em."

Kelly thought as he surveyed the countryside. "With only a hundred of us, it don't seem too smart to go traipsin' after 'em. They could be just layin' an' waitin' for us. There's a good chance Forts Jenkins and Bosley are destroyed. We'd best git back to Fort Augusta an' see if we can't get some reinforcements."

Kelly gave orders to his sergeants. Turning back to Donohue he asked, "You boys need anything?"

"We'll take a little more powder and ammunition to replace what we spent, if you can spare it," answered Donohue. "Other than that, we're fine."

"Stirling, Frederick and Vanderslice, come here a minute," called Kelly.

"Yessir?"

"I want you boys to go around and gather two rounds and powder from each man."

"Yessir,' they replied.

"That'll give each a' your men another ten rounds a piece," said Kelly. "Will that hold you?"

"That'll bring us back to about what we had," answered Donohue. "Thank you, kindly."

"Not at all," said Kelly. "Good luck to ya. And good work holdin' the fort."

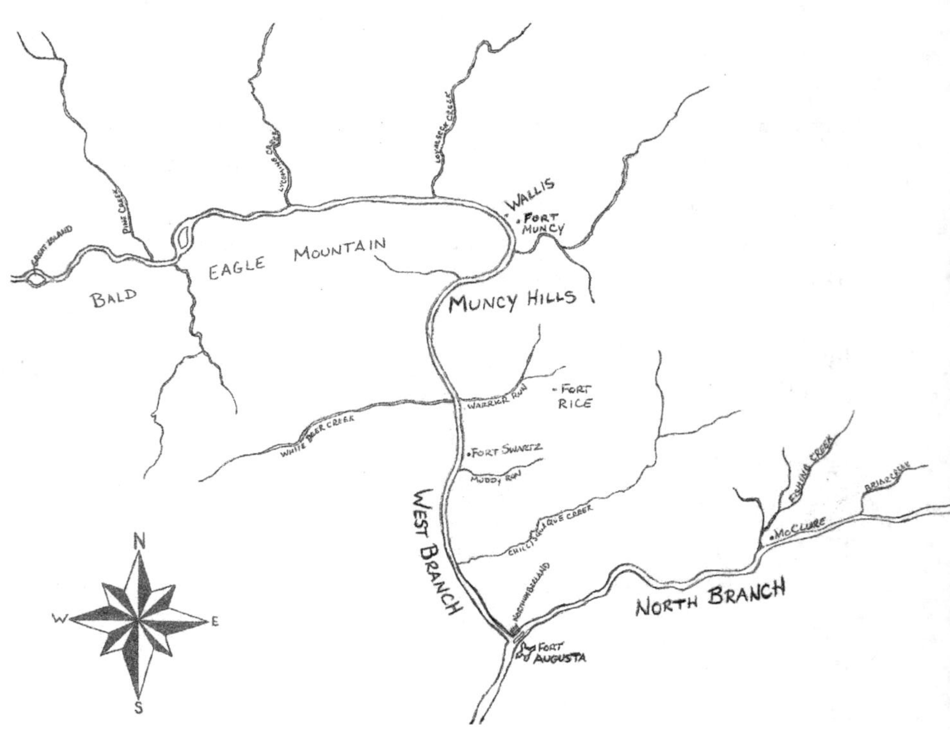

CHAPTER 16

October 1781–November 1782

FORT AUGUSTA

"News! . . . I have news," shouted the rider outside the gate.

"Open the gate!" yelled the sentry.

The rider entered and dismounted. It was Franklin, the kid Hunter sent with the order to evacuate the valley three years ago.

"Take me to Colonel Hunter!" he yelled.

The sergeant led him to the commander's home. Hunter answered and ushered him inside.

Minutes later, Hunter strode onto the parade ground with Franklin and called for the drums to beat assembly. Men hurried from the barracks and gathered from across the fort. Others looked down from their posts on the walls.

"Men," the colonel intoned, "We've just learned General Washington has accepted Cornwallis' surrender at Yorktown."

The din of drums and shouts echoed in the fort.

"Artillery!" shouted Hunter. "Load and prepare to fire."

The gun crews charged the cannon.

"We can spare some powder for such an auspicious occasion," Hunter told Franklin. "Now, would you please lead the men in a salute?"

"It would be an honor, sir," said Franklin.

When they'd loaded the guns and came to attention, Franklin raised his arm.

Hunter shouted, "Huzzah for General Washington and the continentals! Huzzah for freedom and independence. And, huzzah for the United States of America!"

"Huzzah!"

"Huzzah!"

"Huzzah!" shouted the troops as Franklin pumped his fist in the air.

With the last cry hanging in the air, Hunter signaled the guns. A thunderous boom thudded deep within his chest. The sound mushroomed out of the fort, careened off Blue Hill and echoed up the valley.

"The war might not be over," said Hunter, "but victory sure feels closer."

"It sure does, sir," said Franklin, with the same smile Hunter remembered so well.

★ ★ ★ ★ ★

FORT AUGUSTA

The spring melt swelled the river outside the fort. One brisk afternoon, it brought with it a canoe from up the West Branch.

"How goes it, Colonel?" asked Captain Robinson, leader of the ranger company Hunter assigned to rebuild Fort Muncy.

"Fine thanks, Tom . . . and you?" answered Hunter. "Back for supplies?"

Robinson nodded. "It's going well enough," he said. "There's still snow in the passes. Shouldn't see any raids too soon, yet."

"Well," said Hunter, "April's just around the corner. How's the fort coming?"

"So far, so good. I left Lieutenant Van Campen in charge a' half a' the company t' do the buildin' while the other half is out on the trails."

"Good. He'll keep 'em working."

"That he will," agreed Robinson. "Well, I'd better look after them supplies."

"Why don't you stop around the house for supper tonight?" asked Hunter.

"That'd be fine," answered Robinson. "Thank you."

That evening, Hunter greeted the captain at the door.

"Tom, thanks for joining us," he said.

"My pleasure, Sam," answered Robinson, seeing a third man in the room.

Though only middle-aged, the man's face was etched and weathered. Beneath his worn coat, he wore homespuns and stockings that had seen better days.

"Tom, this is Jonas Culbertson," said Hunter good-naturedly.

"Glad to know you," said Culbertson, awkwardly extending a large, rough-hewn hand.

"And you, too, sir," answered Robinson as they shook. "Tom Robinson."

"Culbertson is just up from Cumberland County," Hunter explained. "His brother owned a place near the Great Island. Early in the war they were raided, and his brother was killed."

"My sympathies, Mr. Culbertson," said Robinson.

"Thank you, sir," the man answered.

Hunter continued, "Before the raid, Mr. Culbertson's brother took the precaution to let him know he buried the family's valuables in a particular spot on the property. Mr. Culbertson would like to retrieve them and was hoping to accompany the next scouting party headed that way."

"I don't want t' be no inconvenience," added Culbertson quickly. "I got my own rifle an' supplies, an' I can do my part. I jist thought rather than goin' alone . . ."

"Why certainly," said Robinson. "Don't give it another thought. My men and I would be pleased to have you with us."

"Thank you, sir," said Culbertson.

"It's my pleasure," Robinson replied. "We'll leave for Fort Muncy first thing in the morning."

"Much appreciated," said the man, turning to leave.

"Mr. Culbertson," said Hunter, stopping him at the door.

"Yessir?"

"Captain Robinson and myself are about to dine with my wife. Would you care to join us?"

Culbertson looked both grateful and embarrassed. Almost imperceptibly, he glanced down at his rough clothing and then looked Hunter straight in the eye.

"I thank you, sir," he said. "It's a most kind and generous invitation. As I said, I don't want t' be no imposition to nobody . . . I'm grateful . . . grateful t' you both."

Culbertson turned and left the office. Hunter, not wanting to prolong the man's discomfort, didn't insist and allowed him to go.

★　★　★　★　★

The following morning, Culbertson was waiting for Robinson at the gate.

"Good morning, Mr. Culbertson," Robinson greeted him.

"Good morning, sir."

"Are you ready to go to Muncy?"

"Ready."

The men shouldered their belongings and set off.

By the time Robinson returned, his men had completed the blockhouse.

"Cap'n Robinson," called Van Campen as he saw the men entering camp.

"Well done, Lieutenant," greeted Robinson, surveying his men's handiwork.

"Thank you, sir," said Van Campen. "It's a little bigger project than puttin' that stockade around McLure's on the North Branch was, but it's comin' along."

"Any signs of the enemy?" asked Robinson.

"We saw some tracks from their scouts."

"Well, they're sure to be back," said the captain.

"I'd say so, sir."

"Van Campen, meet Jonas Culbertson."

"Pleased to meet ya," said Van Campen.

"And you, sir," answered Culbertson.

"Mr. Culbertson's brother had a place up by the Great Island," explained Robinson. "They was raided and his brother was killed early in the war."

Van Campen glanced at Culbertson with an understanding look.

"He'd like to venture up to the property and retrieve some of the family's valuables that were buried there."

"Sounds like you had a smart brother, Mr. Culbertson," said Van Campen. "Many didn't bother to safeguard their belongings."

"My brother was a shrewd man, Lieutenant," replied Culbertson. "But not shrewd enough to take himself and his family out of harm's way."

"Most who settled that area wouldn't a' left too easy," answered Van Campen. "That was a tough bunch a settlers. They had to be."

"Well, that's so," said Culbertson. "Once he decided on somethin', nothin' was about t' change his mind. I'm grateful he told me about the valuables. It was sorta his will, I guess you could say."

"Like I said, smart fella," answered Van Campen. "Well, I was plannin' on takin' a detachment out there soon. Would you like t' come along?"

"That's exactly what I was hoping for. Thank you, sir," said Culbertson. Then, he hesitated and said, "I'd be willing t' pay a fee for the service."

Van Campen looked at Culbertson, bemused. Then, he asked, "Can ya use that rifle ya got there?"

"I'm a fair shot," answered Culbertson.

"If we get in a scrape, you can pay your fee with lead. Any property you retrieve is yours," said Van Campen.

"You won't find a better deal than that, Mr. Culbertson," said Robinson.

"I'm sure I won't," he answered. "Nor a better man to pay it to, I venture," he said, extending his hand to Van Campen.

The men clasped hands, and the matter was settled.

"Mr. Culbertson," said Robinson, "Please make yourself as comfortable as possible."

"Thank you," said Culbertson, who turned and walked off.

"Poor man," said Van Campen when Culbertson was out of earshot.

"Looks like he could use whatever's buried there," said Robinson.

"He must need it, or he wouldn't be takin' the chance now," agreed Van Campen. "Jonas, huh? I hope that ain't no indication a' how this one's gonna go."

Robinson smiled wryly. "Didn't know you was superstitious, Mose. Ah, hell. You're too damn lucky anyhow," he said. "Might as well make it a fair fight for once'd."

Van Campen chose twenty men for his patrol and drew supplies from the company's new storehouse.

The next morning, Van Campen detailed three men to escort Culbertson upstream in a boat while the rest walked along the riverbank. After a long day's march, they came within sight of the Great Island. Van Campen sent flankers out on both sides of the path, but there was no sign of the enemy.

They ferried across to the island. The men carefully hid the boat in the underbrush and headed inland. Now late afternoon, Van Campen led his men up a wooded knoll.

"We'll camp here," he said. "And I don't got t' tell ya, it's a cold supper tonight. No fires."

The men groaned, but none of them would have risked a fire.

"Henderson, McRee, Stewart an' Craton, you're on sentry. Go out at least forty yards."

The men nodded and turned off into the woods.

"Culbertson," said Van Campen, "we'll git ya there first thing in the mornin'."

"Much obliged," he answered.

The men spent the last hour before sunset shielding themselves from the damp spring breeze. When they'd finished eating, they passed around a tobacco twist and talked before turning in.

The predawn hours were always the worst. Huddled on a bed of leaves with his back against a log, Van Campen pulled his blanket tight around him to stave off the cold.

"Indians!" someone shouted.

Van Campen awoke as a rifle cracked nearby. He jumped to his feet and saw one of his sentries running into camp, followed closely by raiders. Van Campen's men were stirring. Burwell was already reloading, preparing for his next shot.

Now, coming fully to his senses, Van Campen grabbed his rifle. He fell in next to Burwell and took aim at a warrior who was close on Craton's heels.

Van Campen loosed his rifle ball just as the warrior brought his heavy war-club down on Craton's head. Through the sulfurous smoke, Van Campen saw Craton pitch forward and blood seep out of his ears and nose. The warrior twisted and fell behind him.

Van Campen reloaded as the other sentries came leaping through the misty underbrush. One of them fell, shot through the throat.

A swarm of raiders came crashing in on the rangers. With barely time to raise his rifle, Van Campen shot at the nearest one and watched him crumple to the ground.

Then, he grabbed his rifle by the muzzle and swung it wildly at the next. The blow landed squarely across the warrior's jaw.

Van Campen reached into his belt and pulled his tomahawk. His men also emptied their rifles, and the fight was now a vicious hand-to-hand combat. The rangers soon gained the advantage and the raiders fell back. But, it wasn't in defeat.

As more raiders arrived, they encircled Van Campen's position. Seeing what was happening, three of Van Campen's men decided to make their escape before the circle closed. They bounded off through the woods and got away.

The rest of the rangers remained in position, but Van Campen and his men were no match for the numbers of the enemy, who simply stood back and decimated his ranks with rifle fire.

Van Campen watched his men fall around him. He realized they had no chance to escape. He also noticed green uniforms through the woods. Seeing a Tory officer, he thought maybe he could surrender and save the lives of his remaining men.

Van Campen pulled off his shirt and tied it to the end of his rifle. He waved it over his head and shouted, "Quarter! . . . Quarter! We surrender."

"Cease fire!" shouted the officer.

The firing died away and smoke rose before the morning sun, as streams of light cascaded eerily through the trees.

Van Campen rose, untied his shirt and replaced it. "Everybody up. Form ranks," he called to his men.

Only nine men answered the call. Eight of his men lay dead around him. Of the nine, only he and two others remained unwounded.

The Tory officer advanced toward Van Campen, followed closely by an aide and a throng of warriors.

"Leftenant Nellis," said the officer matter-of-factly.

"Smith," responded Van Campen. "Lieutenant Bill Smith." Van Campen's men heard the reply, but none made the slightest reaction.

"Mr. Smith. Ask your men to stack their arms."

"You heard 'em," said Van Campen to his men.

They stepped forward and dropped their rifles, tomahawks and knives to the ground. When the last of the weapons was tossed on the pile, the Indians rushed in to secure their prisoners. They culled the wounded men from the group and Stewart and Wallace were instantly tomahawked and scalped.

Dazed from the crushing blow he received from the war-club, Craton stared into the distance while fresh blood oozed over the dried and crusted trail coming from his ears and nose. Four Indians grabbed him and pulled him off to a nearby boulder. They sat him down, backed off a few steps, raised their rifles and pulled the triggers.

Culbertson, who'd been wounded in the shoulder, sat propped against a tree. The deepening red stain on his shirt stood out like a beacon. Van Campen watched Culbertson's eyes grow large as a warrior stepped forward and swung his tomahawk, burying it deep into the side of his head.

Burwell had also been wounded in the fight. As he'd raised his rifle to fire, he was hit by an enemy ball that passed along the length of his upper arm. When he lowered his arm, the wound wasn't easily seen, but he was beginning to lose a lot of blood.

Van Campen saw an Indian notice the blood staining Burwell's shirt and dripping to the ground at his feet. When the Indian raised his tomahawk and rushed at Burwell, Van Campen wrenched free, lunged toward the attacker and punched the Indian in the stomach. Caught unprepared, the Indian collapsed to the ground and gasped for breath.

Four Indians reached for their tomahawks and ran for Van Campen. But, others admired his bravery and jumped in to stop the attack. Van Campen and Burwell were both spared.

The raiders buried their dead and led their captives away. They followed the Susquehanna to Pine Creek and turned north.

Van Campen and his men couldn't plan an escape like the one he'd made two years ago. At almost twenty to one, the odds were too great.

Two days into the journey, Van Campen watched two Indians drag Henderson off to the edge of camp. Henderson lost some fingers during the fight but, crossing his arms, he managed to conceal his injury during the death spree on the wounded. Once on the trail, the Indians noticed the wound but allowed him to continue.

Now, however, the hand was festering badly. Bright red streaks traveled up Henderson's swollen arm and a putrid odor announced infection. Henderson seemed resigned to his fate.

He didn't struggle or try to run off. He noticed Van Campen watching and simply stared back at him as he awaited the inevitable.

Van Campen wasn't positive, but he was pretty sure he saw Henderson grin at him in the final moment. It was as if Henderson was saying, "Oh well. I gave it a good try."

Van Campen admired his bravery, but that grin haunted him worse than the execution that followed.

That night, Burwell's wound was also showing signs of infection. Doing his best to show no weakness, Burwell kept pace on the trail, but he was beginning to fade. At the end of the day's march, Burwell was led to the fire.

To his surprise, the Indians had a kettle boiling and they were dropping in plants they'd gathered in the woods. As Burwell stared into the flames, more Indians arrived from the other side of camp with Van Campen. The two men exchanged subtle but quizzical looks.

As the potion simmered, the Indians picked up a long quill. They soaked it in the kettle, grabbed Burwell by the wounded arm and opposite shoulder, and held him steady.

"Don't show any pain, Burwell," warned Van Campen.

The Indian by the kettle withdrew the feather from the liquid and carefully inserted the base of it into Burwell's wound. Pushing it carefully along the length of the quill until it emerged from the hole near his shoulder, the feather was slowly pulled all the way through to the other side. Though excruciating, Burwell didn't wince. His placid face won the admiration of his captors and of Van Campen.

Covered with thick dark-yellow globs of pus, the feather was returned to the kettle. When boiled clean, the practice was repeated. Again, the infection-covered feather was returned to the kettle and the cycle continued.

Each time, Burwell controlled his agony, and each time the feather emerged a little less contaminated until, finally, no trace of infection remained. Van Campen nodded his thanks to those who cared for Burwell and then to those who brought him to witness the procedure.

"Good man, Burwell," said Van Campen.

Burwell nodded back, not yet trusting his voice not to waver. Slowly, the pain in his arm began to subside and, by morning, the wound was showing signs of healing. He had no trouble keeping pace with the group from then on.

The party reached the Genessee River and followed it north. The raiders quickened their pace and Van Campen realized they were entering an Indian village.

"Pigeon Woods," said Nellis to Van Campen. "The fields and forest around here are rife with pigeons and the Indians come here to hunt."

From what Van Campen could make out, there were about forty Indians in the camp - undoubtedly, raiders headed to the valley. Five of them came walking out to meet the newcomers. As they arrived, the leaders of both groups greeted one another.

The raiders spoke loudly as they recounted the battle. Now and then, they gestured toward Van Campen and, to a lesser degree, Burwell. The story concluded, the leaders of the camp motioned Van Campen forward.

"What's this?" Van Campen asked of Nellis.

"They want to ask you some questions," he said.

Two Indians from the camp led Van Campen to the fire. A warrior emerged from a cabin, accompanied by an unkempt white man dressed in worn clothes. The warrior looked directly at Van Campen and spoke in his native language.

Before he could decipher what was being asked, the shabby man asked him, "What were you doin' on the West Branch?"

Van Campen glanced at the man for a moment and then looked directly back at the warrior. "Scoutin' party," he answered.

Again the warrior spoke, staring at Van Campen, and again the shabby man interpreted. "What's yer name?"

"Bill Smith."

The interpreter grinned slightly as the warrior spoke, and then said, "Draw us a picture of the West Branch Valley an' include the creeks that empty into it."

Van Campen picked up a stick and drew a faithful rendering of the valley and its streams in the dirt.

Satisfied with Van Campen's cooperation, the warrior came to the point.

"Where was yer base?" asked the shabby man.

Van Campen hesitated. He knew there'd been scouts in the valley and that they'd know the correct answer. "Fort Muncy," he replied. "We're rebuildin' it."

"How many forts are there on the West Branch, now?" asked the Indian.

Van Campen again was honest. The Indians would know that, too.

Now, the questions got to the crux of the issue. "How many defenders are in each fort?"

"A hundred an' twenty at Muncy, a hundred at Rice, a hundred at McClure on the North Branch, an' five hundred at Augusta," he said matter-of-factly.

Van Campen stayed true to the geographic and structural details, but exaggerated the number of defenders, inhabitants and arms.

"There's also a few hundred militia in Northumberland. We got 'em takin' turns mannin' the forts whilst the rangers covers the ground in between," he concluded.

The warrior stared at Van Campen. Van Campen stared back.

Then the warrior stood, turned and walked back inside the cabin, followed by the other Indians.

When no one remained but the interpreter, he looked Van Campen in the eye and said in a low, eerie voice, "Yer the man that kill't all them Indians when you was taken captive a couple years ago."

Van Campen asked, "What's your name?"

"Jones. Cap'n Horatio Jones. I'm a pris'ner too. I recognize ya from Wyomin'. I was a ensign back durin' Sullivan's raid. You was the quartermaster."

"Don't worry; I won't tell nobody," continued Jones. "But, fer God's sake, don't tell nobody who ya are. Mohawk, the Indian ya hit in the neck with the tommyhawk, run away that night and tole everybody yer name. They know yer Van Camp."

"I already said my name is Bill Smith," said Van Campen.

Jones smiled, broadly. "Glad to make yer acquaintance, Mr. Smith," he said with a wink. "If you can make it t' Niagara, you'll be in the hands a' the British. Then you'll be alright."

Van Campen was grateful for the information. He'd suspected it, but now he knew for sure the Indians knew his name and that he was a marked man.

Two more days brought the party to another village. The raiders raised a triumphal war cry as they approached. Villagers came tumbling out of cabins from all directions and ran to meet them.

Van Campen noticed they were mostly women, with some children and old men sprinkled among them. They were carrying clubs and whips. He and his fellow captives were going to run the gauntlet.

"Clubs and whips," thought Van Campen. "It could be worse."

He'd heard of instances where warriors lined up with tomahawks and knives. Facing women and old men with clubs and whips seemed like a good break.

The villagers closed in and grabbed the prisoners. They shoved them back and forth between them. The preliminaries concluded, the four captives were led to the front of the throng.

The mob pounded the ground with their clubs and cracked their whips as menacingly as possible. The warriors ambled off to the side to watch the proceedings and Nellis worked his way through to the prisoners.

"You know about running the gauntlet, Smith?" he asked.

"I heard tell of it," replied Van Campen.

Nellis pointed off in the distance. Some two hundred yards away was a rectangular building, the village council house. "If you can make it there, you'll have won your lives. All the while, you'll be chased by them," he said, turning to gesture at the mob.

"You good to run, Burwell?" asked Van Campen.

"I'm good," he answered. Burwell's wound had healed nicely.

"All we got t' do is outrun 'em, boys," said Van Campen.

Nellis stood to the side of the mob and raised his arm. The Indians behind the prisoners began growling and yelling as intimidatingly as possible. The warriors laughed.

"Make ready," called Nellis.

The captives assumed a running stance.

"Go!" shouted Nellis.

The captives were off, with the mob on their heels. Van Campen pulled ahead and broke into full stride, with his men just behind. He heard the whips cracking and the yelp of one of his men.

About a quarter of the way along, Van Campen noticed two women come out of a cabin up ahead. They were carrying whips and stood directly in his path, about forty yards before the council house. The prisoners were outpacing the mob, and Van Campen knew this would be the last obstacle.

As he closed the distance between them, he considered his strategy. Should he try to run around them, or push his way through? Then, he decided, if he could remove the women from the path entirely, his men would have a free run to the council house.

As he got to the women, Van Campen leapt forward. The whips cracked. One grazed his arm. Van Campen plowed into the women, tumbled and landed entangled with them on the ground.

He quickly jumped up and followed his men as they sped past. The dazed women sat on the ground while the mob ran around them. Van Campen and his men stood gasping at the council house, with their hands on their knees, when Nellis arrived.

"Well done, Smith," said Nellis, chuckling.

In a few days, the group was back on the trail.

Arriving at Fort Niagara was a relief for Van Campen. He'd made it through without being discovered. He and his and men were led through the looming gates into a large, open room in one of the barracks. A table with three chairs faced across the room to two rows of benches on the other side.

Nellis, Van Campen and his men took seats in the first row of benches. Their Indian escort filed in on each side of them and in the row behind.

A Tory colonel soon entered the room flanked by two adjutants. All wore pressed uniforms of evergreen, trimmed with brass buttons and insignia. Nellis rose. Van Campen and his men followed suit.

"Leftenant Nellis," he said crisply, announcing himself to the colonel.

"Yes. Well done, Leftenant."

"Thank you, Colonel Butler."

Van Campen and his men exchanged a quick glance. So, this was Colonel Butler, commander of Butler's rangers and the designer of six years of devastating raids on the valley. What followed was a curious mix of military pomp and Indian ceremony.

Since Van Campen and his men survived the journey to Niagara, they'd now be adopted into an Indian family or become official military prisoners. Butler and Nellis discoursed with the Indians while Van Campen saw his men, one by one, led off to stand beside a particular warrior.

When only Van Campen remained, a long conversation took place. If he, too, was adopted into an Indian family, he'd have to maintain his identity as Bill Smith. It might only be a matter of time until someone recognized him.

Finally, the haggling ceased when Nellis took Van Campen by the arm and led him around the table to stand next to Butler. The ceremonies concluded, Van Campen's men left with Nellis and the Indians.

"I've adopted you myself, Smith," said Butler to Van Campen. "I've heard of your bravery in the battle and your leadership on the trail. I believe you'll find opportunities here."

Van Campen wasn't sure what Butler was driving at, but he was relieved to be out of the hands of the Indians.

"Cholerton . . . set Smith up with a comfortable room," said Butler to one of his aides.

"Yes sir," the man obeyed. "This way, Mr. Smith."

For the next few days, Van Campen enjoyed an officer's room in the fort. He was given new clothes, excellent food and provided a decanter of whiskey. He wasn't sure why he was receiving this treatment, but it was better than the guardhouse. Then, things became complicated.

An Indian party showed up at the fort and told Butler that Lieutenant Smith was really Van Campen. Somehow, Mohawk learned Van Campen lead the rangers to the Great Island. Mohawk knew he was among the captives and had been following Van Campen ever since.

The raiders were furious at having been fooled and they demanded Van Campen's return.

"Lieutenant Van Campen," said Cholerton, entering Van Campen's room.

Van Campen stared back and calmly answered, "Who?"

"You are Lieutenant Van Campen," continued Cholerton. "Leader of the detachment of Robinson's Rangers who was rebuilding

Fort Muncy . . . leader of the scouting party taken at the Great Island . . . and the same Van Campen who butchered nine Indians in an escape back in 1780."

Van Campen realized he'd been found out. He looked at Cholerton and said, "I escaped in '80. Me an' two other captives was bein' led up the Susquehanna. We woulda bin the first captives taken after Sullivan's raid. You say I butchered those men. What woulda happened t' us if we was taken all the way back t' the villages?"

Cholerton reflected silently.

Van Campen continued, "I'm a soldier, jest like you. We're at war. It's a prisoner's duty t' escape, an' that's what I done. I killed five a' them raiders, and I wounded Mohawk in the neck . . . that's what I done."

Cholerton considered what Van Campen just told him. "Very well. I'll tell the colonel your position," said Cholerton, turning to leave.

"Leftenant," said Van Campen.

"Yes?"

"Under the circumstances, I'd like t' request a knife."

Cholerton looked back, incredulous.

"Hear me out," continued Van Campen. "There are Indians constantly in and out of the fort. It don't take much imagination t' think one of 'em might take matters into his own hands. All I'm askin' is t' have the chance t' defend myself. Bring me a knife an' a string so I can keep it 'round my neck. No one'll ever know."

Cholerton left without answering.

More Indians arrived to demand the return of Van Campen, and the pressure on Butler built. For years, he maintained a delicate balance between military strategy and political prudence. In deference to his allies, he wasn't always able to handle every situation the way he would have liked.

Now, Van Campen put that balance in jeopardy. Butler thought Van Campen could be valuable to him, but he couldn't risk alienating the Indians.

"I've got good news for you, Lieutenant," said Cholerton on his next visit.

Van Campen stared back, waiting.

"Colonel Butler has offered to spare you from the mercies of the Indians. All you need do is accept a British commission. You'll be given your current rank and a command. A man of your fortitude will rise quickly. . ."

"Stop right there," interrupted Van Campen. "That's the *good* news?"

"It certainly is," Cholerton snapped. "It's a great honour to be thought worthy to . . . "

"It's an honor I'll not accept," Van Campen interrupted. "To stain honor with honor is a concept beyond my understandin'. I don't care what the Indians do t' me. They can torture me and burn what's left fer all I care.

"My honor is t' my country. My honor is t' my men, who I watched get murdered jist because they'd been wounded in a battle they fought honorably. My honor is t' my family . . . my father who was butchered an' left layin' unburied in front of his home . . . my little brother who was thrown still livin' across a fire an' left strugglin' to get out.

"They were honored t' live in a country a' freedom. They were honored t' buy land, an' work it, an' t' make of it what they could. I was honored t' escape from them that killed 'em an' t' keep fightin' fer the country they were honored t' live in. No, *Left*enant, my honor says that's an honor I'll never accept. I'll not take a British commission."

Cholerton hadn't expected Van Campen to immediately accept the offer, but he also hadn't expected such a complete rebuke. Still, he couldn't help but admire Van Campen's character. Now, he understood the whole story of Van Campen's escape and the killing of his captors.

Cholerton stepped to the door and placed his hand on the knob. Then, he turned back. Van Campen fixed him with a steely gaze.

Cholerton walked to a nearby table, reached inside his shirt and pulled at a piece of rawhide tied around his neck. A sheathed knife appeared from beneath his uniform. Cholerton placed the knife on the table, then turned and left the room.

Van Campen had little contact with anyone in the coming days, except for those who brought his meals. When questioned, they said they had no information.

Then, one afternoon, there was a knock on Van Campen's door.

"Come in," he said.

The door opened and he was shocked to see a woman enter. She was dressed very finely and carried herself with grace and dignity.

"Moses?" queried the woman.

"Yes?"

"It's me, Mary Daniels. Well, Mary *Pry*, now."

Van Campen looked closer and recognized his childhood classmate.

"Mary Daniels from Northampton?" he asked.

"The same," she said.

"What on earth are ya doin' here?"

"Well, not long after you and your family moved from the Delaware, my family moved downriver, close to Philadelphia. It was terrifying when the British occupied the city. I wasn't sure what would become of us. But, then, things continued on pretty much as usual.

"One day I went with my family to take some produce to market. I met an officer, Captain Pry. He was very kind, and we began to talk. Then, over the next few months, he showed up each week, and we'd renew our conversation.

"We ... well, we fell in love. My father wasn't happy, but politics had nothing to do with it. We were just in love. Eventually, I accepted his proposal, and we got married. Then, after the British left Philadelphia, he was stationed here."

"Oh, I see," said Van Campen.

"Don't think ill of me, Moses. I didn't switch sides. I never really had a side. I'm weary of the war and just want things to be the way they were before it all started. Besides, I told you, we were in love. He's my husband."

"I'm not judgin' ya Mary," said Van Campen.

"Thank you."

"So, how did you find out I was here?" he asked.

"It would be hard for anyone within fifty miles not to know you were here," she said. "It's quite the news."

"That big, huh?"

"Yes," she said.

Mary paused.

"Well . . ." she continued. "When I heard you were here, I asked permission to come and visit you. Being old classmates and all, I thought it would be nice to see you again and to wish you well."

"Thank you, Mary. It's nice to see you too."

"Moses," she said timidly, "I understand they've offered you a chance for protection if you take a British commission."

"Oh, Mary; you too?"

"Moses, I don't want to see you handed over to the Indians to be . . . to be . . . who knows what. You might even end up in my husband's command. There are lots of pretty girls here. You could settle down and we could all become friends like we were in the old days."

"Mary," said Van Campen gently. "Thank you for your concern. I know yer worried for me an' I appreciate it. But it could never be that way.

"For you, it's not political. For me, it's much more. I believe in what I'm fightin' for. I believe in this cause. I'll never switch sides."

"Oh, Moses. I was afraid you'd say that. But I did want to see you again."

"I'm glad you did, Mary."

"Me too. Good luck to you, Moses," she said.

"And to you," he answered.

Days later, Van Campen heard the sound of troops in the hallway. His door burst open, and a sergeant called to him across the room.

"On your feet," he shouted.

Van Campen knew the moment had come. He stood and walked to the door.

"Come along," said the sergeant.

Van Campen found himself in the middle of a ten-man detail. Heavily armed, with bayonets fixed, the men marched him hurriedly from his room, out of the barracks, across the parade ground and out the front gate. The Indians encamped outside recognized Van Campen and began shouting. Van Campen was sure he'd be delivered to them, but they continued on.

The Indians followed along, gathering in numbers as they went. They pressed close around the detail, shouting for Van Campen. The soldiers in the front of the detail leveled their bayonets waist-high and continued forward.

They marched straight through the town and headed for the docks. Van Campen wasn't sure what was happening. The crowd around them strung out along the narrow street, and it was obvious the detail wouldn't be stopped.

As they reached the docks, they made for a nearby ship. They formed around the end of the gangplank, and the sergeant motioned to Van Campen to board.

He didn't hesitate. As Van Campen reached the top and stepped on deck he was greeted by Mary Pry. She stood, smiling, next to a tall British captain.

"Moses, meet my husband, Captain Pry."

"Captain," said Van Campen, nodding. "I take it you had somethin' t' do with this?"

"I did, Lieutenant, at my wife's behest. I also spoke with

Leftenant Cholerton, and I believe I understand the situation. We both discussed the matter with Colonel Butler, and he agreed to this solution."

"Well, thank you," said Van Campen. "I appreciate yer help."

"Not at all," answered the captain. "We've all got a duty. You were doing yours."

"So where am I goin'?" Van Campen asked the captain.

"Montreal. You'll be held there as a prisoner with the other Americans who've been captured over the years. It won't be comfortable, but you'll be in British hands, and you'll stay alive."

Captain Pry turned to the ship captain. "Captain Sheffield, this is Lieutenant Moses Van Campen. As you know, he is an American prisoner. However, he is also a personal friend of ours and I would appreciate it if you showed him every courtesy on your journey."

"If he is a friend of yours, Captain Pry, I will certainly do so."

Captain Pry and Mary bid Moses goodbye. Captain Sheffield took Van Campen below decks and supplied him with provisions that would be more than sufficient for the journey. Then he showed him to his room and made sure he was comfortable.

FORT AUGUSTA

"It's been such a nice summer," said Susanna Hunter at supper one evening. "It's almost as if everything were back to normal."

"Not quite, Susie," said Hunter. "Folks is still bein' raided here and there. It's just not as regular or as organized as it was."

"Still, it's been pretty quiet around here."

"Well, it's about to get a little busier," said Hunter.

"How do you mean?"

"This goes no further than this table, right?" asked Hunter.

Susanna nodded.

"I just received orders to get ready to supply another raid into

New York State. General Washington feels one more strong blow might just put an end to the raids here."

"It's already so late in the season," said Susanna. "When will this happen?"

"Soon," said Hunter. "General Potter will leave from here and target the villages along the Genessee. At the same time, a party will leave from Fort Pitt and march on the Sandusky Valley, in the Ohio country, and a third prong will set out from Albany and make for Oswego. All three will push toward their targets at once."

Supply-laden boats soon came and went, new troops filled Fort Augusta and Hunter worked to organize everything in the weeks that followed. General Potter arrived to take command, and, then, days prior to the raid, Washington cancelled everything.

"Cancelled?" exclaimed Potter.

"Yes," said Hunter reading the orders. "It says the British had a change in command. General Carlton's in charge now. He ordered an end to raids on the frontiers and sent runners to try to find any raiders on the trail and turn 'em back."

"Well, I'll be damned," said Potter.

"I've been waiting to hear that for the last seven years," said Hunter. "No more raids."

★ ★ ★ ★ ★

CHILLISQUAQUE VALLEY

"Just a few more," said John Martin to his wife.

They were just finishing a hard day's work of planting a new orchard.

"In a few years, we'll be spendin' our time makin' cider," he said as he patted the dirt around the last seedling. Rising from the ground, John stretched his back. He raised his face to the sky and felt the warm autumn breeze. The fresh scent of fall leaves was in the air, and the evening star sparkled overhead.

He never felt the tomahawk . . . or heard his wife scream.

Ten days later, Sergeant Edward Lee and Robert Caruthers left Fort Rice to scout the surrounding area. They spent the day making a wide circle around the fort and through the neighboring settlements. By late afternoon, they were crossing the Martins' farm.

As they crested the top of a hill, shots rang out. Caruthers heard two raiders' shots sail just past his ear. Another hit Lee in the head.

Caruthers turned toward the shots and saw four raiders rushing out of the nearby tree line. He returned fire with the shot he had loaded, but it did no harm. He turned to run, but the four raiders closed the gap quickly.

He only made it about twenty yards from where he'd started when the first of the raiders caught up and tackled him. The remaining three were on him in an instant. The raiders pulled Caruthers to his feet and took him with them as they headed back north.

★ ★ ★ ★ ★

FORT AUGUSTA

It had been a year since Cornwallis surrendered to Washington. Now, in the first week of November, Colonel Hunter received a dispatch. He pulled a document from the pouch that carried the seal of the Continental Congress.

Eyebrows raised, he broke the sealing wax and read:

A Proclamation

It being the duty of all Nations to offer supplications to ALMIGHTY GOD for his gracious assistance in a time of distress: The United States in Congress assembled, taking into consideration the many instances of divine goodness to these States in the conflict in which they have been so long engaged; the present happy and promising state of public affairs; the success of the arms of the United States, and those of their Allies, and the acknowledgement of their independence by another European power: ------- Do hereby recommend to the inhabitants of these States the observation of THURSDAY the twenty-eighth day of NOVEMBER next, as a day of solemn THANKSGIVING to GOD for all his mercies: and they do further recommend to all ranks, to testify to their gratitude to GOD for his goodness, by a cheerful obedience of his laws, and by promoting the practice of true and undefiled religion, which is the great foundation of public prosperity and national happiness.

Done in Congress, at Philadelphia, the eleventh day of October, AD 1782.

John Hanson, President
Charles Thomson, Secretary

A broad smile crossed Hunter's face. His mind reeled with such warm and comforting thoughts that he couldn't recall the last time he'd felt this happy.

He'd known the war had turned a corner. He knew the British changed their policy about harassing the frontiers. But, somehow, seeing the words written down brought the reality home; the Continental Congress was acknowledging the end of hostilities.

Hunter savored the moment. He wandered across the parade and out the western gate, the document still clutched in his hand. He strolled down to the riverbank, looked to the sky and breathed in great measured lungfuls of clean, crisp air.

Looking past Blue Hill, he stared up the West Branch. The breeze rushed over the surface of the water and caught him full in the face.

His mind repeated, *"the present happy and promising state of public affairs; the success of the arms of the United States. . ."*

He reflected on the past seven years. He thought of those

who'd been lost. He thought of those who'd struggled and given everything so their families, so their countrymen . . . so *he* could live a life of freedom.

He thought of John Brady and his young son James. He thought of Hawkins Boone. He thought of the countless others who'd dared to stand up to tyranny no matter the consequences.

"They were the foundation," he thought to himself. "They were the ones who laid down their lives as the bedrock of freedom. We're the ones who must now build on that foundation and advance the cause they began. We're the ones who must safeguard the great gift that's been given."

Hunter turned back toward the fort. Above the wall, the flag of the new republic stood out against a crisp blue sky and snapped in the breeze.

. . . THURSDAY the twenty-eighth day of NOVEMBER . . . a day of solemn THANKSGIVING . . . he read.

"We'll have a dandy," he said to himself. "We'll have a dandy."

★ ★ ★ ★ ★

And then . . .

COLONEL SAMUEL HUNTER

Colonel Hunter died in June 1784. He is buried along with members of his family in the little cemetery that stands on the site of Fort Augusta.

SAMUEL BRADY

Colonel Brodhead chose Samuel to lead a ranger unit through Western Pennsylvania until the close of the war. Samuel married and started a family in Washington County, PA.

When an Indian war broke out in 1788, General Anthony Wayne called on him to reorganize his rangers and defend the frontier. Many exploits of great attacks, narrow escapes, and rescued captives are attributed to Samuel and his men.

Samuel died of natural causes in 1795 at his home in West Liberty, VA (now WV). He was 39.

MARY BRADY

When Mary left Muncy after John's death, she traveled to her parents' home in Cumberland County. She stayed only five months before returning to the family's property across the river from Derr's. Mary and the children worked the farm. She died in October 1783.

The Brady military legacy continued for many generations as Mary and John's descendants played important roles in the War of 1812, the Civil War and beyond.

LIBERTY BRADY

Upon her mother's death, Liberty remained on the family farm with the other children. Mary, the oldest Brady daughter, married in 1795. Liberty and the remaining children went to live with her in Sunbury.

Liberty eventually married William Dewart, a congressman from Sunbury. She died in 1851.

THE DEATH OF JOHN BRADY

For almost two hundred years after John Brady was killed, it was assumed he'd been ambushed and killed by Indian raiders. The monument that stands near the site says as much. But modern historians believe he was assassinated.

Brady's scalp would have been prized by the Indians. So would the ammunition, watch and money he carried that was left on his body. There was ample time and opportunity to take these things, but none of them were disturbed.

Brady stood directly in the path of Wallis' plans. He was

a respected leader and a force in rallying settlers to the cause of freedom.

Robert Robb had his greatest humiliation in Brady's home, and he lost a great deal of local standing because of it.

Peter Smith's debt to the Brady family remained, but Brady wasn't there to collect it. Smith's life after Brady was killed is unclear, but some believe he retired in Canada where he came into property and fortune.

TIM MURPHY

Many considered Tim's shot that killed General Fraser to be the turning point of the battle of Saratoga. That victory brought the French into the war on the American side and largely determined the outcome of the conflict.

When his enlistment expired in 1779, Tim continued to fight with militia units. He reenlisted in the Continental Army toward the end of the war. He served with the Pennsylvania regulars and was there when Cornwallis surrendered to Washington at Yorktown.

Tim returned to Schoharie in 1782, married, and started a large family. He was a farmer, owned a grist mill and went into local politics.

Tim died in 1818. He was 67.

MOSES VAN CAMPEN

Van Campen and some of his fellow prisoners in Montreal were moved to New York City in 1782. There, they were released, and Van Campen returned to Northumberland in January 1783.

After the war, Van Campen married and began farming near Northumberland. Moses also became a surveyor, and he moved several times with his family to various locations across Northern Pennsylvania and New York State.

There are many stories of Van Campen meeting with Mohawk late in life. Most tell of how they recounted old times.

Van Campen died in Angelica, NY in October 1849. He was 92.

SAMUEL WALLIS

Wallis was never suspected of his treason during his lifetime. A well-respected resident of the West Branch, he lived well for many years and continued to acquire land.

Wallis entered into a business deal with Supreme Court Justice and signer of the Declaration of Independence, James Wilson, in which Wallis highly leveraged his estate. When Wilson delayed payment, Wallis traveled to visit him.

Wallis had the papers that would save his estate drawn up and ready for Wilson's signature. Wilson held the pen in his hand but hesitated. Saying he wasn't feeling well, Wilson went to bed. The next morning, he was found dead from an overdose of laudanum.

Ruined and devastated, Wallis began his trip home and spent the night at an inn. The room he was given had been occupied the previous night by someone with yellow fever. Wallis contracted the disease and died before he ever reached Muncy. It was 1798.

In 1941, Wallis' treachery was finally made public in Van Doren's *Secret History of the American Revolution*. He discovered the evidence by examining the Secret Service papers of British Headquarters in North America.

References to *The Gentleman from Philadelphia* shed light on Wallis' wartime activities, as did Andre's ledger entry for September 13, 1780: "Captain Beckwith for W. for Moore 210 pounds." Wallis' personal papers also revealed a receipt dated January 6, 1781, signed by Peggy Shippen that said, "Received of Daniel Coxe for . . . Mr. Samuel Wallace of Pennsylvania, the sum of two hundred guineas, ordered to be paid by Mr. Wallace to General Arnold."

LOCHABAR (FORT FORESTER)

The Hessian soldier buried in the basement was discovered in 1876, when the home was being updated with a steam-heating system. Although a mess kit and some personal belongings were found with the body, the mystery was only partially solved when the sword was identified as that of a Hessian soldier from the revolutionary period.

The account presented here is offered as a likely scenario of how a lone Hessian soldier could have ended up sealed in the basement at Lochabar.

THE PINE CREEK DECLARATION

The Pine Creek Declaration took place on July 4, 1776, with none of the participants aware that a similar declaration was being undertaken by the Continental Congress in Philadelphia on the same day.

Living in the Fair Play territory, these settlers were not recognized citizens of Pennsylvania. They lived beyond the law of the state and were forced to create their own society.

The declaration was signed beneath the Tiadaghton Elm, which last blossomed in 1973 and has since been cut down.

No record of the Pine Creek Declaration remains. The document presented in chapter one was created to be as likely a representation as possible.

CORRESPONDENCE

The letters shared in *Liberty's Land* are pulled from historical records. They present a fascinating look into the mindset of the characters in their own words. Only minor changes to some spelling and wording were made to the originals for the sake of clarity and modern understanding.

DANIEL VINCENT

Daniel was captured at the fall of Fort Freeland. He was marched to Fort Niagara with the other captives while the women and children were freed.

Vincent's wife Anglechy went back to her parents' home in New Jersey and heard nothing of her husband for the next three years. One winter evening, as she was about to join her neighbors for a sleigh ride, another neighbor pulled up with a stranger.

They approached Anglechy and the neighbor said, "I have someone here with news of your husband."

The stranger was roughly dressed and had a large beard. He stepped forward and took her hand.

"What news do you have of my husband, sir?"

The conversation continued for a short time when the stranger finally said, "Angel, don't you know me?"

She looked into his eyes for a long moment and let out a sudden cry of recognition. It was Daniel.

The two embraced as the snowflakes fell magically around them and erased the years of separation they'd endured.

With deepest appreciation to:

My wife Nicole, who was there from the moment *Liberty's Land* was a new idea, through the years of research, drafts and finalization. Her perspective has been invaluable and her inspiration a constant guide. It remains so, each and every day . . .

Ilse and Atticus, who patiently spent many years listening to stories of my latest research discovery. And, for cheerfully enduring the planned road trips and unexpected detours to visit the sites where they occurred. But, most of all, for all the fun we had while doing so.

The Strand Magazine Managing Editor Andrew Gulli for his endless encouragement, guidance and professional insight.

The Masthof Press team, who shared the vision and goal of restoring the heroes of the West Branch to their rightful place in the pantheon of American History . . . especially Liz Petersheim, whose constant support, cheerful collaboration and consummate professionalism made the entire publishing process the overwhelmingly positive and creative experience I always hoped it would be.

Editor Marla Kipp for thoughtfully and meticulously working through a detailed and unconventional manuscript.

My parents, Chuck and Peggy, for the countless weekend car trips to museums, battlefields and historic sites . . . each of which was a new and exciting adventure which fired my imagination and instilled the love of history I've known my whole life. I'm still always looking forward to the next one.

And . . . to John, Mary and James Brady, Hawkins and Jane Boone, Samuel and Susanna Hunter and to the countless determined and steadfast Americans like them, who, from that day to this, sacrificed so much that we might have the independence and freedom we enjoy, today.

CHRIS YOHN

Chris grew up on the West Branch of the Susquehanna River and has been a history fanatic since childhood. He and his wife Nicole moved to New York City after college to pursue a career in the performing arts. For the next 10 years, Chris regularly appeared on daytime television. He was a founding member of the North Country Rock band *Parker Hill*, which played in some of the city's better-known venues and best-forgotten dives. He also worked on stage and in film before leaving New York with a Broadway national tour. He's written for the *Journal of the American Revolution* and is a recipient of the Sons of the American Revolution (SAR) Patriot Medal, the SAR Gold 250th Anniversary Medal, the Daughters of the American Revolution Good Citizenship Medal and two International Association of Business Communicators (IABC) Gold Quill awards.

Love what you see?
Share the story!

Find more great books or
grab another copy for a friend.

**Enjoy FREE shipping
on your first order!**

Use promo code: SHIP4FREE

www.masthof.com

9 7 9 8 8 9 6 7 4 0 2 6 1